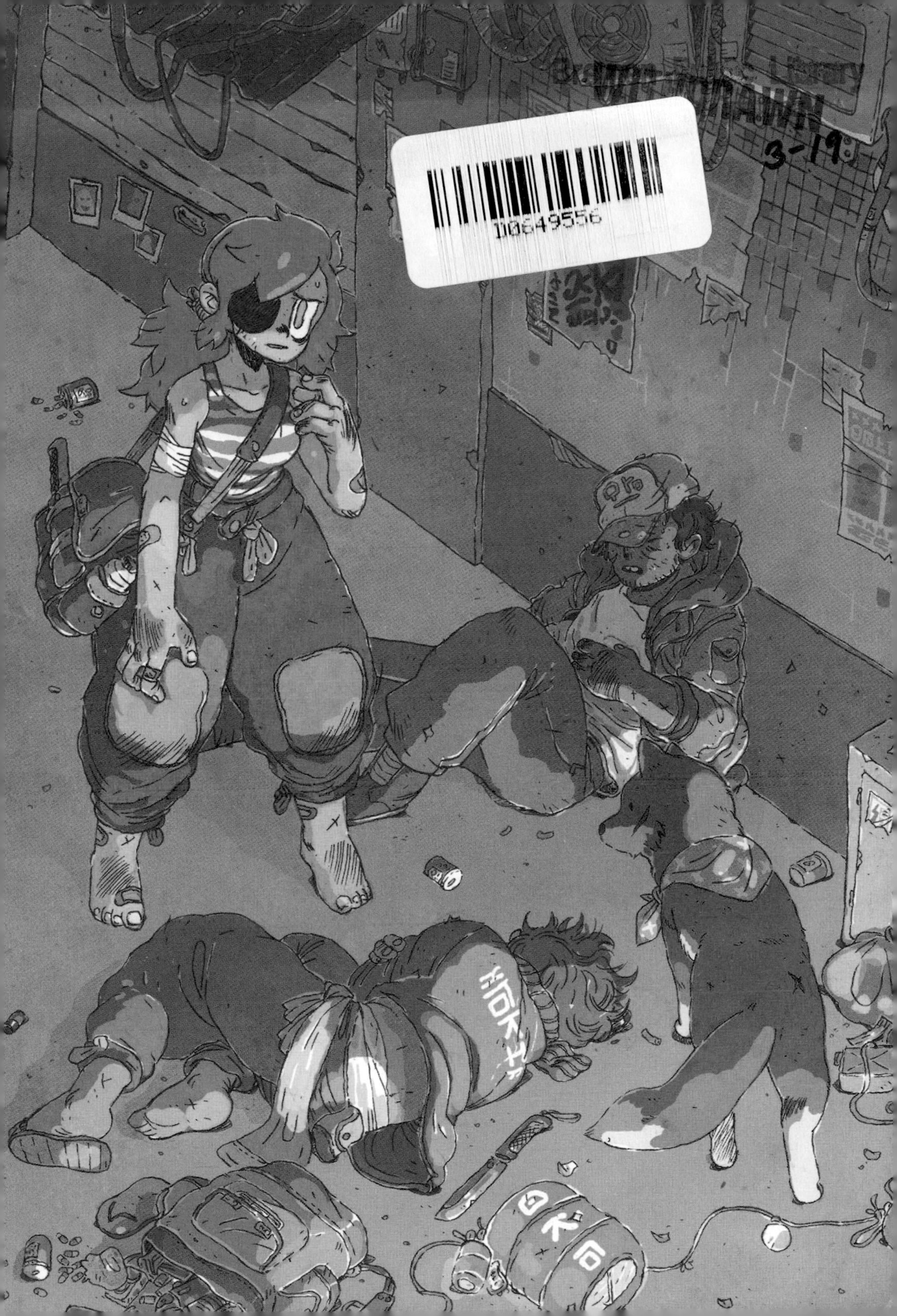

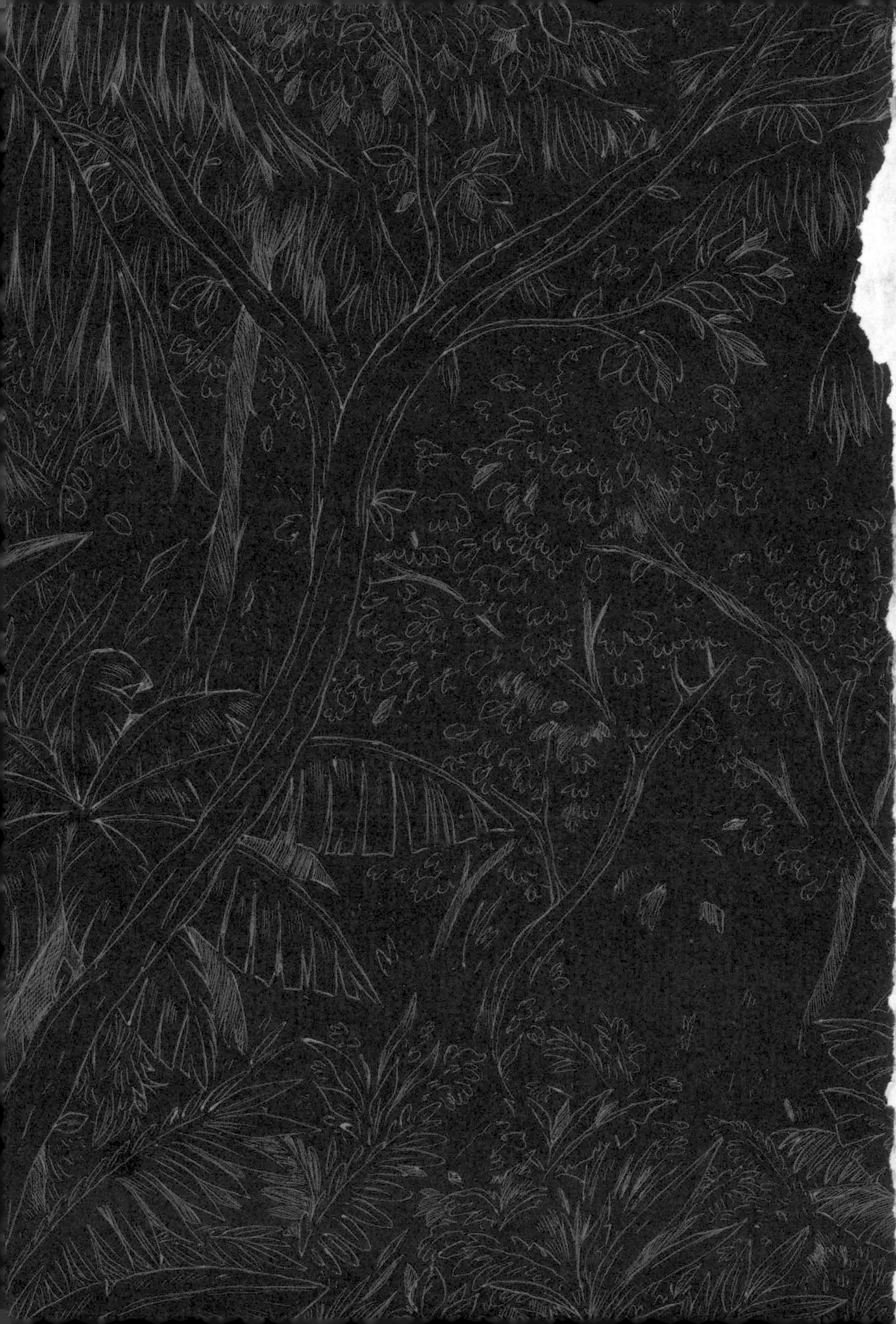

PTSD

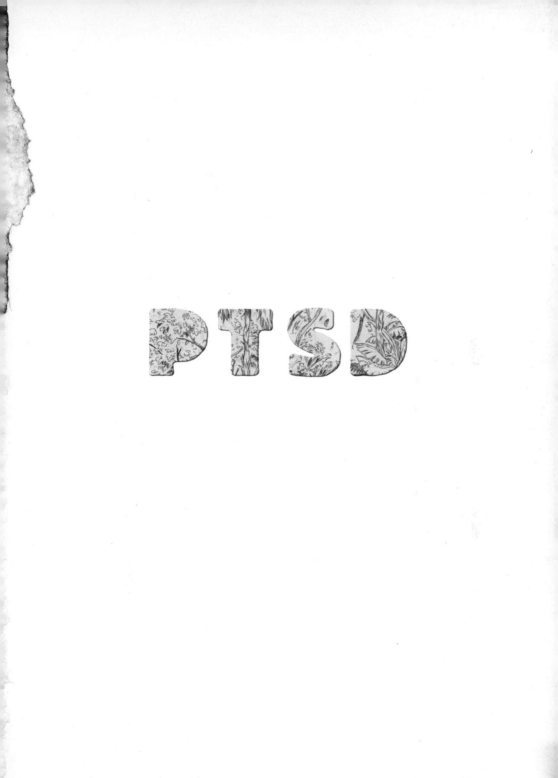

GUILLAUME SINGELIN

First Second
New York

First Second

Published by First Second
First Second is an imprint of Roaring Brook Press,
a division of Holtzbrinck Publishing Holdings Limited Partnership
175 Fifth Avenue, New York, NY 10010

Don't miss your next favorite book from First Second!
For the latest updates go to firstsecondnewsletter.com and sign up for our enewsletter.

Library of Congress Control Number: 2018938082

ISBN: 978-1-62672-318-4

Our books may be purchased in bulk for promotional, educational, or business use.
Please contact your local bookseller or the Macmillan Corporate and Premium Sales Department
at (800) 221-7945 ext. 5442 or by email at MacmillanSpecialMarkets@macmillan.com.

```
FIRST
```

```
EDITION
```

First edition, 2019

Edited by Mark Siegel and Casey Gonzalez
Book design by Chris Dickey

Printed in China

Penciled with a red Col-Erase pencil. Inked with a Pilot BP-S Matic ballpoint pen.

10 9 8 7 6 5 4 3 2 1

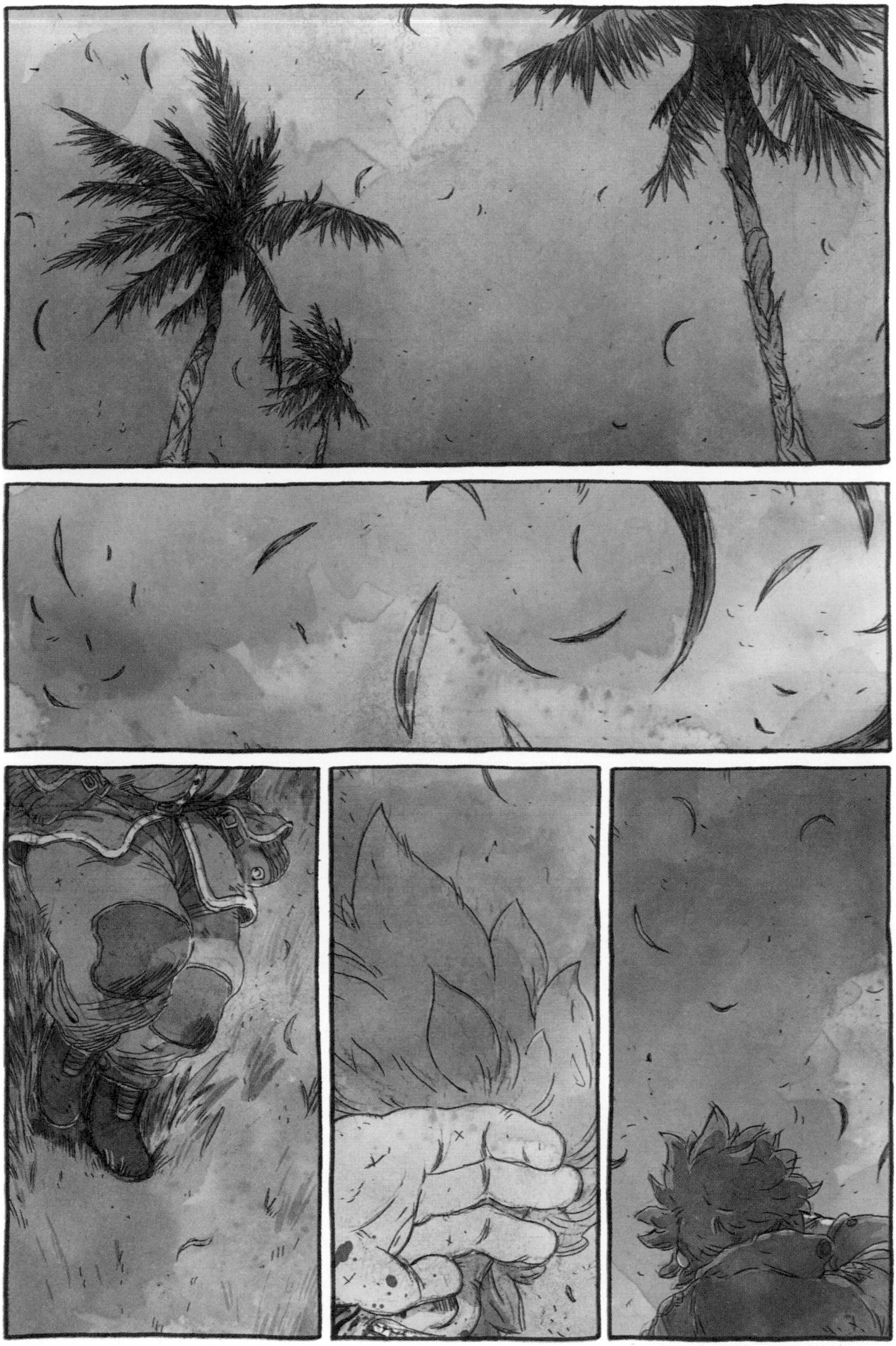

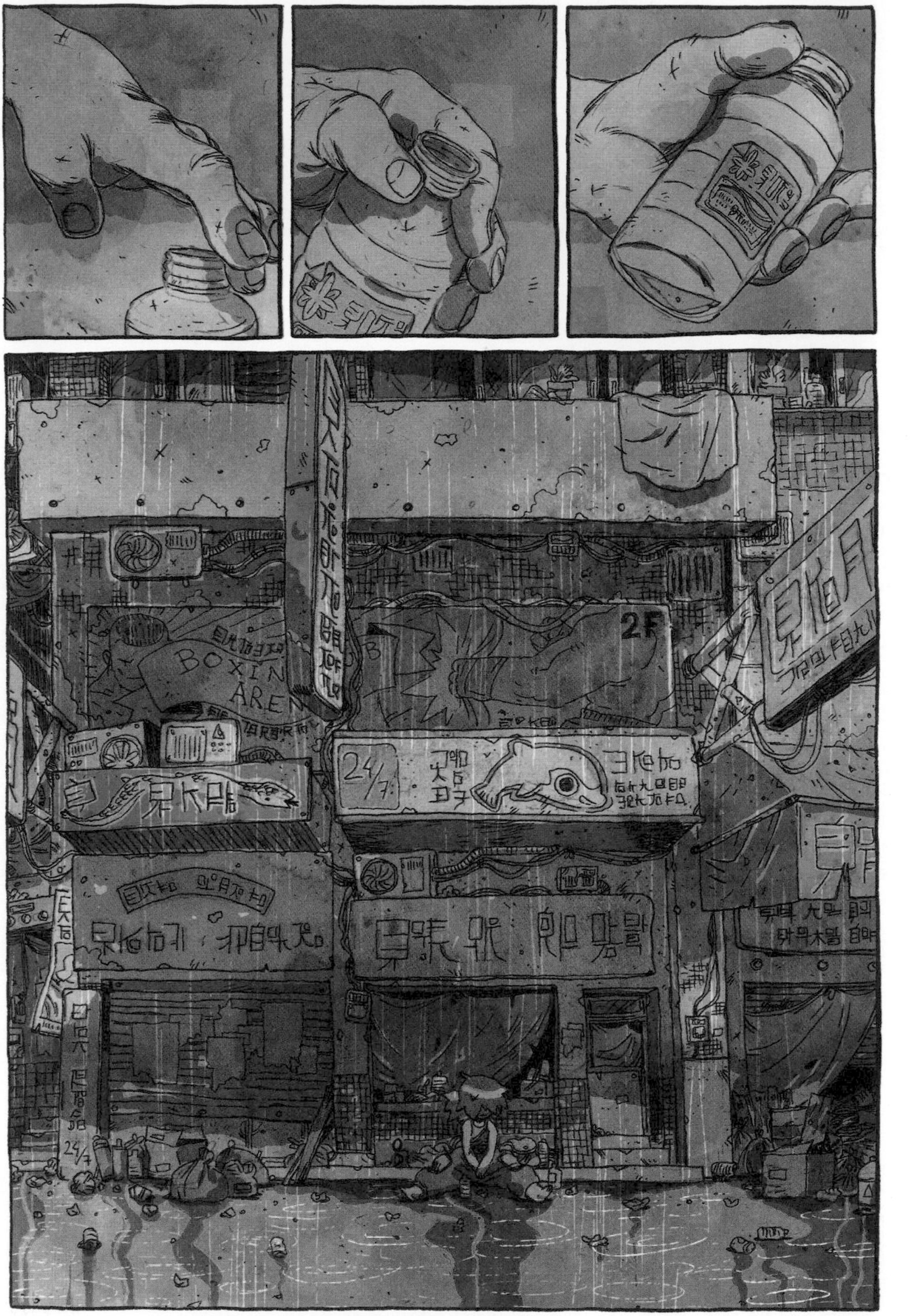
BOXIN
AREN
2F
24/7

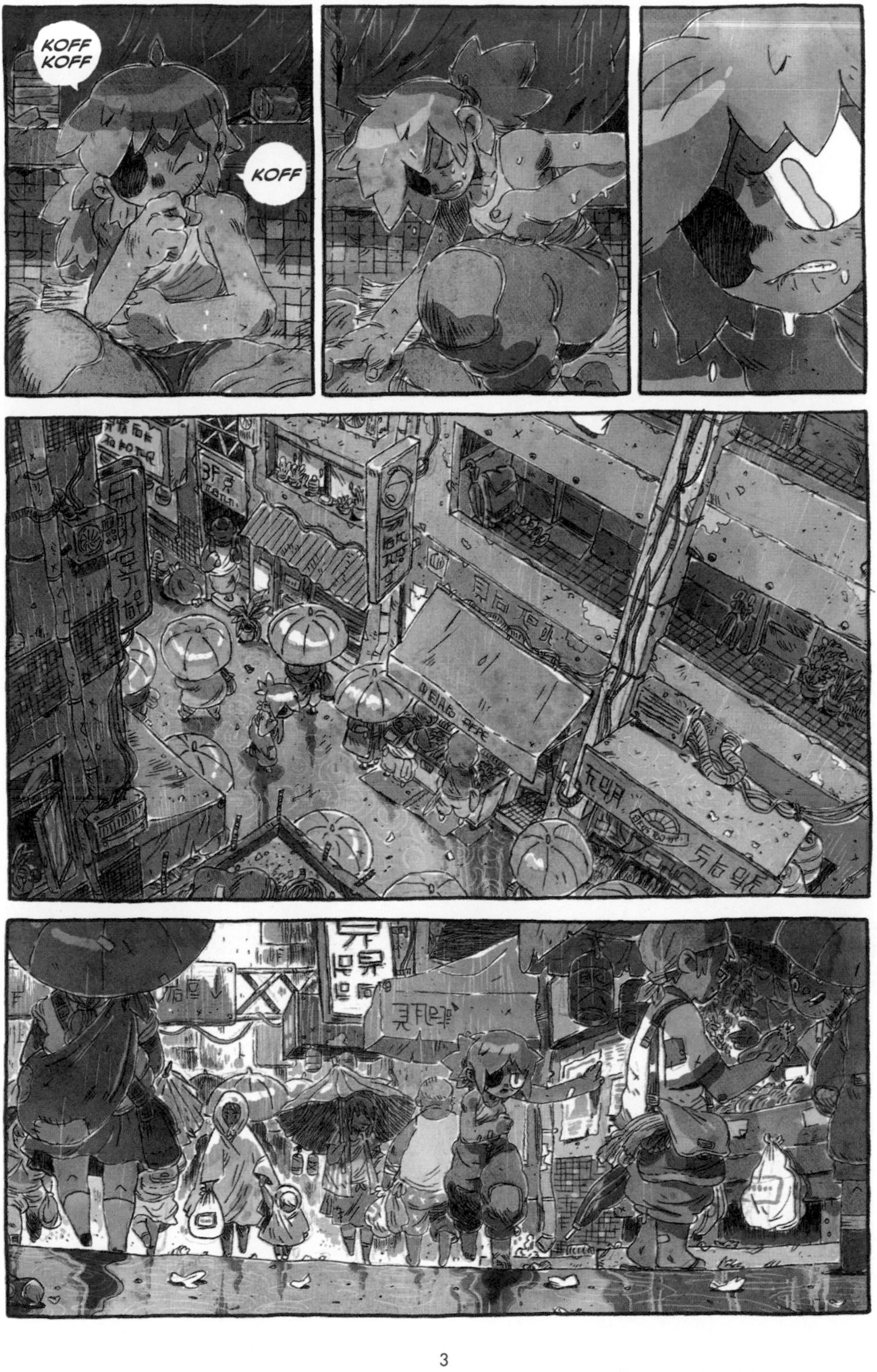
KOFF
KOFF
KOFF

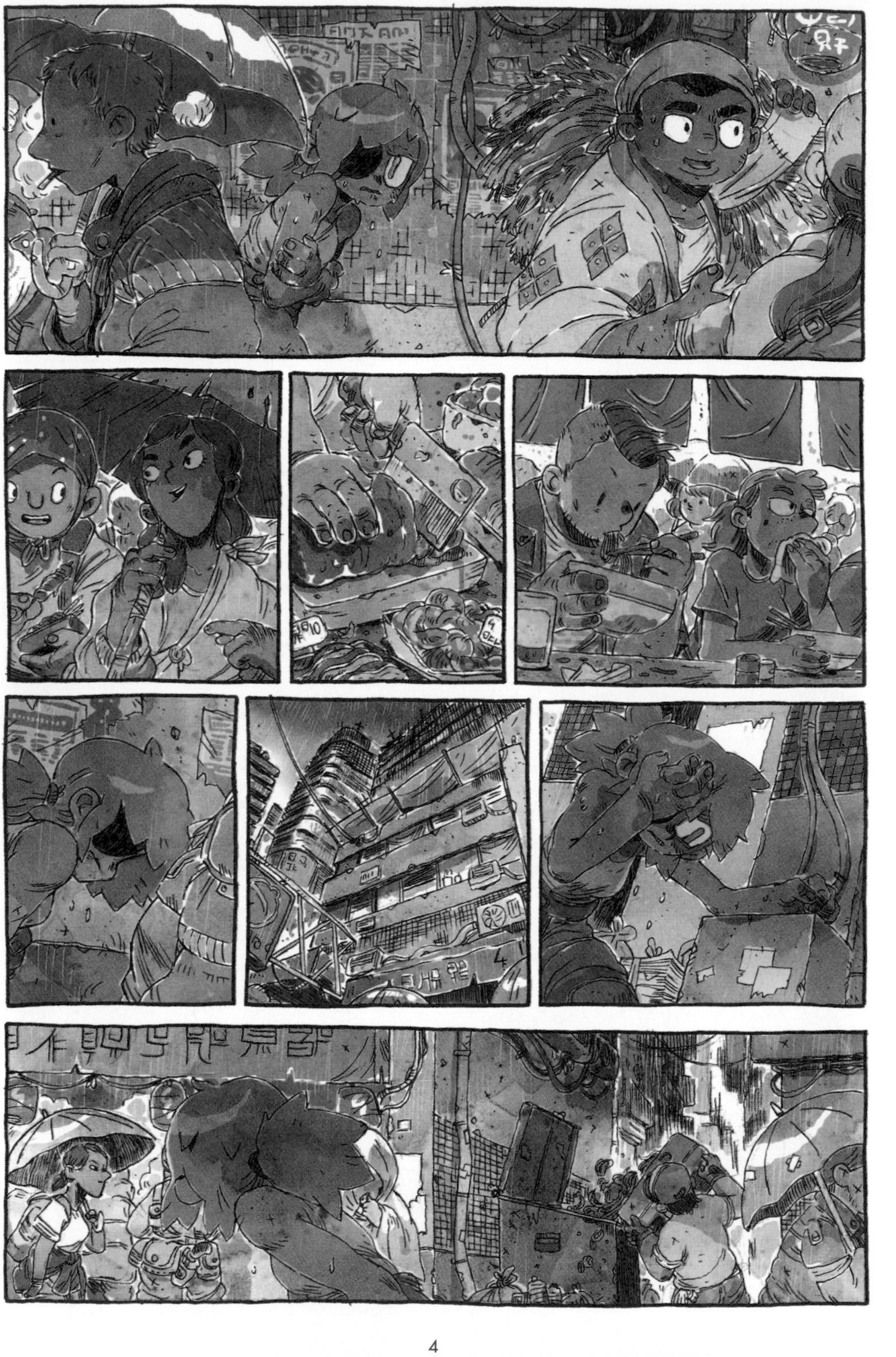

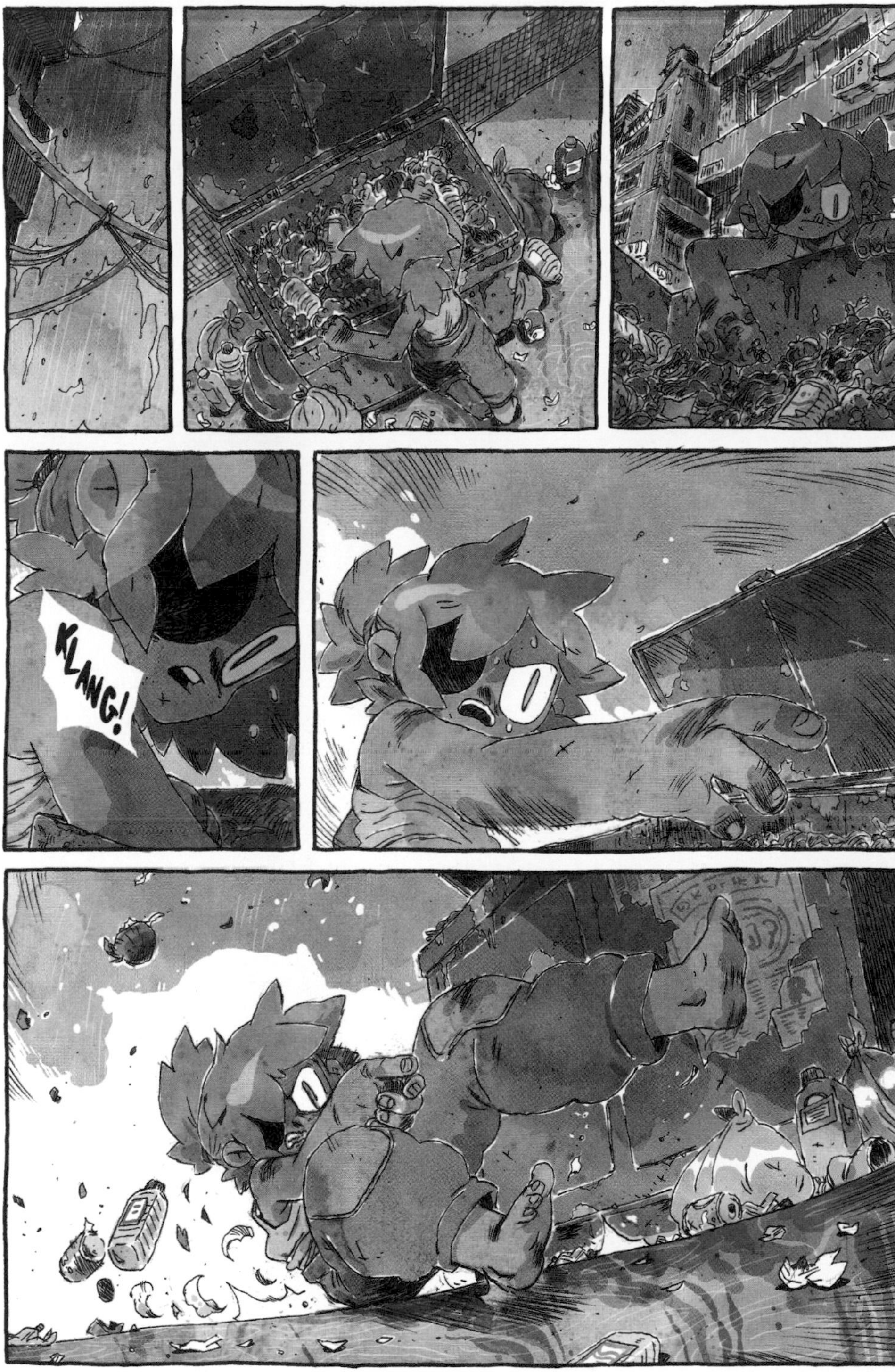
KLANG!

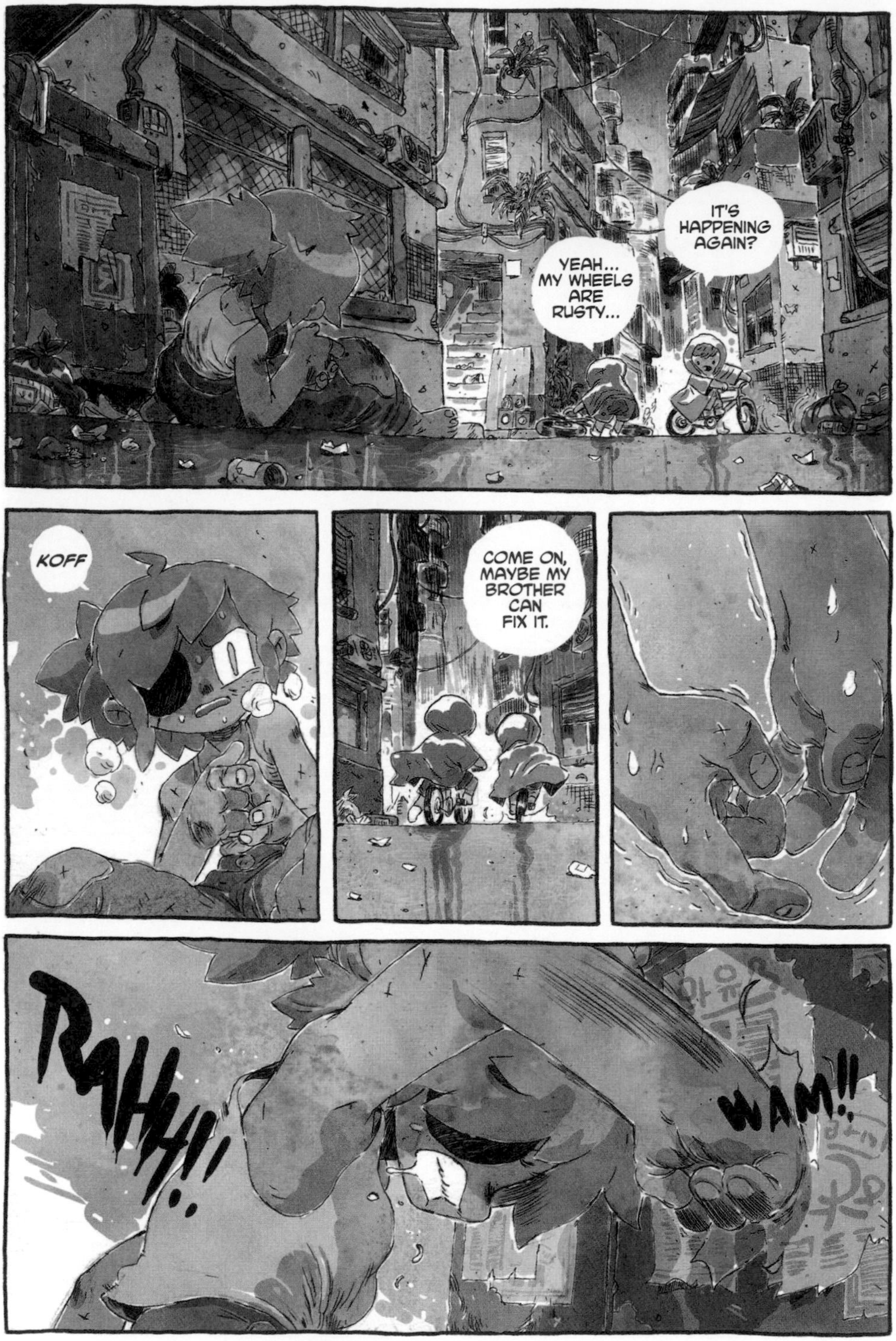
IT'S HAPPENING AGAIN?
YEAH... MY WHEELS ARE RUSTY...
KOFF
COME ON, MAYBE MY BROTHER CAN FIX IT.
RAHH!!
WAM!!

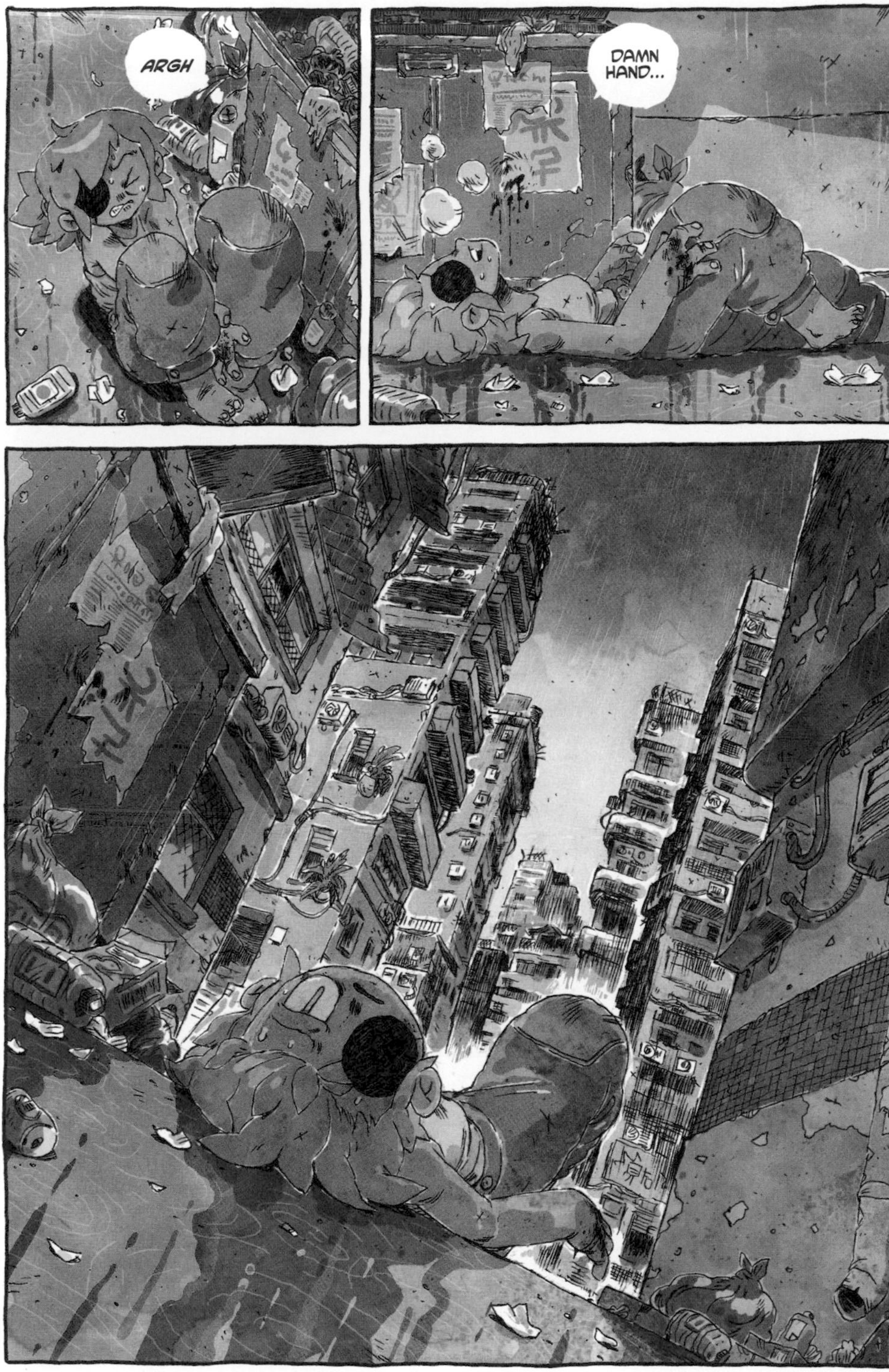
ARGH
DAMN HAND...

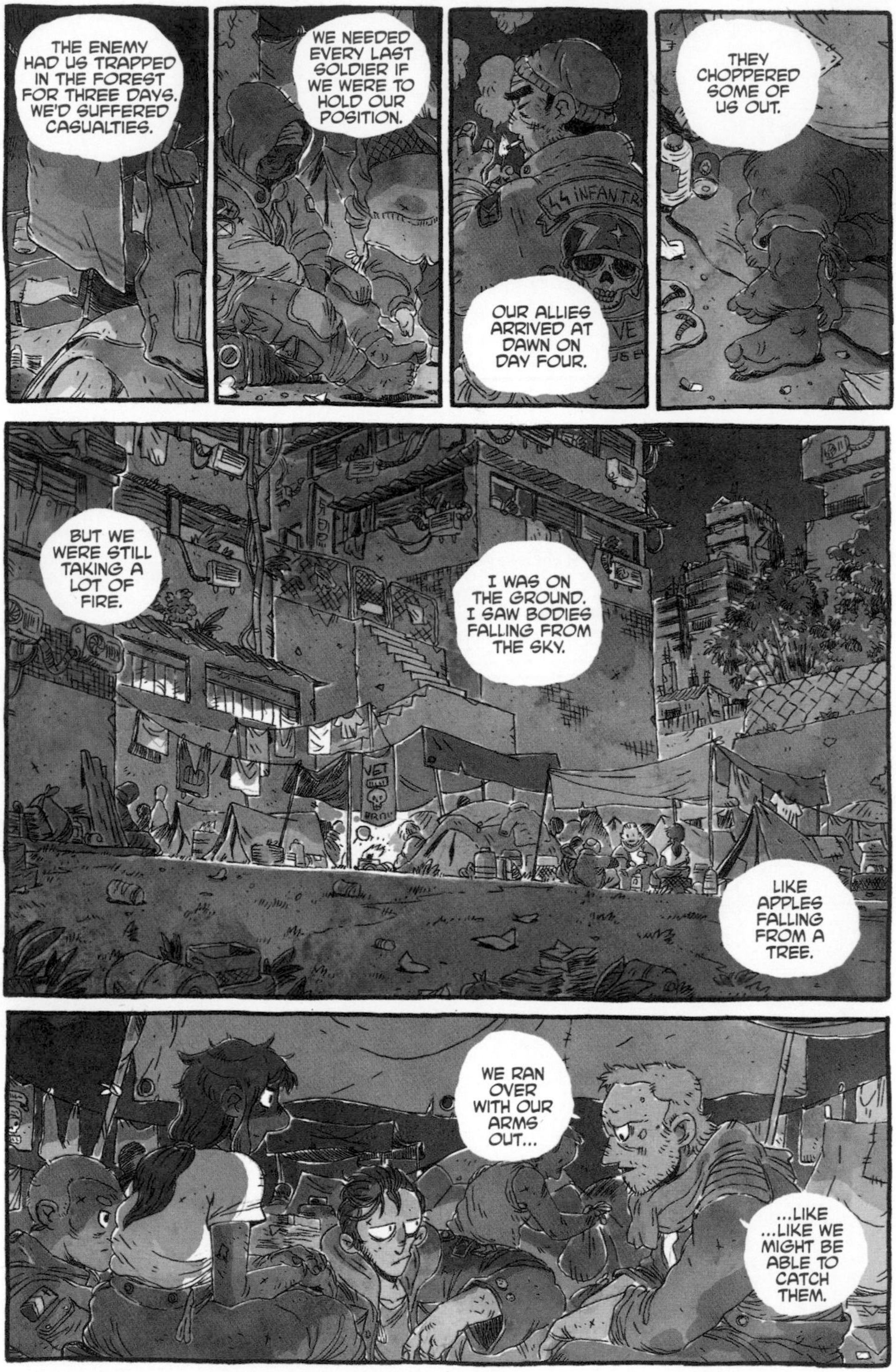
THE ENEMY HAD US TRAPPED IN THE FOREST FOR THREE DAYS. WE'D SUFFERED CASUALTIES.
WE NEEDED EVERY LAST SOLDIER IF WE WERE TO HOLD OUR POSITION.
OUR ALLIES ARRIVED AT DAWN ON DAY FOUR.
THEY CHOPPERED SOME OF US OUT.
BUT WE WERE STILL TAKING A LOT OF FIRE.
I WAS ON THE GROUND. I SAW BODIES FALLING FROM THE SKY.
VET
LIKE APPLES FALLING FROM A TREE.
WE RAN OVER WITH OUR ARMS OUT...
...LIKE ...LIKE WE MIGHT BE ABLE TO CATCH THEM.

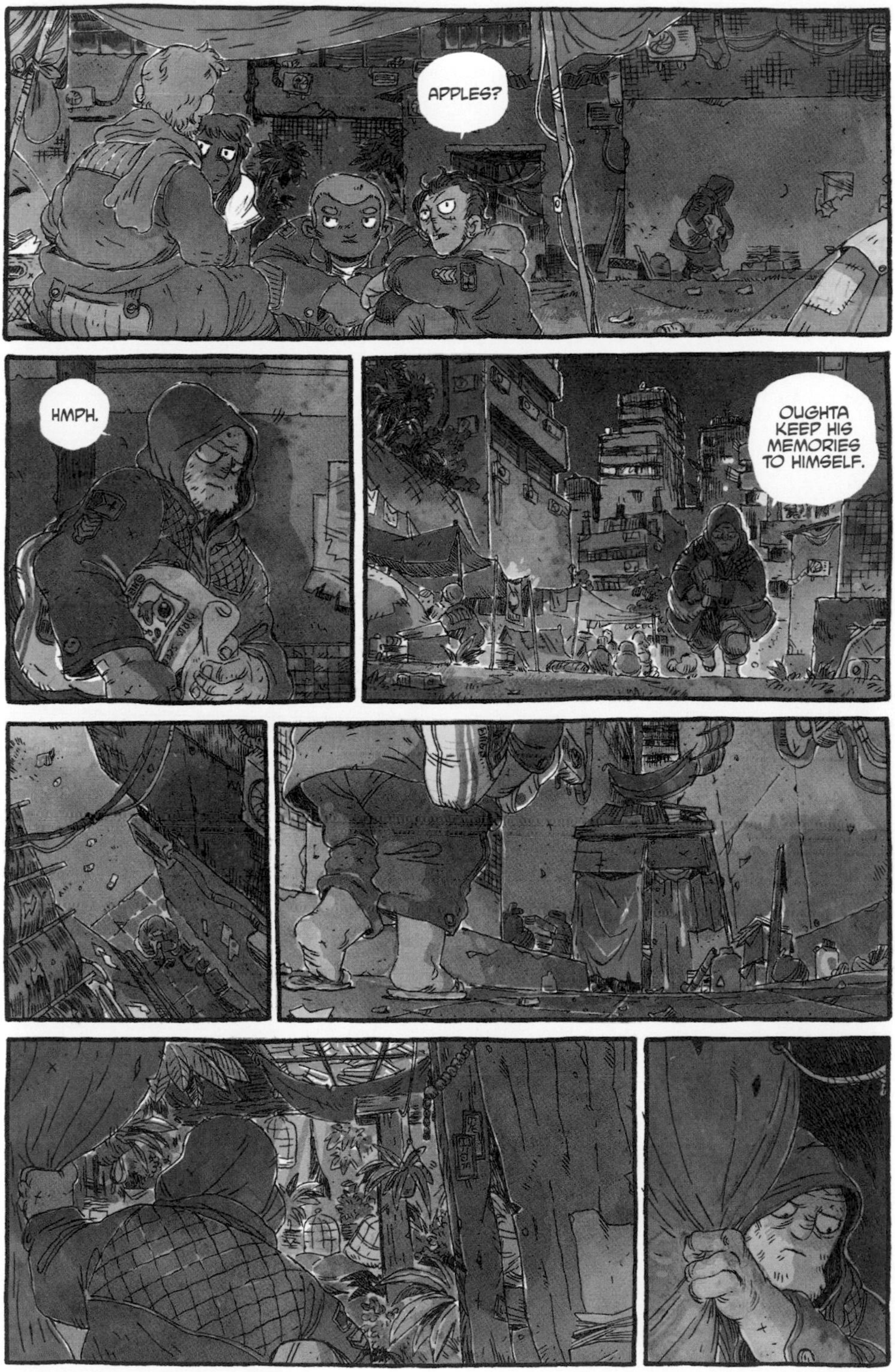

APPLES?
HMPH.
OUGHTA KEEP HIS MEMORIES TO HIMSELF.

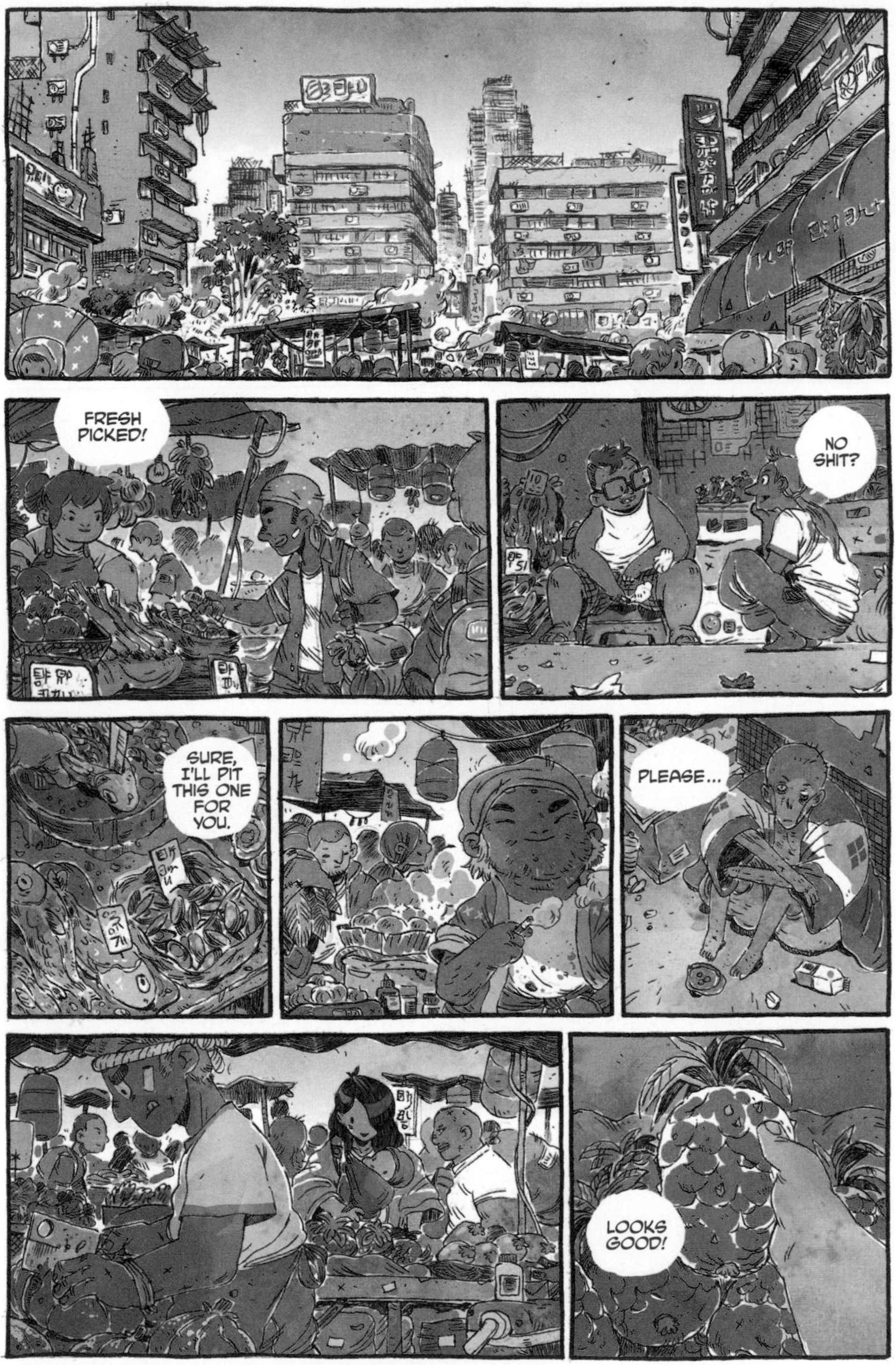
FRESH PICKED!
NO SHIT?
SURE, I'LL PIT THIS ONE FOR YOU.
PLEASE...
LOOKS GOOD!

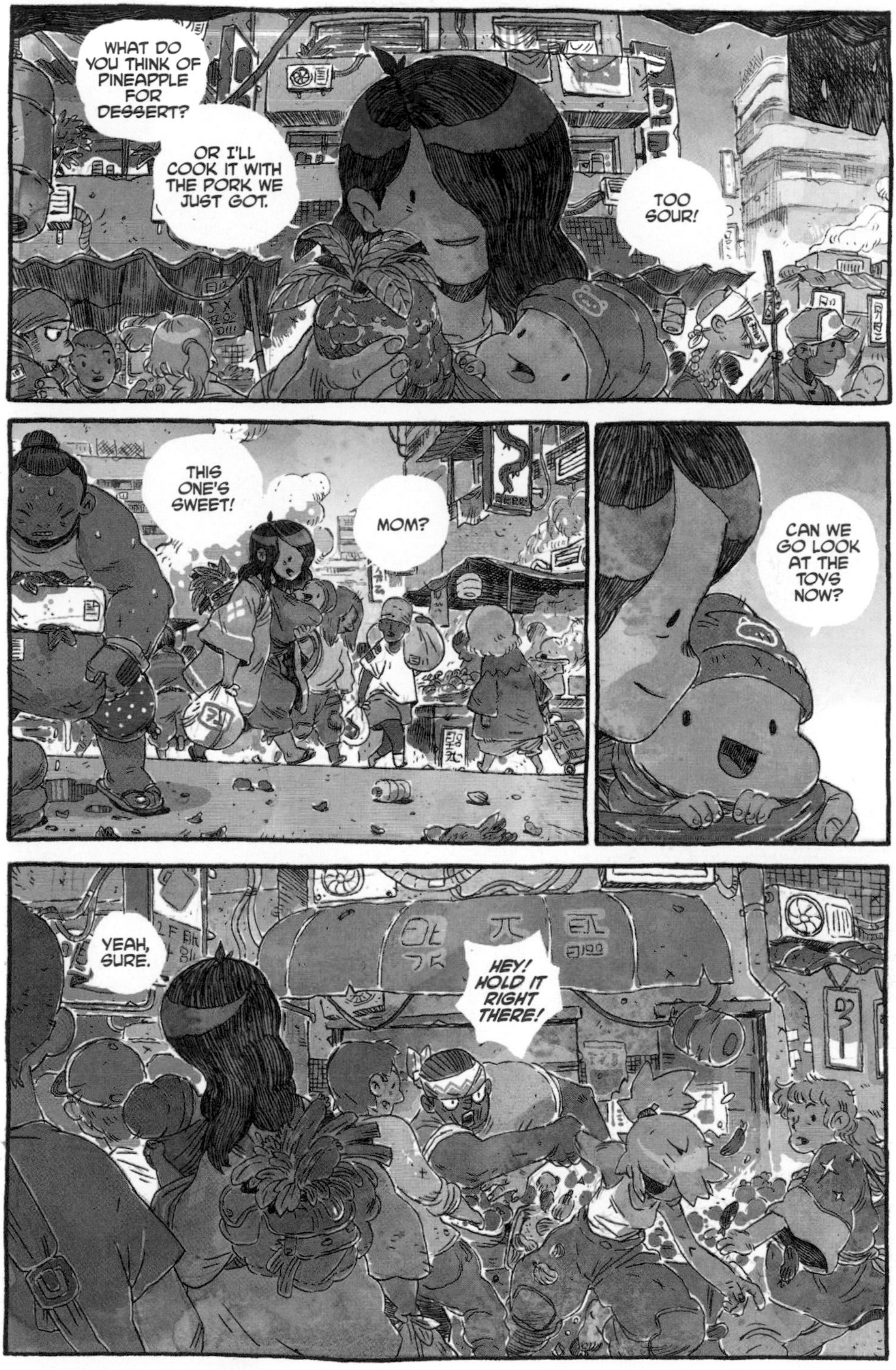
WHAT DO YOU THINK OF PINEAPPLE FOR DESSERT?
OR I'LL COOK IT WITH THE PORK WE JUST GOT.
TOO SOUR!
THIS ONE'S SWEET!
MOM?
CAN WE GO LOOK AT THE TOYS NOW?
YEAH, SURE.
HEY! HOLD IT RIGHT THERE!

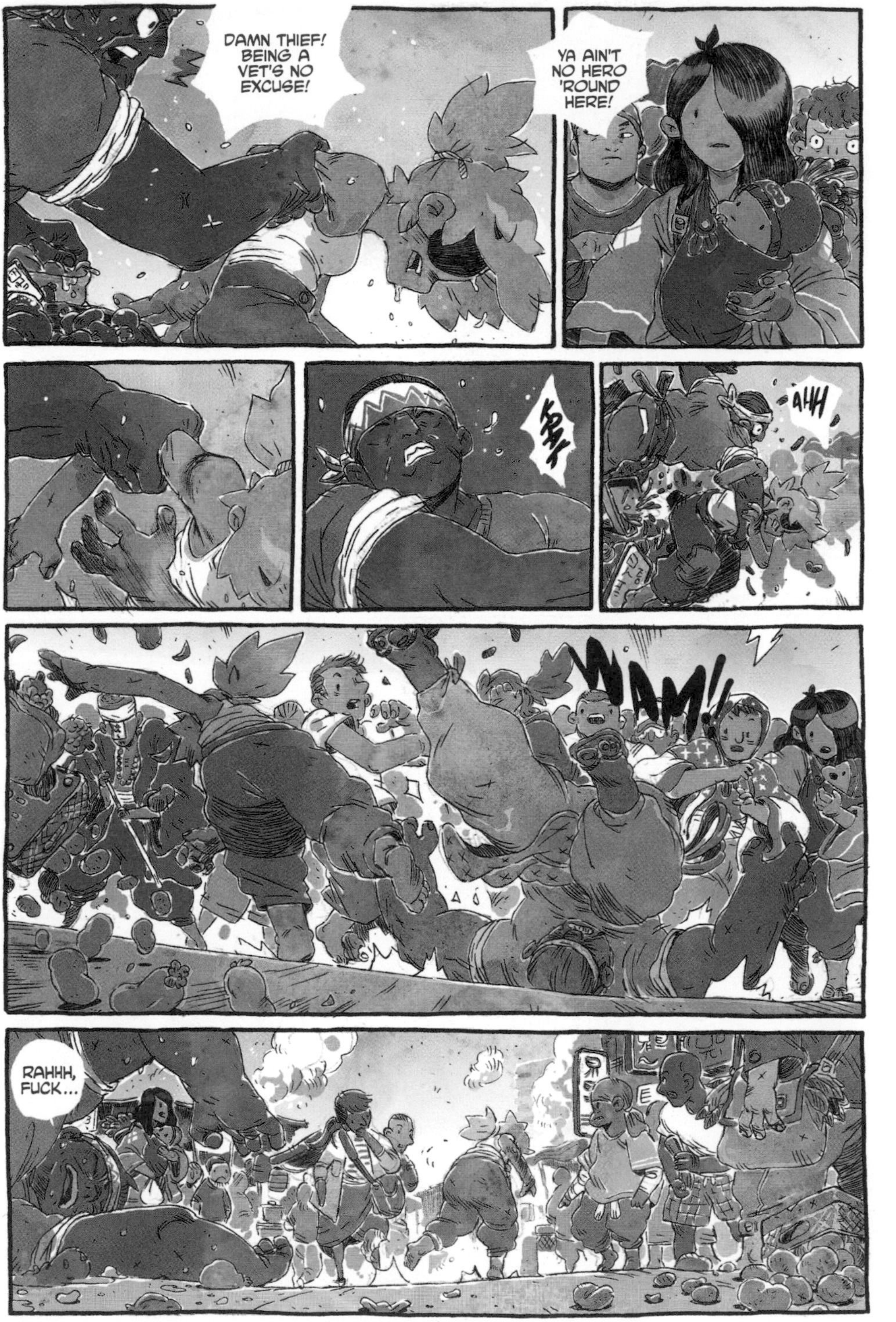
DAMN THIEF! BEING A VET'S NO EXCUSE!
YA AIN'T NO HERO 'ROUND HERE!
AHH
WAM!!
RAHHH, FUCK...

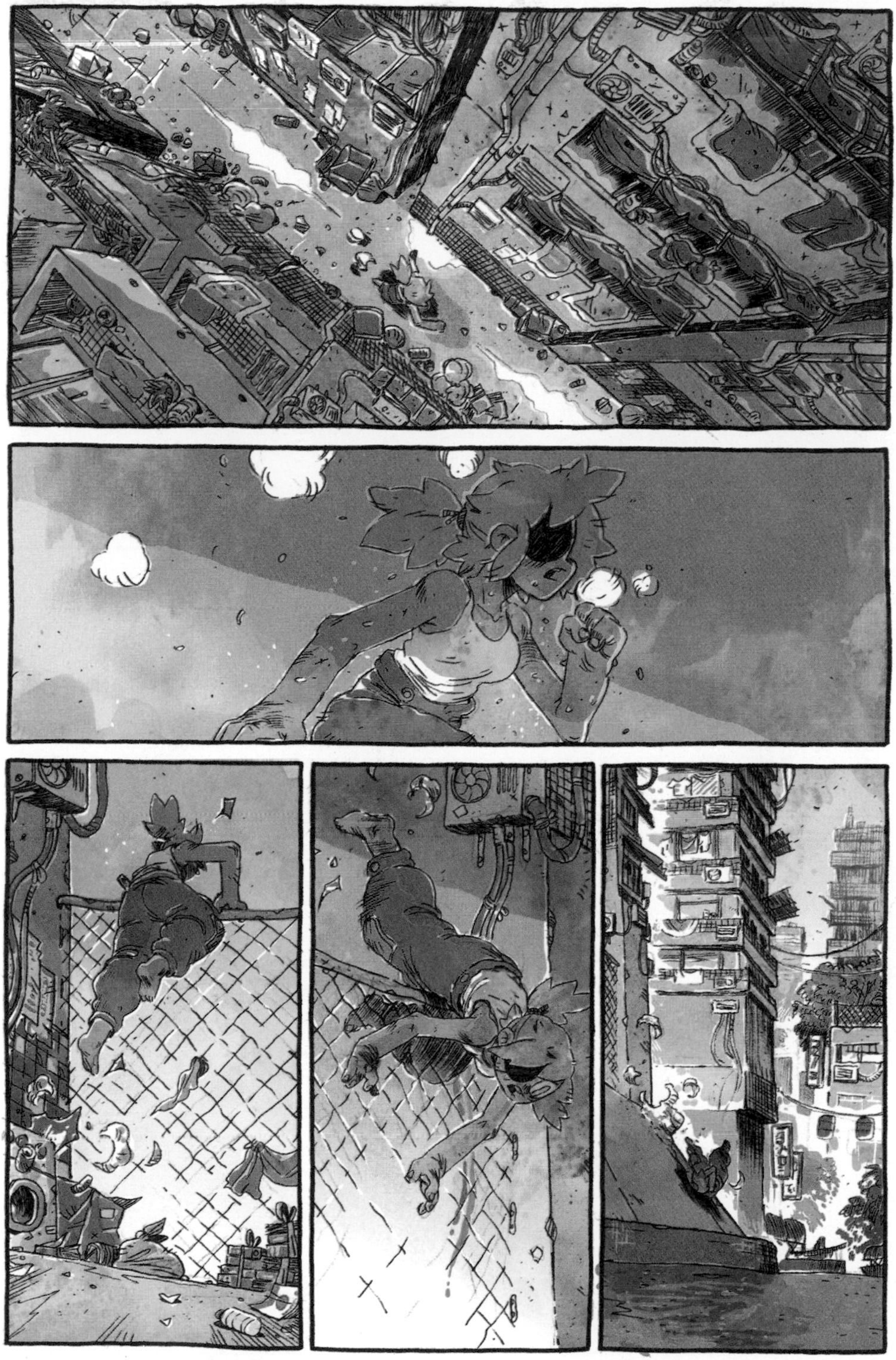

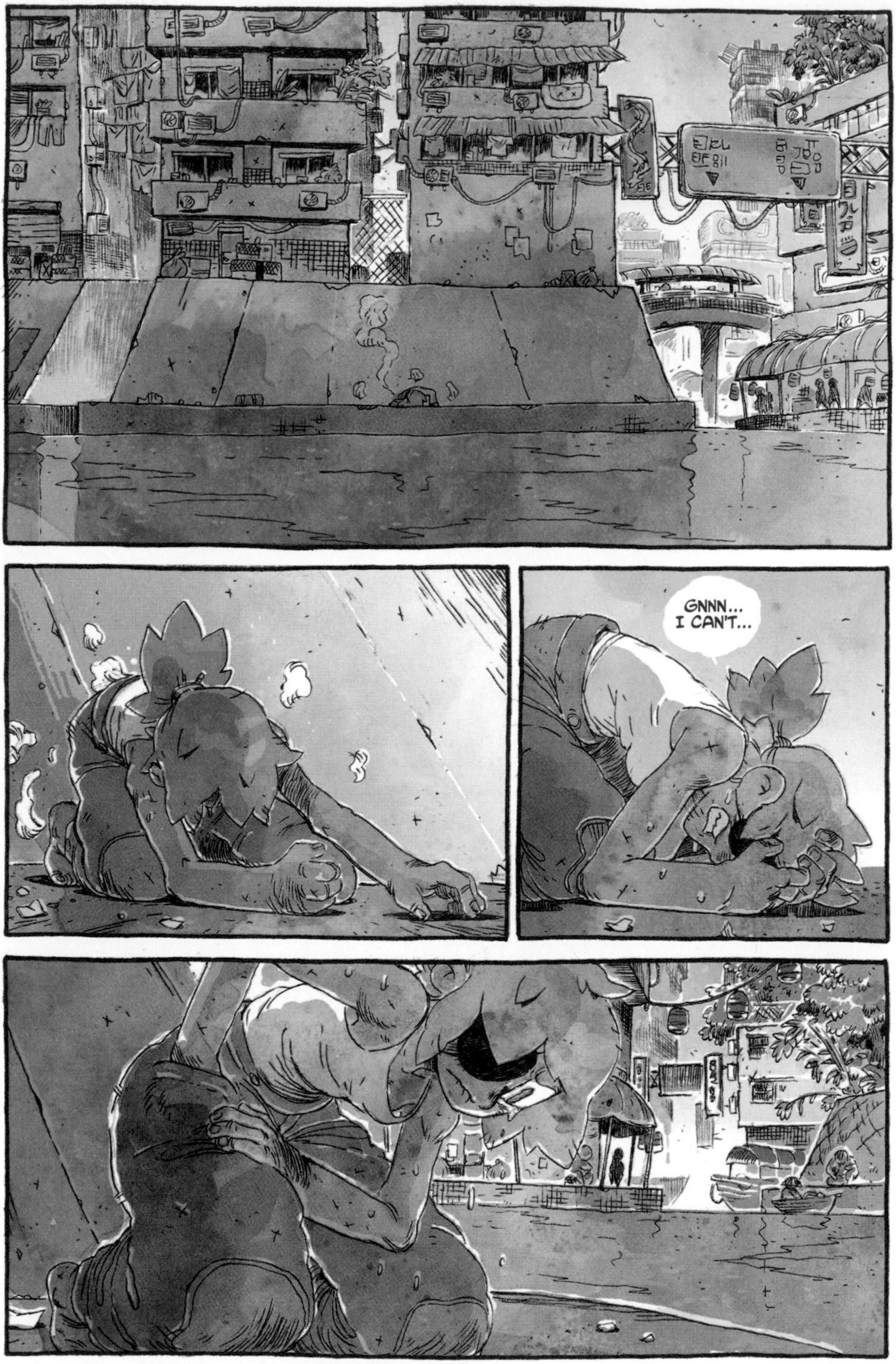
GNNN...
I CAN'T...

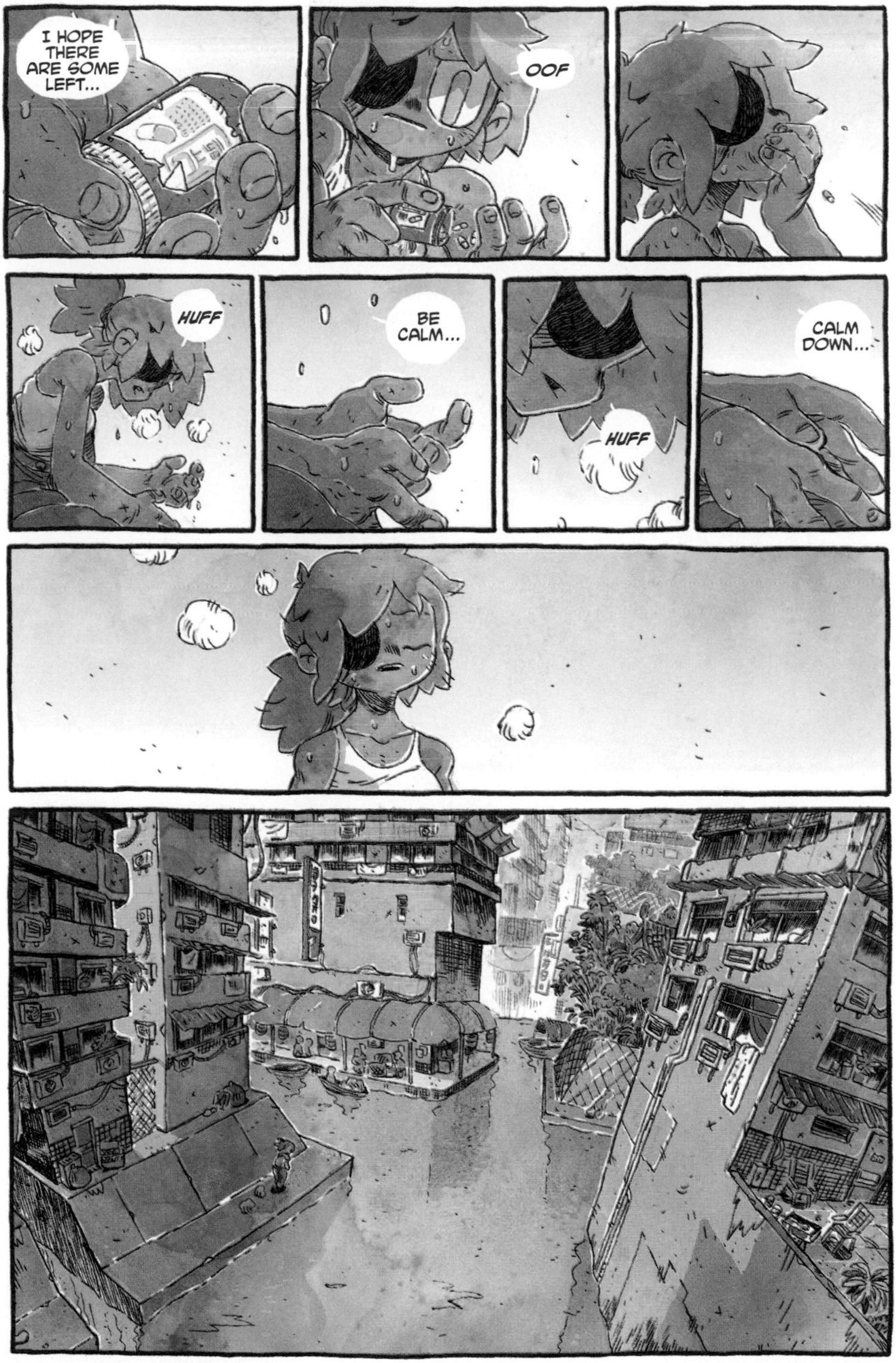
I HOPE THERE ARE SOME LEFT...
OOF
HUFF
BE CALM...
HUFF
CALM DOWN...

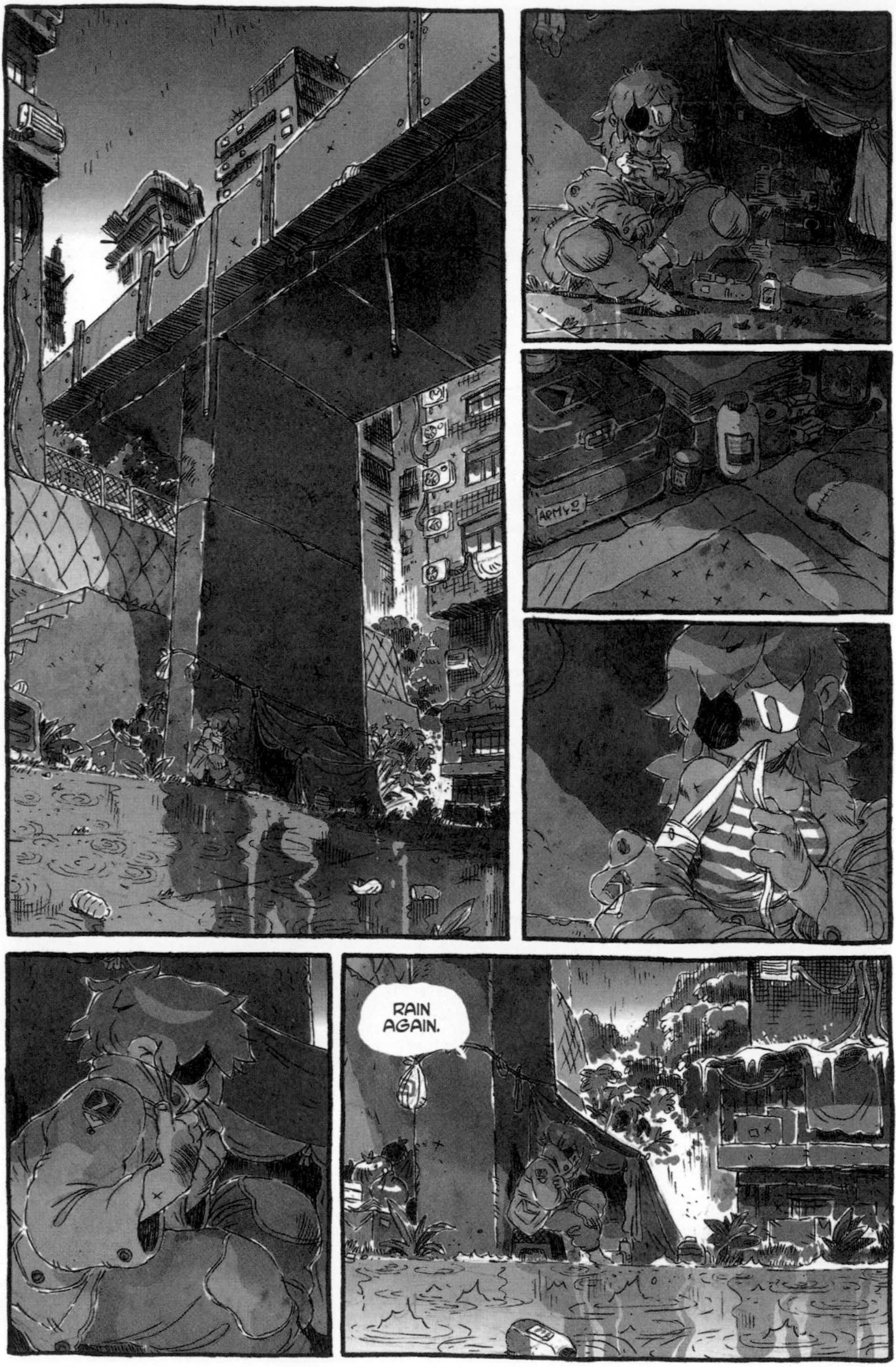
RAIN AGAIN.

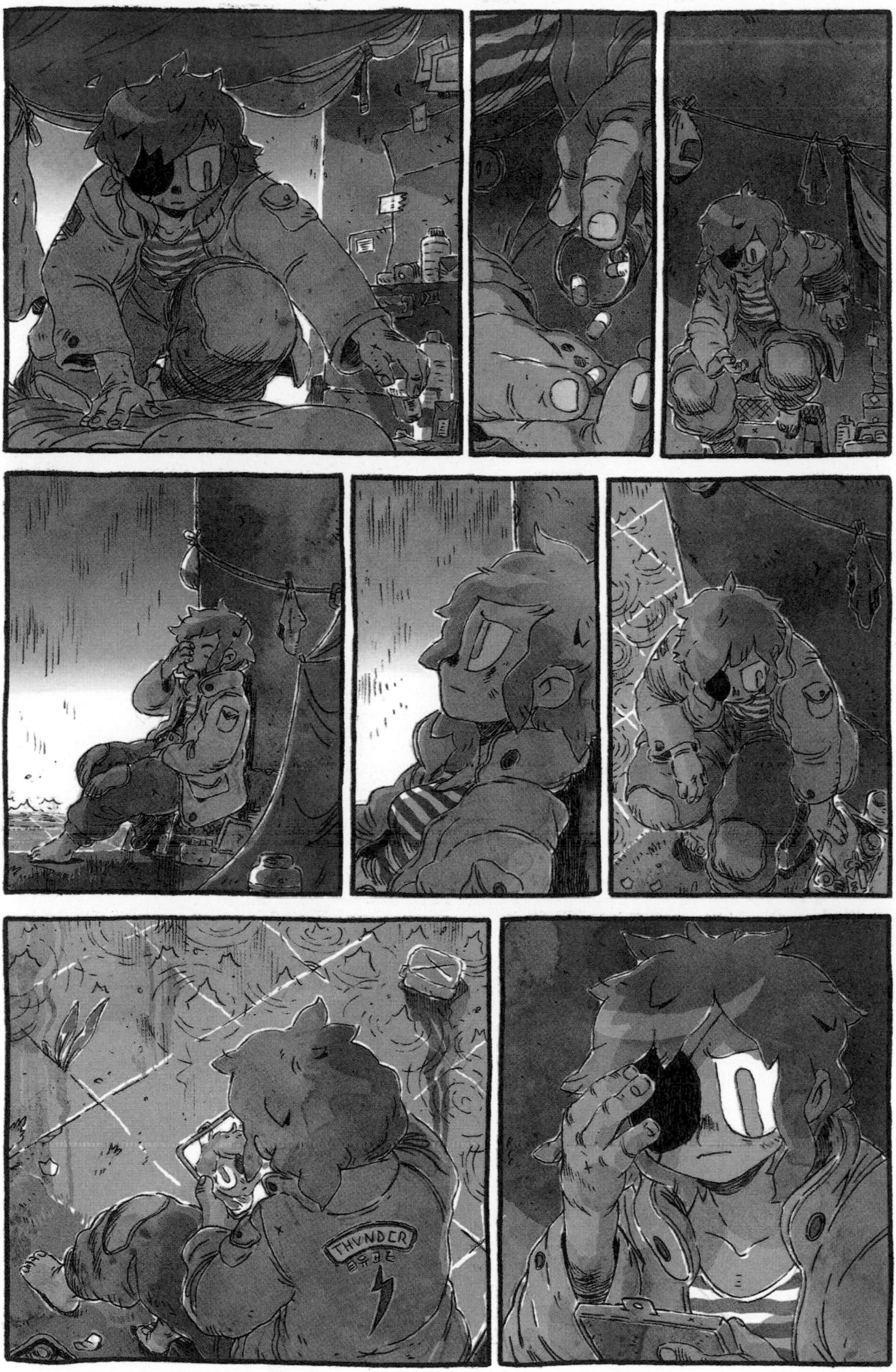
THVNDER

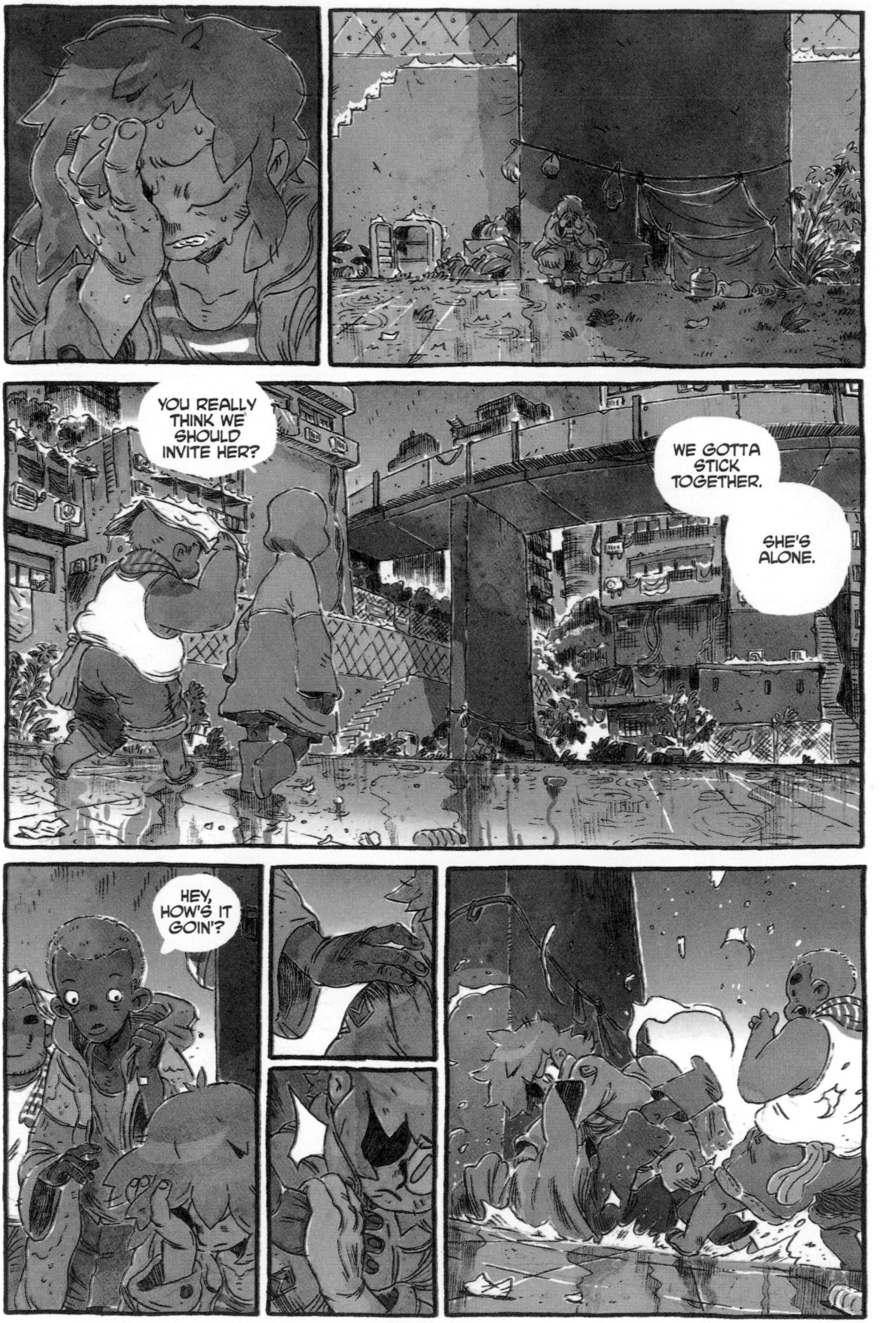
YOU REALLY THINK WE SHOULD INVITE HER?
WE GOTTA STICK TOGETHER.
SHE'S ALONE.
HEY, HOW'S IT GOIN'?

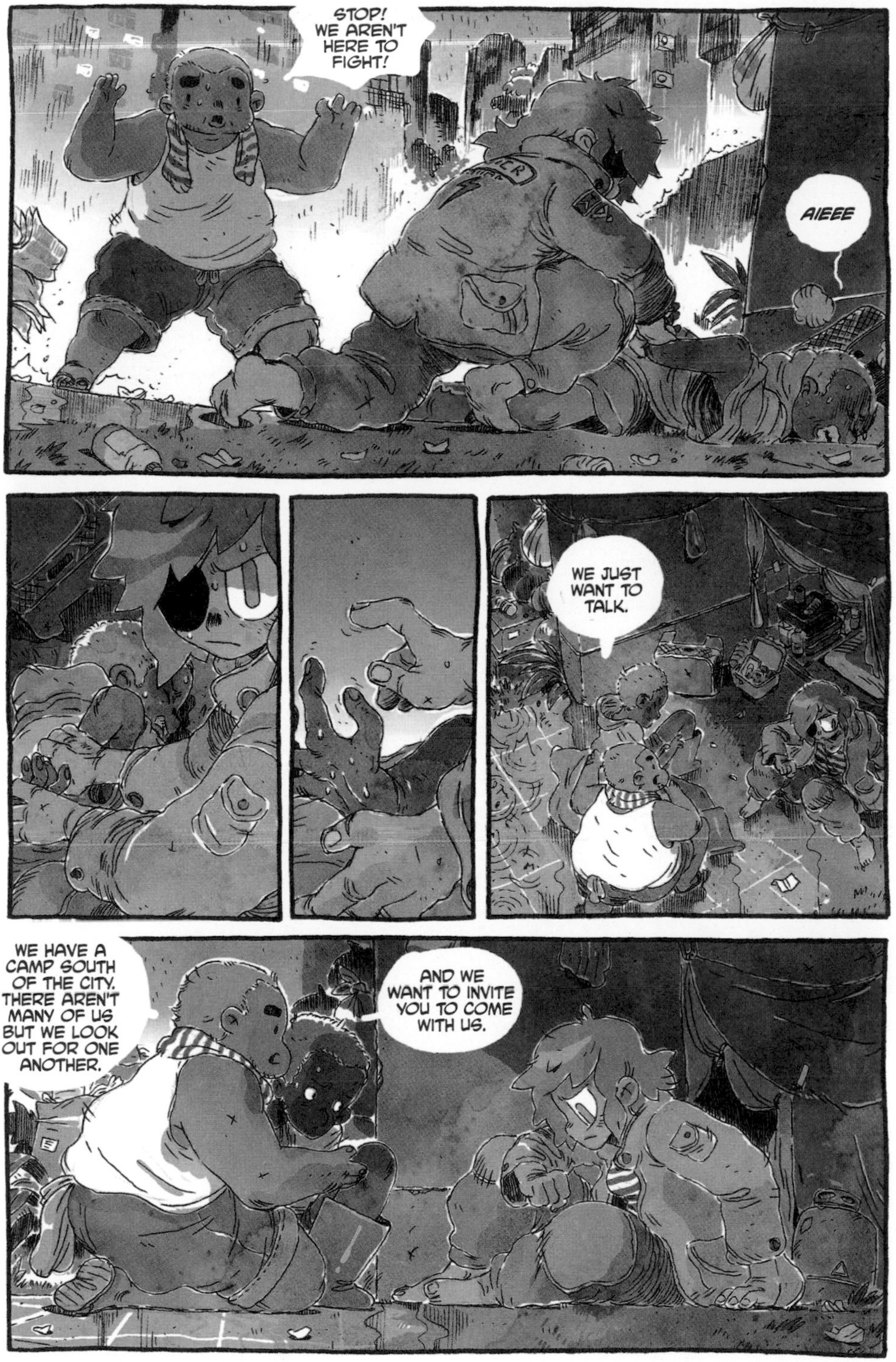
STOP! WE AREN'T HERE TO FIGHT!
AIEEE
WE JUST WANT TO TALK.
WE HAVE A CAMP SOUTH OF THE CITY. THERE AREN'T MANY OF US BUT WE LOOK OUT FOR ONE ANOTHER.
AND WE WANT TO INVITE YOU TO COME WITH US.

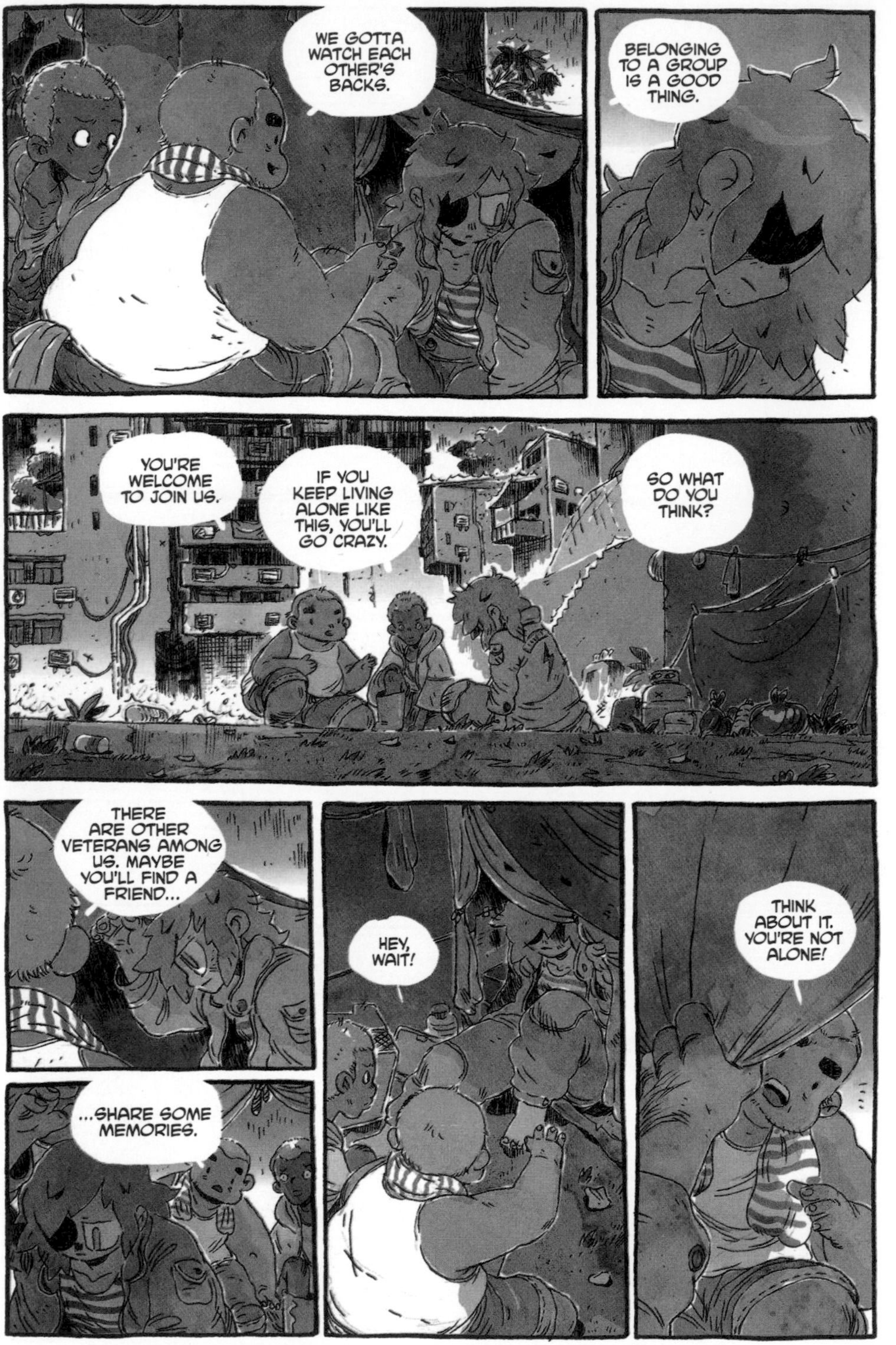
WE GOTTA WATCH EACH OTHER'S BACKS.
BELONGING TO A GROUP IS A GOOD THING.
YOU'RE WELCOME TO JOIN US.
IF YOU KEEP LIVING ALONE LIKE THIS, YOU'LL GO CRAZY.
SO WHAT DO YOU THINK?
THERE ARE OTHER VETERANS AMONG US. MAYBE YOU'LL FIND A FRIEND...
...SHARE SOME MEMORIES.
HEY, WAIT!
THINK ABOUT IT. YOU'RE NOT ALONE!

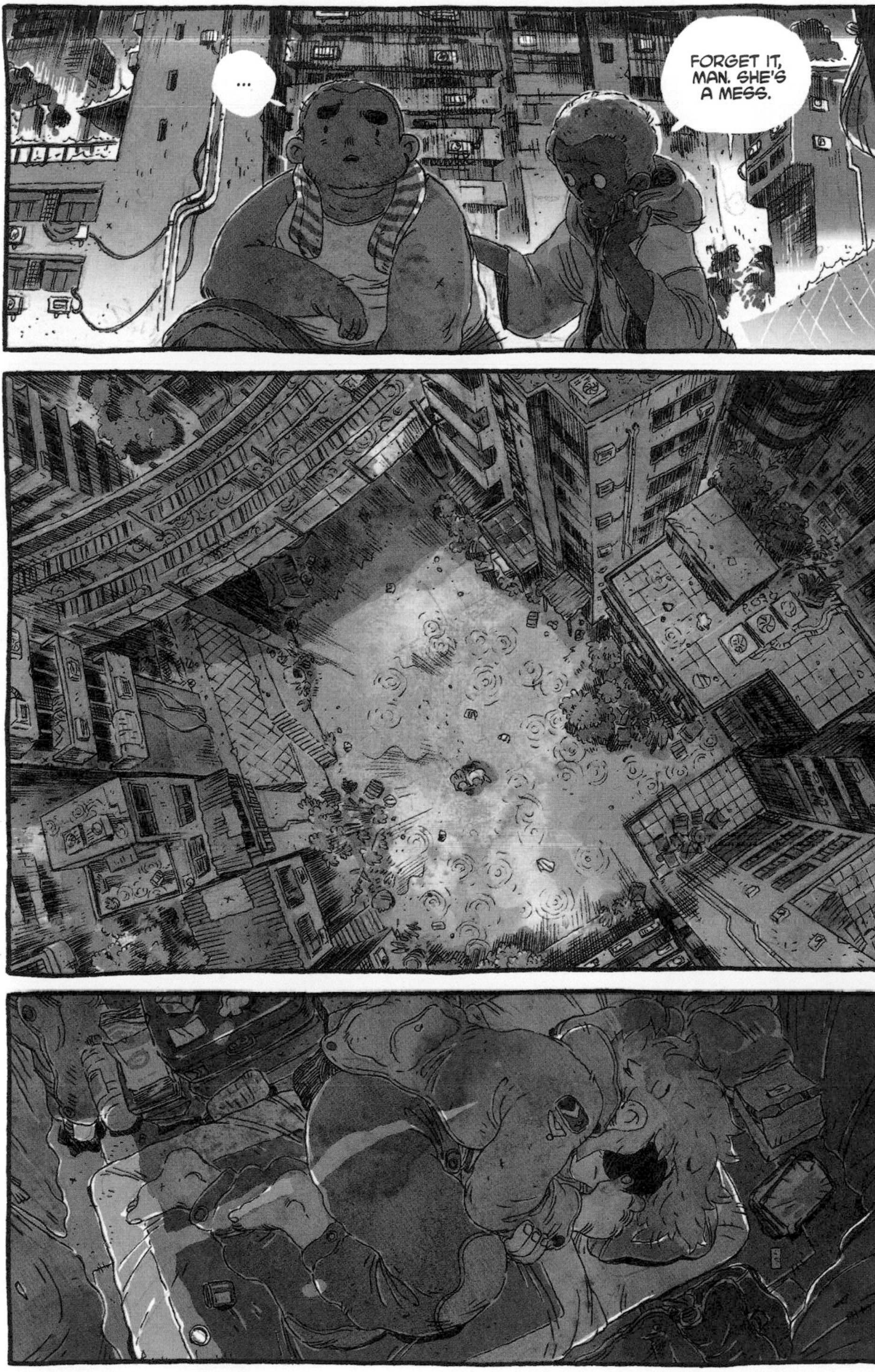
...
FORGET IT, MAN. SHE'S A MESS.

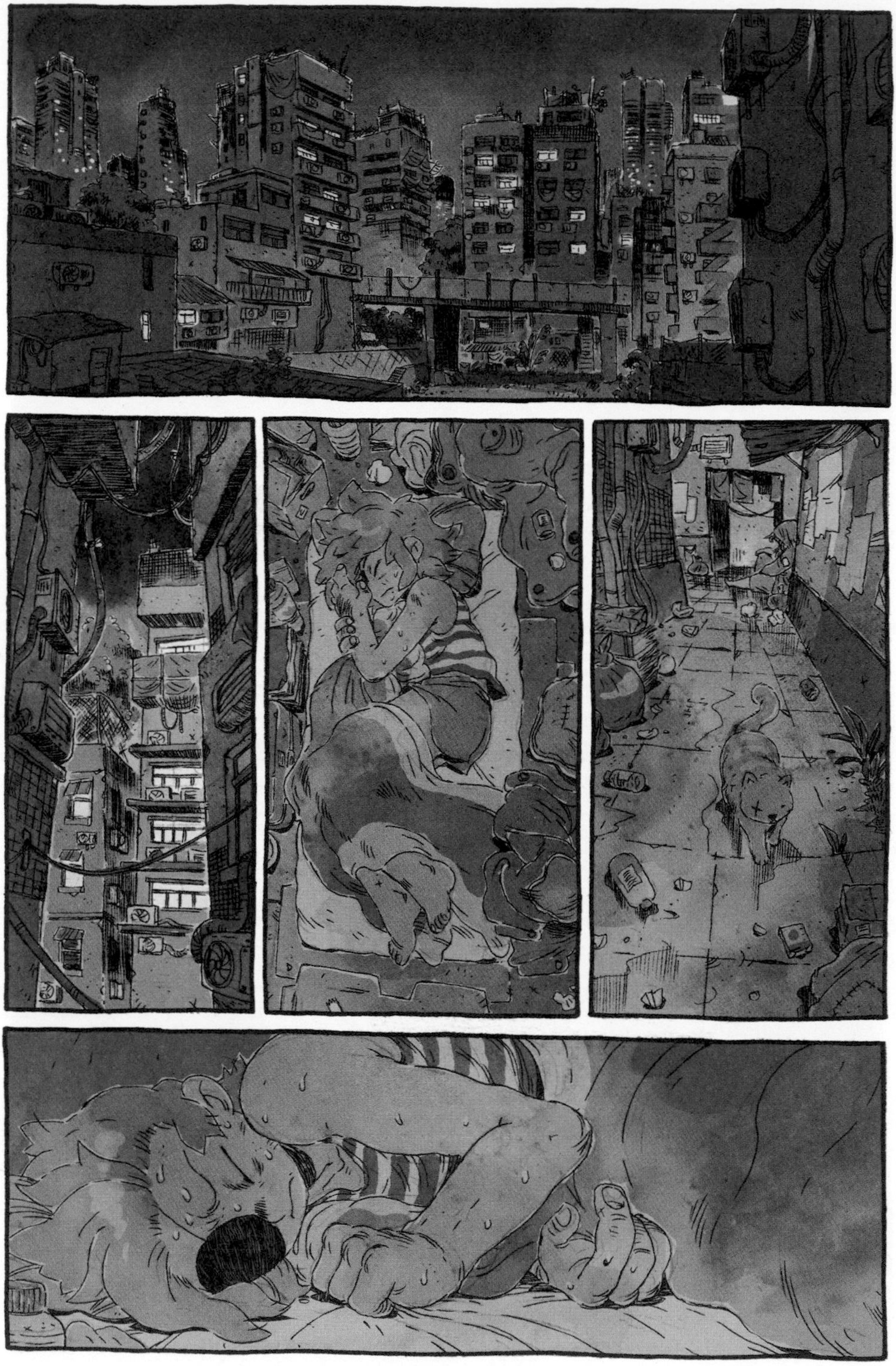

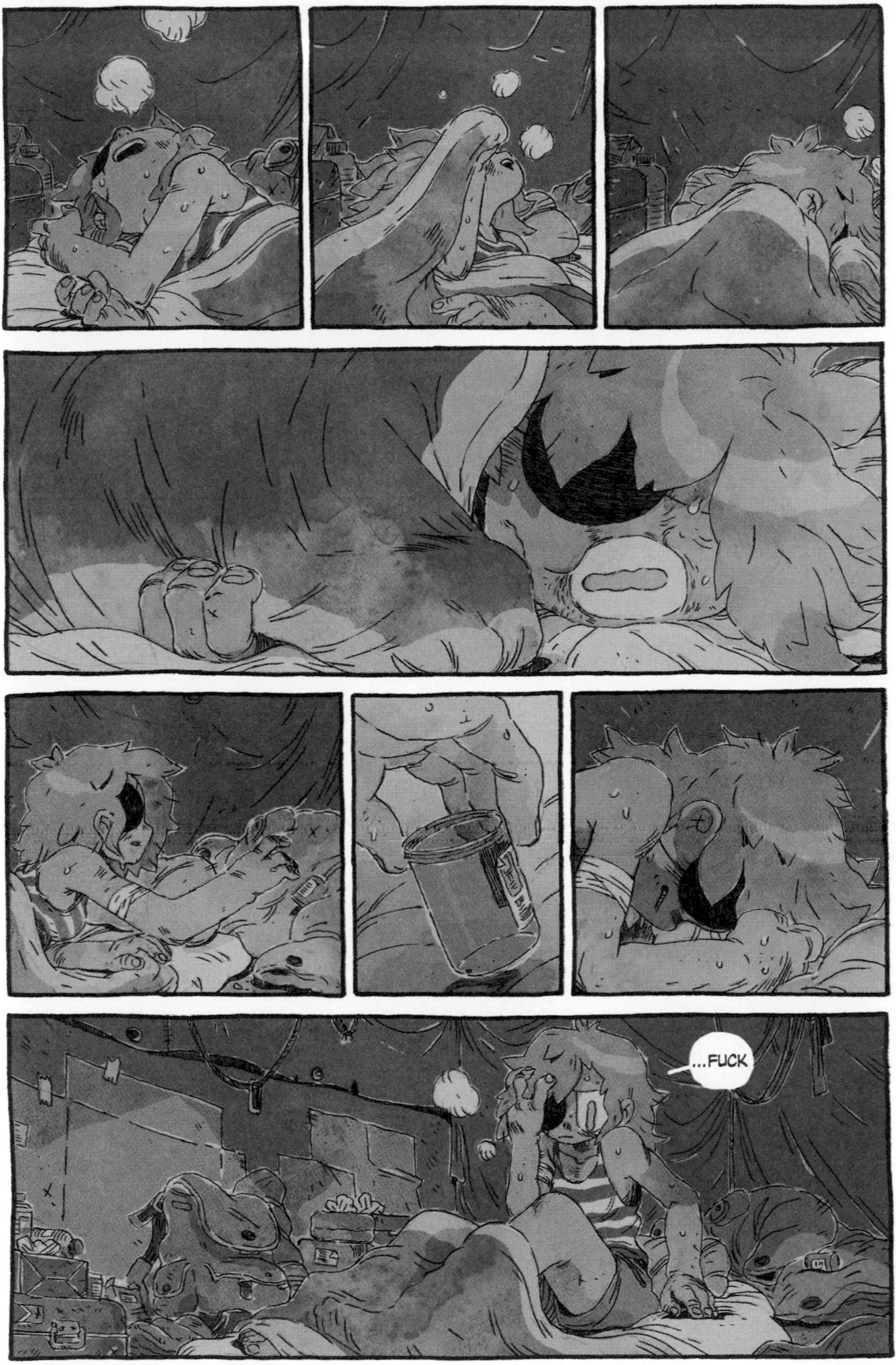
...FUCK

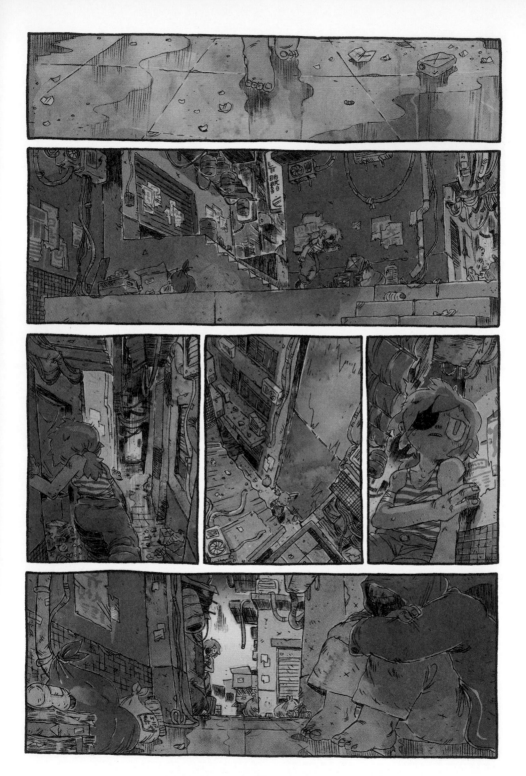

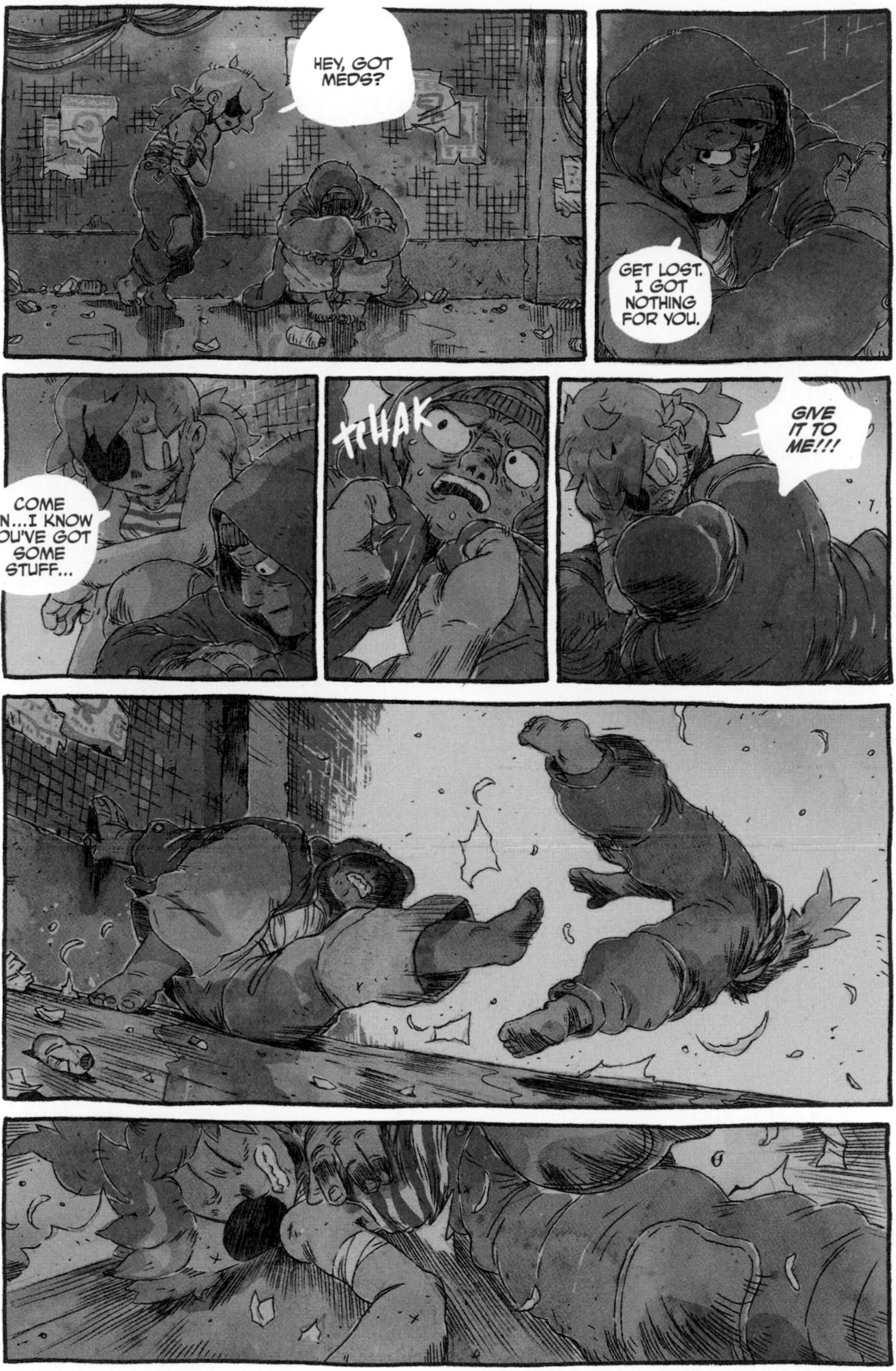
HEY, GOT MEDS?
GET LOST. I GOT NOTHING FOR YOU.
COME ON...I KNOW YOU'VE GOT SOME STUFF...
TCHAK
GIVE IT TO ME!!!

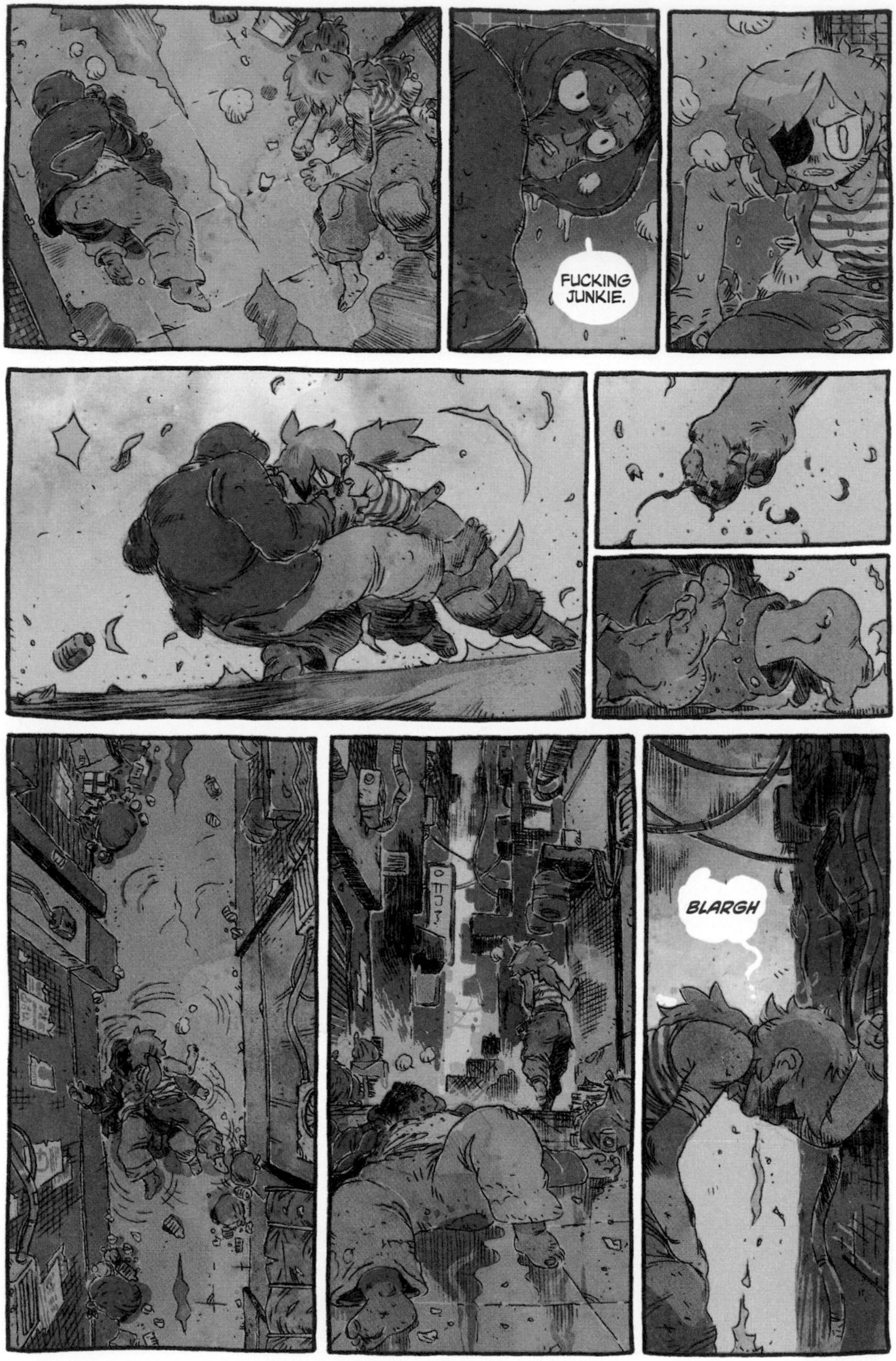
FUCKING JUNKIE.
BLARGH

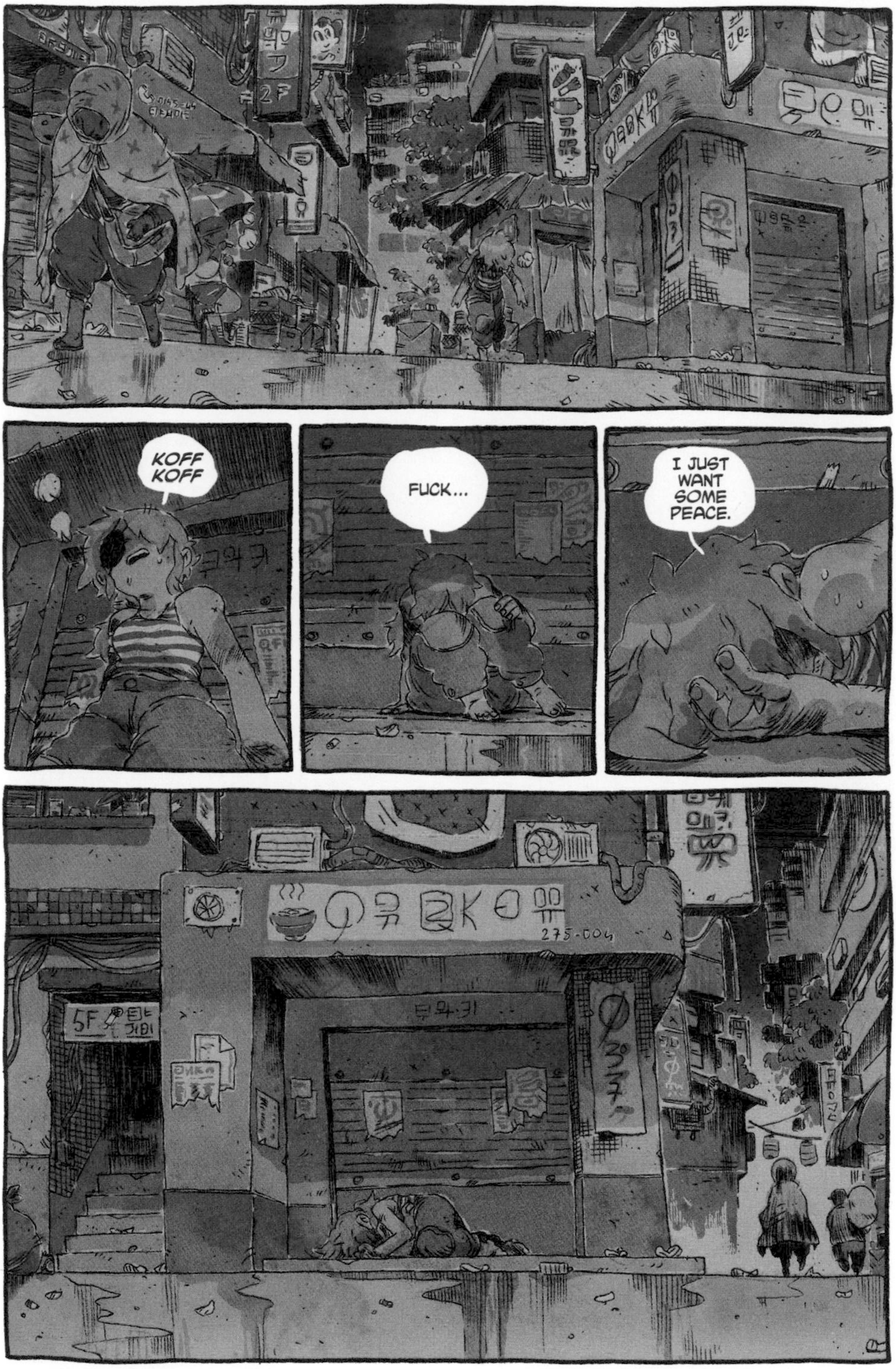

KOFF KOFF
FUCK...
I JUST WANT SOME PEACE.

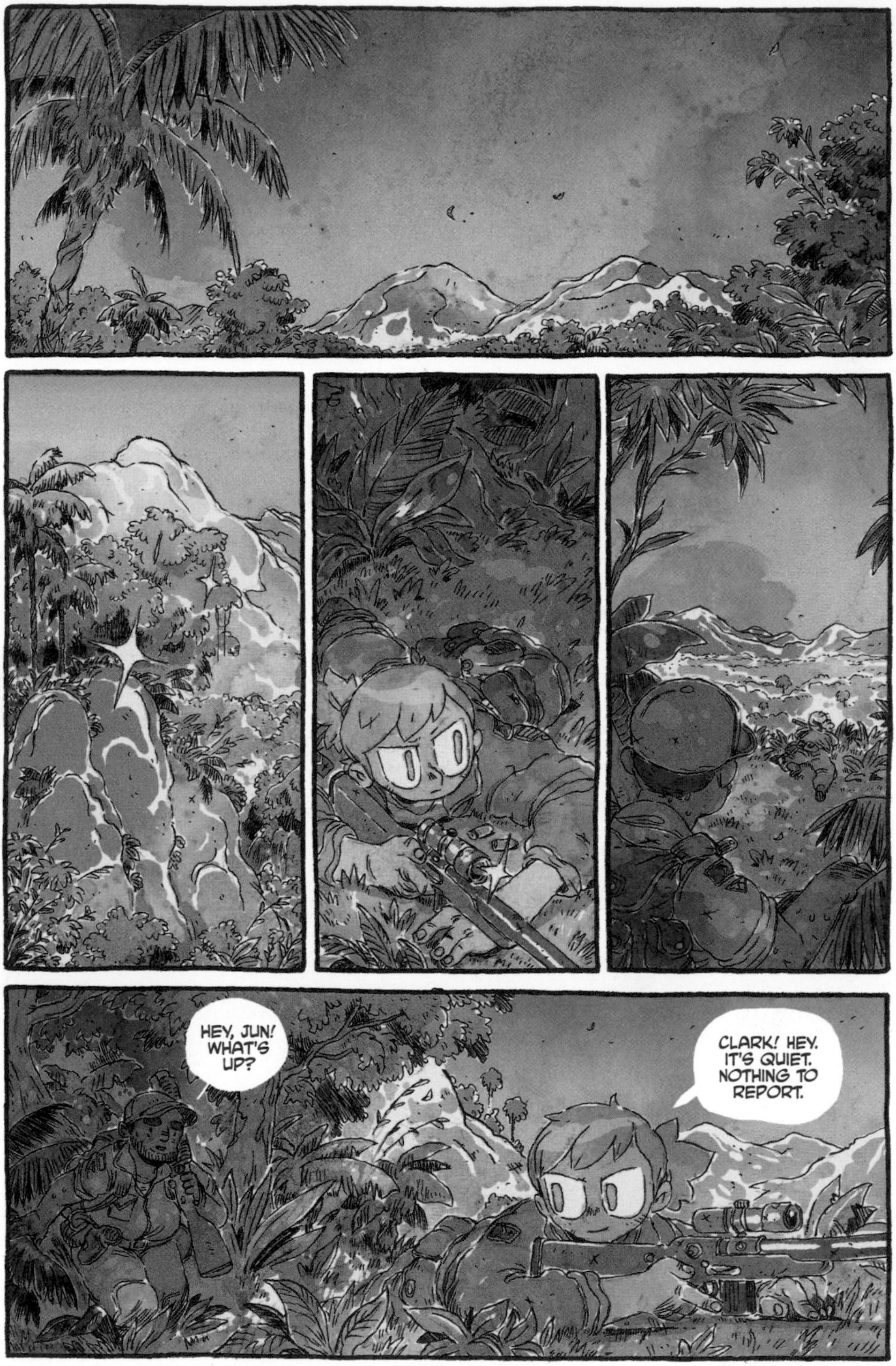
HEY, JUN! WHAT'S UP?
CLARK! HEY. IT'S QUIET. NOTHING TO REPORT.

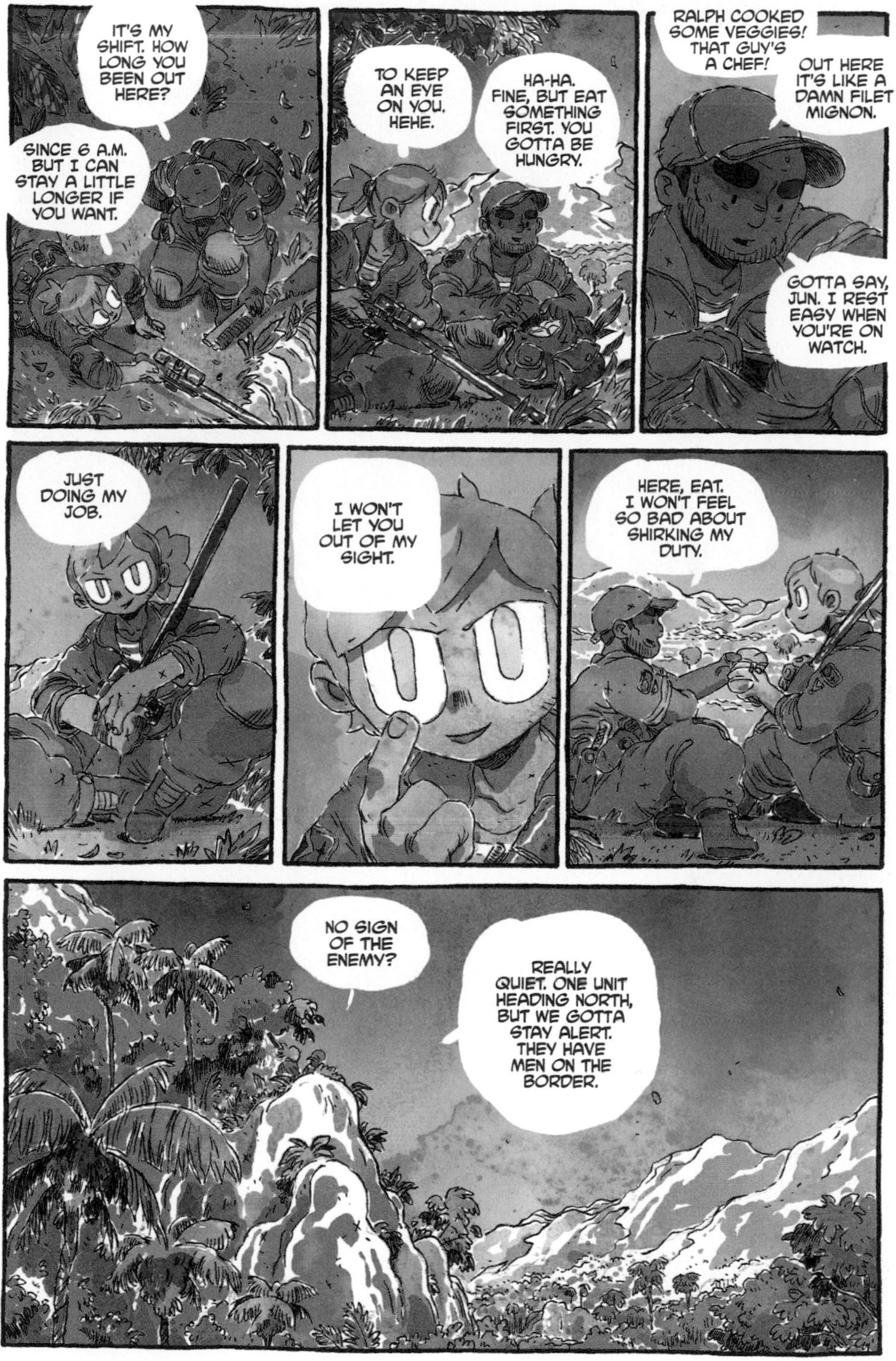
IT'S MY SHIFT. HOW LONG YOU BEEN OUT HERE?
SINCE 6 A.M. BUT I CAN STAY A LITTLE LONGER IF YOU WANT.
TO KEEP AN EYE ON YOU. HEHE.
HA-HA. FINE, BUT EAT SOMETHING FIRST. YOU GOTTA BE HUNGRY.
RALPH COOKED SOME VEGGIES! THAT GUY'S A CHEF!
OUT HERE IT'S LIKE A DAMN FILET MIGNON.
GOTTA SAY, JUN. I REST EASY WHEN YOU'RE ON WATCH.
JUST DOING MY JOB.
I WON'T LET YOU OUT OF MY SIGHT.
HERE, EAT. I WON'T FEEL SO BAD ABOUT SHIRKING MY DUTY.
NO SIGN OF THE ENEMY?
REALLY QUIET. ONE UNIT HEADING NORTH, BUT WE GOTTA STAY ALERT. THEY HAVE MEN ON THE BORDER.

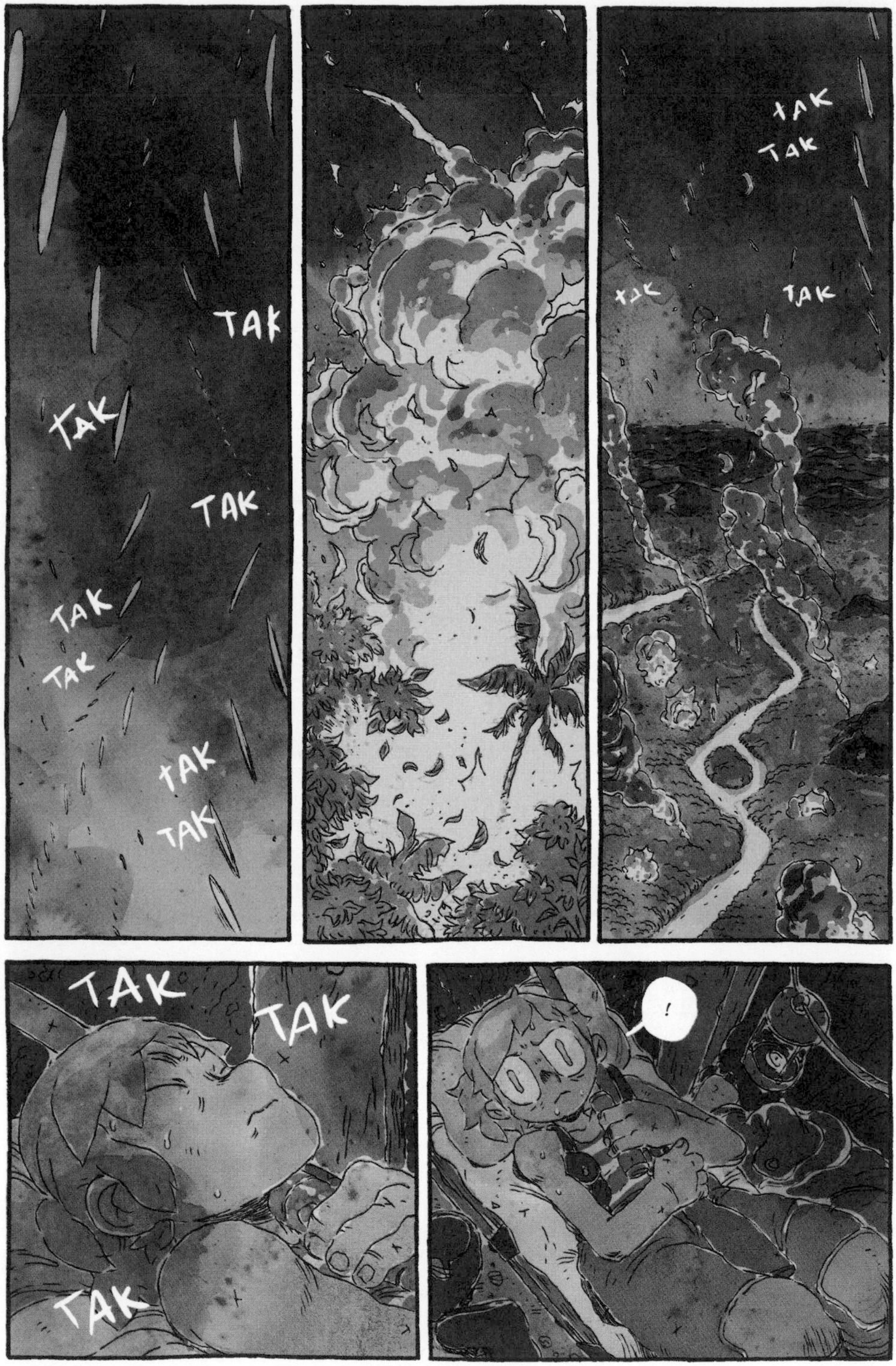
TAK
TAK
TAK
TAK
TAK
TAK
TAK
TAK
TAK
TAK
TAK
TAK
TAK
TAK
TAK
!

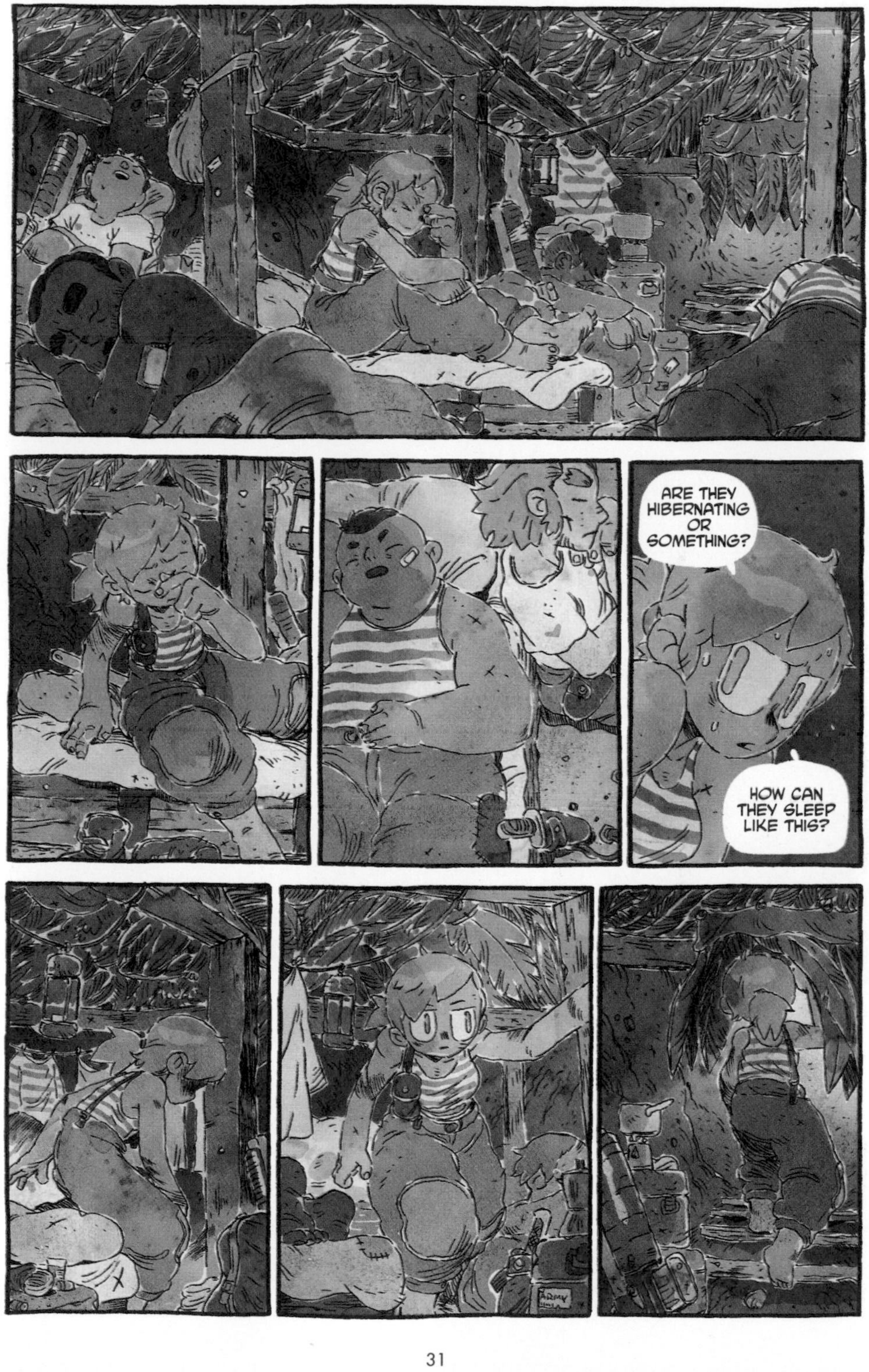
ARE THEY HIBERNATING OR SOMETHING?
HOW CAN THEY SLEEP LIKE THIS?

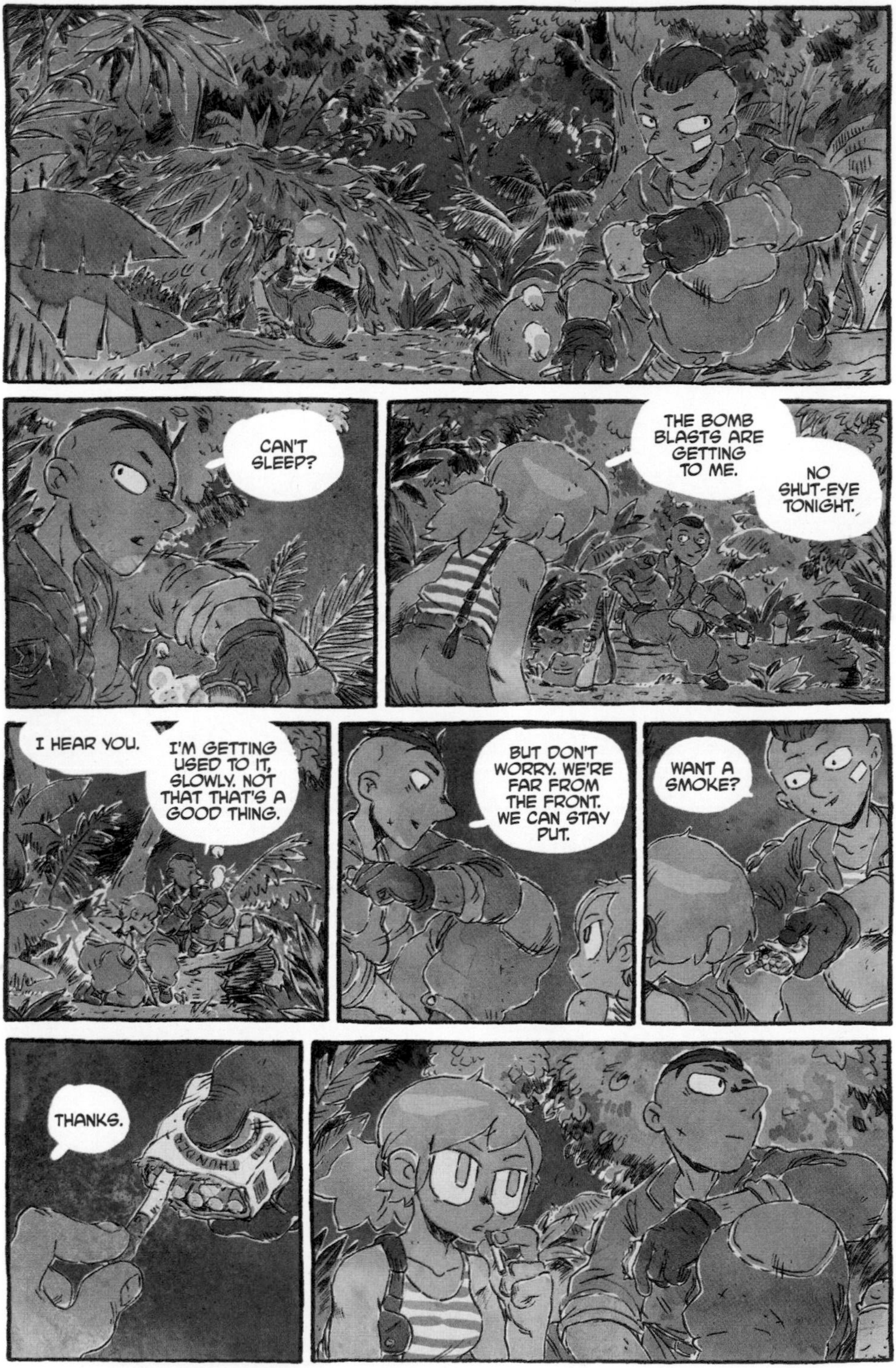
CAN'T SLEEP?
THE BOMB BLASTS ARE GETTING TO ME.
NO SHUT-EYE TONIGHT.
I HEAR YOU.
I'M GETTING USED TO IT, SLOWLY. NOT THAT THAT'S A GOOD THING.
BUT DON'T WORRY. WE'RE FAR FROM THE FRONT. WE CAN STAY PUT.
WANT A SMOKE?
THANKS.

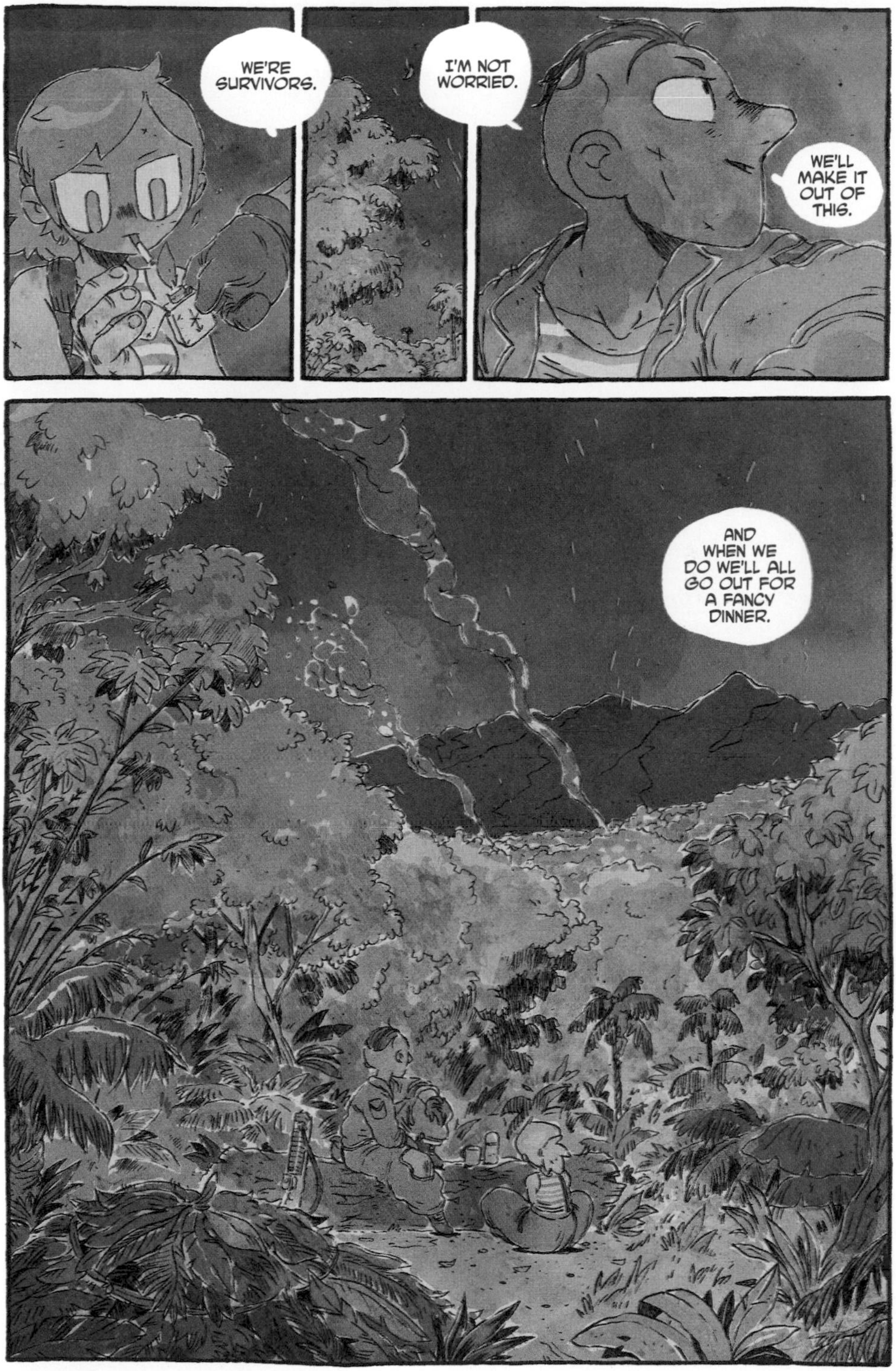
WE'RE SURVIVORS.
I'M NOT WORRIED.
WE'LL MAKE IT OUT OF THIS.
AND WHEN WE DO WE'LL ALL GO OUT FOR A FANCY DINNER.

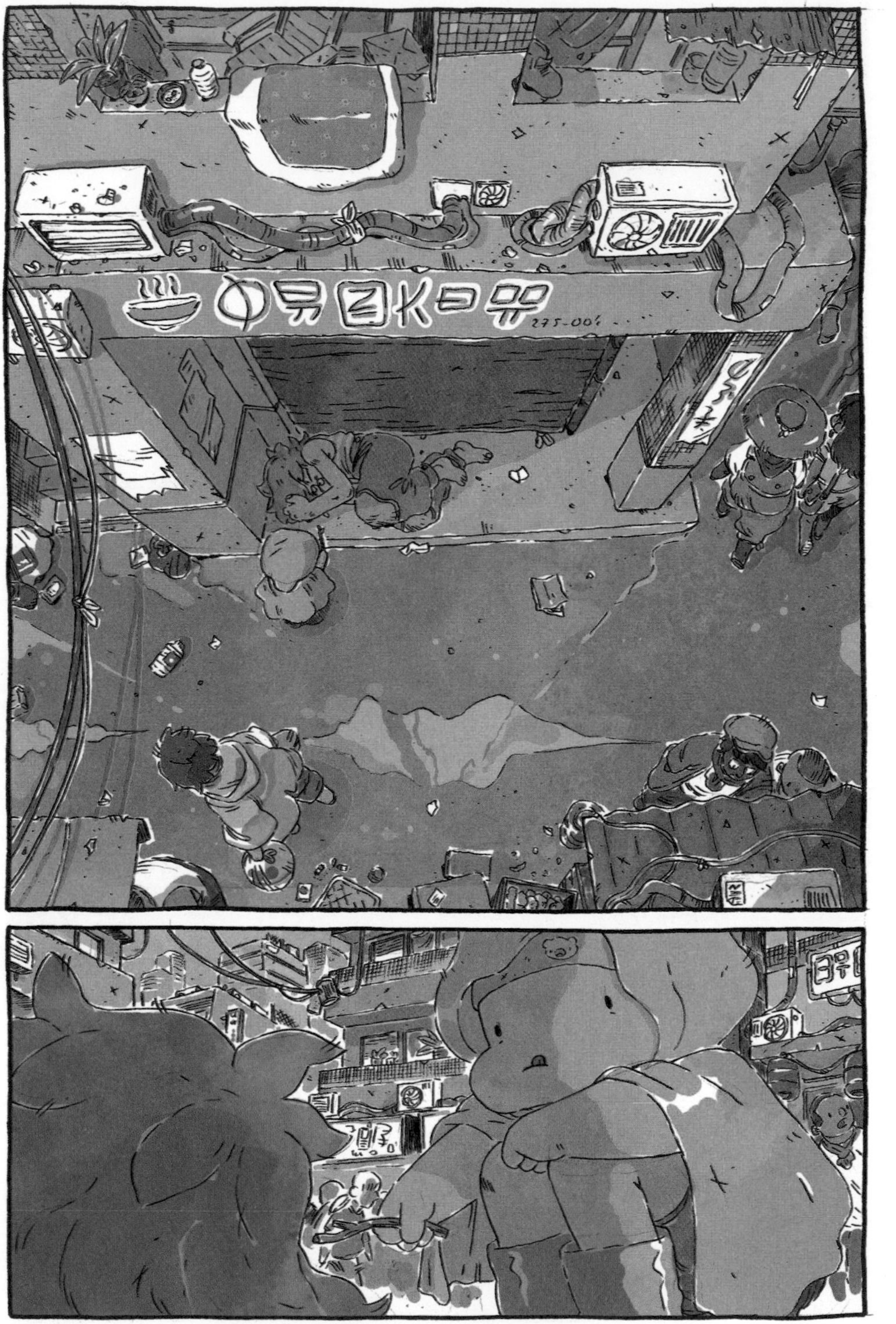

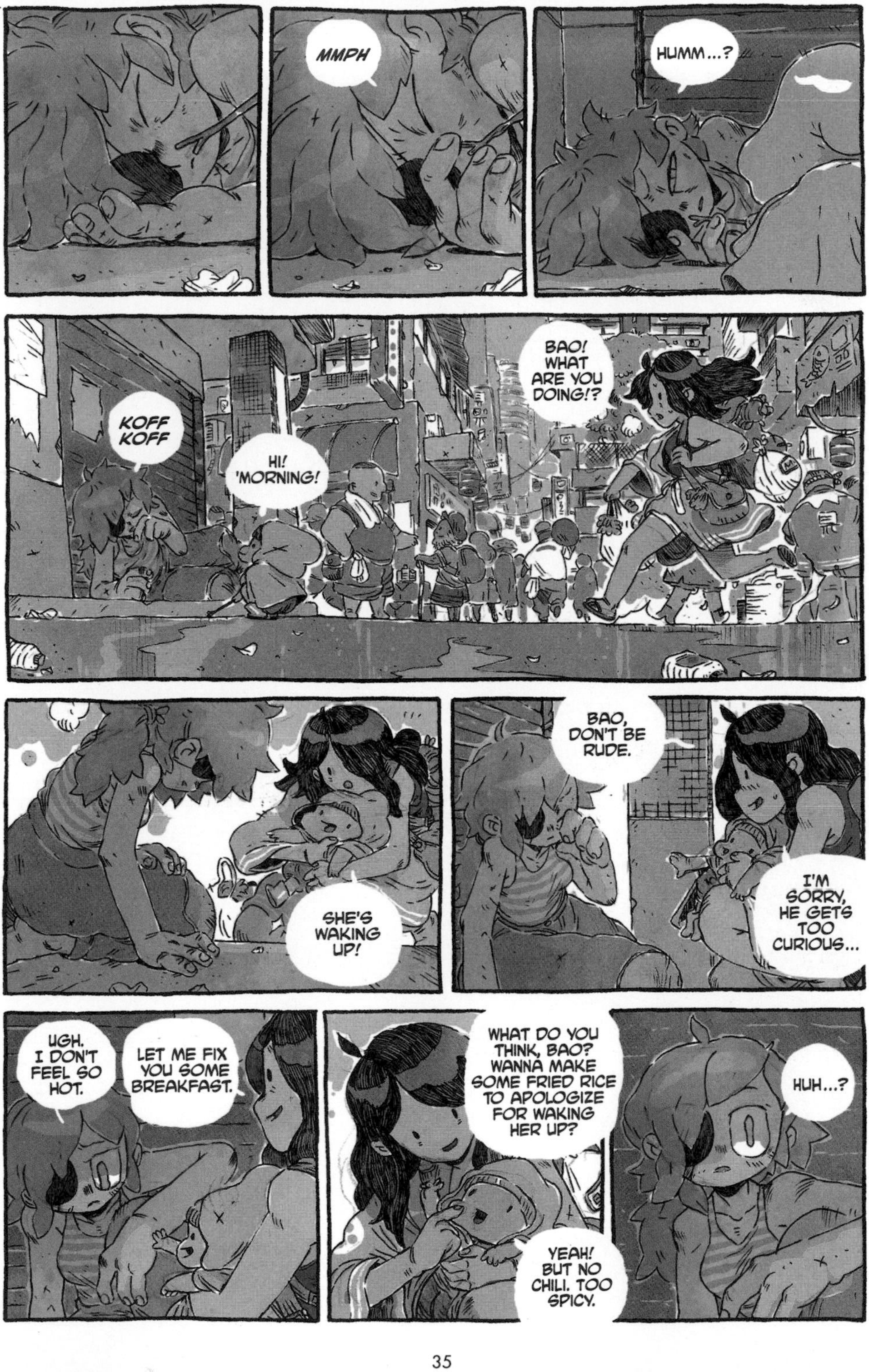

MMPH
HUMM...?
KOFF KOFF
HI! 'MORNING!
BAO! WHAT ARE YOU DOING!?
SHE'S WAKING UP!
BAO, DON'T BE RUDE.
I'M SORRY, HE GETS TOO CURIOUS...
UGH. I DON'T FEEL SO HOT.
LET ME FIX YOU SOME BREAKFAST.
WHAT DO YOU THINK, BAO? WANNA MAKE SOME FRIED RICE TO APOLOGIZE FOR WAKING HER UP?
YEAH! BUT NO CHILI. TOO SPICY.
HUH...?

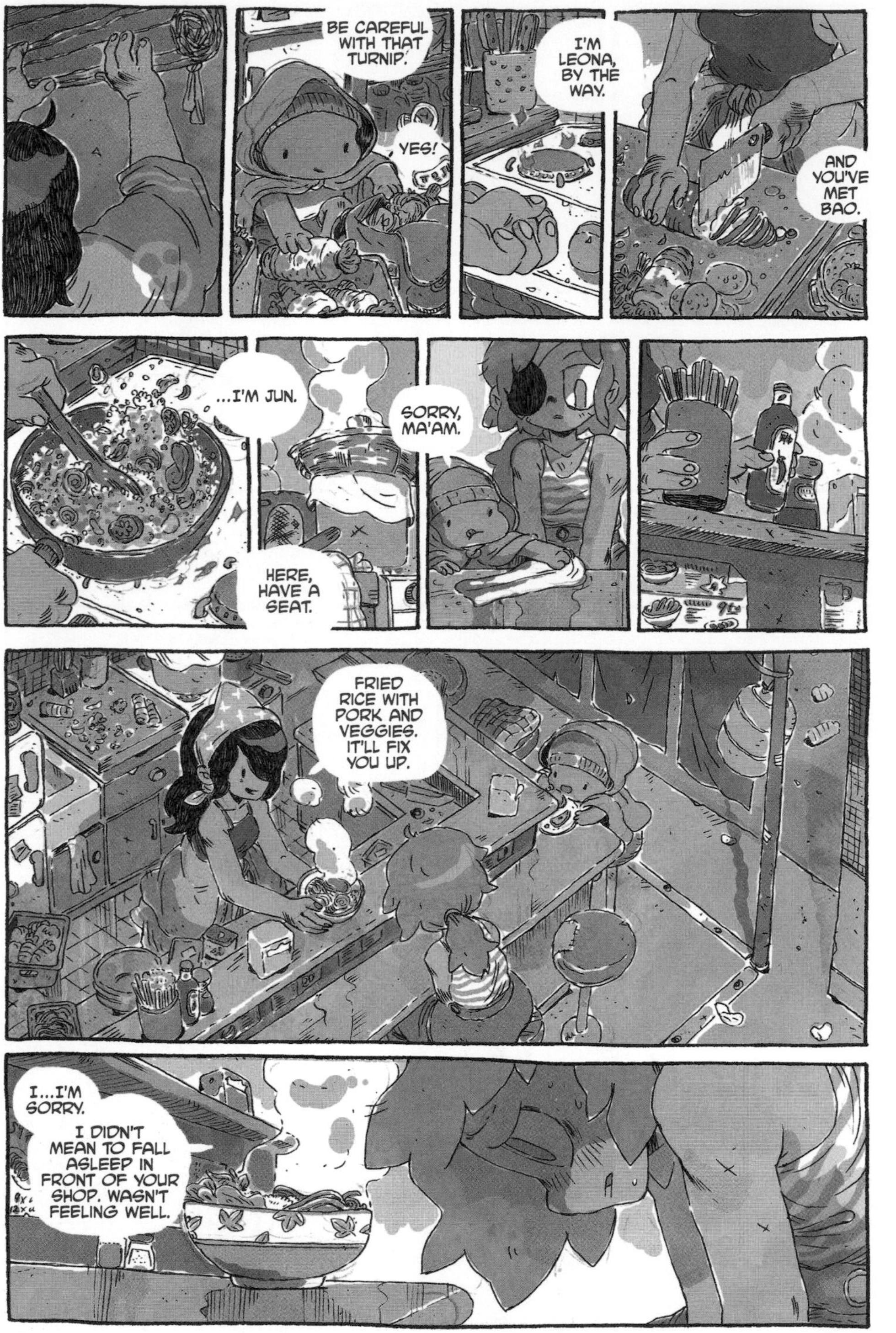

BE CAREFUL WITH THAT TURNIP.
YES!
I'M LEONA, BY THE WAY.
AND YOU'VE MET BAO.
...I'M JUN.
SORRY, MA'AM.
HERE, HAVE A SEAT.
FRIED RICE WITH PORK AND VEGGIES. IT'LL FIX YOU UP.
I...I'M SORRY.
I DIDN'T MEAN TO FALL ASLEEP IN FRONT OF YOUR SHOP. WASN'T FEELING WELL.

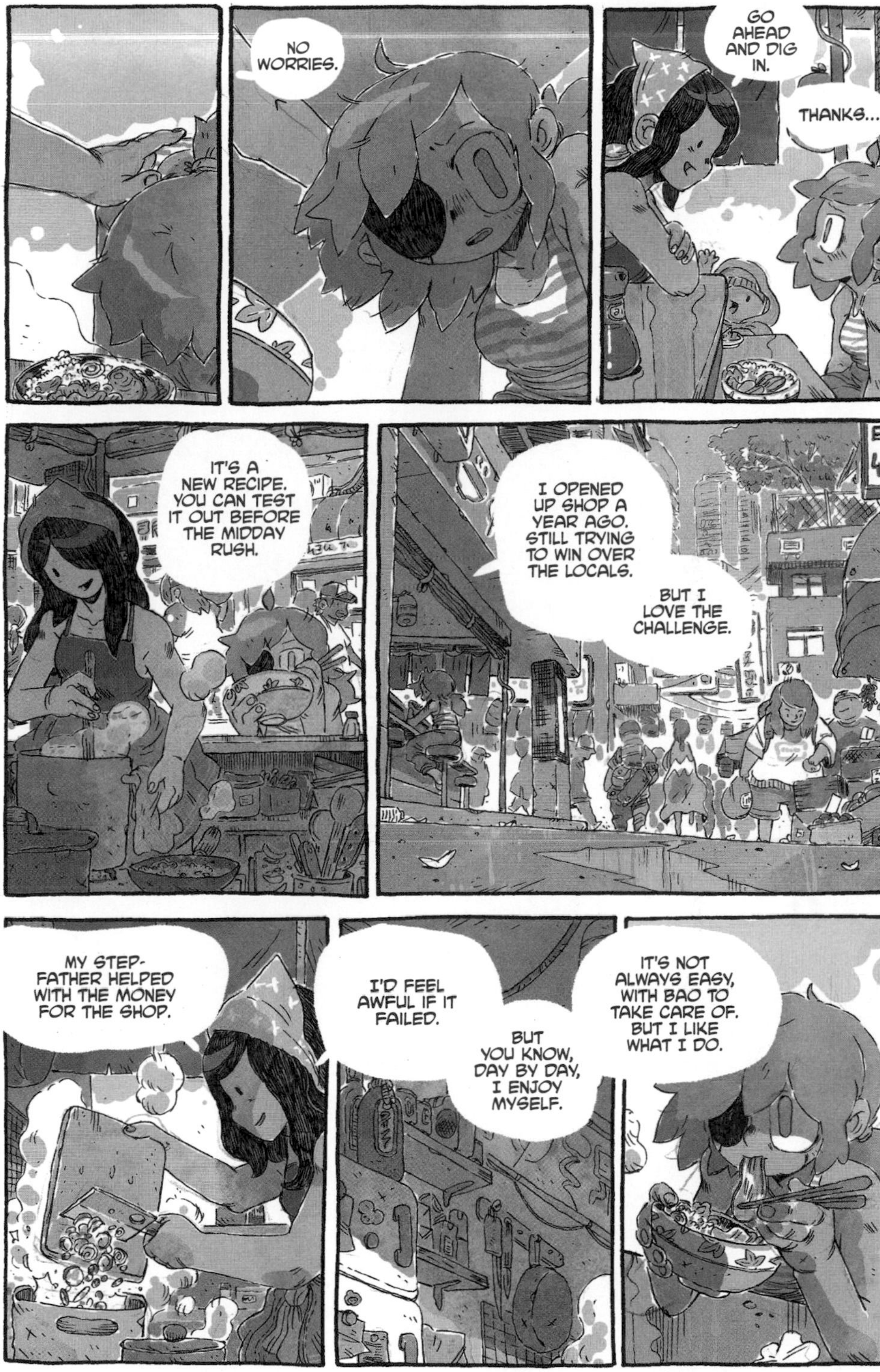
NO WORRIES.
GO AHEAD AND DIG IN.
THANKS...
IT'S A NEW RECIPE. YOU CAN TEST IT OUT BEFORE THE MIDDAY RUSH.
I OPENED UP SHOP A YEAR AGO. STILL TRYING TO WIN OVER THE LOCALS.
BUT I LOVE THE CHALLENGE.
MY STEP-FATHER HELPED WITH THE MONEY FOR THE SHOP.
I'D FEEL AWFUL IF IT FAILED.
BUT YOU KNOW, DAY BY DAY, I ENJOY MYSELF.
IT'S NOT ALWAYS EASY, WITH BAO TO TAKE CARE OF. BUT I LIKE WHAT I DO.

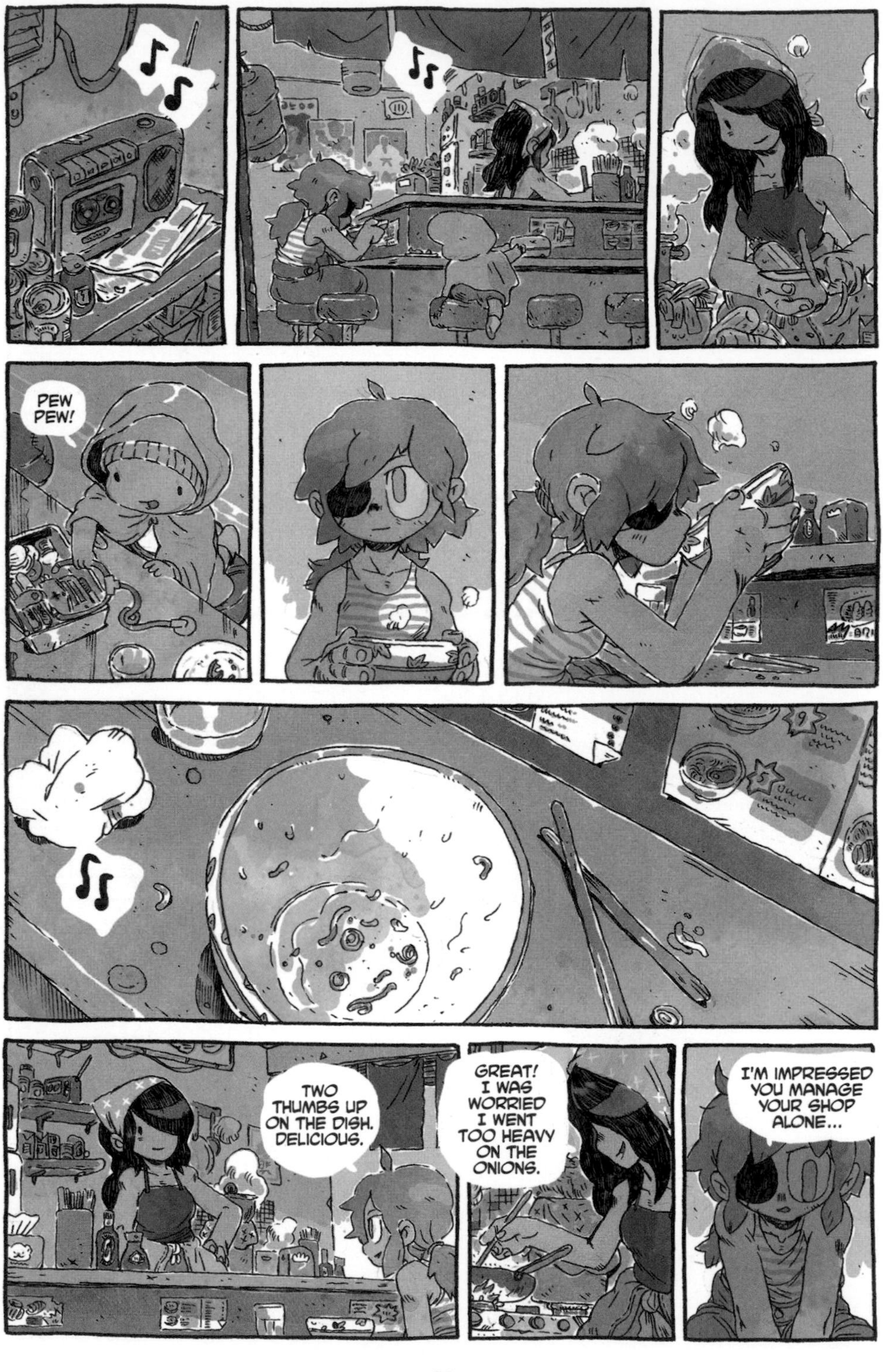
PEW PEW!
TWO THUMBS UP ON THE DISH. DELICIOUS.
GREAT! I WAS WORRIED I WENT TOO HEAVY ON THE ONIONS.
I'M IMPRESSED YOU MANAGE YOUR SHOP ALONE...

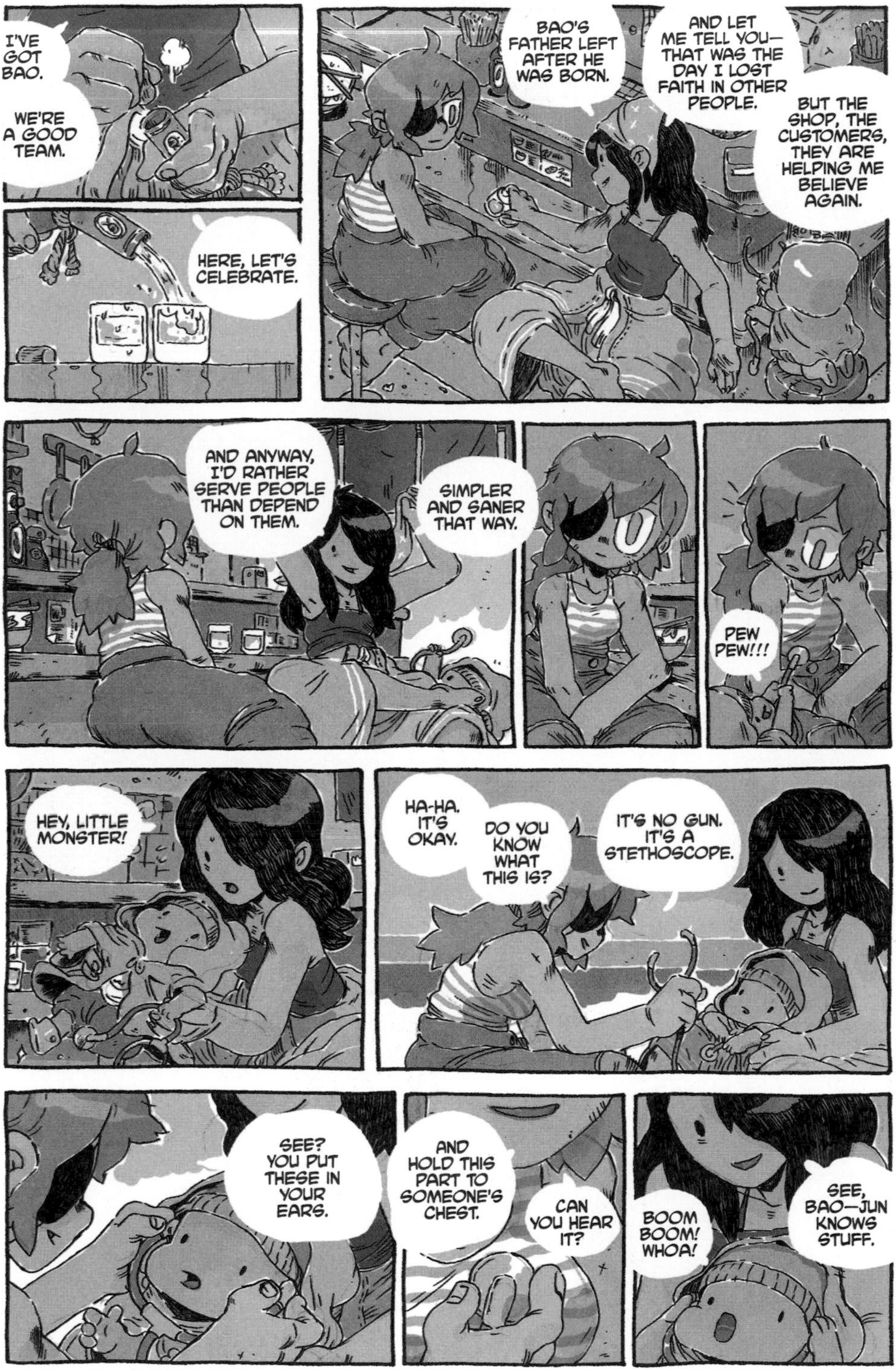
I'VE GOT BAO.
WE'RE A GOOD TEAM.
HERE, LET'S CELEBRATE.
BAO'S FATHER LEFT AFTER HE WAS BORN.
AND LET ME TELL YOU— THAT WAS THE DAY I LOST FAITH IN OTHER PEOPLE.
BUT THE SHOP, THE CUSTOMERS, THEY ARE HELPING ME BELIEVE AGAIN.
AND ANYWAY, I'D RATHER SERVE PEOPLE THAN DEPEND ON THEM.
SIMPLER AND SANER THAT WAY.
PEW PEW!!!
HEY, LITTLE MONSTER!
HA-HA. IT'S OKAY.
DO YOU KNOW WHAT THIS IS?
IT'S NO GUN. IT'S A STETHOSCOPE.
SEE? YOU PUT THESE IN YOUR EARS.
AND HOLD THIS PART TO SOMEONE'S CHEST.
CAN YOU HEAR IT?
BOOM BOOM! WHOA!
SEE, BAO-JUN KNOWS STUFF.

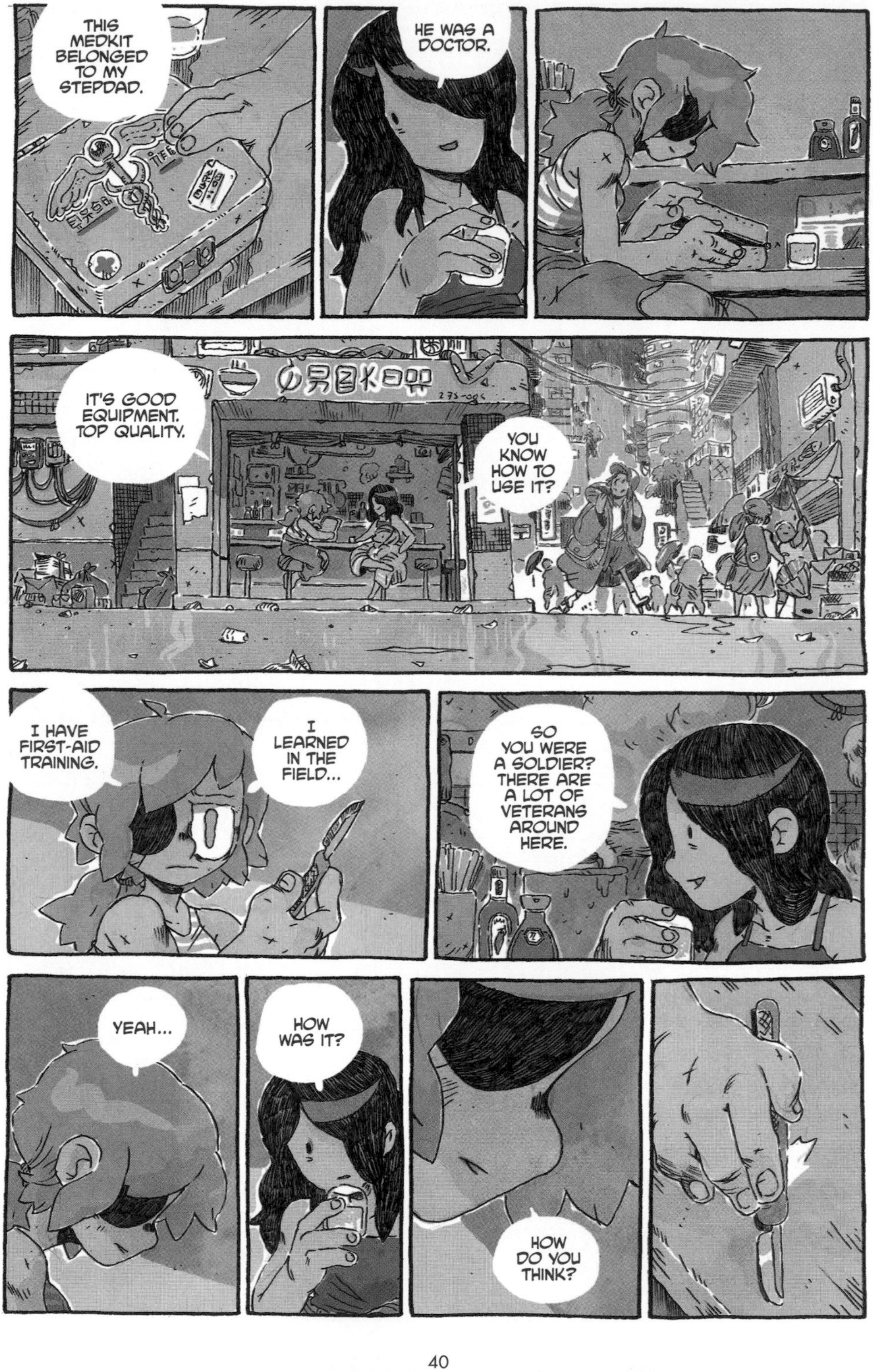
THIS MEDKIT BELONGED TO MY STEPDAD.
HE WAS A DOCTOR.
IT'S GOOD EQUIPMENT. TOP QUALITY.
YOU KNOW HOW TO USE IT?
I HAVE FIRST-AID TRAINING.
I LEARNED IN THE FIELD...
SO YOU WERE A SOLDIER? THERE ARE A LOT OF VETERANS AROUND HERE.
YEAH...
HOW WAS IT?
HOW DO YOU THINK?

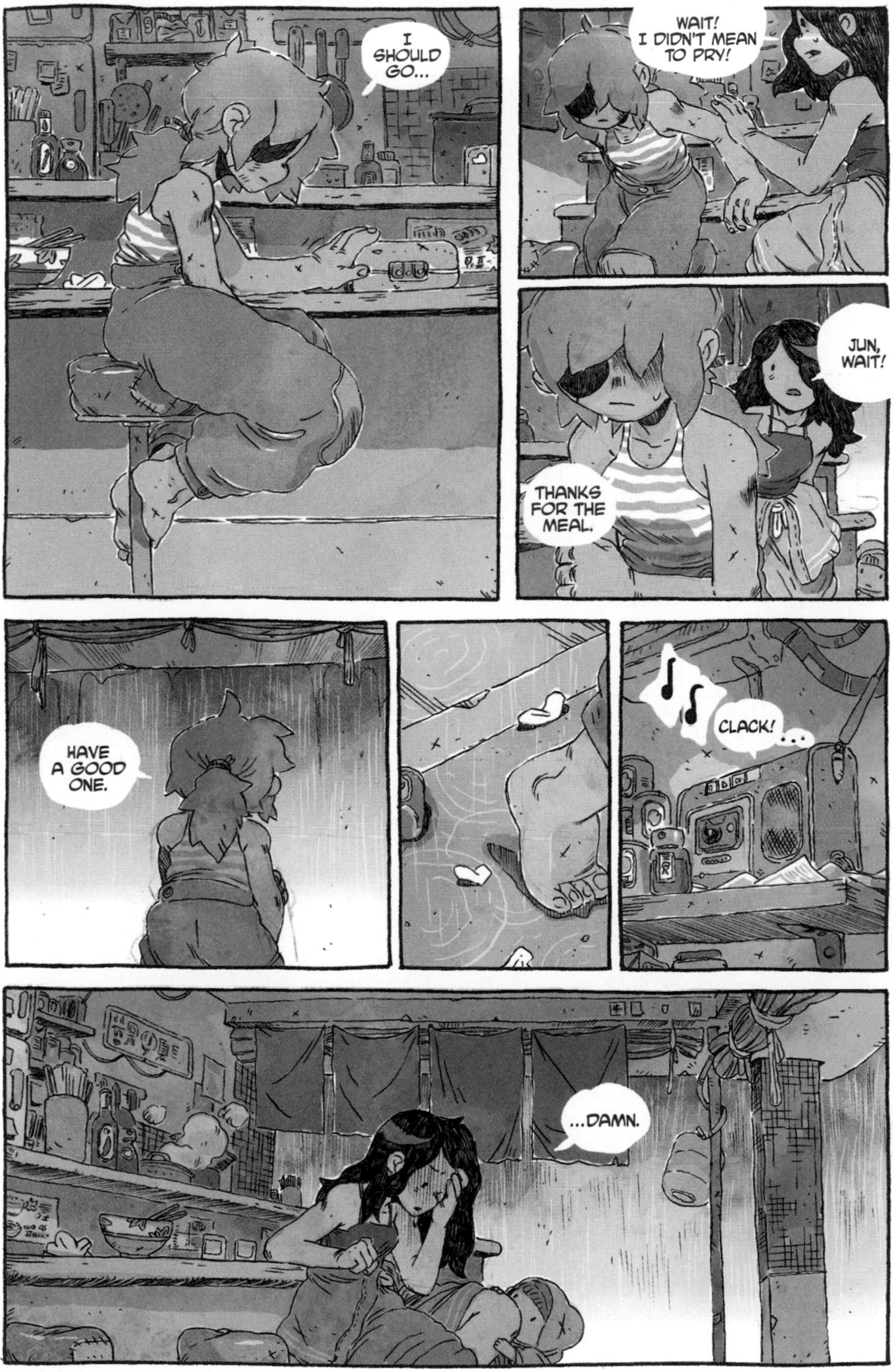
I SHOULD GO...
WAIT! I DIDN'T MEAN TO PRY!
JUN, WAIT!
THANKS FOR THE MEAL.
HAVE A GOOD ONE.
CLACK!
...
...DAMN.

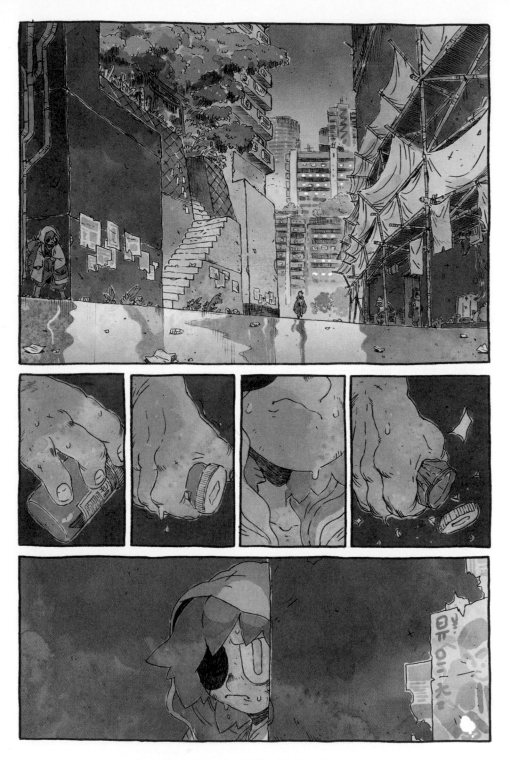

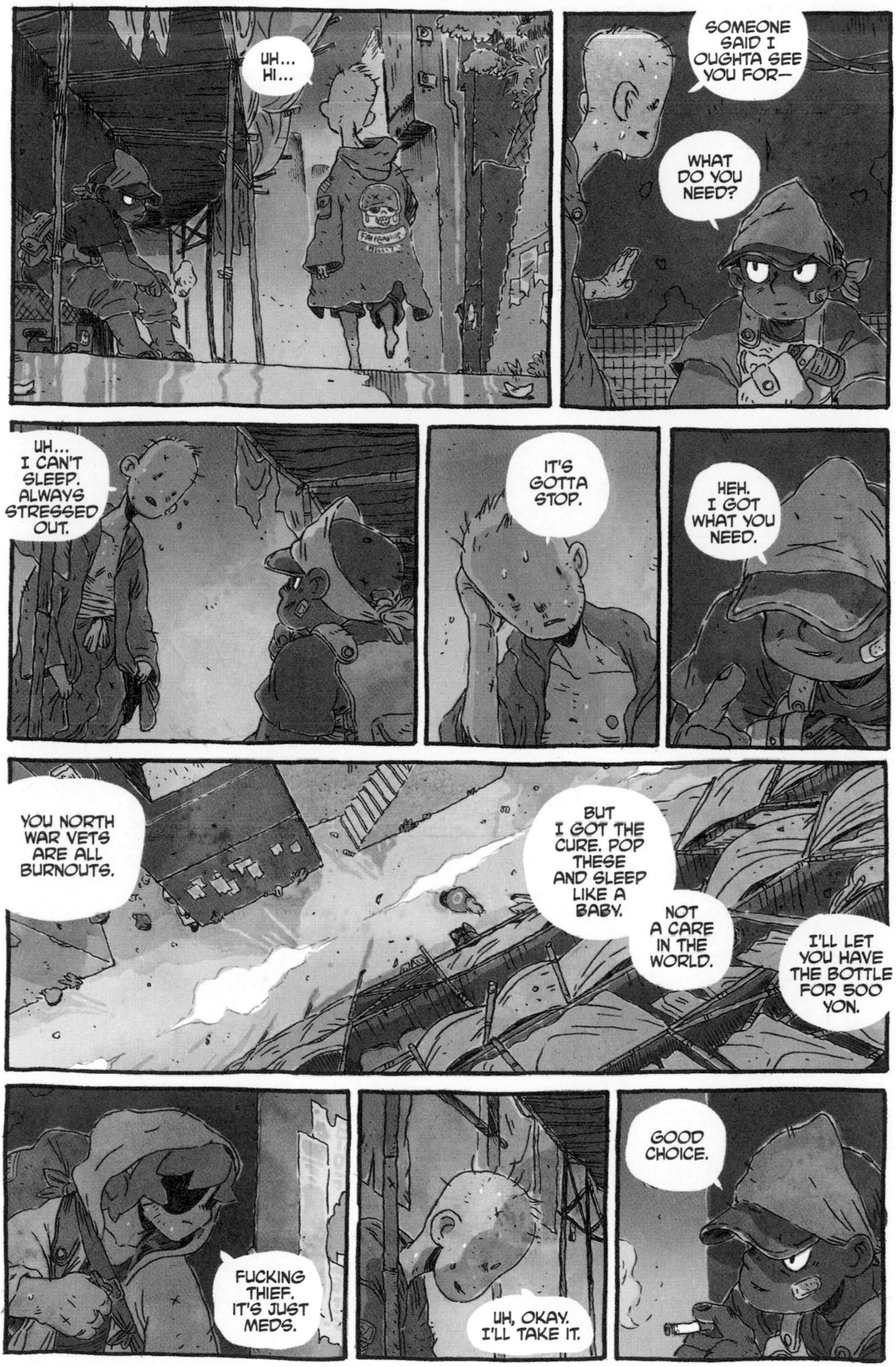
UH... HI...
SOMEONE SAID I OUGHTA SEE YOU FOR—
WHAT DO YOU NEED?
UH... I CAN'T SLEEP. ALWAYS STRESSED OUT.
IT'S GOTTA STOP.
HEH. I GOT WHAT YOU NEED.
YOU NORTH WAR VETS ARE ALL BURNOUTS.
BUT I GOT THE CURE. POP THESE AND SLEEP LIKE A BABY.
NOT A CARE IN THE WORLD.
I'LL LET YOU HAVE THE BOTTLE FOR 500 YON.
FUCKING THIEF. IT'S JUST MEDS.
UH, OKAY. I'LL TAKE IT.
GOOD CHOICE.

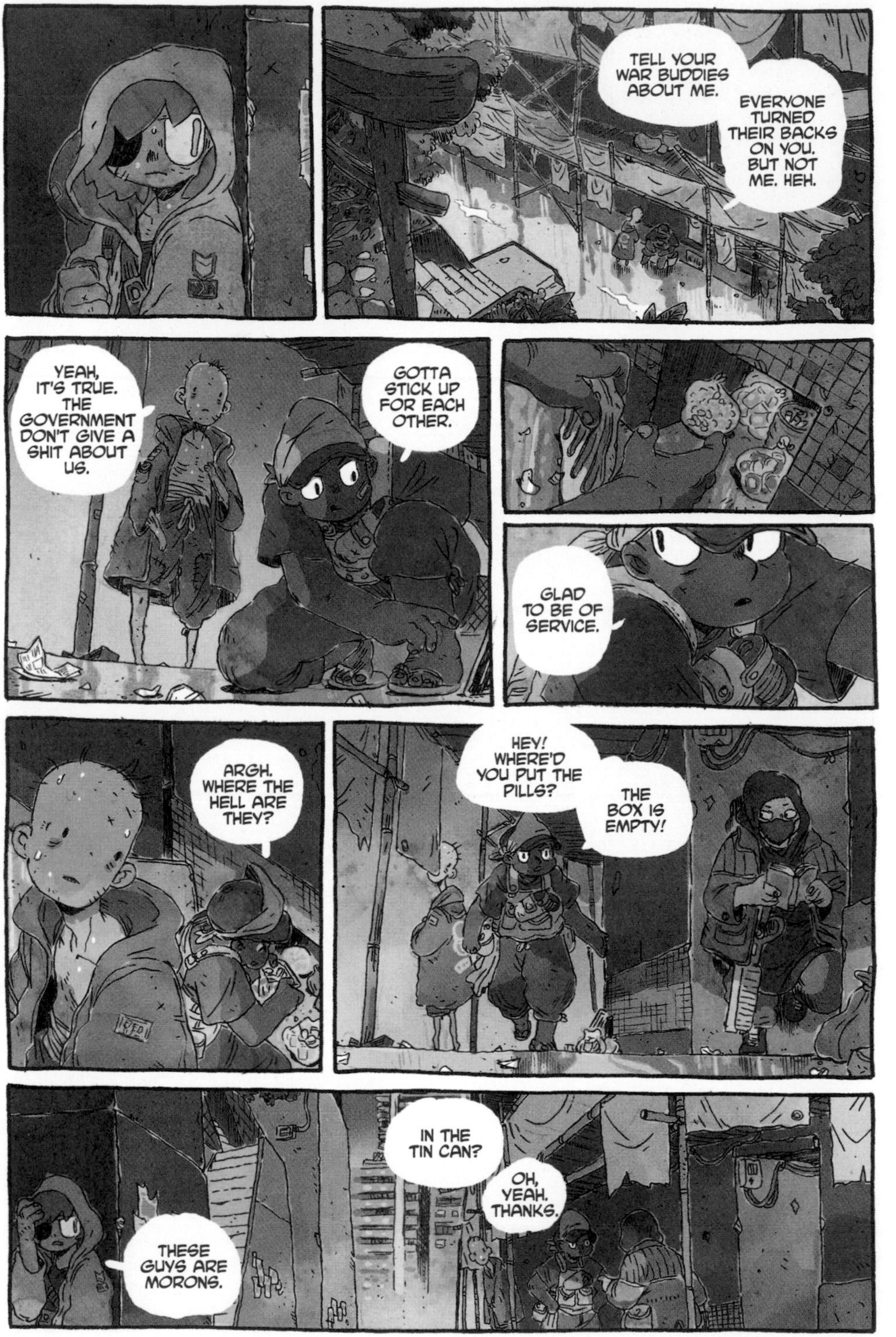
TELL YOUR WAR BUDDIES ABOUT ME.
EVERYONE TURNED THEIR BACKS ON YOU. BUT NOT ME. HEH.
YEAH, IT'S TRUE. THE GOVERNMENT DON'T GIVE A SHIT ABOUT US.
GOTTA STICK UP FOR EACH OTHER.
GLAD TO BE OF SERVICE.
ARGH. WHERE THE HELL ARE THEY?
HEY! WHERE'D YOU PUT THE PILLS?
THE BOX IS EMPTY!
IN THE TIN CAN?
OH, YEAH. THANKS.
THESE GUYS ARE MORONS.

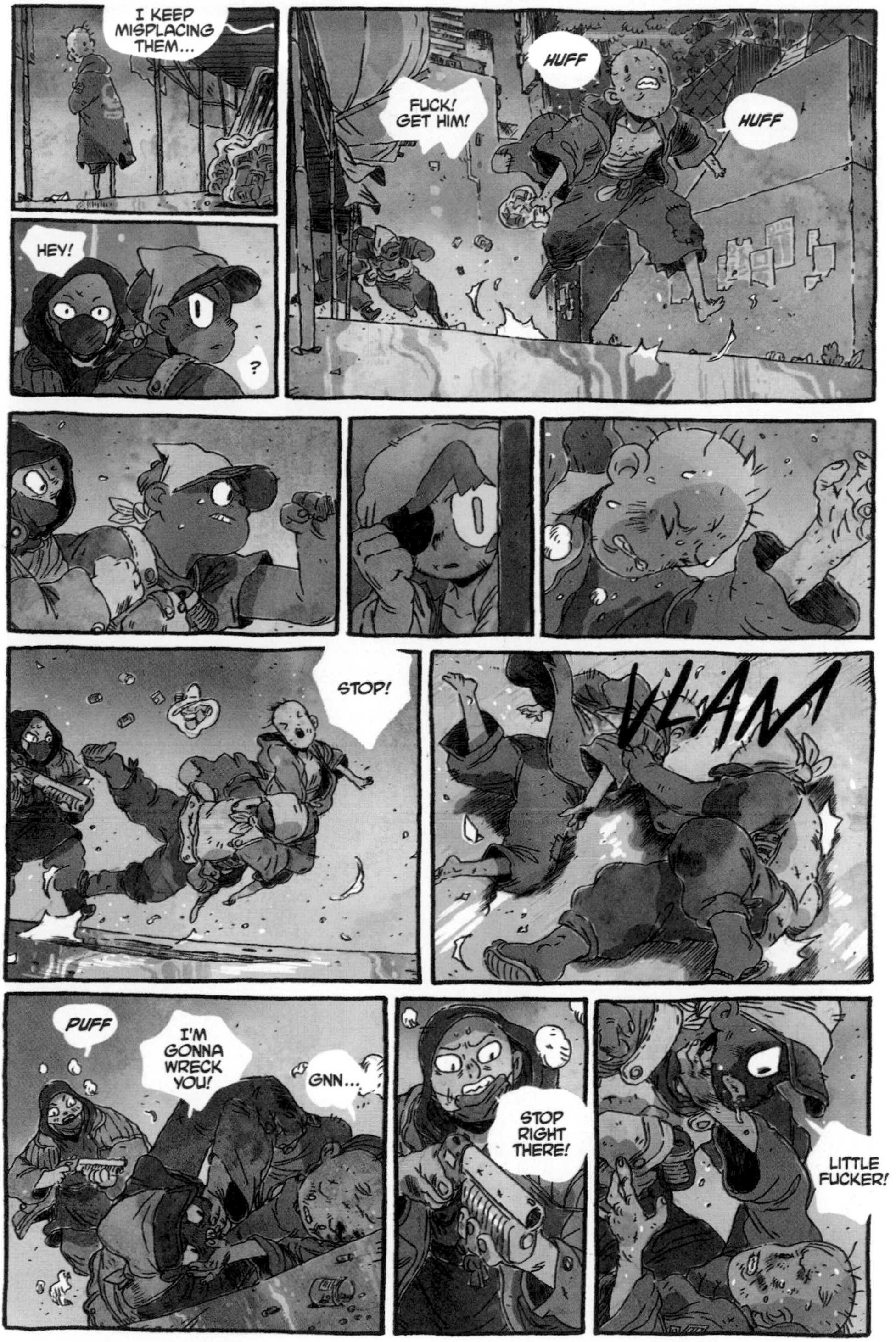
I KEEP MISPLACING THEM...
HUFF
FUCK! GET HIM!
HUFF
HEY!
?
STOP!
VLAM
PUFF
I'M GONNA WRECK YOU!
GNN...
STOP RIGHT THERE!
LITTLE FUCKER!

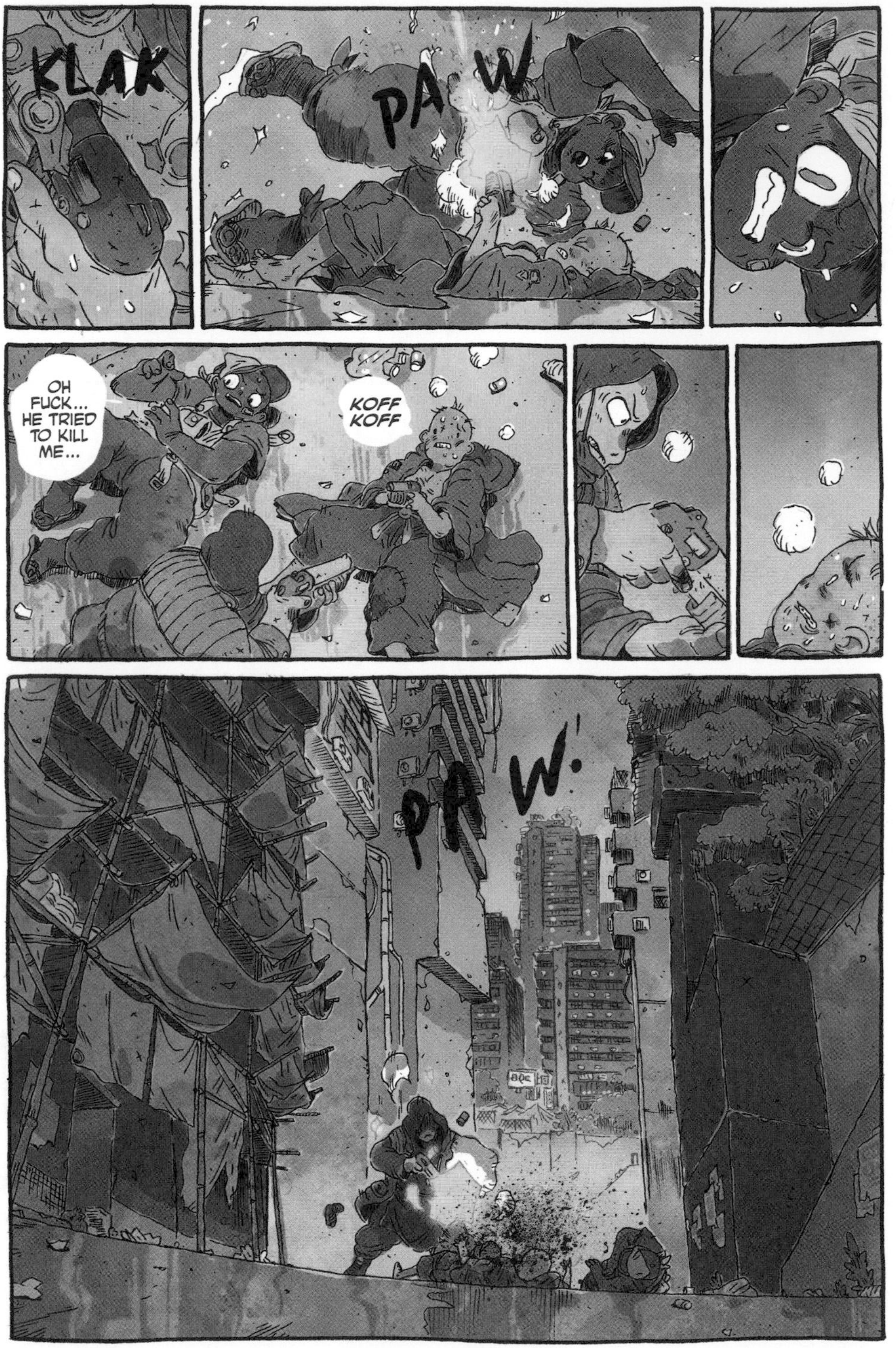
KLAK
PAW
OH FUCK... HE TRIED TO KILL ME...
KOFF KOFF
PAW!

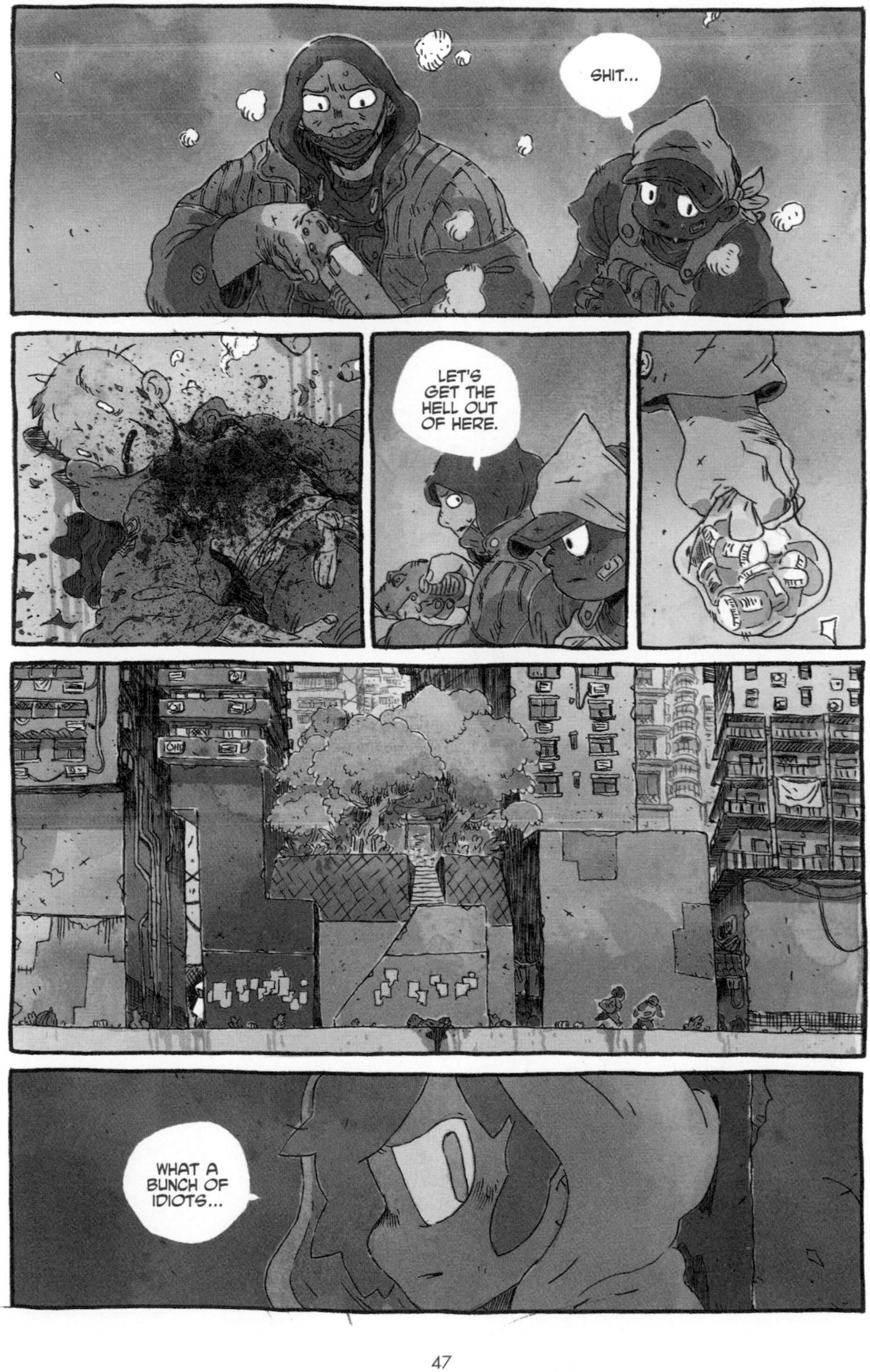
SHIT...
LET'S GET THE HELL OUT OF HERE.
WHAT A BUNCH OF IDIOTS...

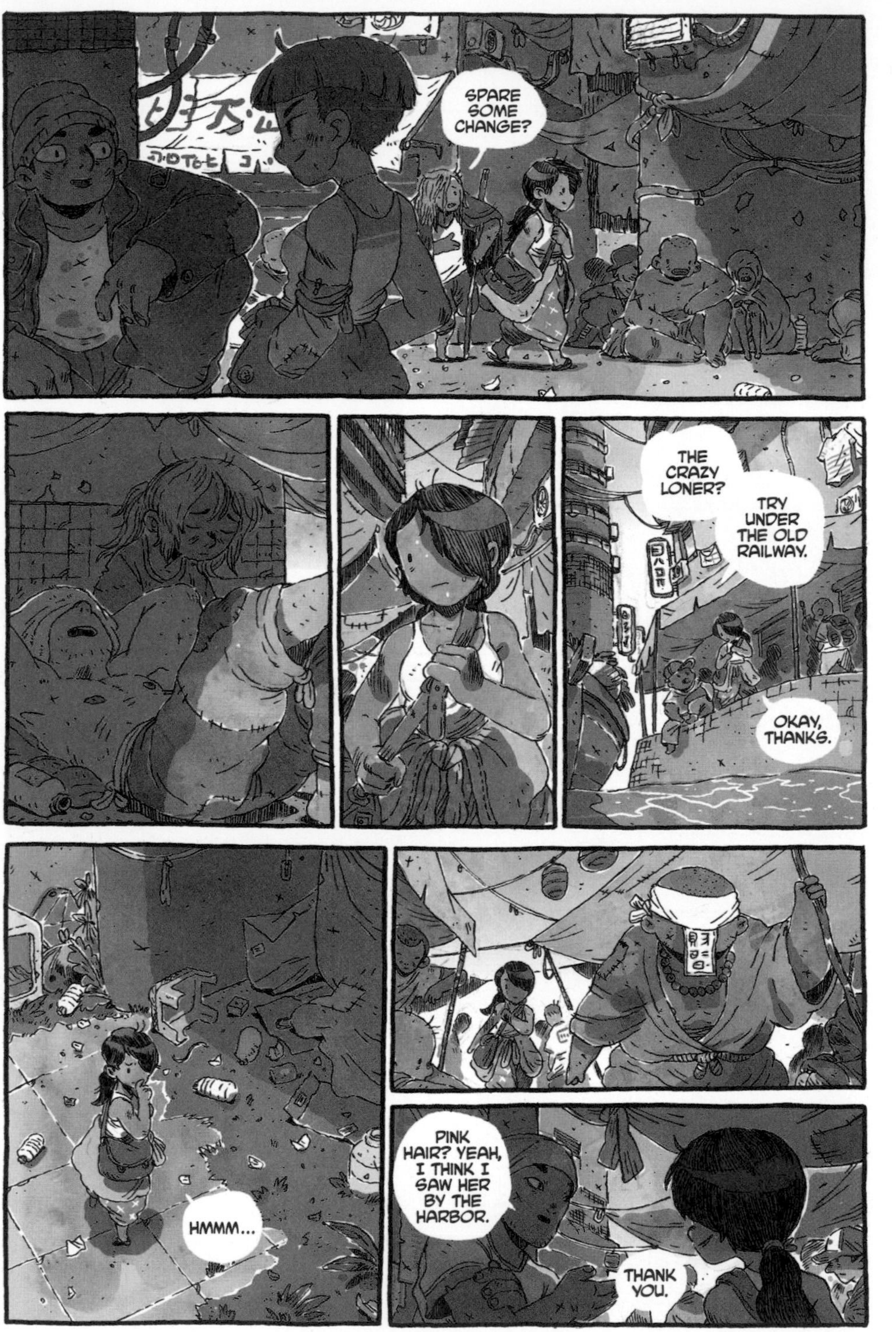
SPARE SOME CHANGE?
THE CRAZY LONER?
TRY UNDER THE OLD RAILWAY.
OKAY, THANKS.
HMMM...
PINK HAIR? YEAH, I THINK I SAW HER BY THE HARBOR.
THANK YOU.

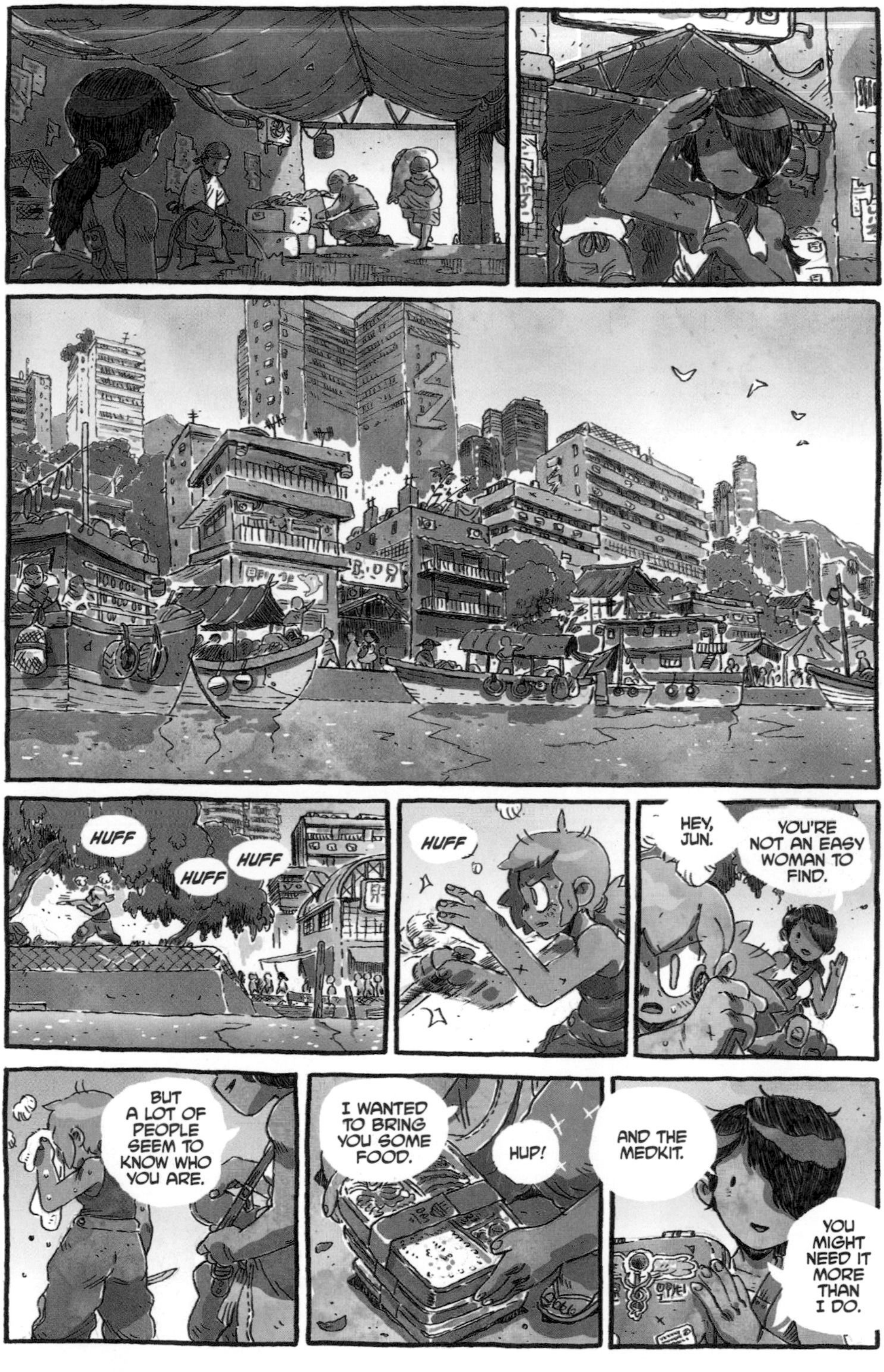
HUFF
HUFF
HUFF
HUFF
HEY, JUN.
YOU'RE NOT AN EASY WOMAN TO FIND.
BUT A LOT OF PEOPLE SEEM TO KNOW WHO YOU ARE.
I WANTED TO BRING YOU SOME FOOD.
HUP!
AND THE MEDKIT.
YOU MIGHT NEED IT MORE THAN I DO.

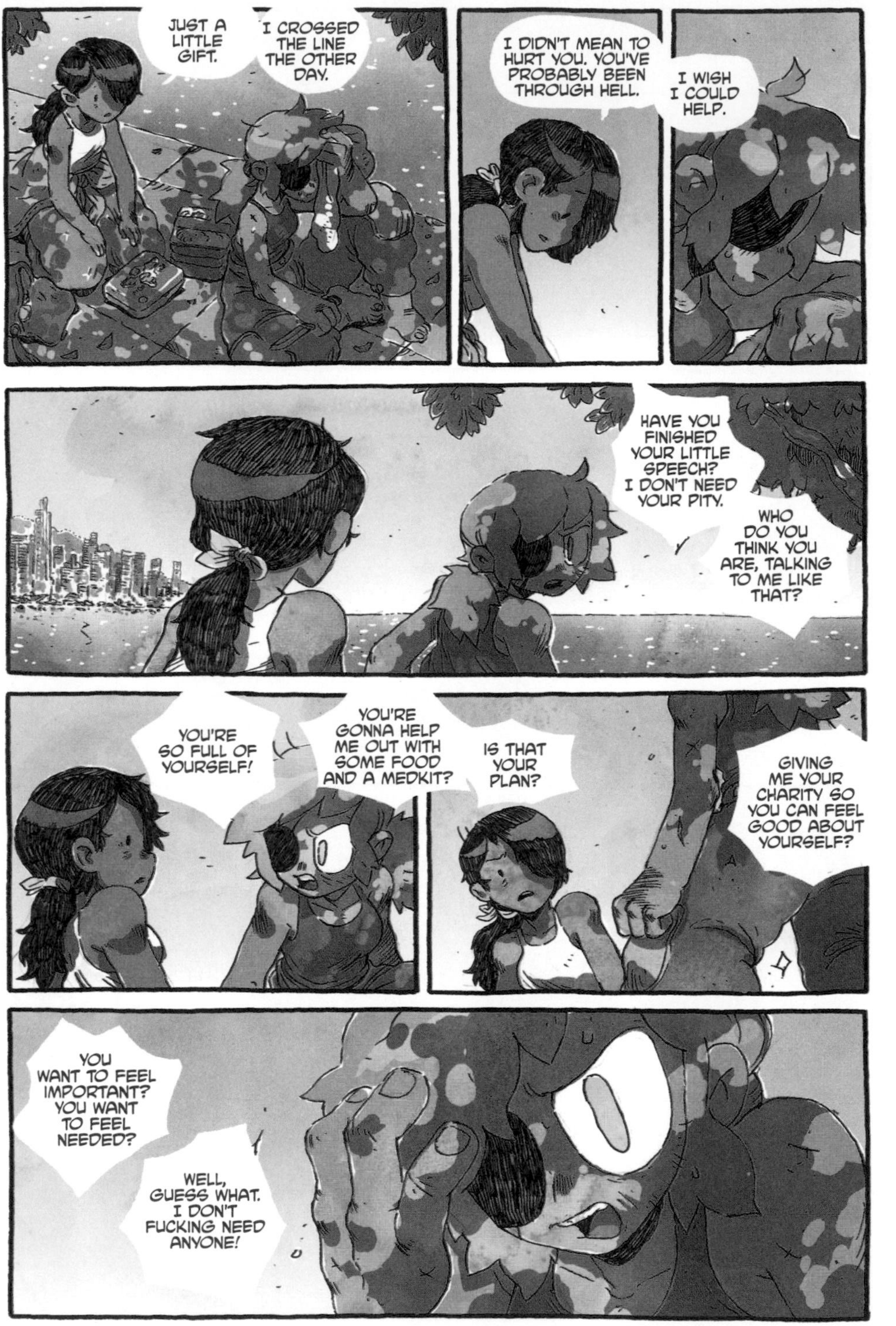
JUST A LITTLE GIFT.
I CROSSED THE LINE THE OTHER DAY.
I DIDN'T MEAN TO HURT YOU. YOU'VE PROBABLY BEEN THROUGH HELL.
I WISH I COULD HELP.
HAVE YOU FINISHED YOUR LITTLE SPEECH? I DON'T NEED YOUR PITY.
WHO DO YOU THINK YOU ARE, TALKING TO ME LIKE THAT?
YOU'RE SO FULL OF YOURSELF!
YOU'RE GONNA HELP ME OUT WITH SOME FOOD AND A MEDKIT?
IS THAT YOUR PLAN?
GIVING ME YOUR CHARITY SO YOU CAN FEEL GOOD ABOUT YOURSELF?
YOU WANT TO FEEL IMPORTANT? YOU WANT TO FEEL NEEDED?
WELL, GUESS WHAT. I DON'T FUCKING NEED ANYONE!

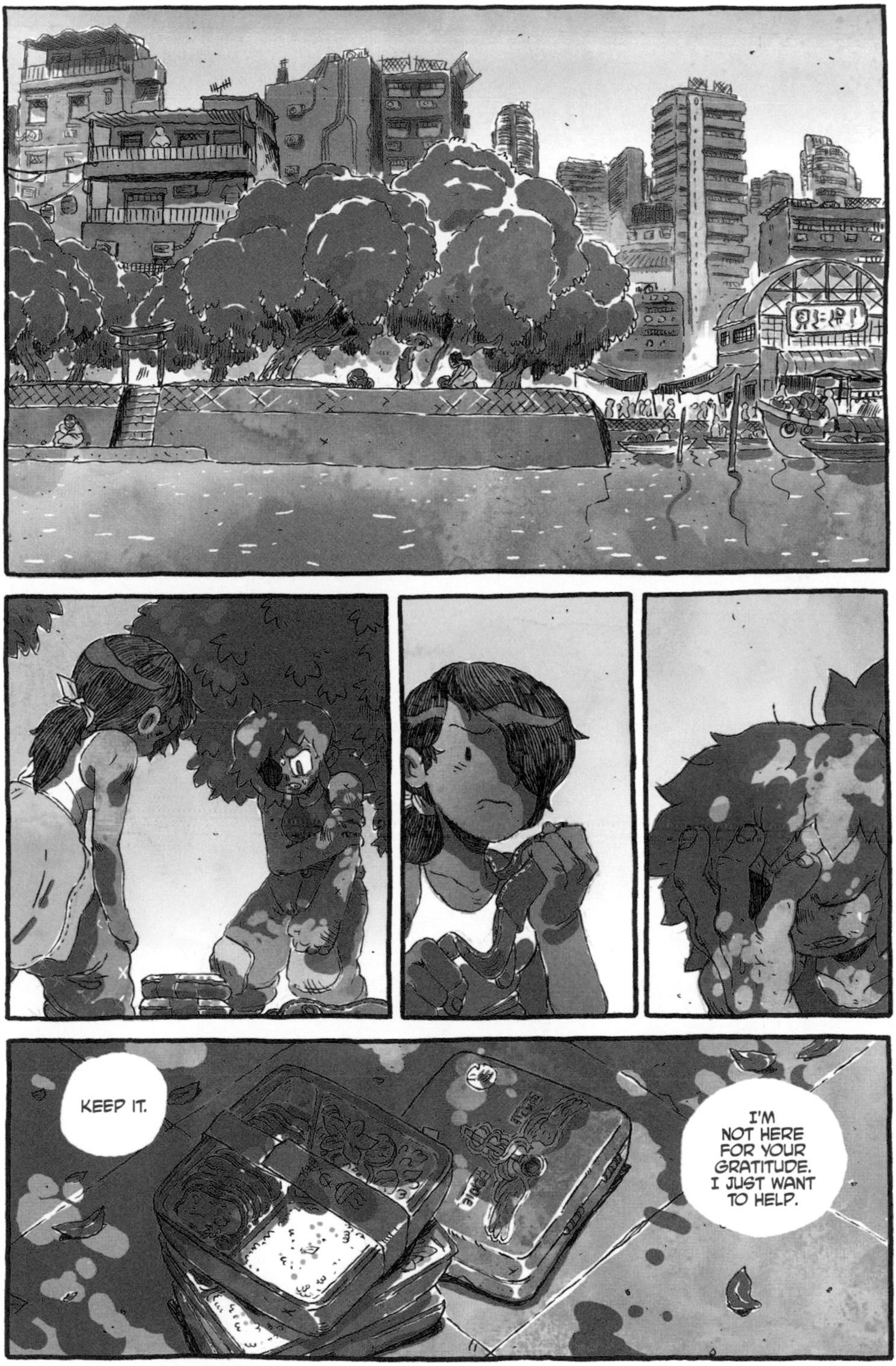
KEEP IT.
I'M NOT HERE FOR YOUR GRATITUDE. I JUST WANT TO HELP.

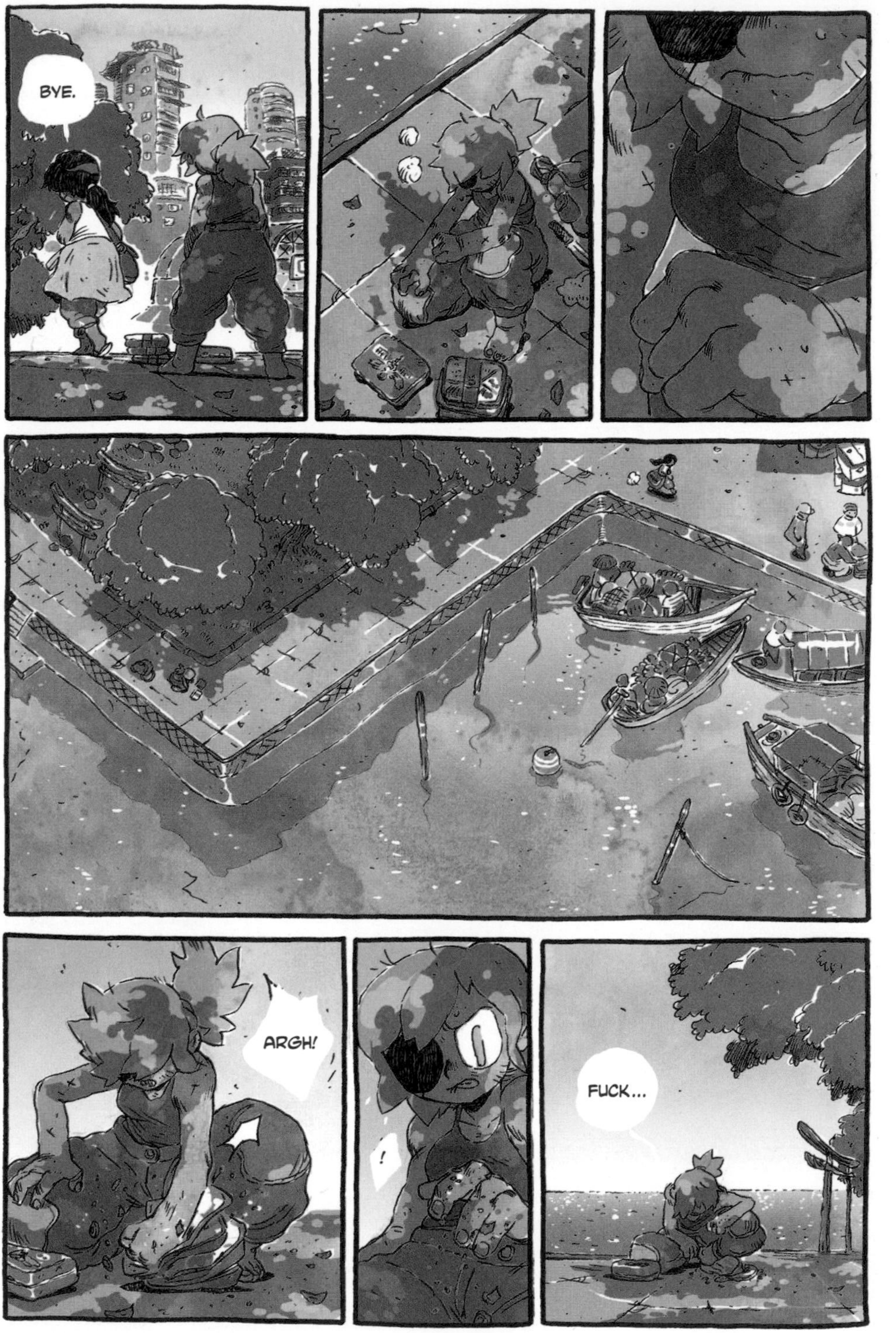
BYE.
ARGH!
!
FUCK...

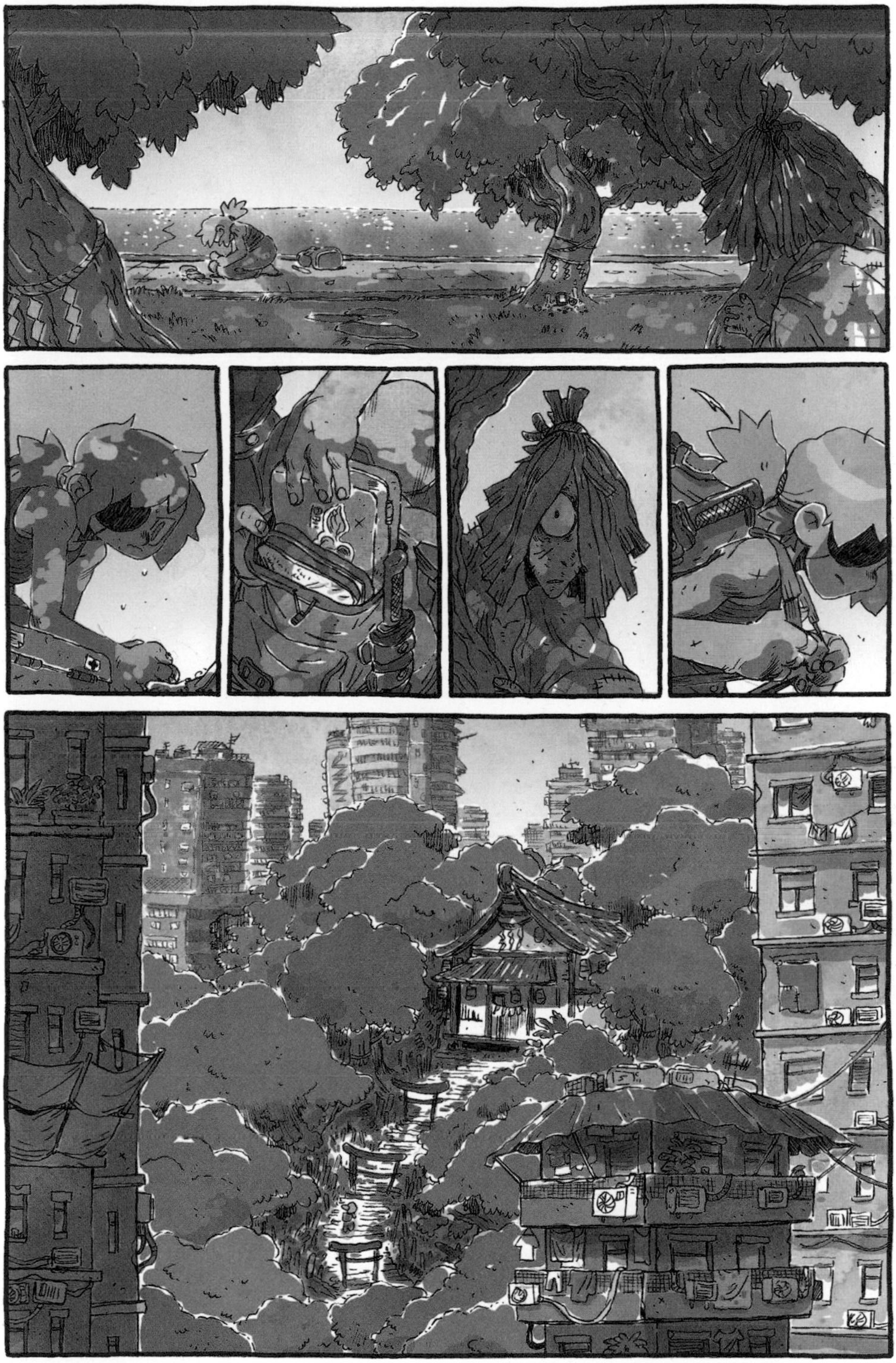

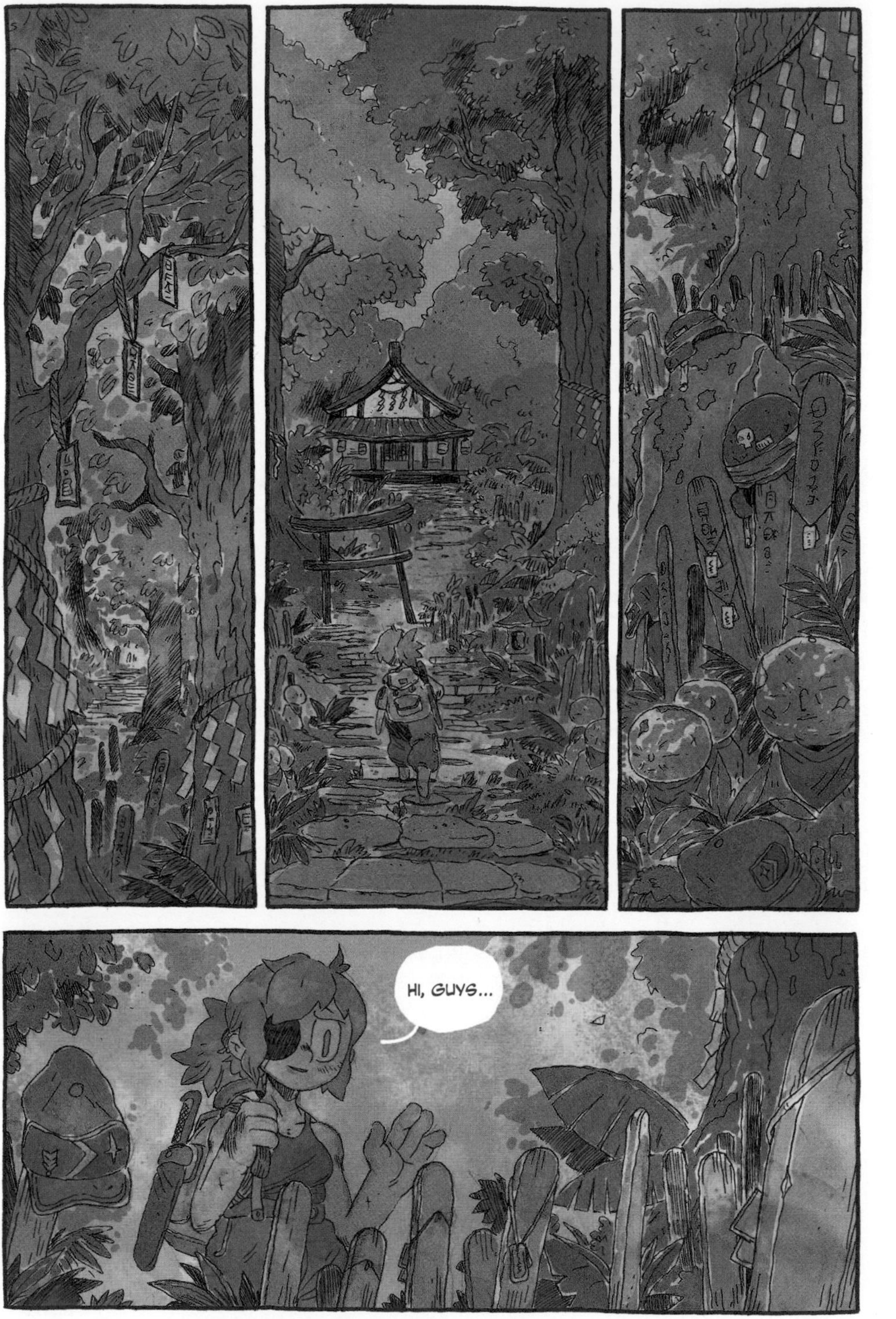
HI, GUYS...

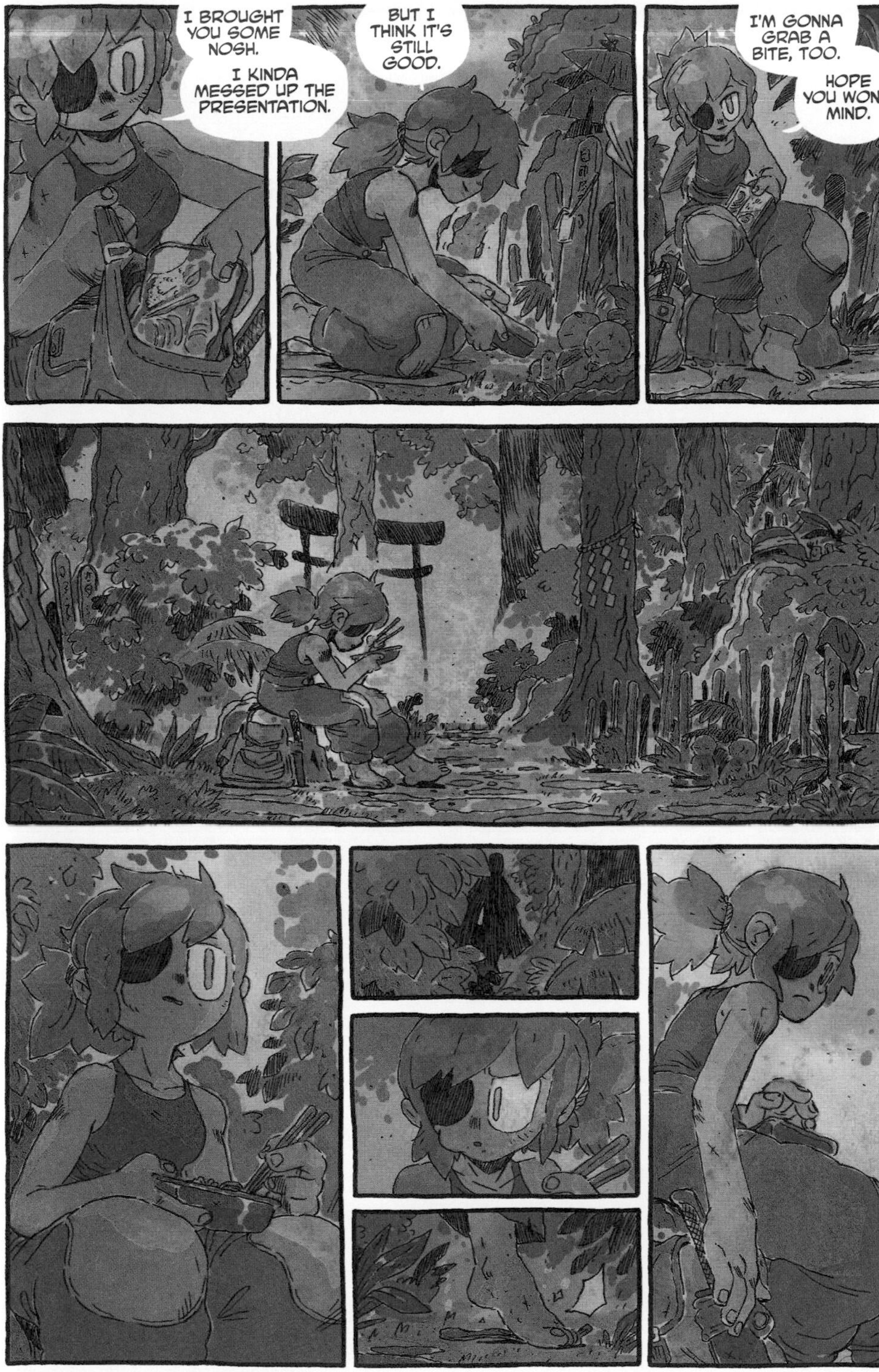
I BROUGHT YOU SOME NOSH.
I KINDA MESSED UP THE PRESENTATION.
BUT I THINK IT'S STILL GOOD.
I'M GONNA GRAB A BITE, TOO.
HOPE YOU WON'T MIND.

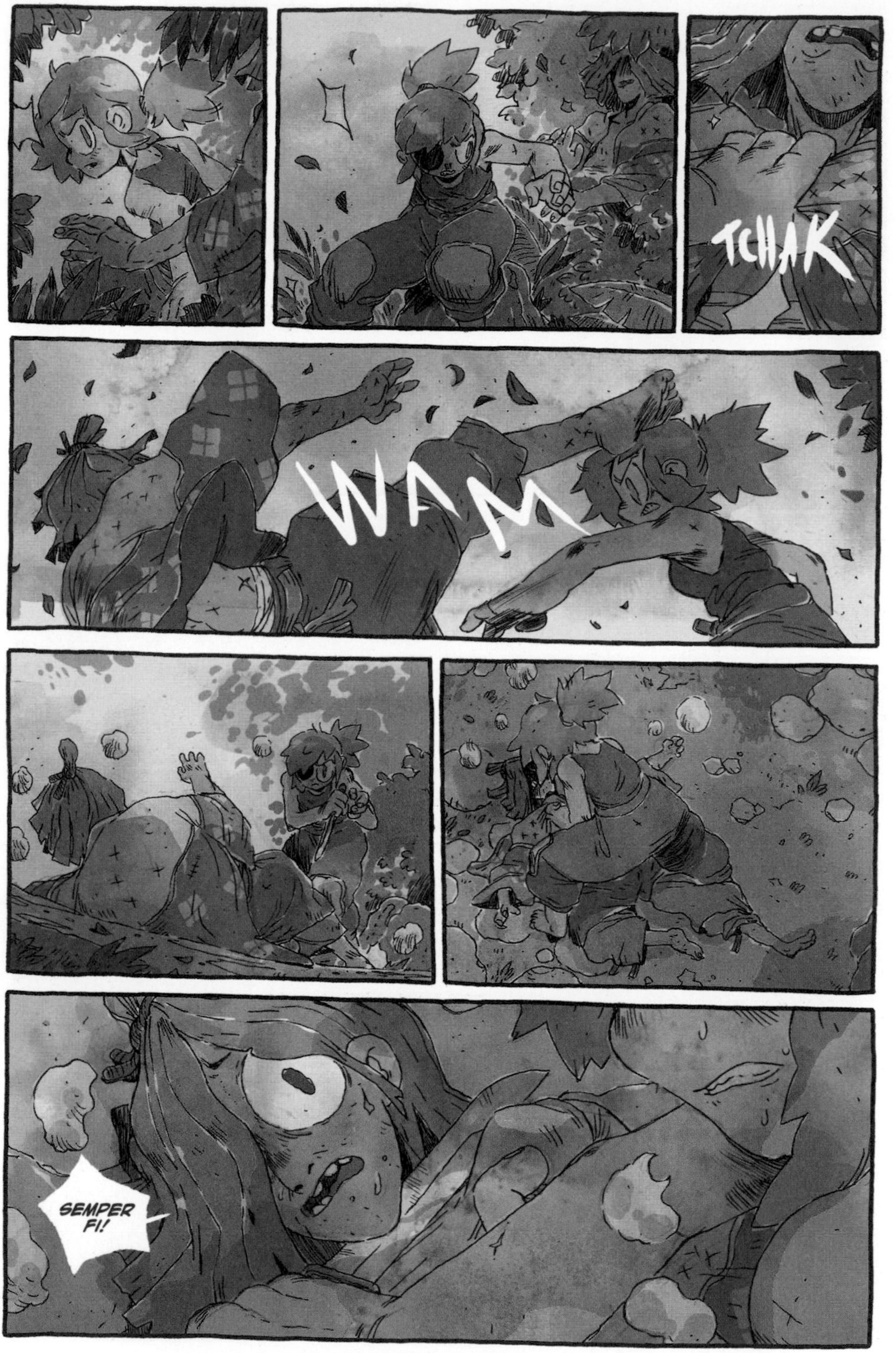
TCHAK
WAM
SEMPER FI!

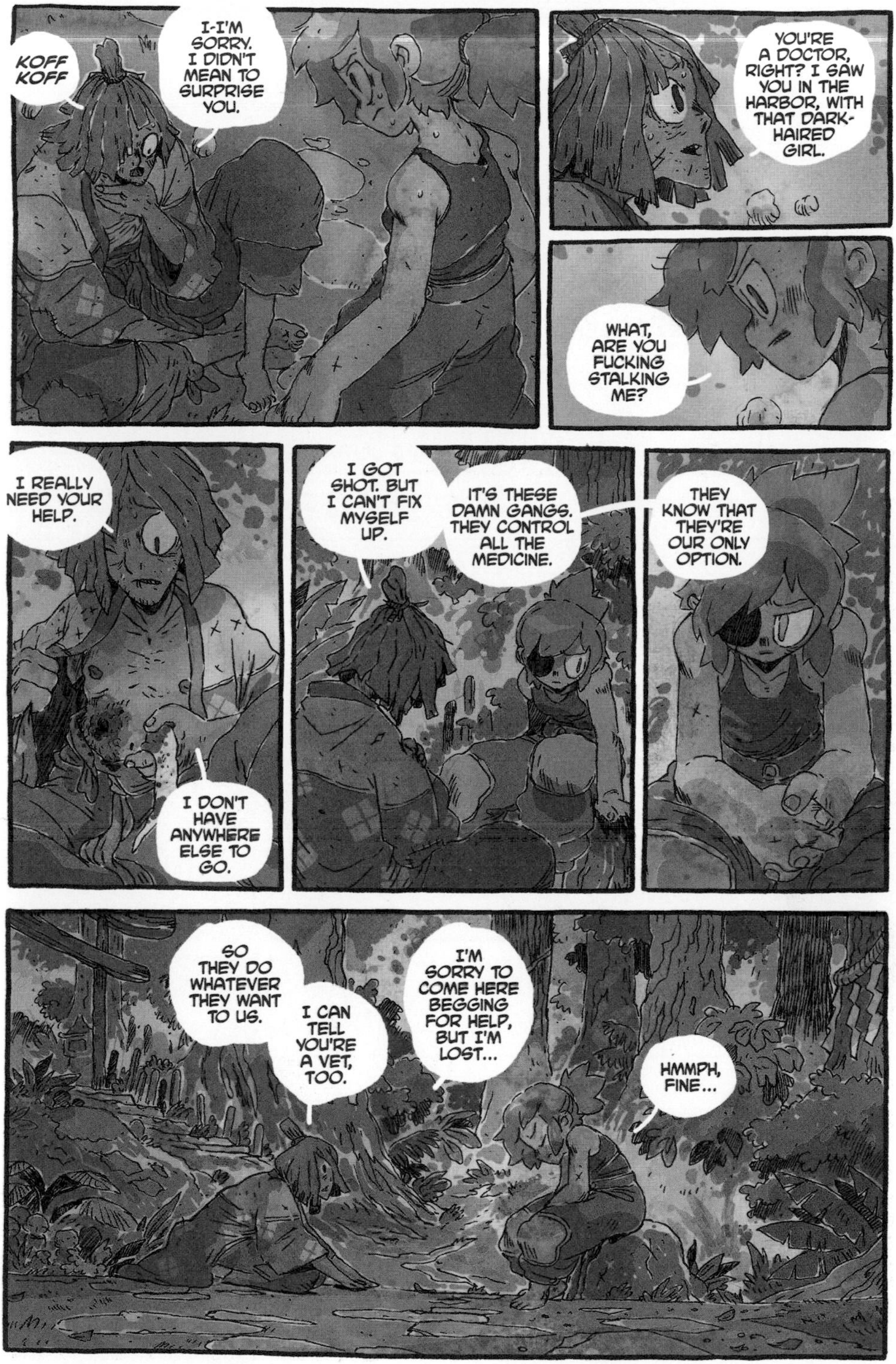
KOFF KOFF
I-I'M SORRY. I DIDN'T MEAN TO SURPRISE YOU.
YOU'RE A DOCTOR, RIGHT? I SAW YOU IN THE HARBOR, WITH THAT DARK-HAIRED GIRL.
WHAT, ARE YOU FUCKING STALKING ME?
I REALLY NEED YOUR HELP.
I DON'T HAVE ANYWHERE ELSE TO GO.
I GOT SHOT. BUT I CAN'T FIX MYSELF UP.
IT'S THESE DAMN GANGS. THEY CONTROL ALL THE MEDICINE.
THEY KNOW THAT THEY'RE OUR ONLY OPTION.
SO THEY DO WHATEVER THEY WANT TO US.
I CAN TELL YOU'RE A VET, TOO.
I'M SORRY TO COME HERE BEGGING FOR HELP, BUT I'M LOST...
HMMPH, FINE...

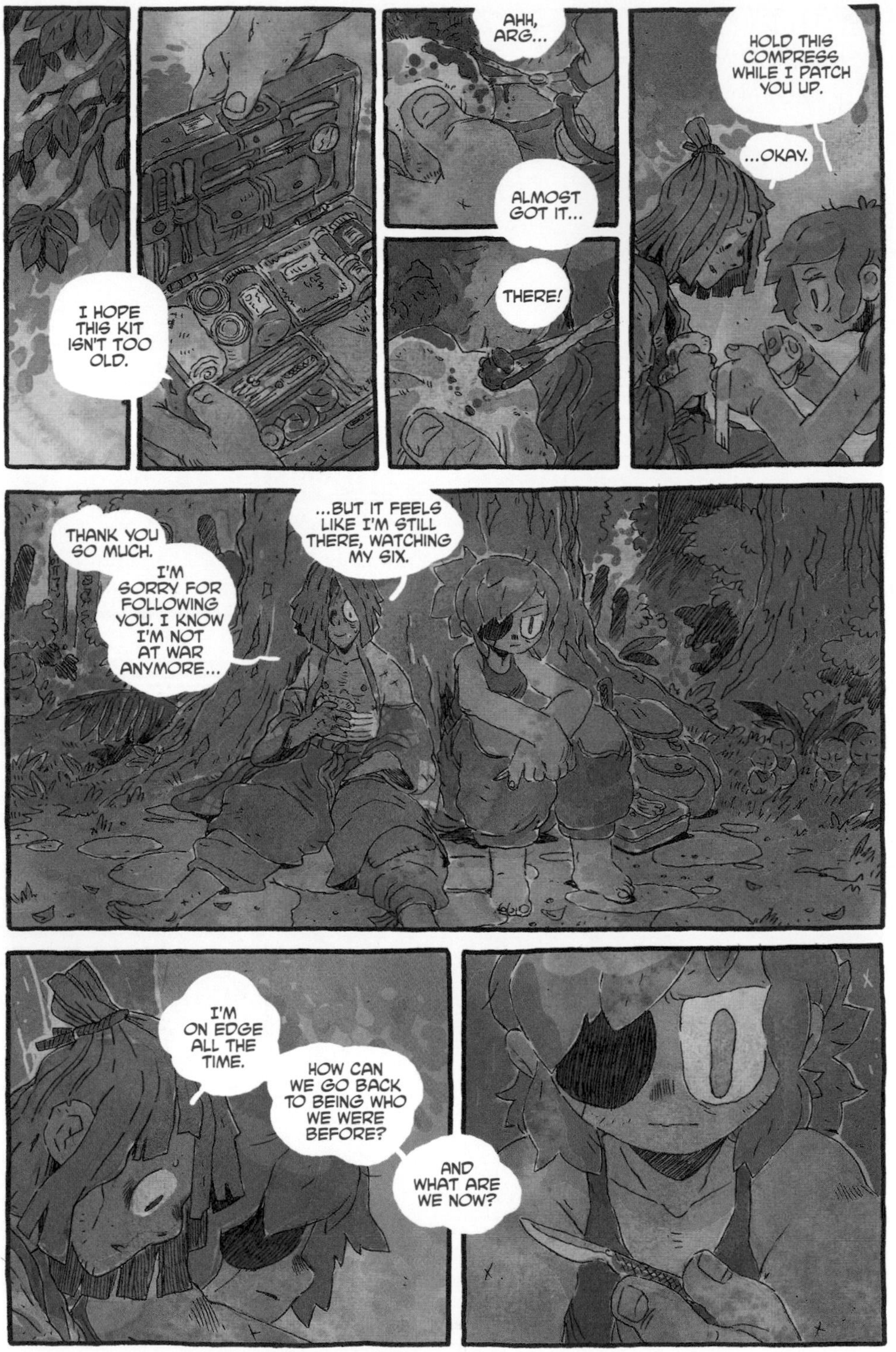

I HOPE THIS KIT ISN'T TOO OLD.
AHH, ARG...
ALMOST GOT IT...
THERE!
HOLD THIS COMPRESS WHILE I PATCH YOU UP.
...OKAY.
THANK YOU SO MUCH.
I'M SORRY FOR FOLLOWING YOU. I KNOW I'M NOT AT WAR ANYMORE...
...BUT IT FEELS LIKE I'M STILL THERE, WATCHING MY SIX.
I'M ON EDGE ALL THE TIME.
HOW CAN WE GO BACK TO BEING WHO WE WERE BEFORE?
AND WHAT ARE WE NOW?

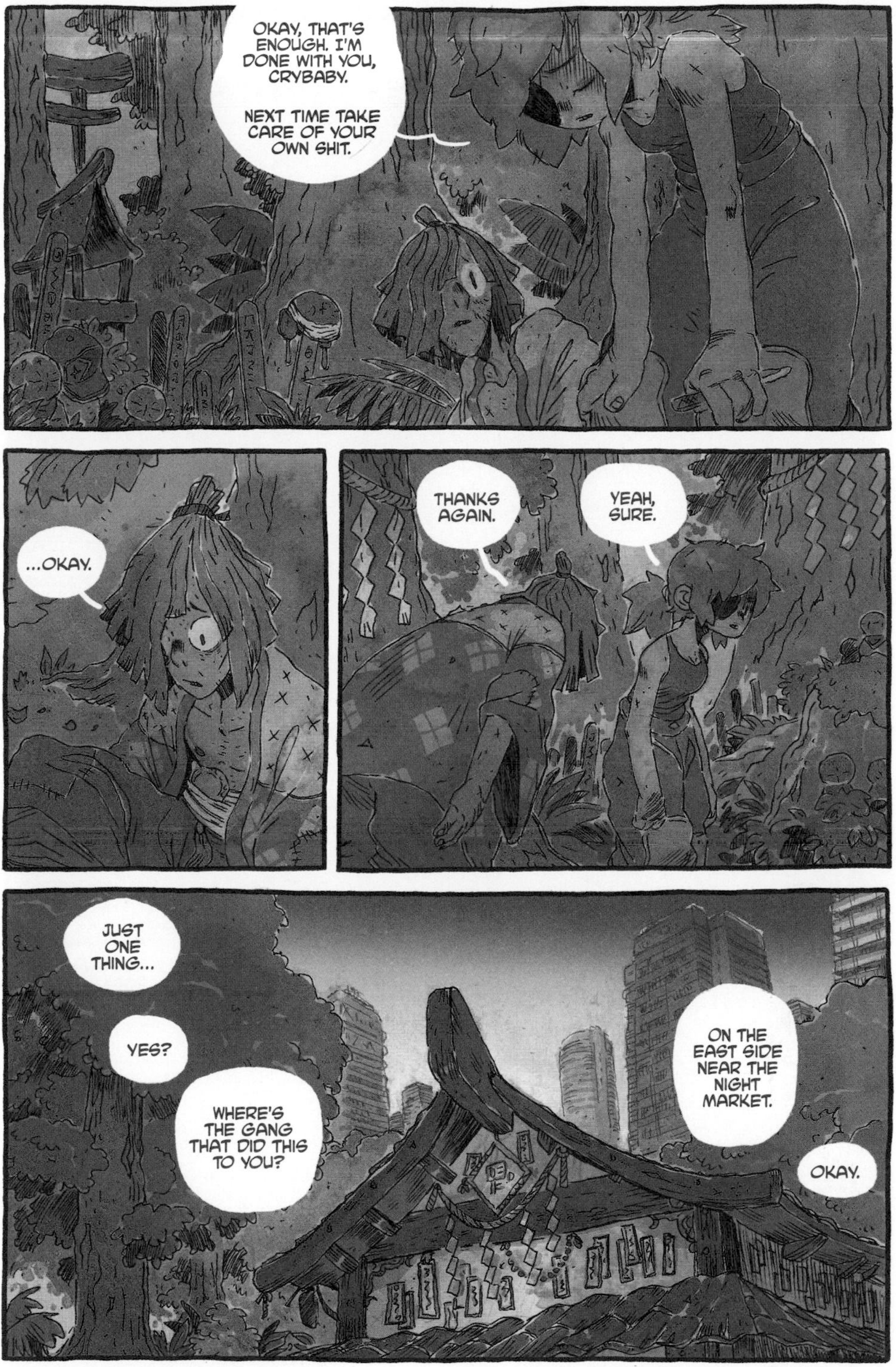
OKAY, THAT'S ENOUGH. I'M DONE WITH YOU, CRYBABY.
NEXT TIME TAKE CARE OF YOUR OWN SHIT.
...OKAY.
THANKS AGAIN.
YEAH, SURE.
JUST ONE THING...
YES?
WHERE'S THE GANG THAT DID THIS TO YOU?
ON THE EAST SIDE NEAR THE NIGHT MARKET.
OKAY.

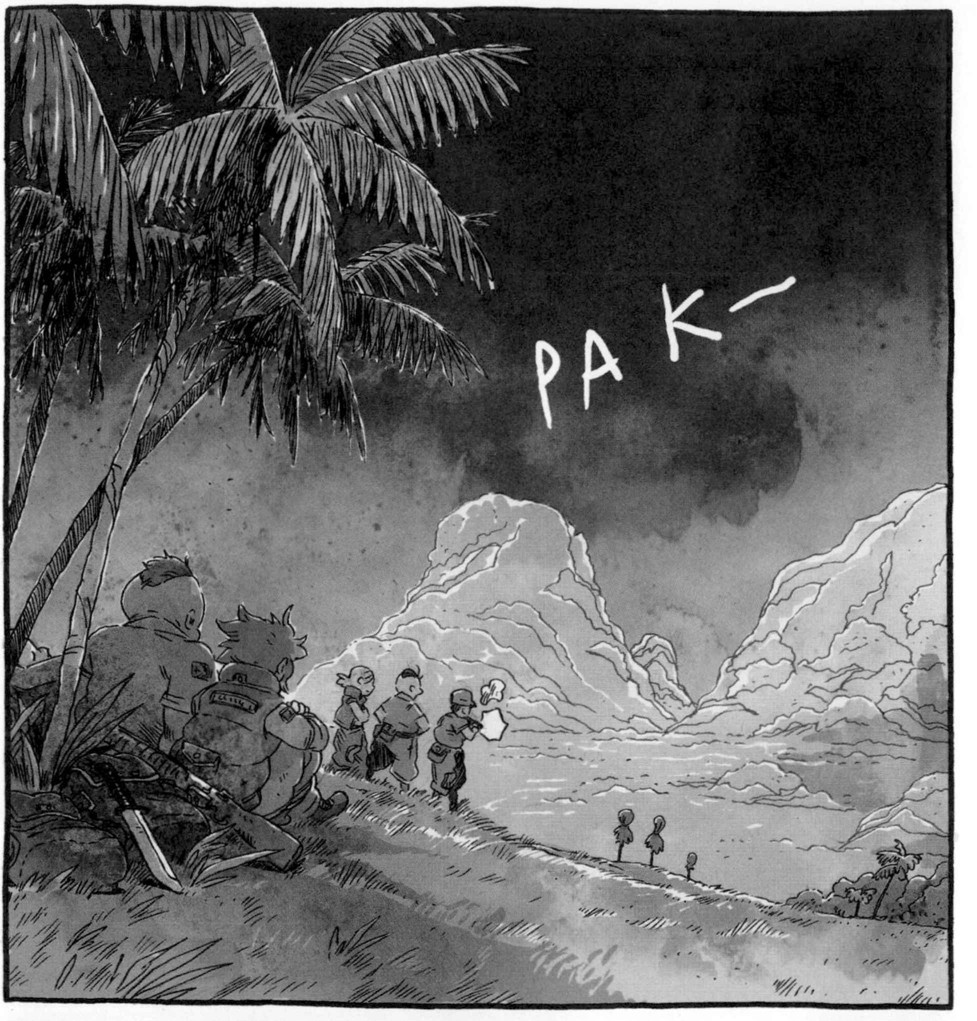
PAK—

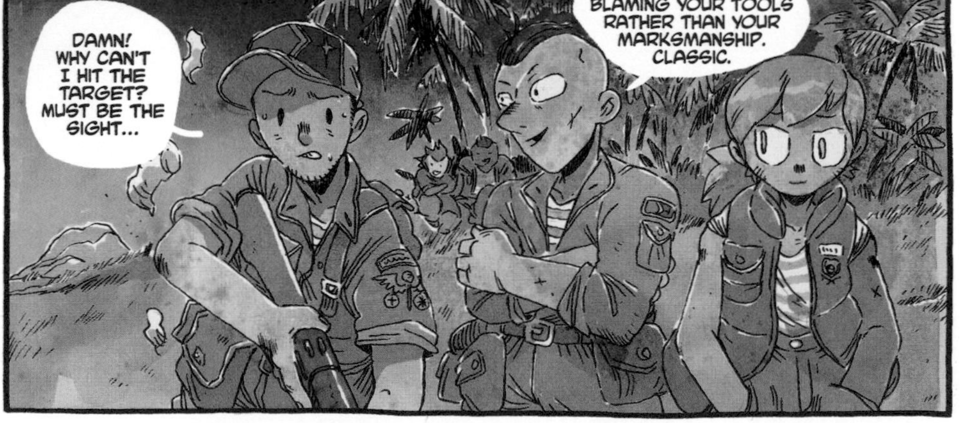
DAMN! WHY CAN'T I HIT THE TARGET? MUST BE THE SIGHT...
BLAMING YOUR TOOLS RATHER THAN YOUR MARKSMANSHIP. CLASSIC.

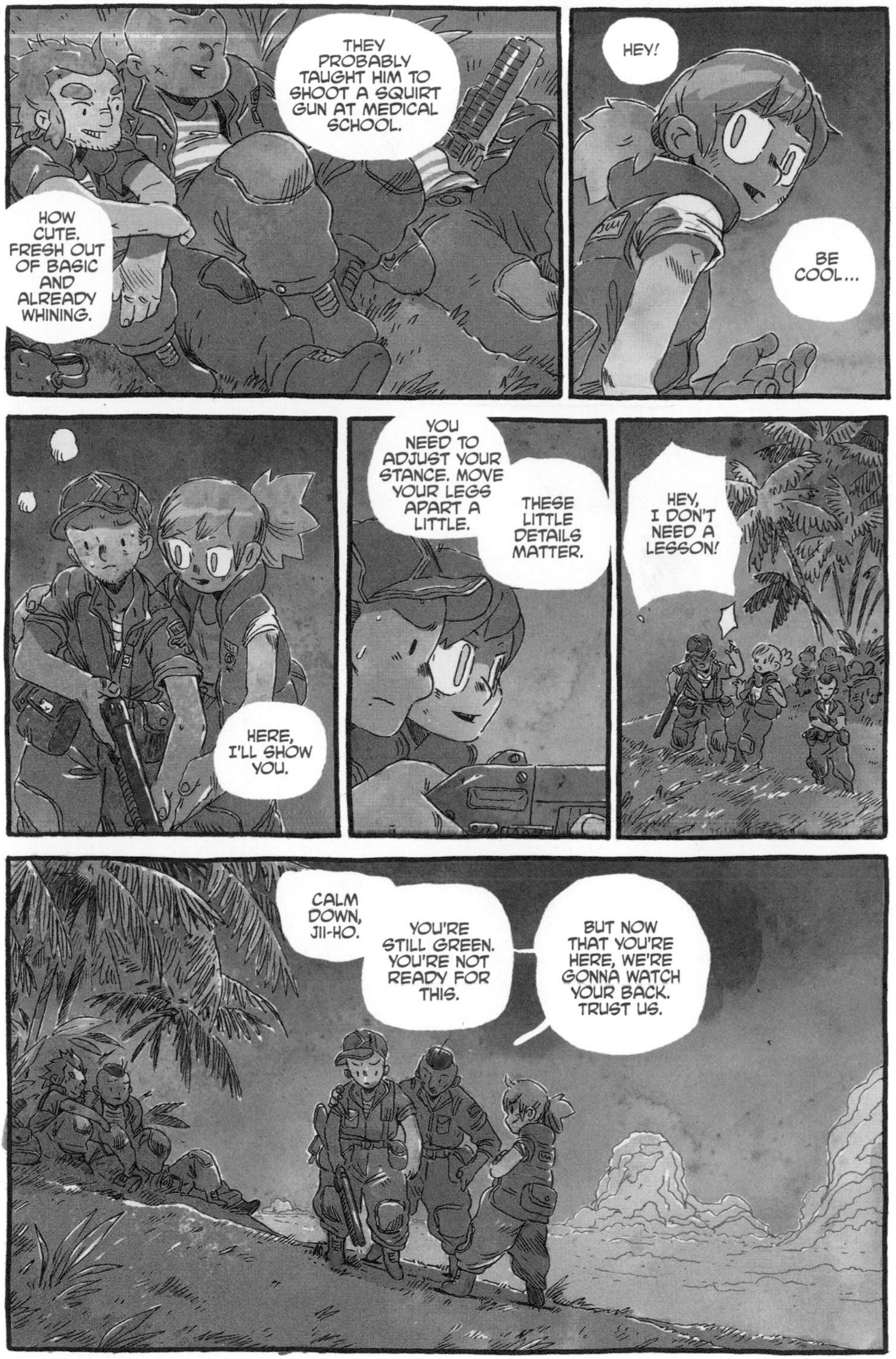
THEY PROBABLY TAUGHT HIM TO SHOOT A SQUIRT GUN AT MEDICAL SCHOOL.
HOW CUTE. FRESH OUT OF BASIC AND ALREADY WHINING.
HEY!
BE COOL...
HERE, I'LL SHOW YOU.
YOU NEED TO ADJUST YOUR STANCE. MOVE YOUR LEGS APART A LITTLE.
THESE LITTLE DETAILS MATTER.
HEY, I DON'T NEED A LESSON!
CALM DOWN, JII-HO.
YOU'RE STILL GREEN. YOU'RE NOT READY FOR THIS.
BUT NOW THAT YOU'RE HERE, WE'RE GONNA WATCH YOUR BACK. TRUST US.

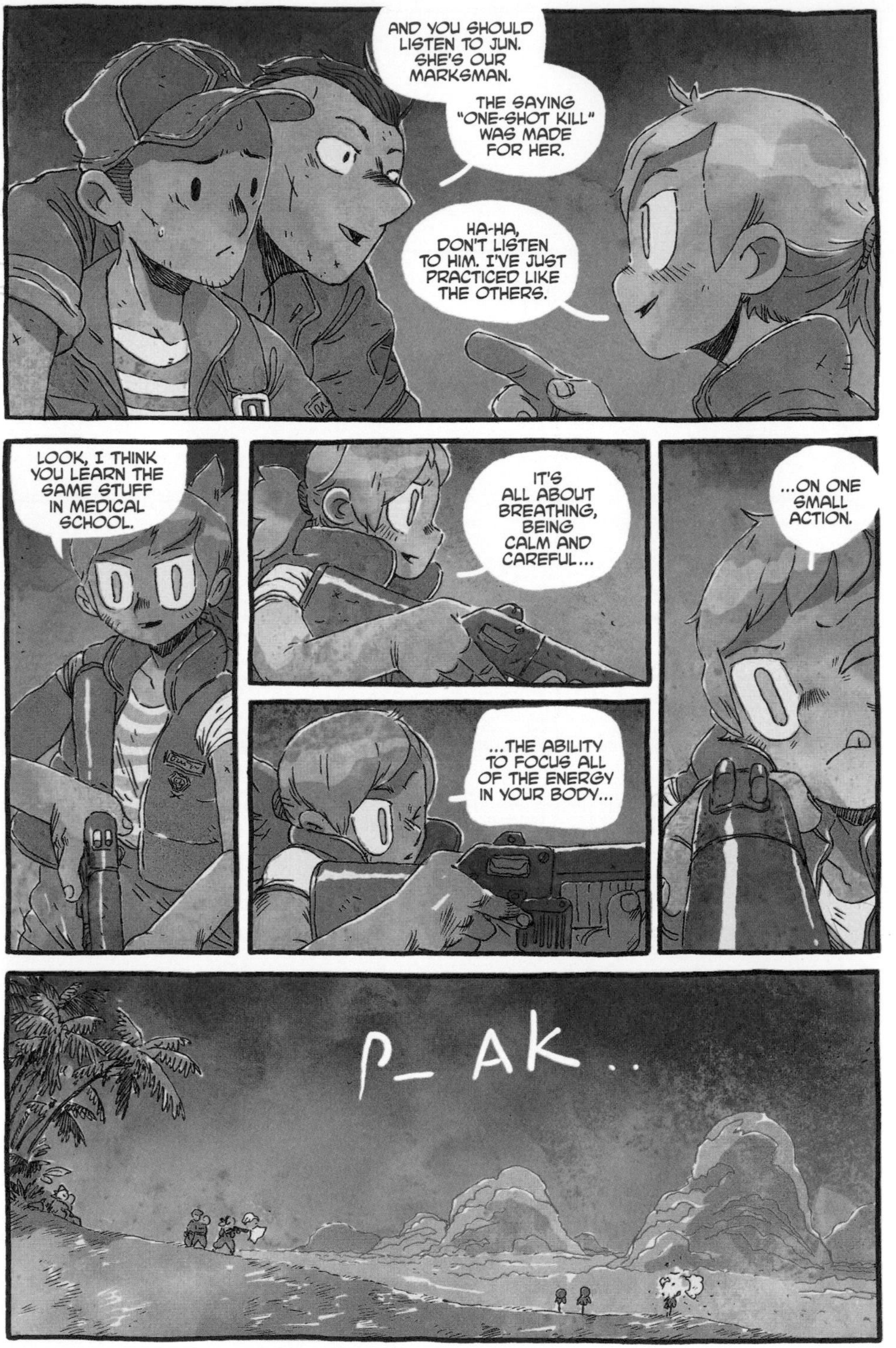
AND YOU SHOULD LISTEN TO JUN. SHE'S OUR MARKSMAN.
THE SAYING "ONE-SHOT KILL" WAS MADE FOR HER.
HA-HA, DON'T LISTEN TO HIM. I'VE JUST PRACTICED LIKE THE OTHERS.
LOOK, I THINK YOU LEARN THE SAME STUFF IN MEDICAL SCHOOL.
IT'S ALL ABOUT BREATHING, BEING CALM AND CAREFUL...
...THE ABILITY TO FOCUS ALL OF THE ENERGY IN YOUR BODY...
...ON ONE SMALL ACTION.
P_AK..

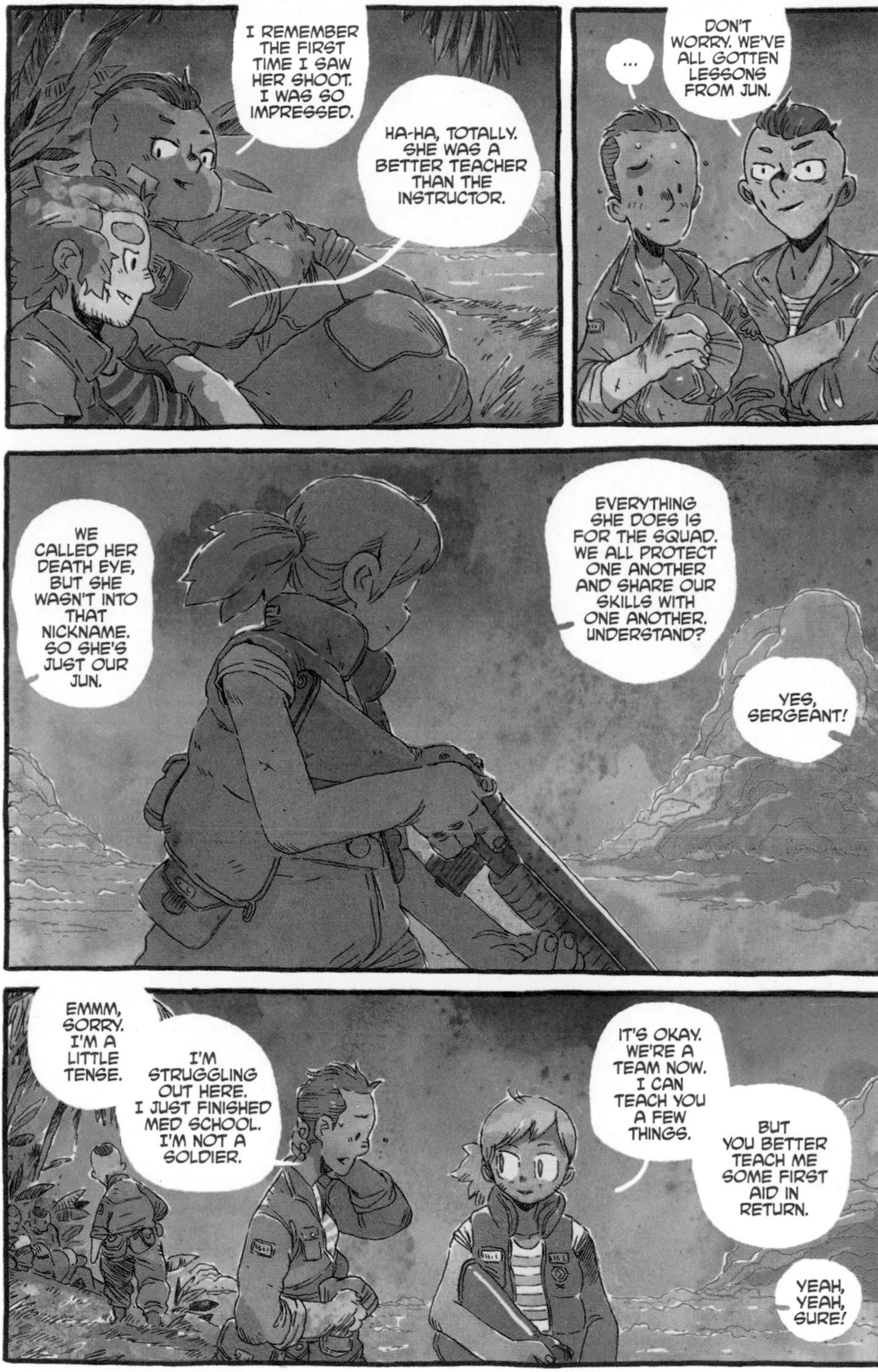
I REMEMBER THE FIRST TIME I SAW HER SHOOT. I WAS SO IMPRESSED.
HA-HA, TOTALLY. SHE WAS A BETTER TEACHER THAN THE INSTRUCTOR.
...
DON'T WORRY. WE'VE ALL GOTTEN LESSONS FROM JUN.
WE CALLED HER DEATH EYE, BUT SHE WASN'T INTO THAT NICKNAME. SO SHE'S JUST OUR JUN.
EVERYTHING SHE DOES IS FOR THE SQUAD. WE ALL PROTECT ONE ANOTHER AND SHARE OUR SKILLS WITH ONE ANOTHER. UNDERSTAND?
YES, SERGEANT!
EMMM, SORRY. I'M A LITTLE TENSE.
I'M STRUGGLING OUT HERE. I JUST FINISHED MED SCHOOL. I'M NOT A SOLDIER.
IT'S OKAY. WE'RE A TEAM NOW. I CAN TEACH YOU A FEW THINGS.
BUT YOU BETTER TEACH ME SOME FIRST AID IN RETURN.
YEAH, YEAH, SURE!

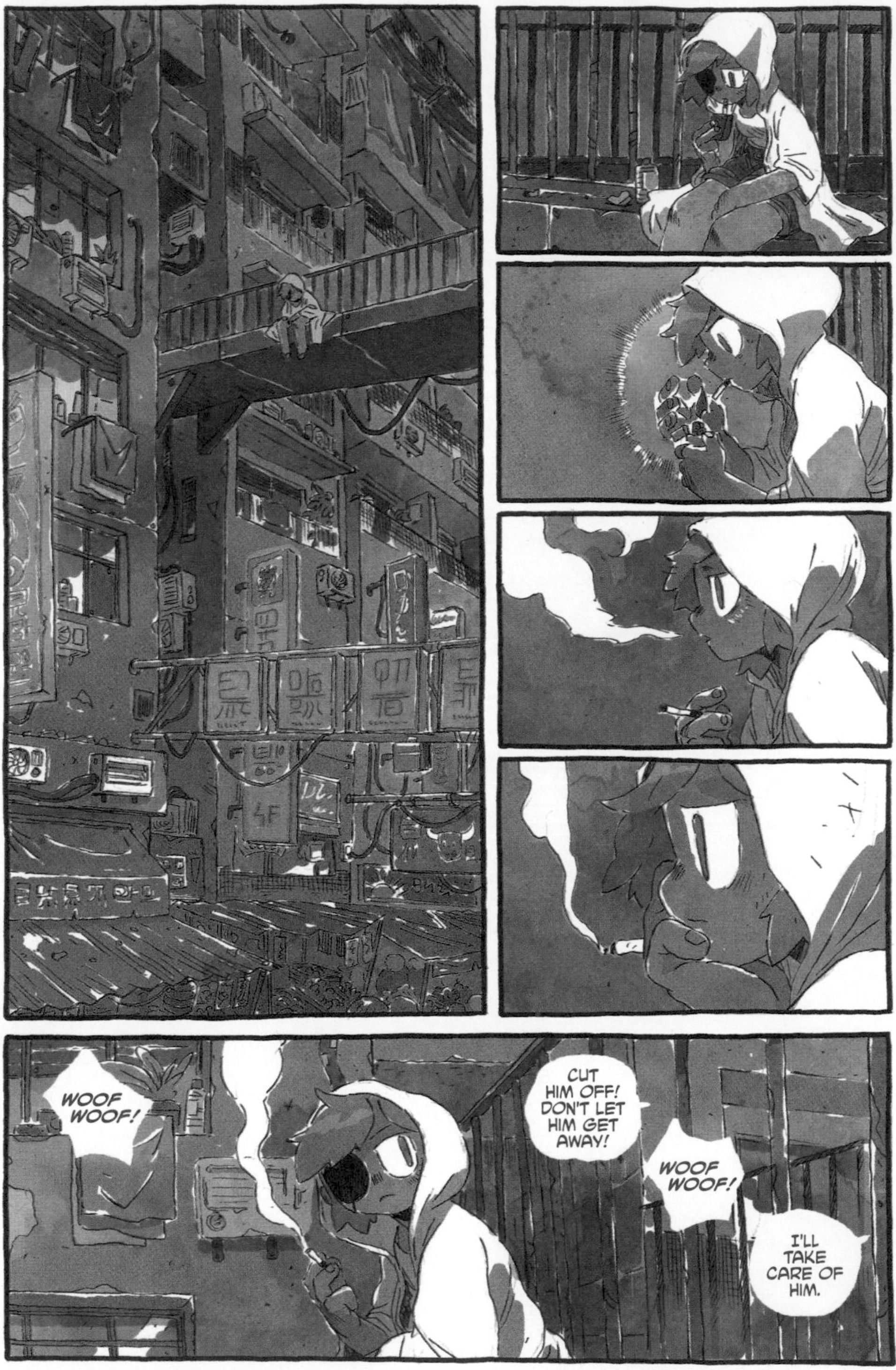
WOOF WOOF!
CUT HIM OFF! DON'T LET HIM GET AWAY!
WOOF WOOF!
I'LL TAKE CARE OF HIM.

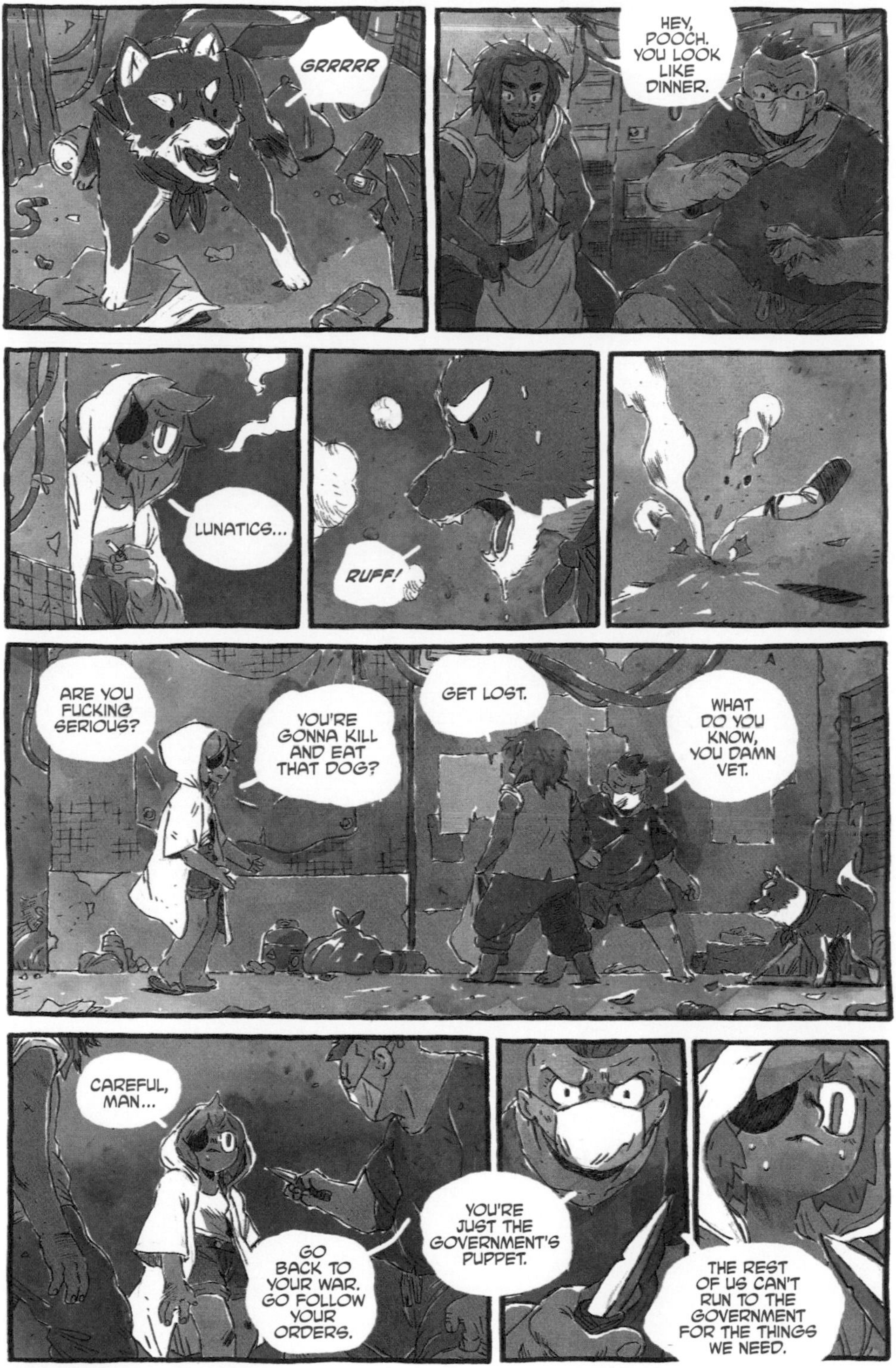
GRRRRR
HEY, POOCH. YOU LOOK LIKE DINNER.
LUNATICS...
RUFF!
ARE YOU FUCKING SERIOUS?
YOU'RE GONNA KILL AND EAT THAT DOG?
GET LOST.
WHAT DO YOU KNOW, YOU DAMN VET.
CAREFUL, MAN...
GO BACK TO YOUR WAR. GO FOLLOW YOUR ORDERS.
YOU'RE JUST THE GOVERNMENT'S PUPPET.
THE REST OF US CAN'T RUN TO THE GOVERNMENT FOR THE THINGS WE NEED.

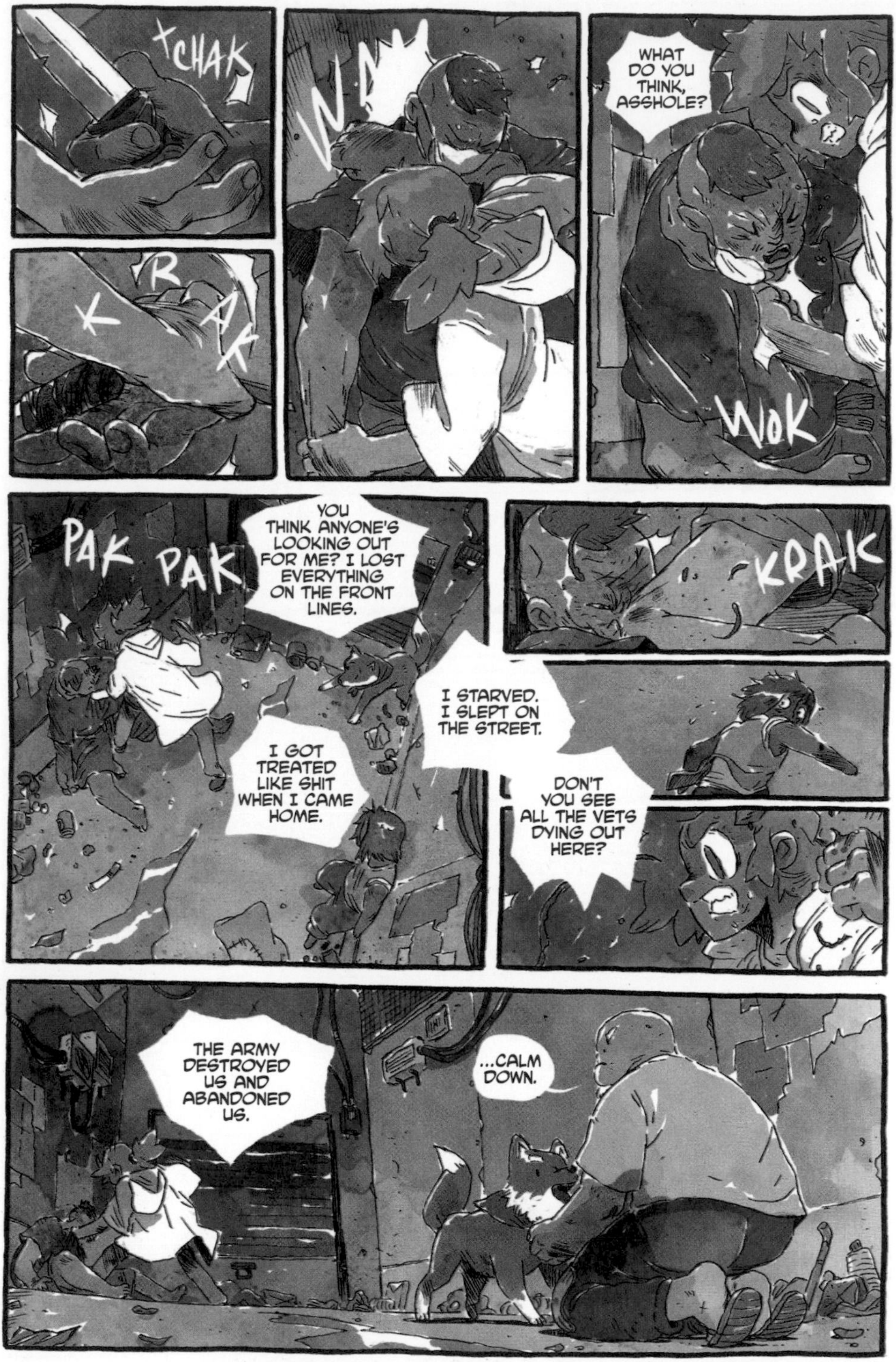

CHAK
KRAK
WHAT DO YOU THINK, ASSHOLE?
WOK
PAK PAK
YOU THINK ANYONE'S LOOKING OUT FOR ME? I LOST EVERYTHING ON THE FRONT LINES.
KRAK
I STARVED. I SLEPT ON THE STREET.
I GOT TREATED LIKE SHIT WHEN I CAME HOME.
DON'T YOU SEE ALL THE VETS DYING OUT HERE?
THE ARMY DESTROYED US AND ABANDONED US.
...CALM DOWN.

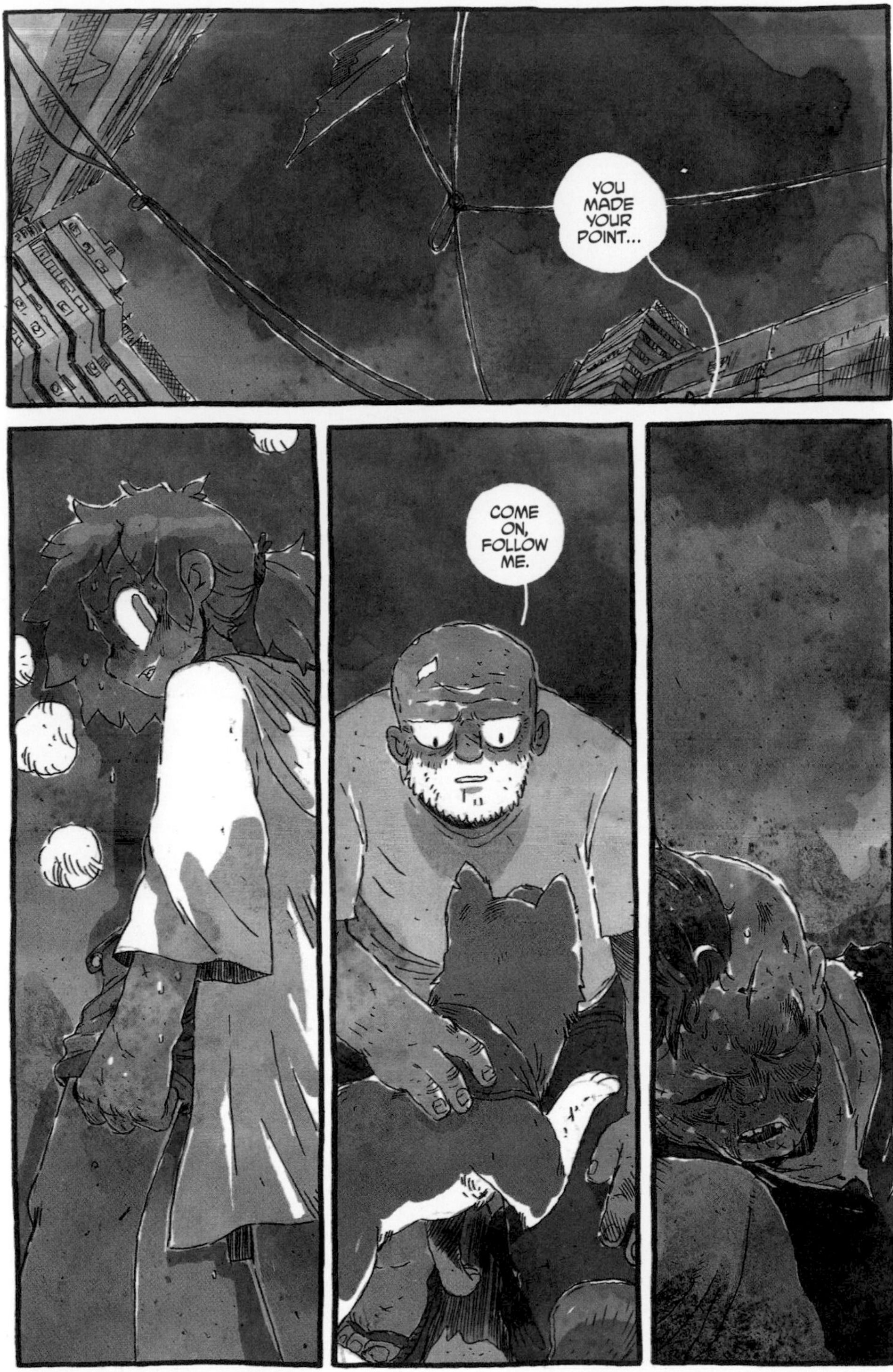
YOU MADE YOUR POINT...
COME ON, FOLLOW ME.

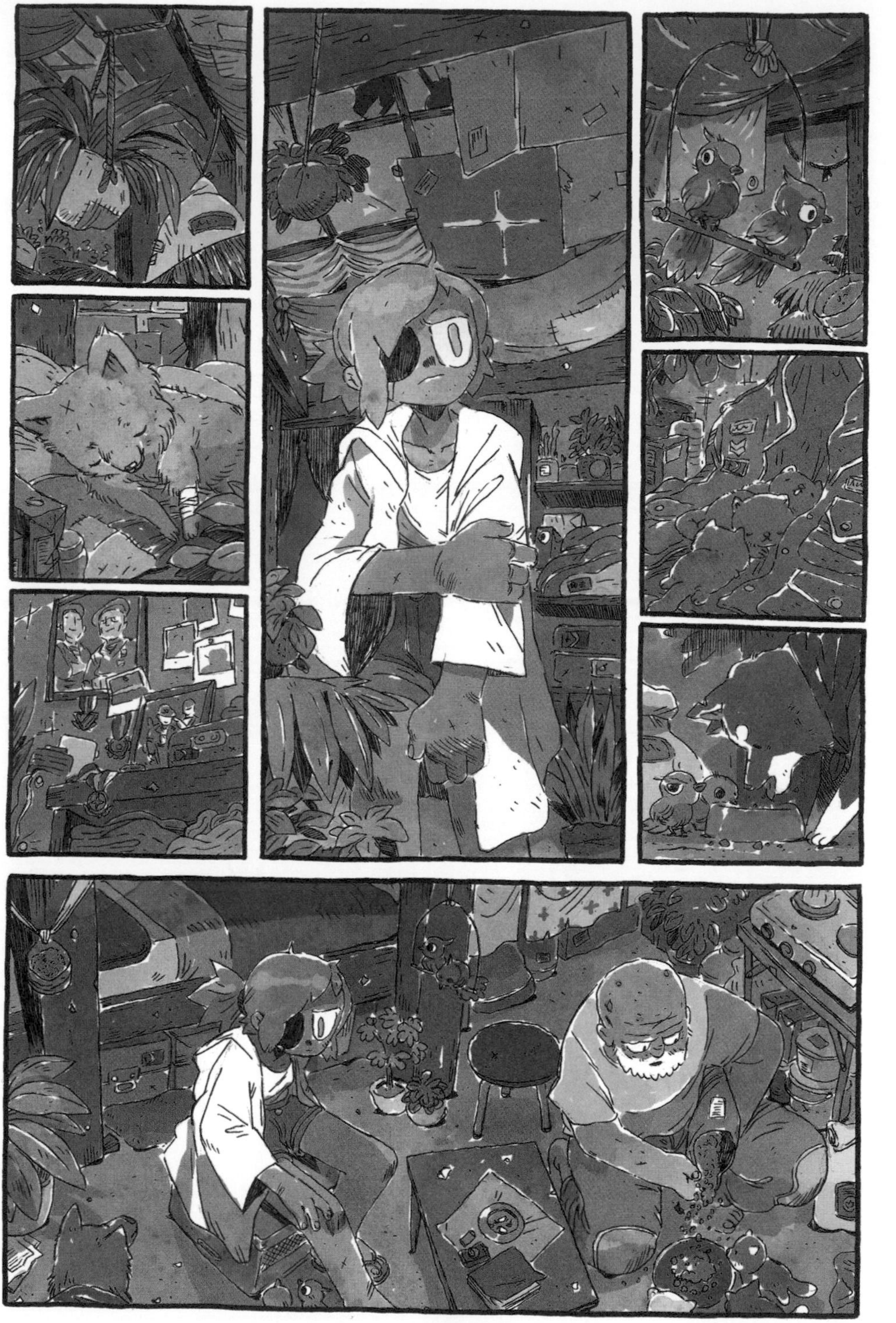

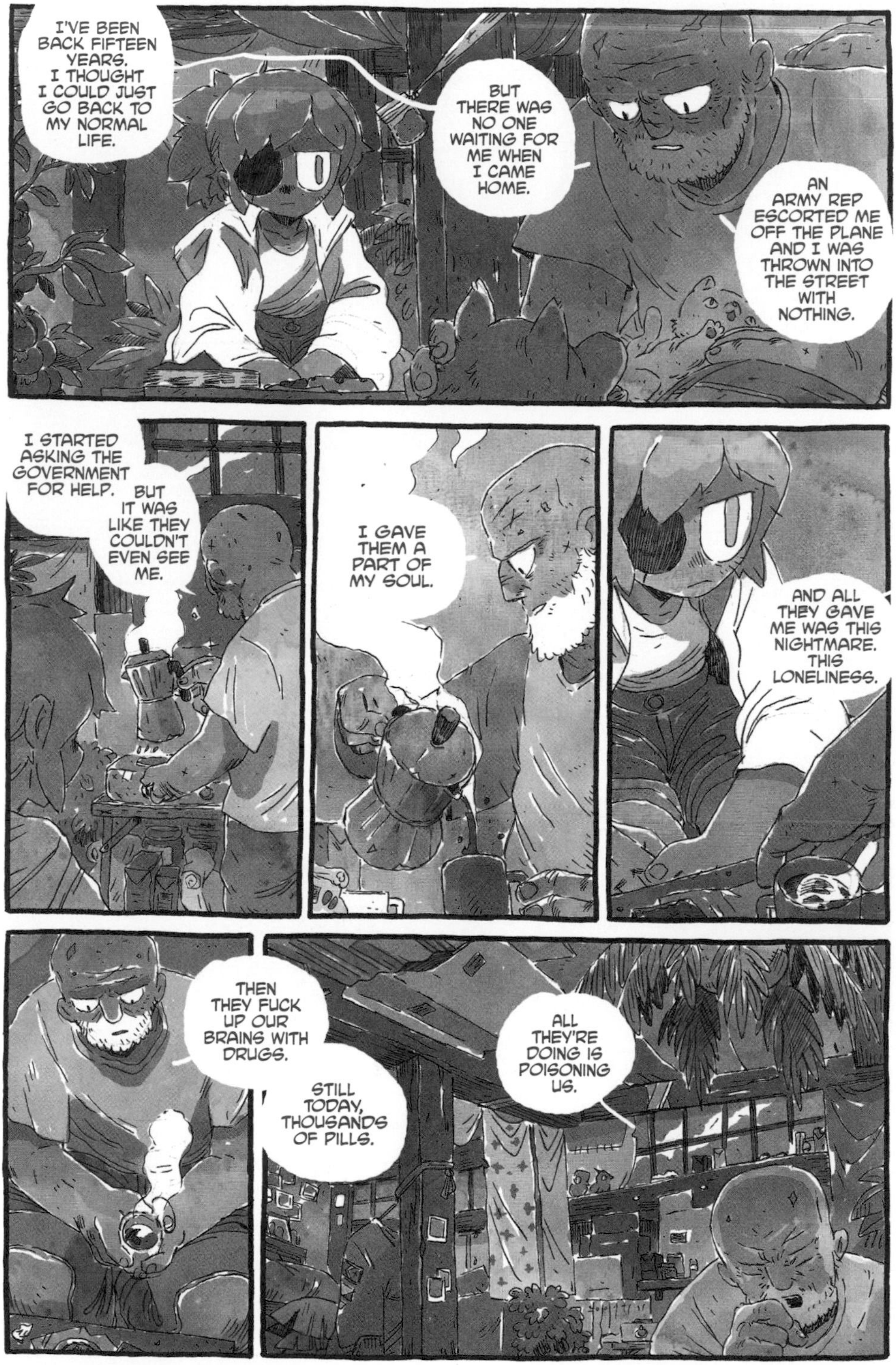
I'VE BEEN BACK FIFTEEN YEARS. I THOUGHT I COULD JUST GO BACK TO MY NORMAL LIFE.
BUT THERE WAS NO ONE WAITING FOR ME WHEN I CAME HOME.
AN ARMY REP ESCORTED ME OFF THE PLANE AND I WAS THROWN INTO THE STREET WITH NOTHING.
I STARTED ASKING THE GOVERNMENT FOR HELP.
BUT IT WAS LIKE THEY COULDN'T EVEN SEE ME.
I GAVE THEM A PART OF MY SOUL.
AND ALL THEY GAVE ME WAS THIS NIGHTMARE. THIS LONELINESS.
THEN THEY FUCK UP OUR BRAINS WITH DRUGS.
STILL TODAY, THOUSANDS OF PILLS.
ALL THEY'RE DOING IS POISONING US.

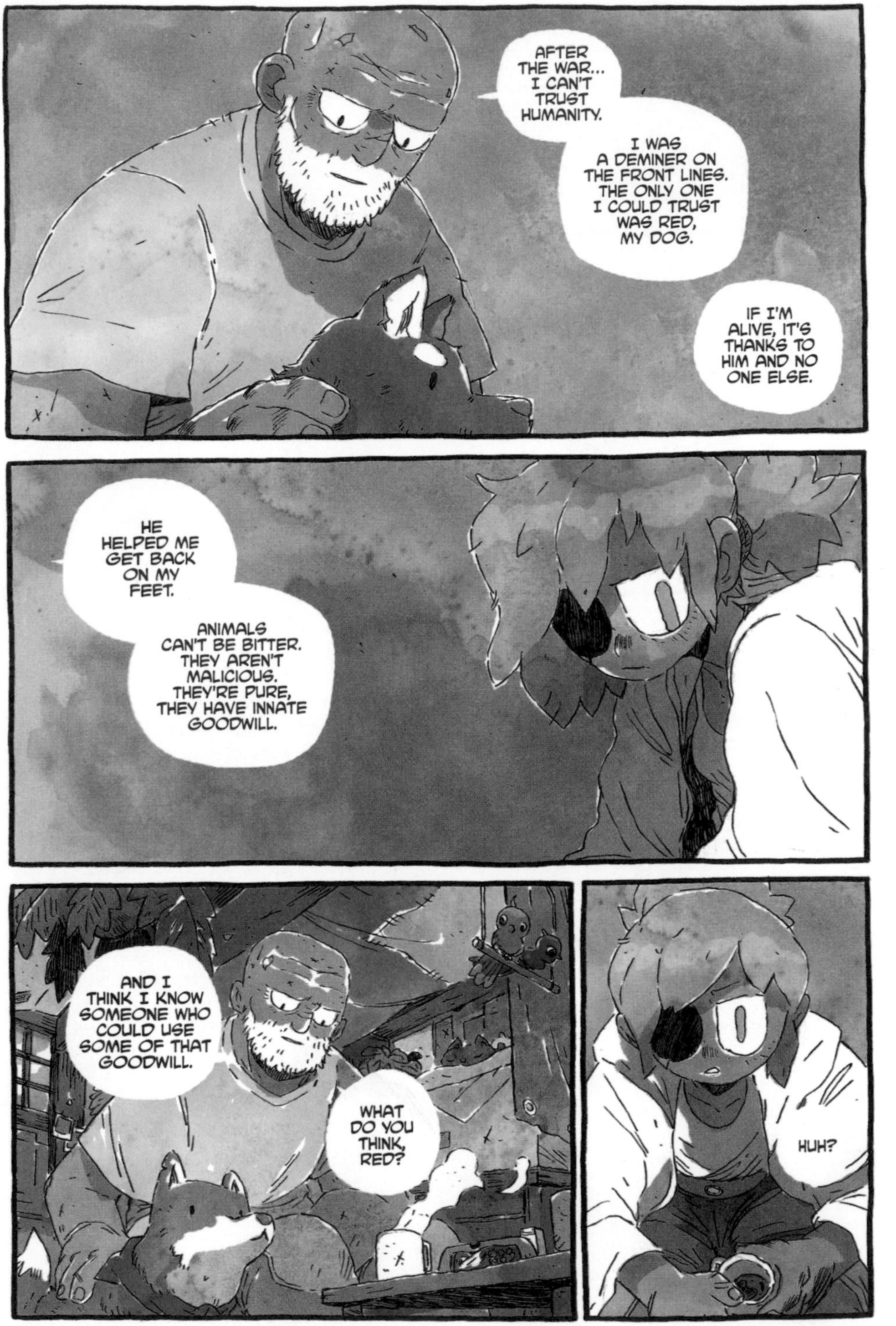
AFTER THE WAR... I CAN'T TRUST HUMANITY.
I WAS A DEMINER ON THE FRONT LINES. THE ONLY ONE I COULD TRUST WAS RED, MY DOG.
IF I'M ALIVE, IT'S THANKS TO HIM AND NO ONE ELSE.
HE HELPED ME GET BACK ON MY FEET.
ANIMALS CAN'T BE BITTER. THEY AREN'T MALICIOUS. THEY'RE PURE, THEY HAVE INNATE GOODWILL.
AND I THINK I KNOW SOMEONE WHO COULD USE SOME OF THAT GOODWILL.
WHAT DO YOU THINK, RED?
HUH?

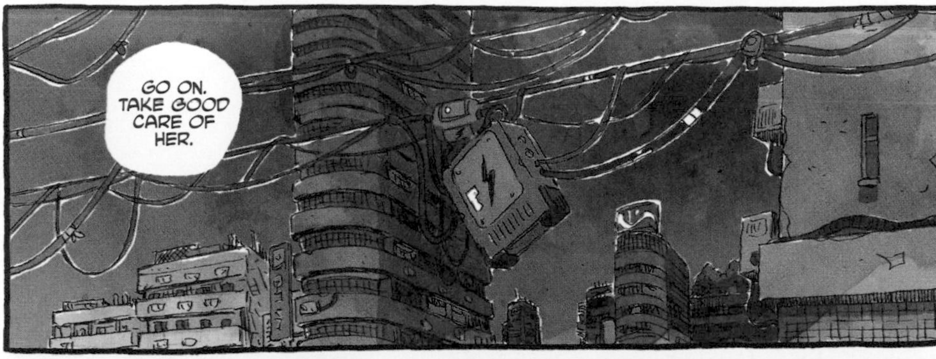
GO ON. TAKE GOOD CARE OF HER.

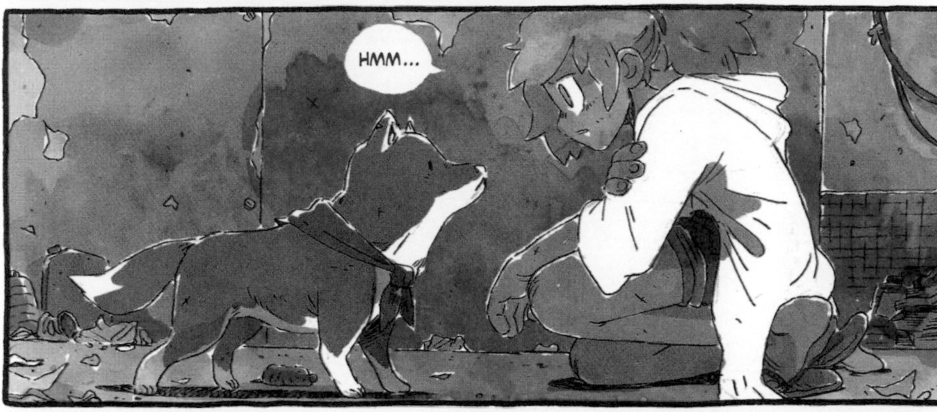
HMM...

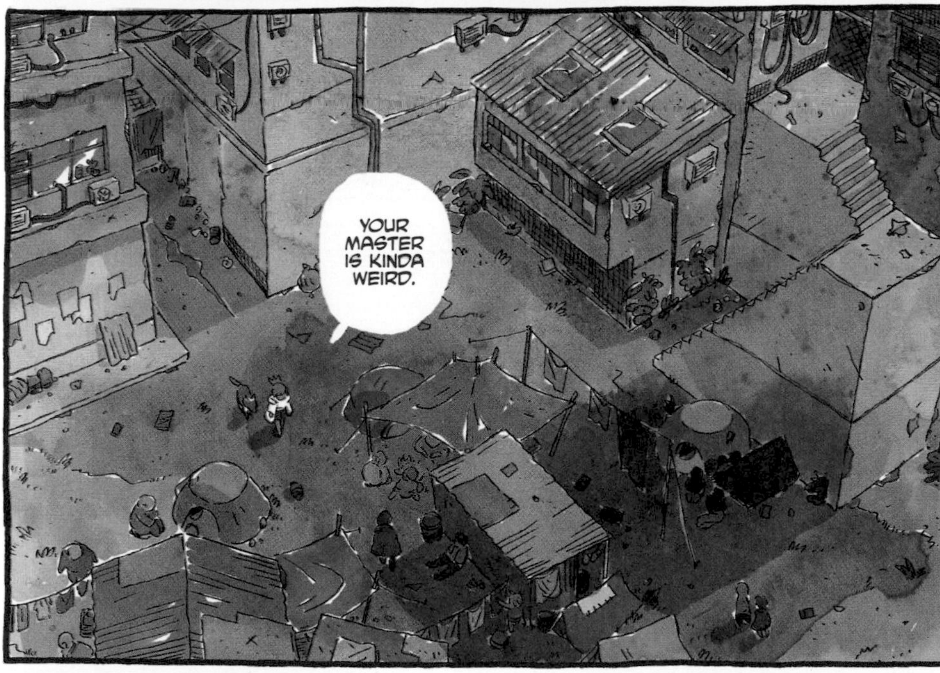
YOUR MASTER IS KINDA WEIRD.

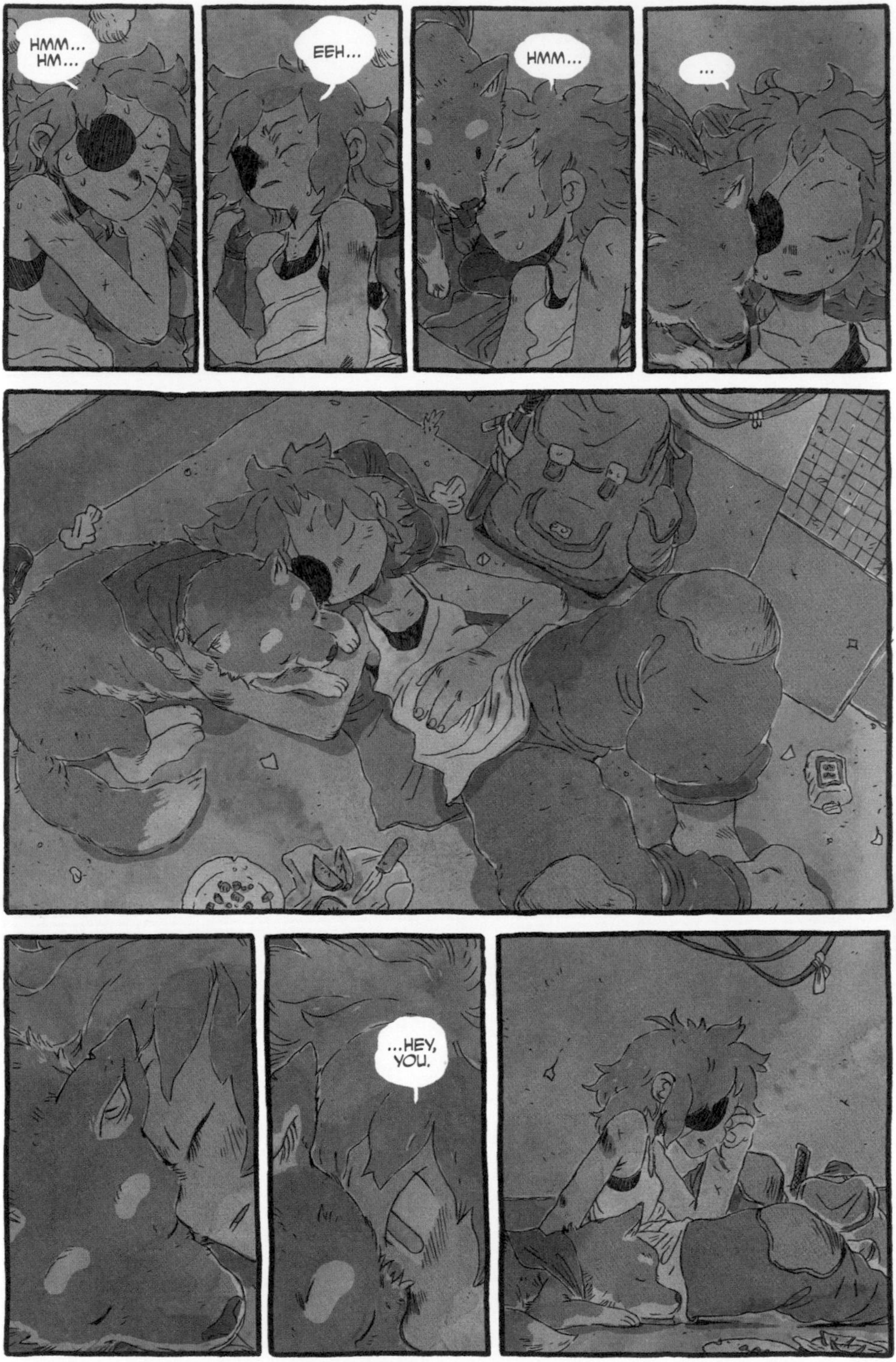

HMM... HM...
EEH...
HMM...
...
...HEY, YOU.

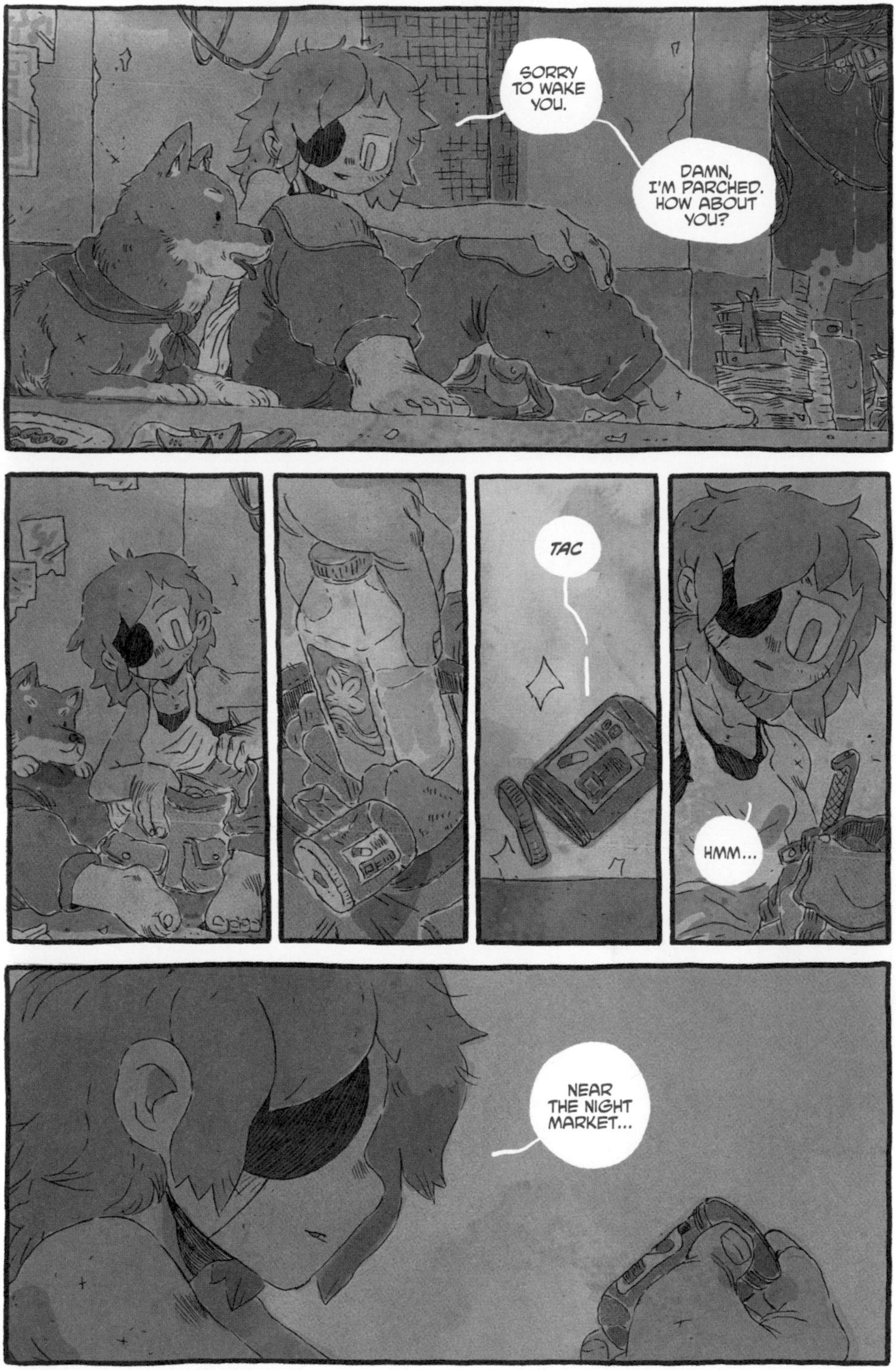
SORRY TO WAKE YOU.
DAMN, I'M PARCHED. HOW ABOUT YOU?
TAC
HMM...
NEAR THE NIGHT MARKET...

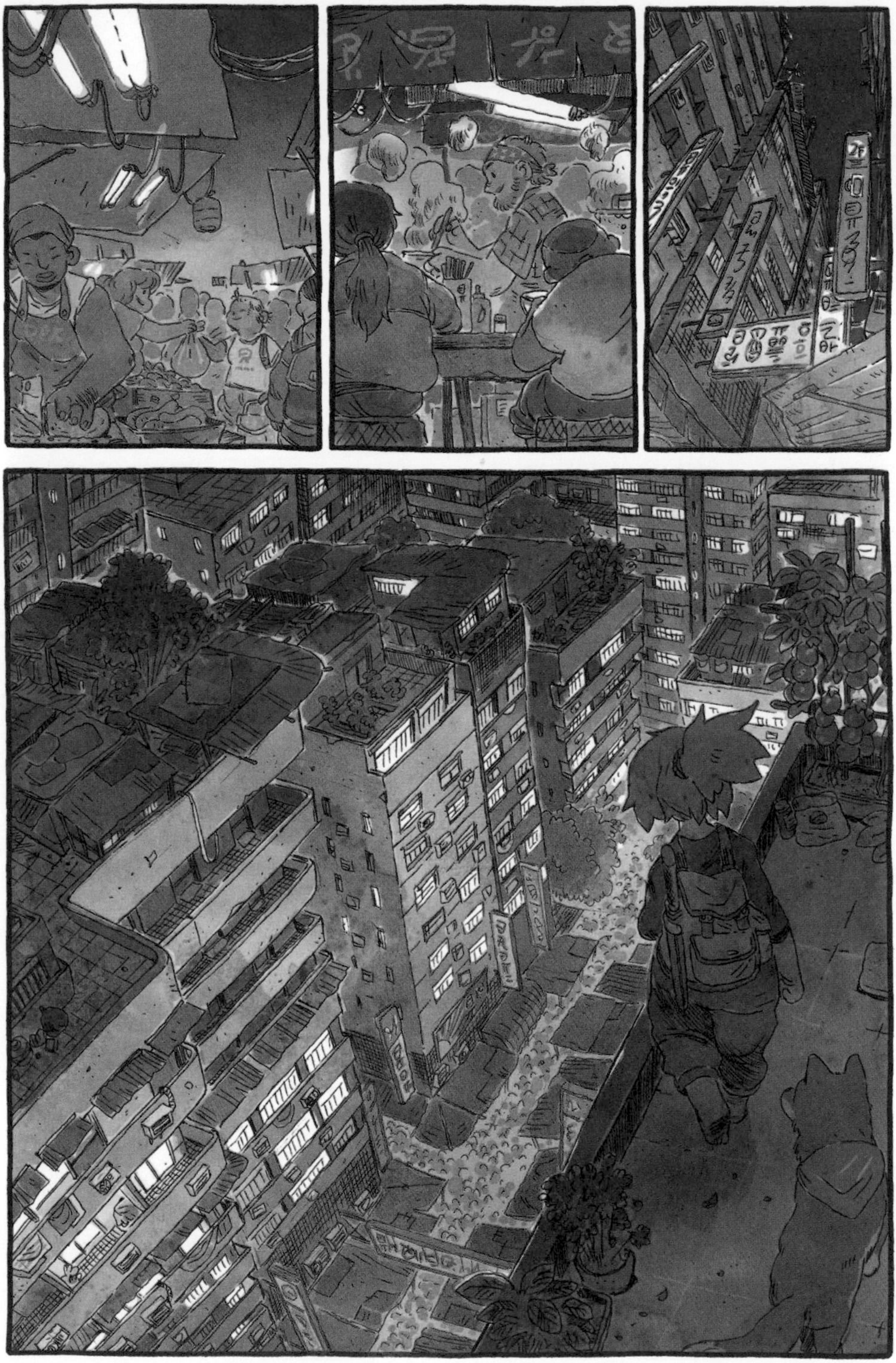

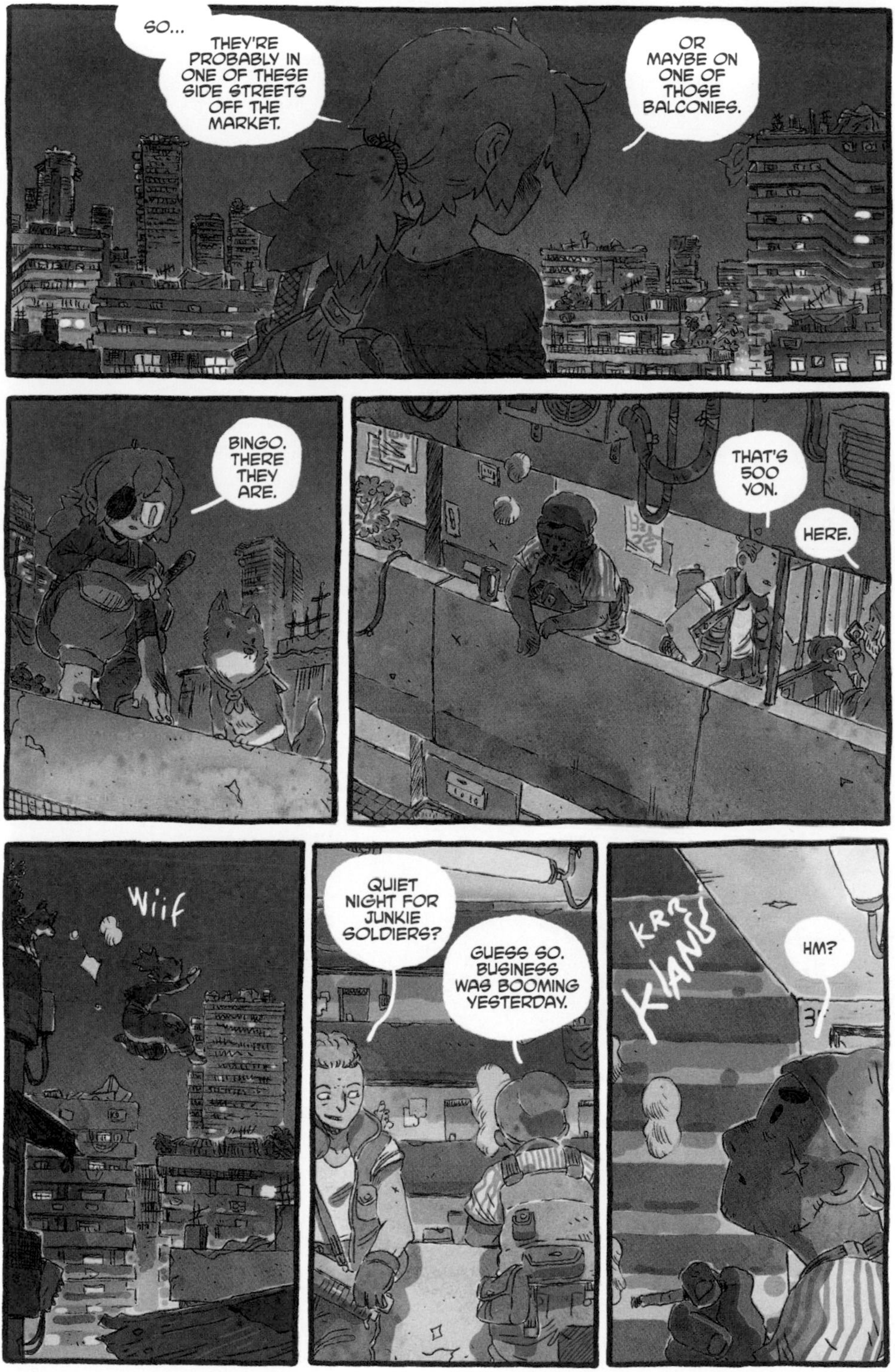
SO...
THEY'RE PROBABLY IN ONE OF THESE SIDE STREETS OFF THE MARKET.
OR MAYBE ON ONE OF THOSE BALCONIES.
BINGO. THERE THEY ARE.
THAT'S 500 YON.
HERE.
Wiif
QUIET NIGHT FOR JUNKIE SOLDIERS?
GUESS SO. BUSINESS WAS BOOMING YESTERDAY.
KRR KIANG
HM?

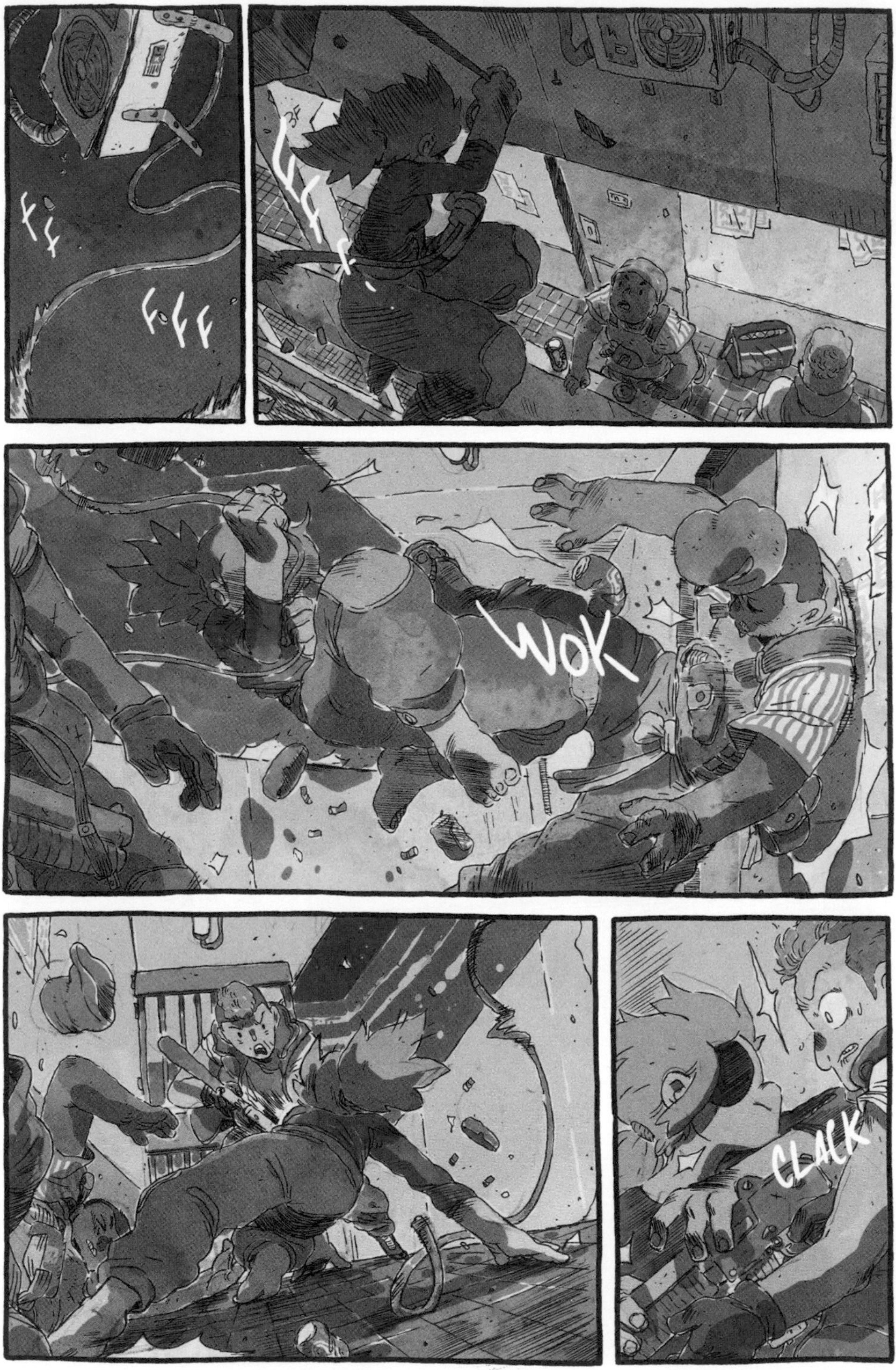
FF
FFF
3F
FFF
WOK
CLACK

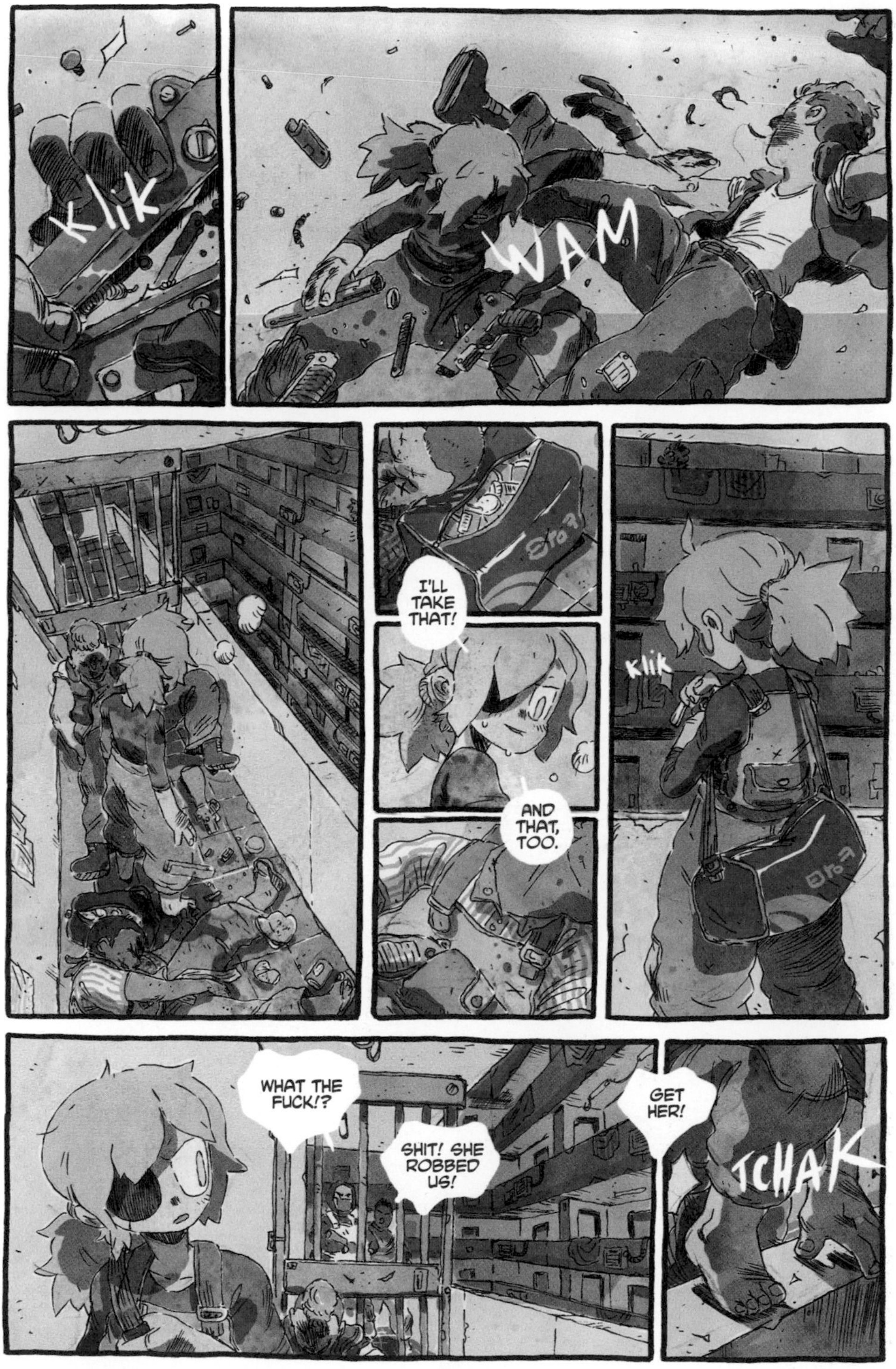
KLIK
WAM
I'LL TAKE THAT!
AND THAT, TOO.
KLIK
WHAT THE FUCK!?
SHIT! SHE ROBBED US!
GET HER!
TCHAK

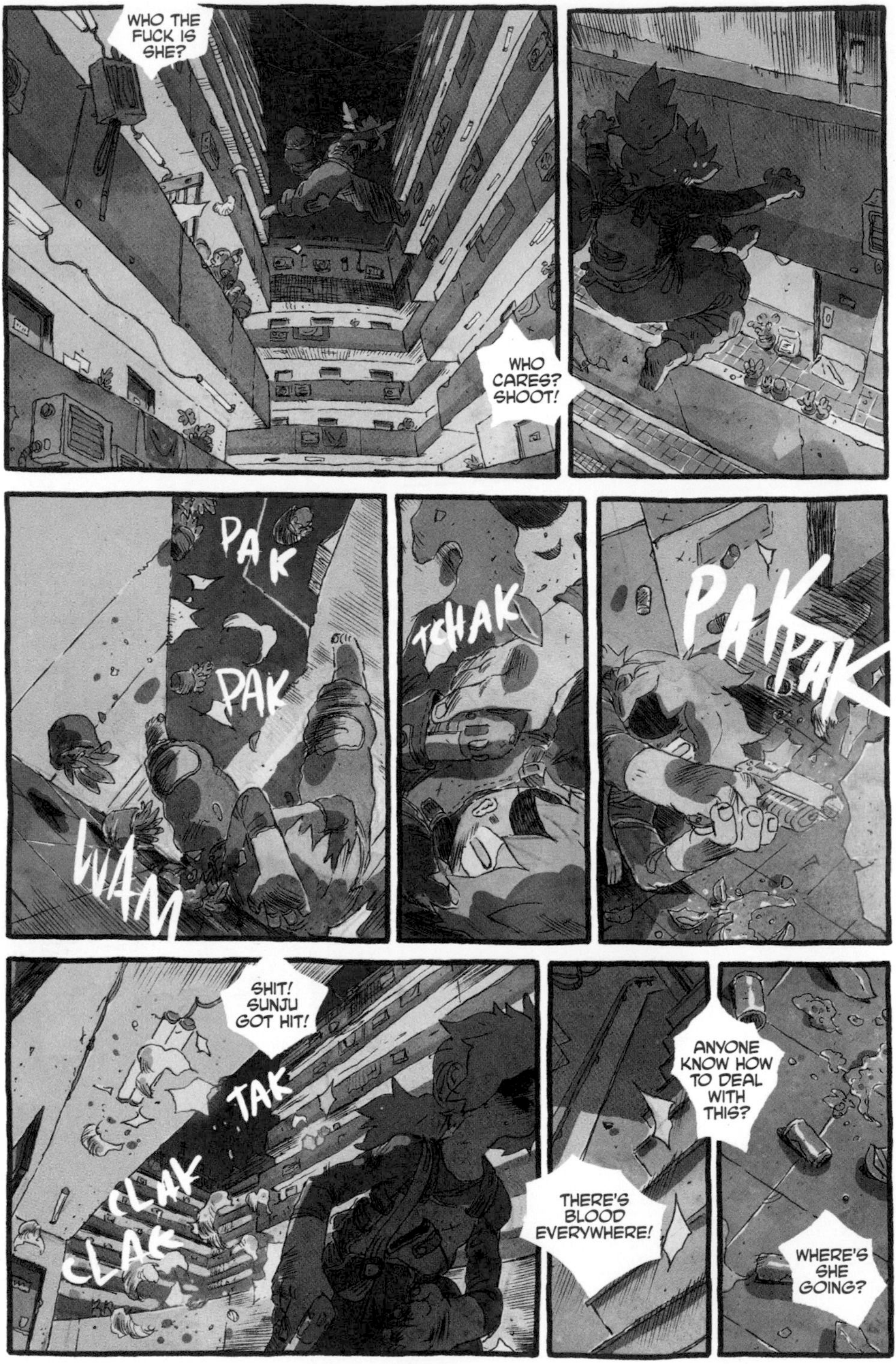
WHO THE FUCK IS SHE?
WHO CARES? SHOOT!
PAK
PAK
WAM
TCHAK
PAK PAK
SHIT! SUNJU GOT HIT!
TAK
CLAK CLAK
ANYONE KNOW HOW TO DEAL WITH THIS?
THERE'S BLOOD EVERYWHERE!
WHERE'S SHE GOING?

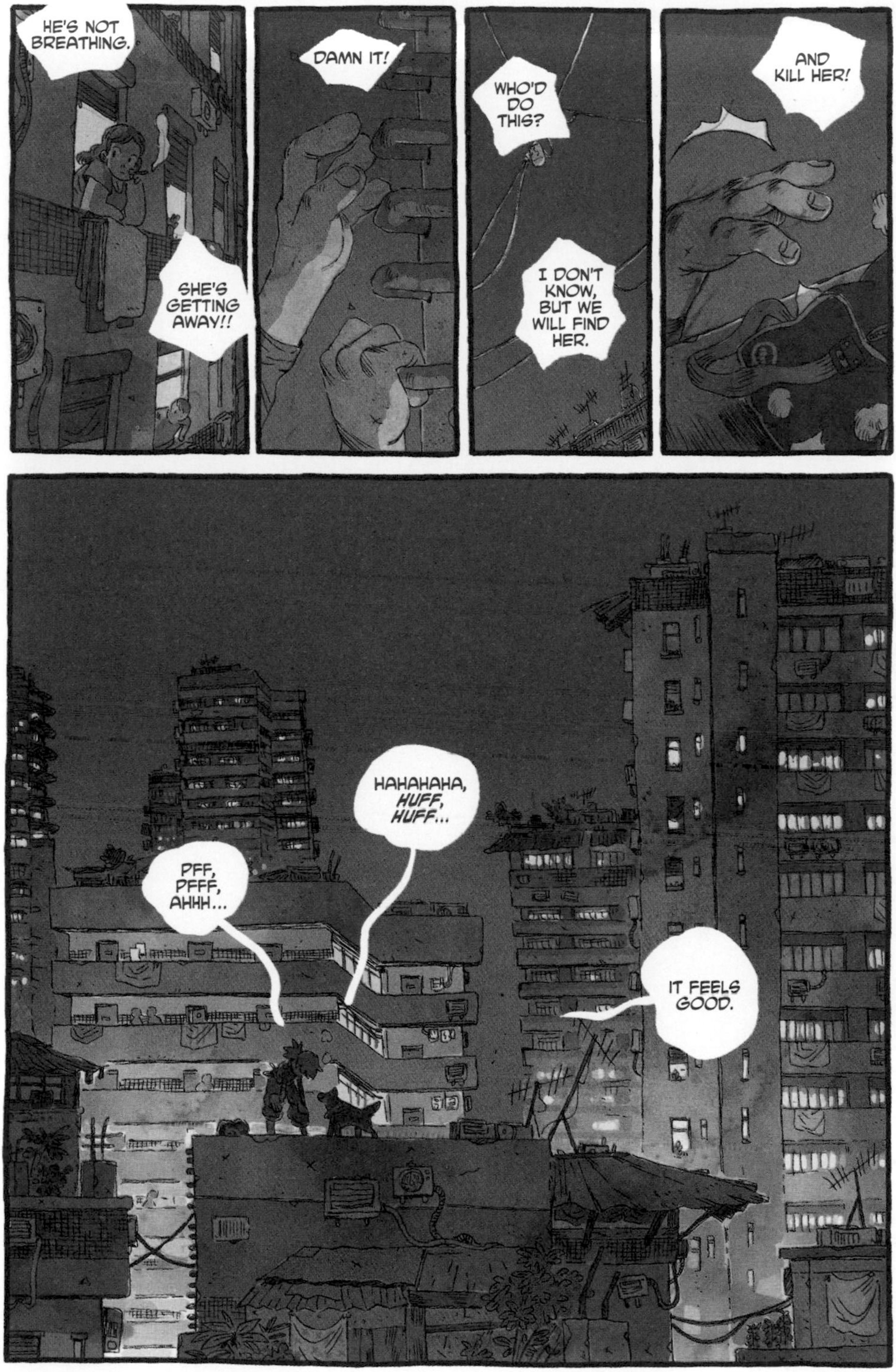
HE'S NOT BREATHING.
SHE'S GETTING AWAY!!
DAMN IT!
WHO'D DO THIS?
I DON'T KNOW, BUT WE WILL FIND HER.
AND KILL HER!
PFF, PFFF, AHHH...
HAHAHAHA, *HUFF, HUFF*...
IT FEELS GOOD.

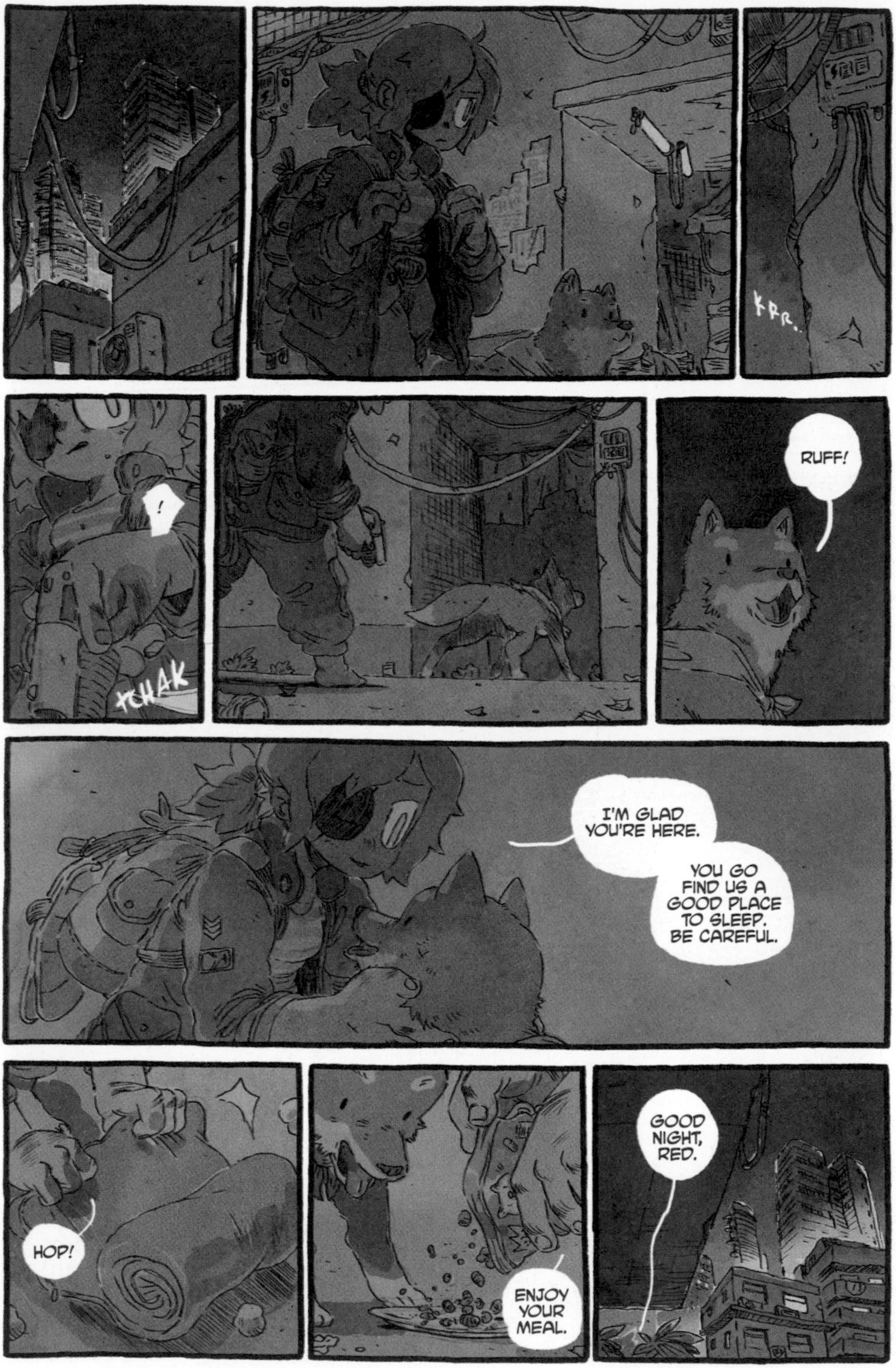
KRR..
!
TCHAK
RUFF!
I'M GLAD YOU'RE HERE.
YOU GO FIND US A GOOD PLACE TO SLEEP. BE CAREFUL.
HOP!
ENJOY YOUR MEAL.
GOOD NIGHT, RED.

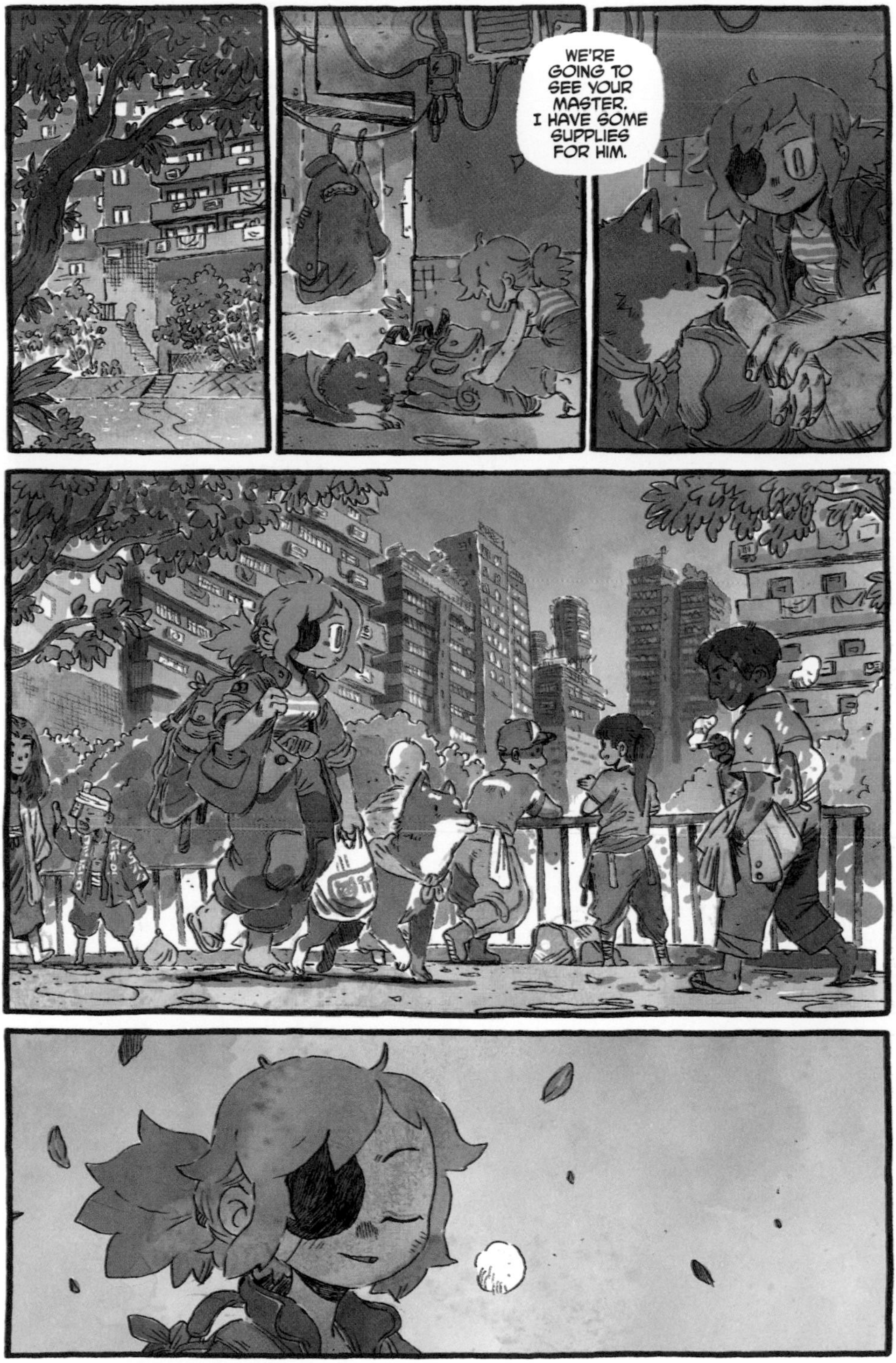
WE'RE GOING TO SEE YOUR MASTER. I HAVE SOME SUPPLIES FOR HIM.

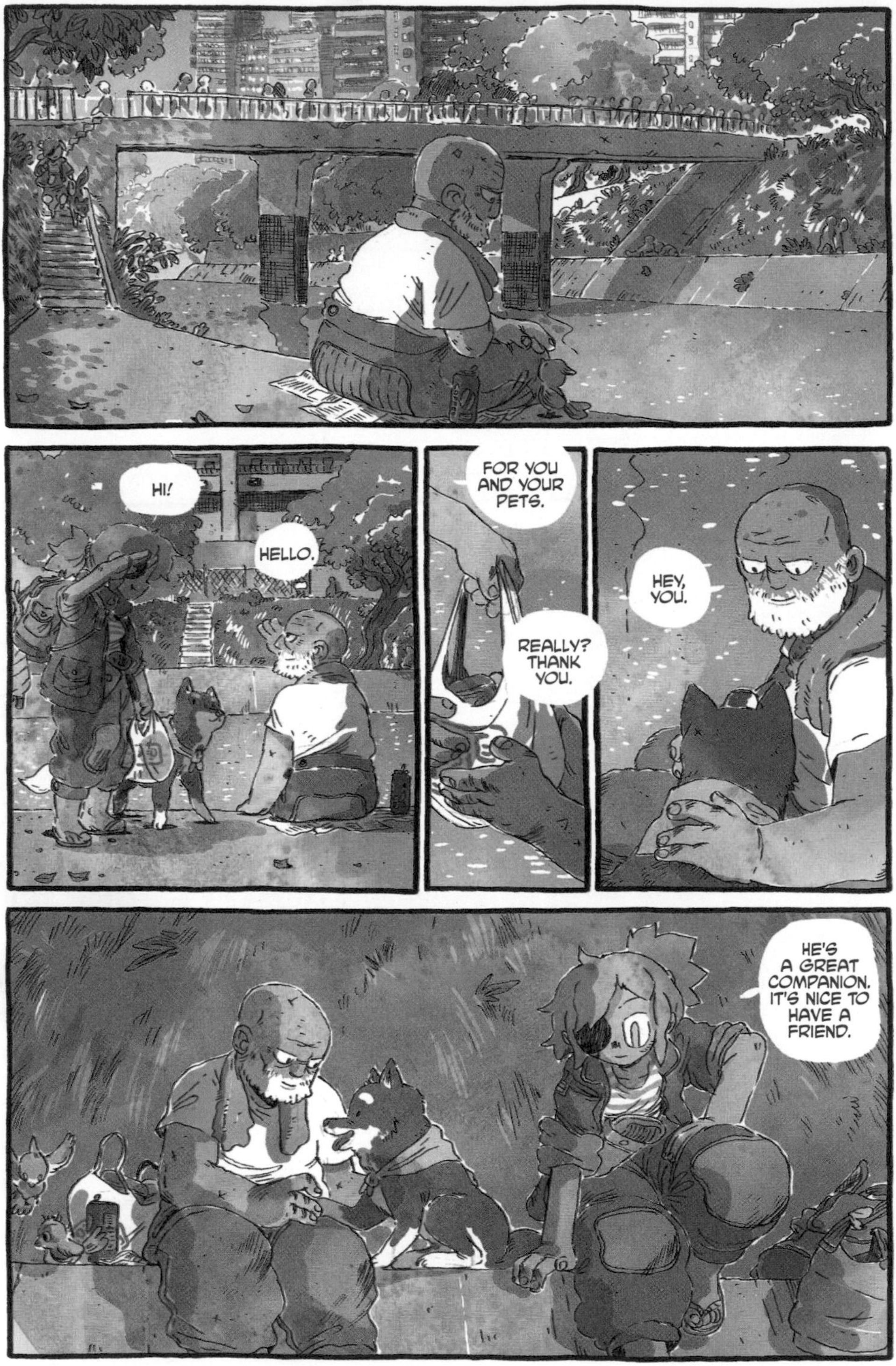
HI!
HELLO.
FOR YOU AND YOUR PETS.
REALLY? THANK YOU.
HEY, YOU.
HE'S A GREAT COMPANION. IT'S NICE TO HAVE A FRIEND.

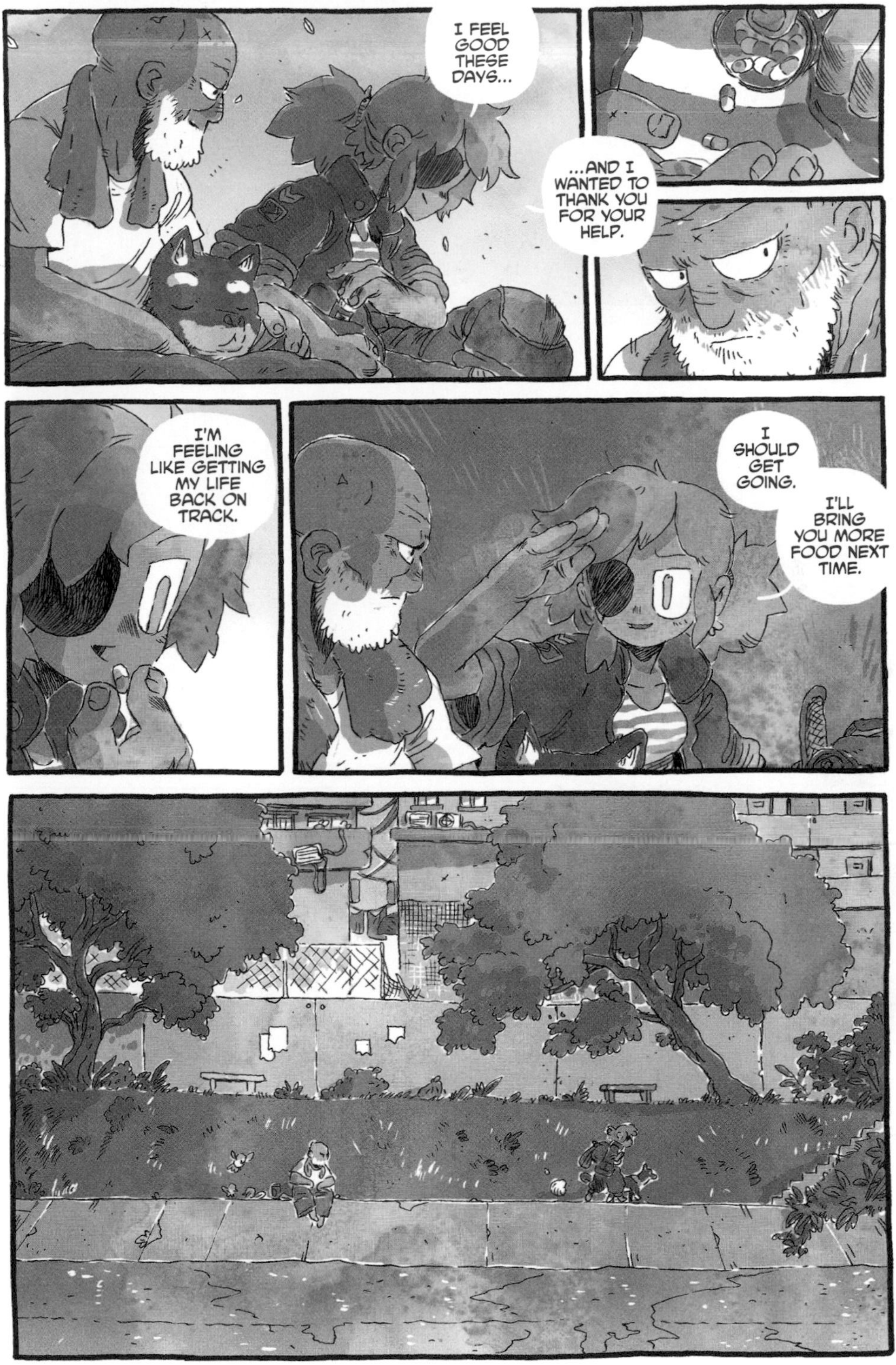
I FEEL GOOD THESE DAYS...
...AND I WANTED TO THANK YOU FOR YOUR HELP.
I'M FEELING LIKE GETTING MY LIFE BACK ON TRACK.
I SHOULD GET GOING.
I'LL BRING YOU MORE FOOD NEXT TIME.

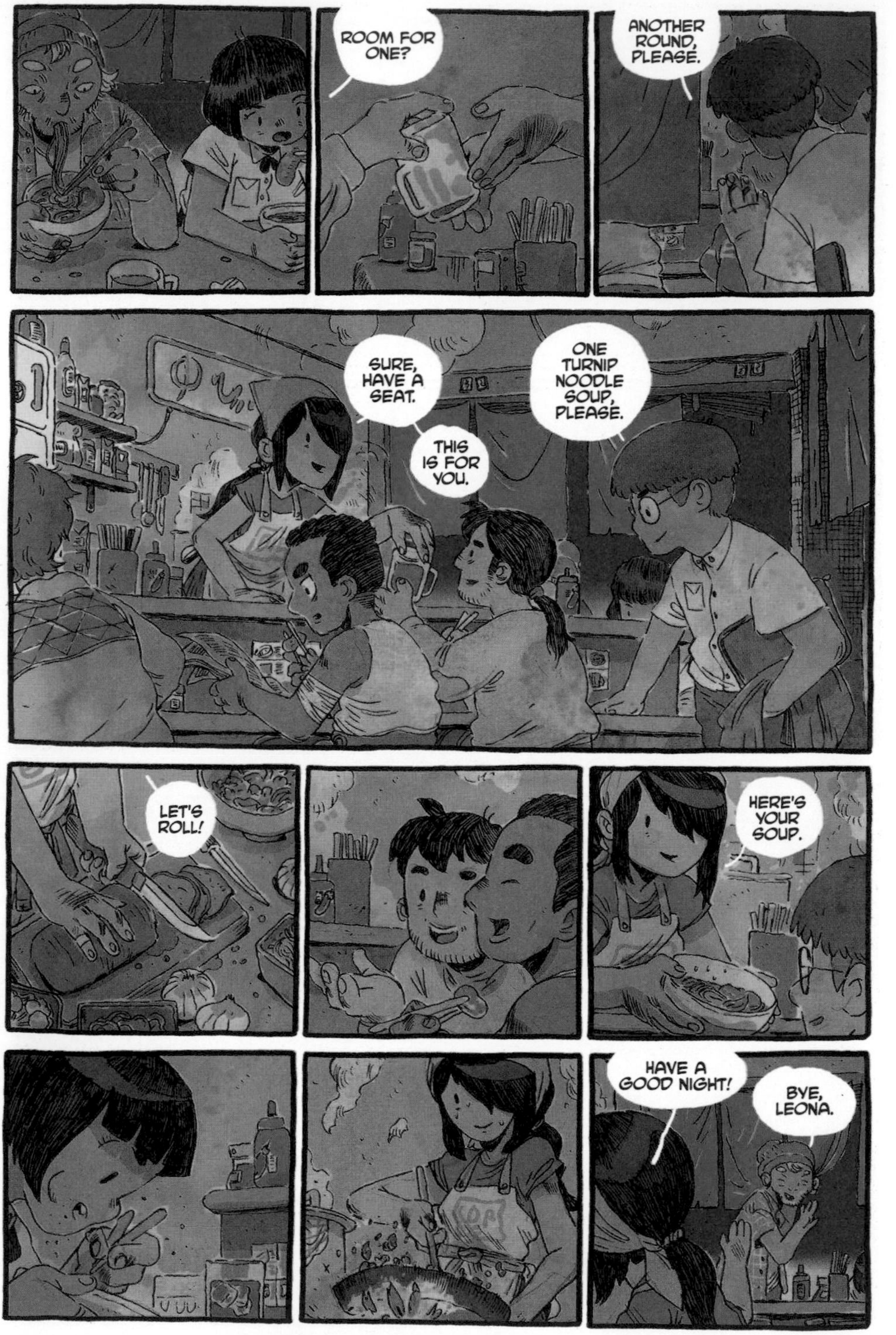
ROOM FOR ONE?
ANOTHER ROUND, PLEASE.
SURE, HAVE A SEAT.
THIS IS FOR YOU.
ONE TURNIP NOODLE SOUP, PLEASE.
LET'S ROLL!
HERE'S YOUR SOUP.
HAVE A GOOD NIGHT!
BYE, LEONA.

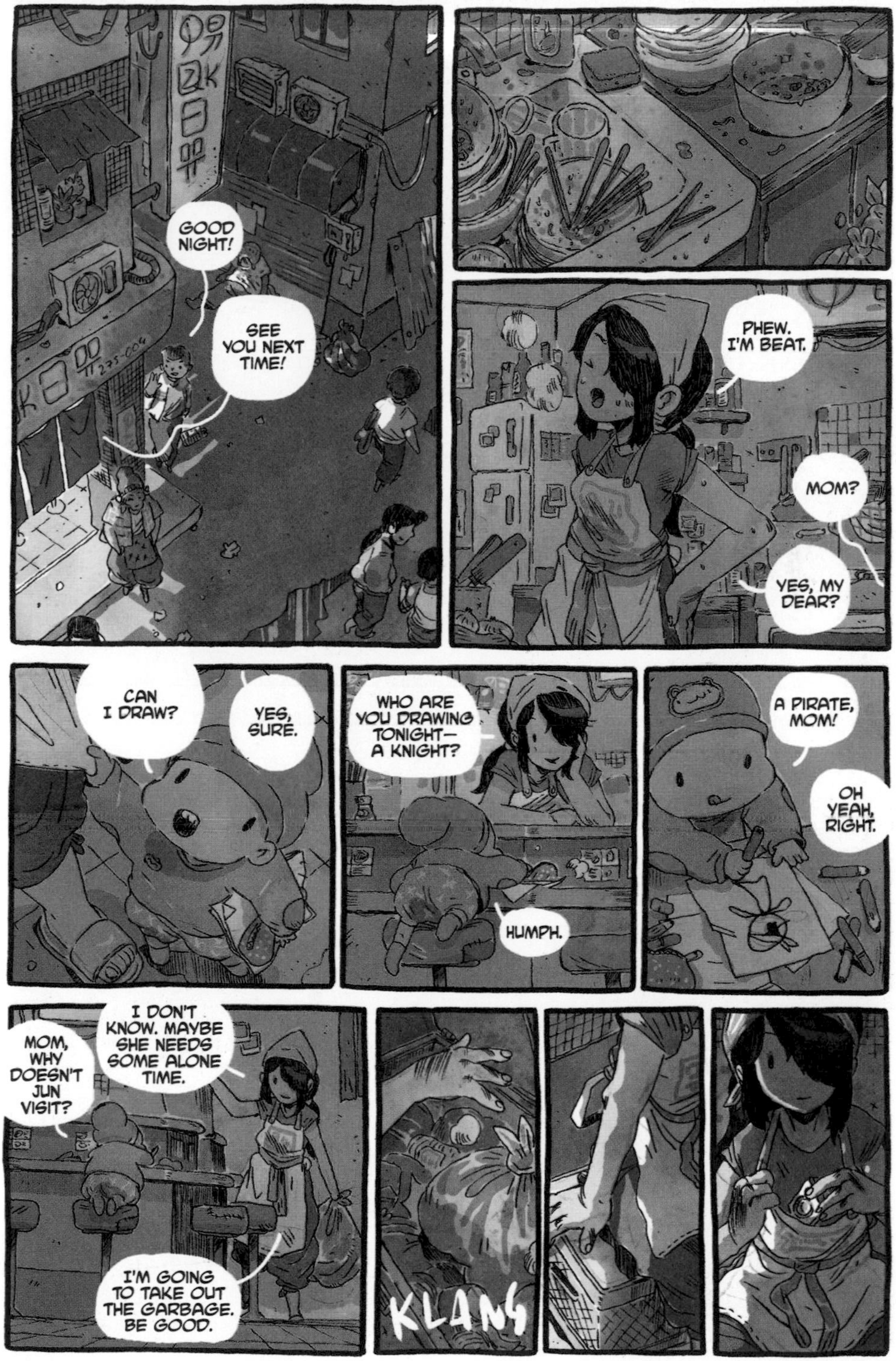

GOOD NIGHT!
SEE YOU NEXT TIME!
PHEW. I'M BEAT.
MOM?
YES, MY DEAR?
CAN I DRAW?
YES, SURE.
WHO ARE YOU DRAWING TONIGHT— A KNIGHT?
HUMPH.
A PIRATE, MOM!
OH YEAH, RIGHT.
MOM, WHY DOESN'T JUN VISIT?
I DON'T KNOW. MAYBE SHE NEEDS SOME ALONE TIME.
I'M GOING TO TAKE OUT THE GARBAGE. BE GOOD.
KLANG

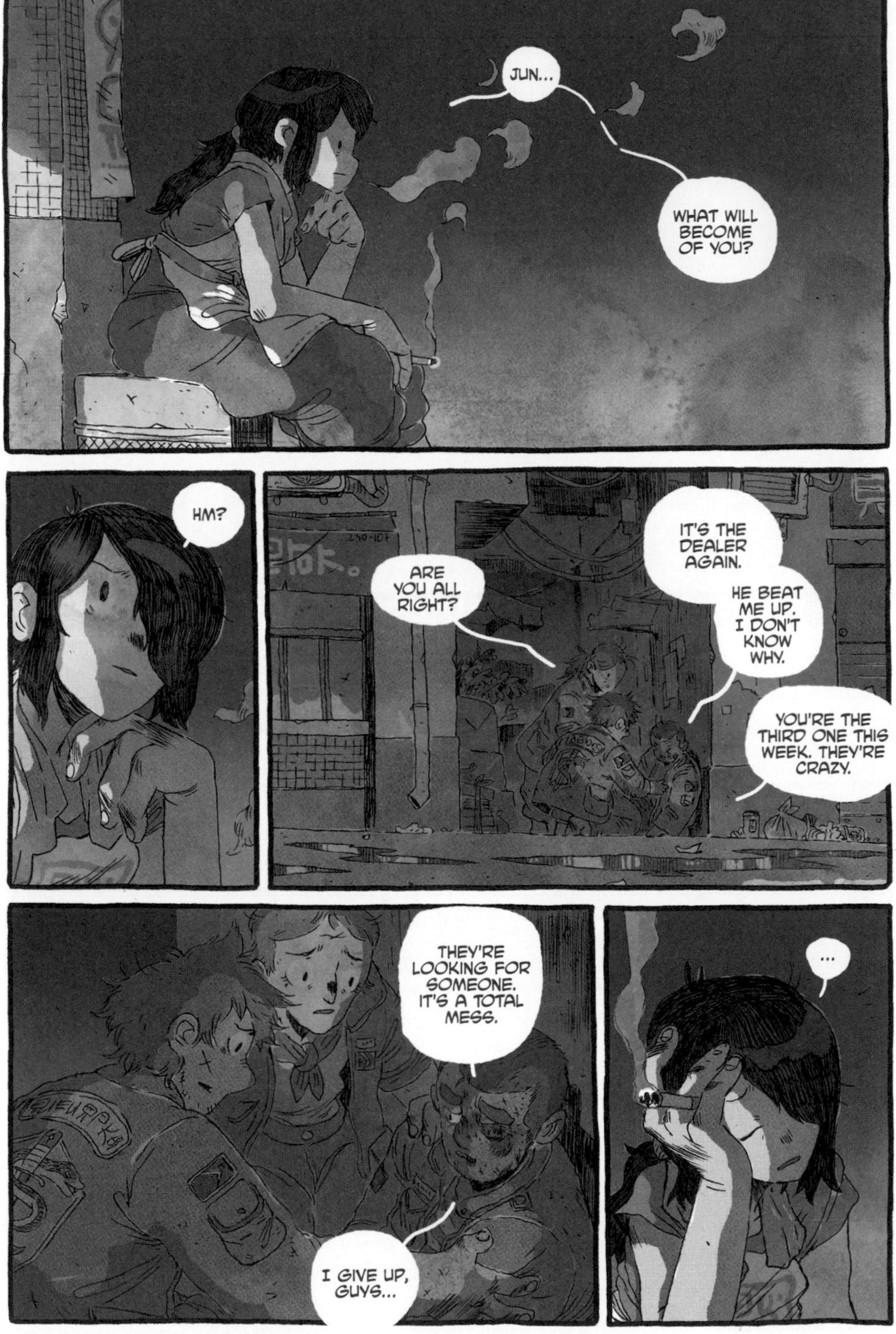
JUN...
WHAT WILL BECOME OF YOU?
HM?
ARE YOU ALL RIGHT?
IT'S THE DEALER AGAIN.
HE BEAT ME UP. I DON'T KNOW WHY.
YOU'RE THE THIRD ONE THIS WEEK. THEY'RE CRAZY.
THEY'RE LOOKING FOR SOMEONE. IT'S A TOTAL MESS.
I GIVE UP, GUYS...
...

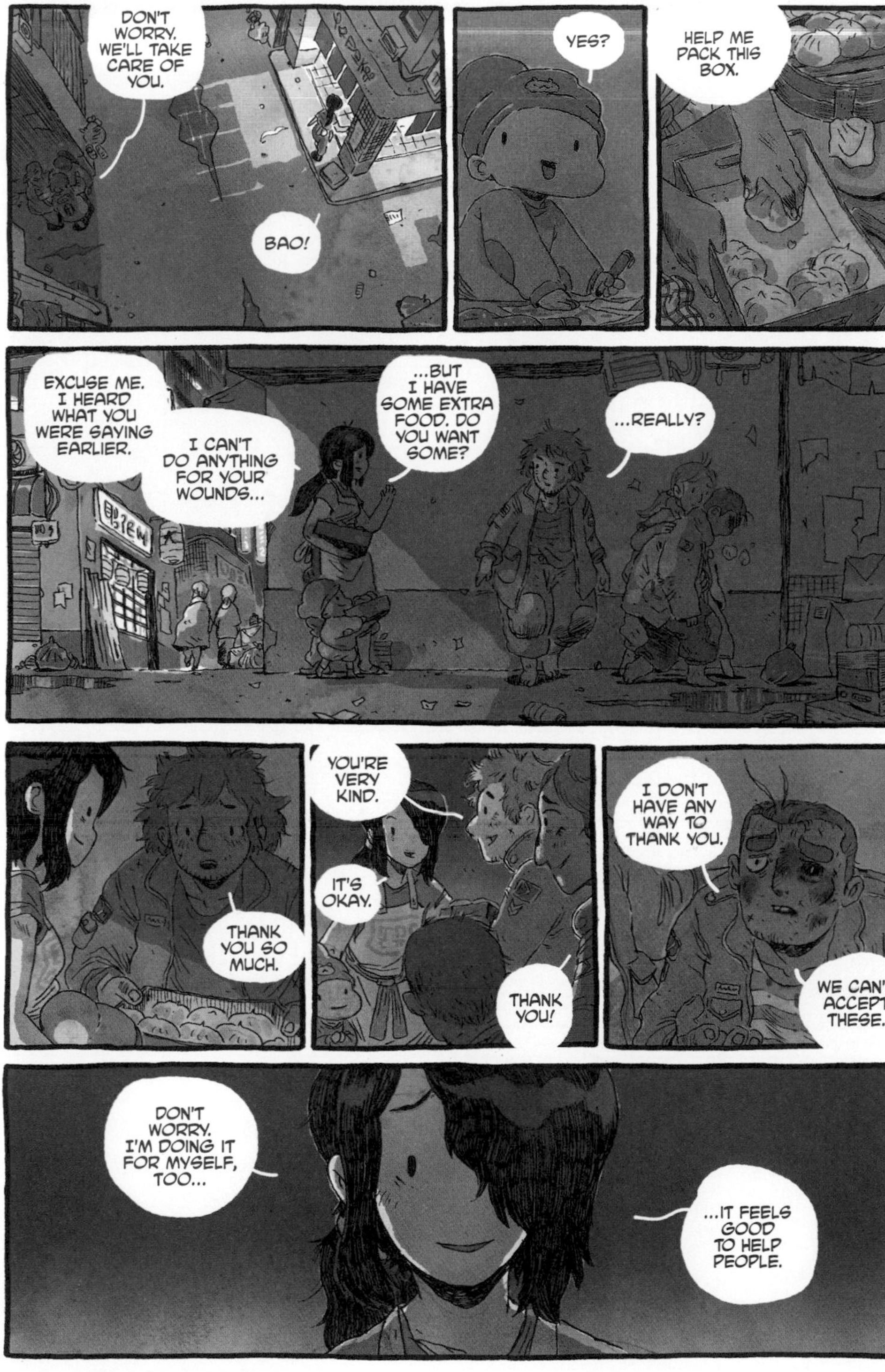

DON'T WORRY. WE'LL TAKE CARE OF YOU.
BAO!
YES?
HELP ME PACK THIS BOX.
EXCUSE ME. I HEARD WHAT YOU WERE SAYING EARLIER.
I CAN'T DO ANYTHING FOR YOUR WOUNDS...
...BUT I HAVE SOME EXTRA FOOD. DO YOU WANT SOME?
...REALLY?
THANK YOU SO MUCH.
YOU'RE VERY KIND.
IT'S OKAY.
THANK YOU!
I DON'T HAVE ANY WAY TO THANK YOU.
WE CAN'T ACCEPT THESE.
DON'T WORRY. I'M DOING IT FOR MYSELF, TOO...
...IT FEELS GOOD TO HELP PEOPLE.

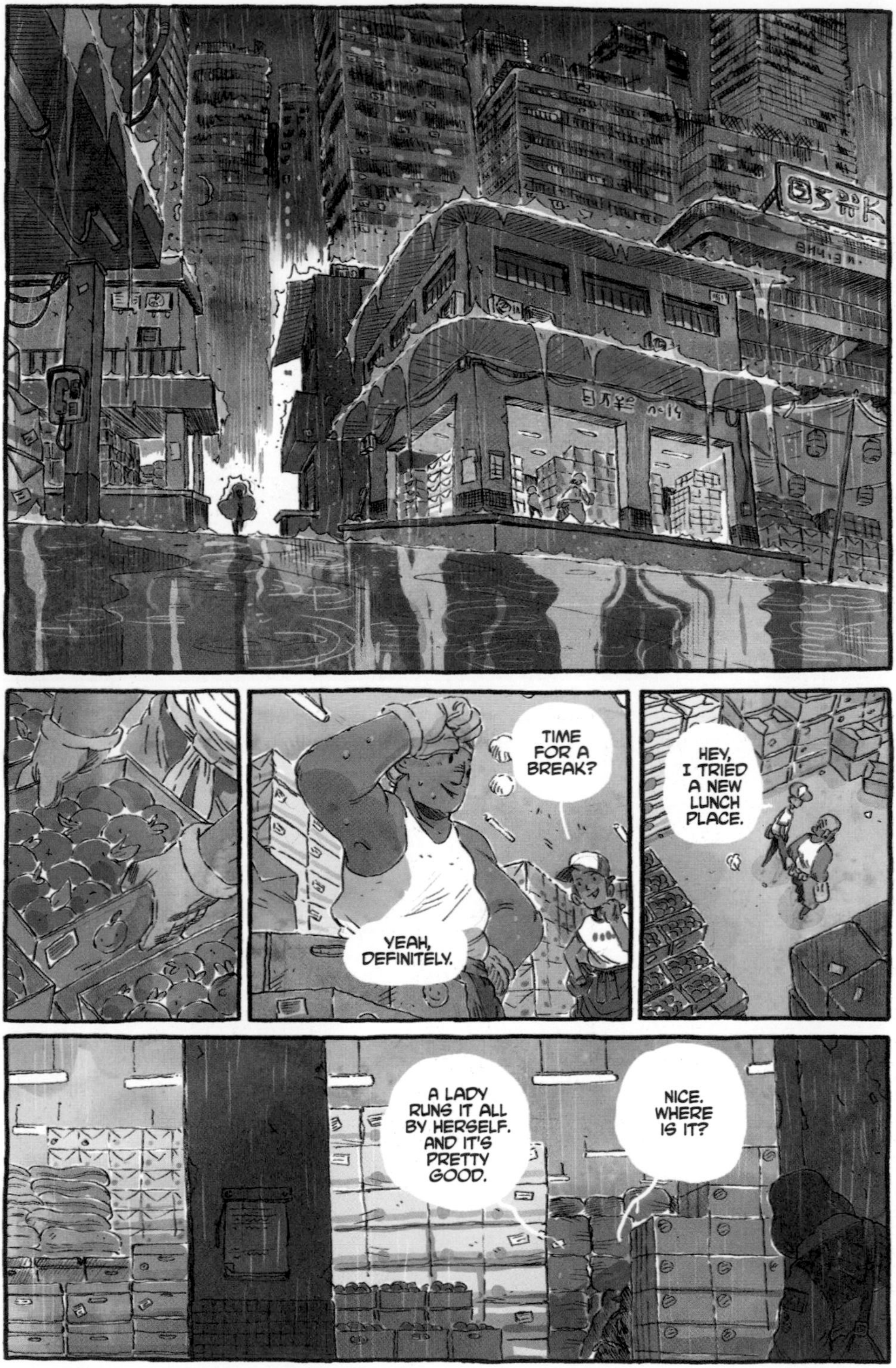
TIME FOR A BREAK?
YEAH, DEFINITELY.
HEY, I TRIED A NEW LUNCH PLACE.
A LADY RUNS IT ALL BY HERSELF. AND IT'S PRETTY GOOD.
NICE. WHERE IS IT?

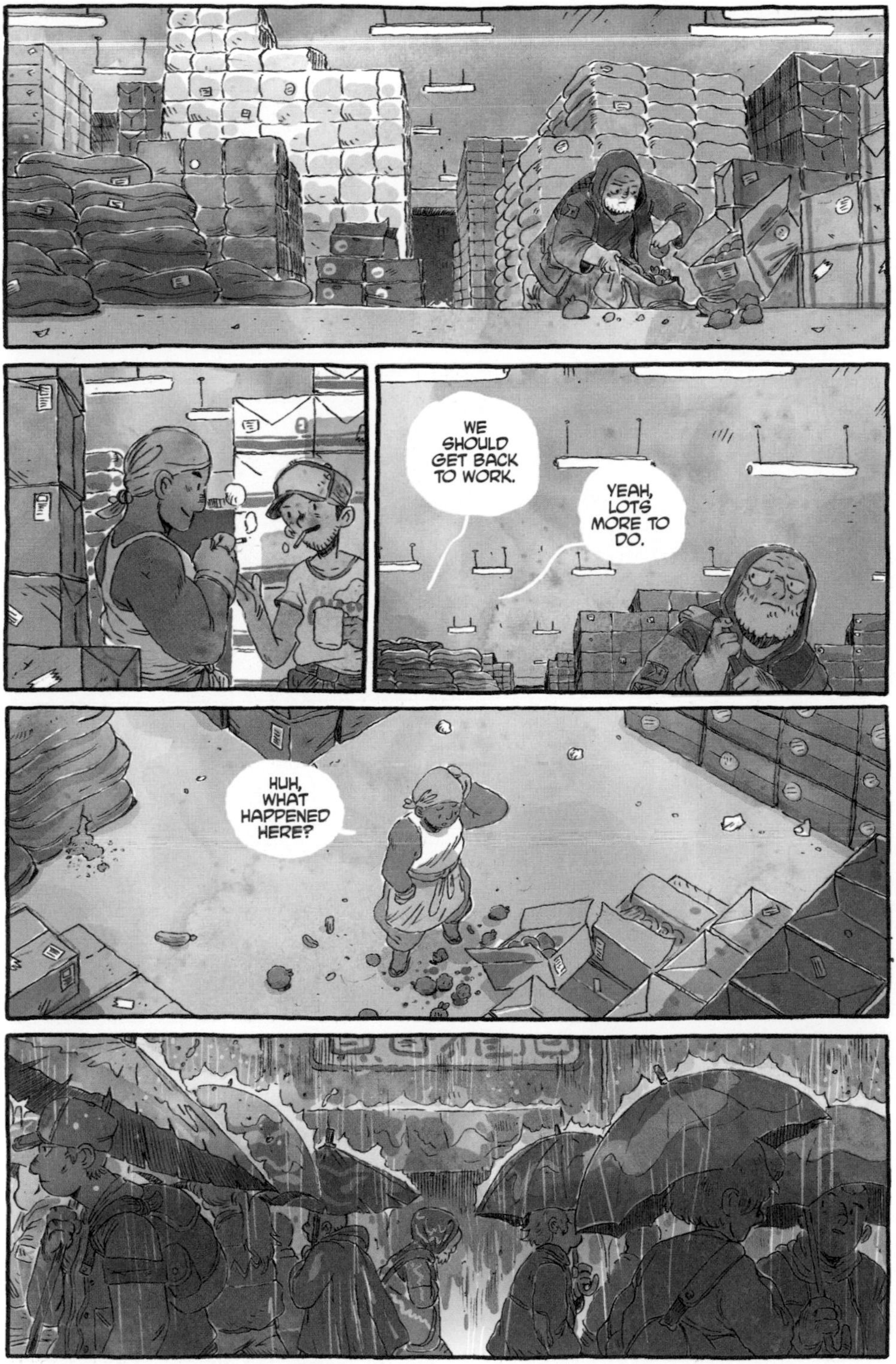
WE SHOULD GET BACK TO WORK.
YEAH, LOTS MORE TO DO.
HUH, WHAT HAPPENED HERE?

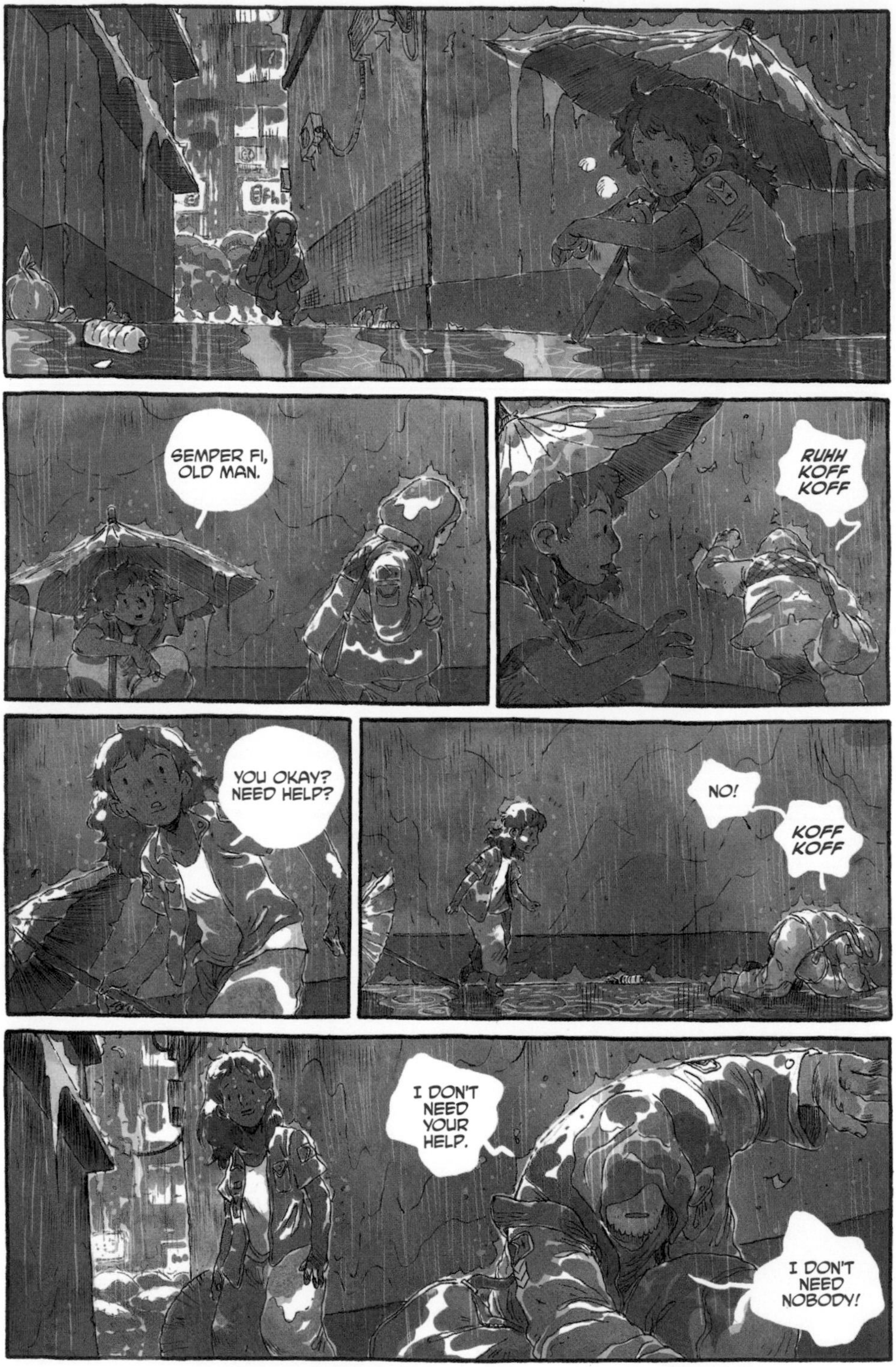
SEMPER FI, OLD MAN.
RUHH KOFF KOFF
YOU OKAY? NEED HELP?
NO!
KOFF KOFF
I DON'T NEED YOUR HELP.
I DON'T NEED NOBODY!

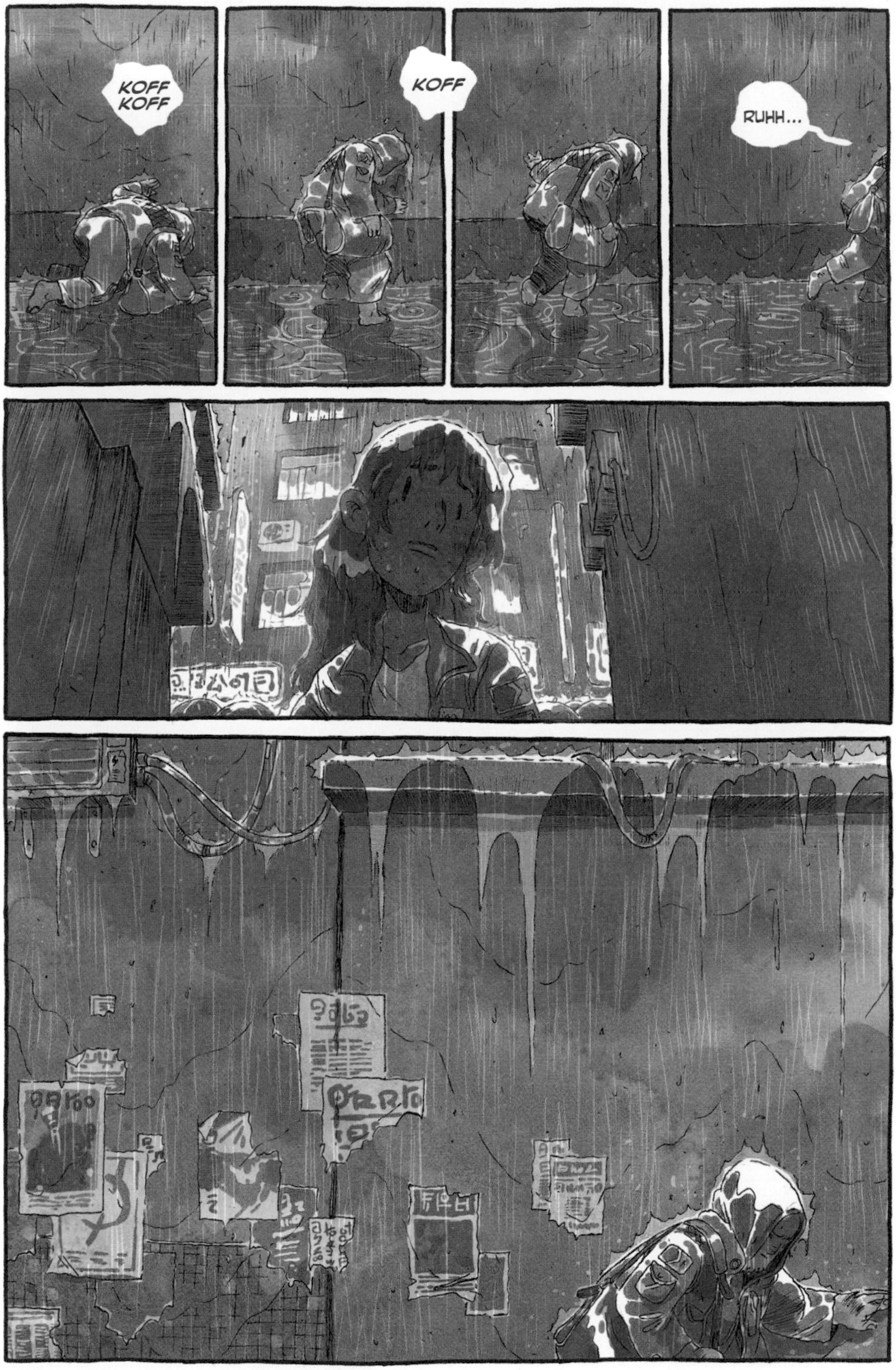
KOFF
KOFF
KOFF
RUHH...

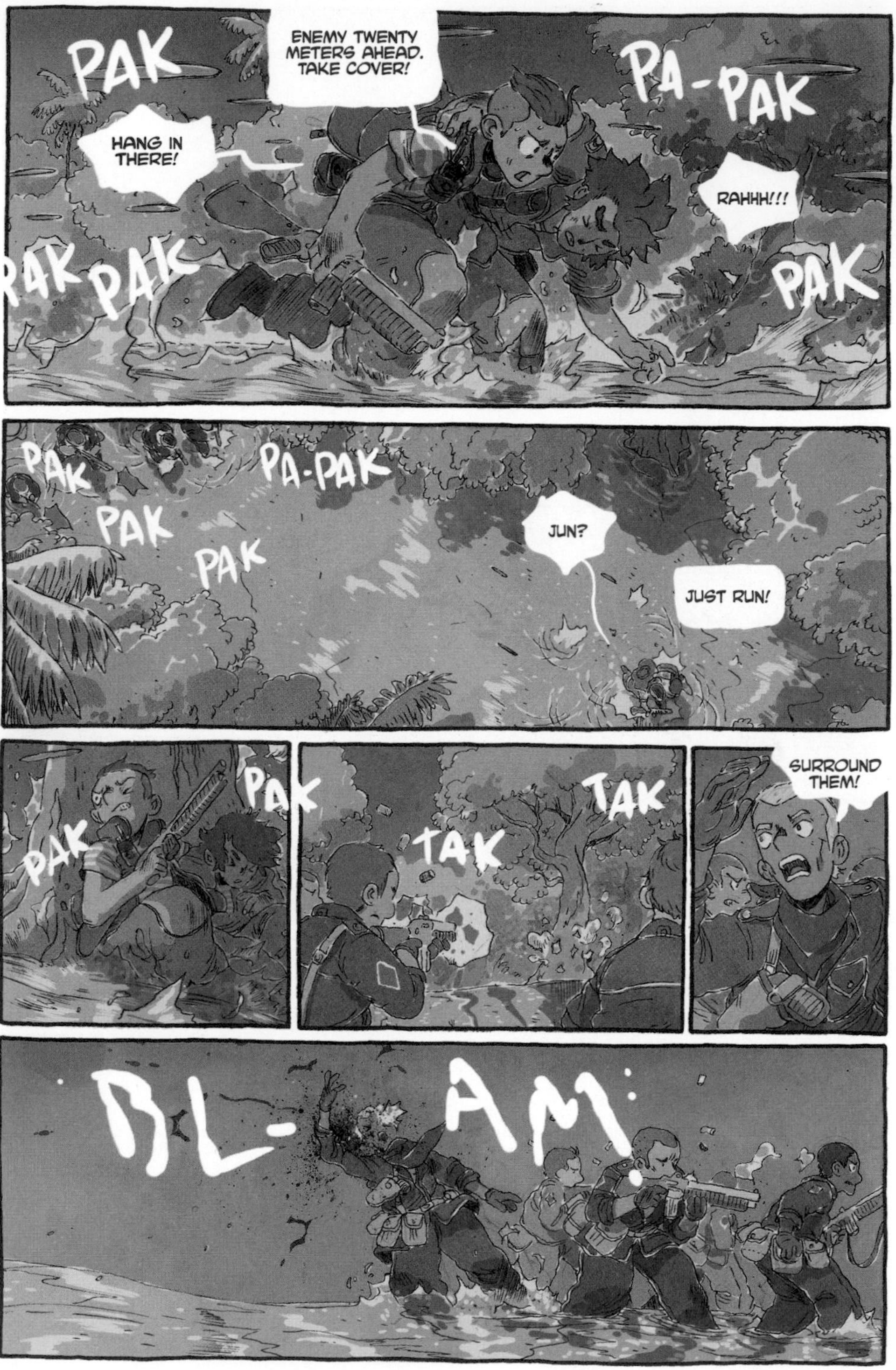
PAK
ENEMY TWENTY METERS AHEAD. TAKE COVER!
PA-PAK
HANG IN THERE!
RAHHH!!!
PAK
PAK
PAK
PAK
PA-PAK
PAK
PAK
JUN?
JUST RUN!
PAK
PAK
TAK
TAK
SURROUND THEM!
BL-AM

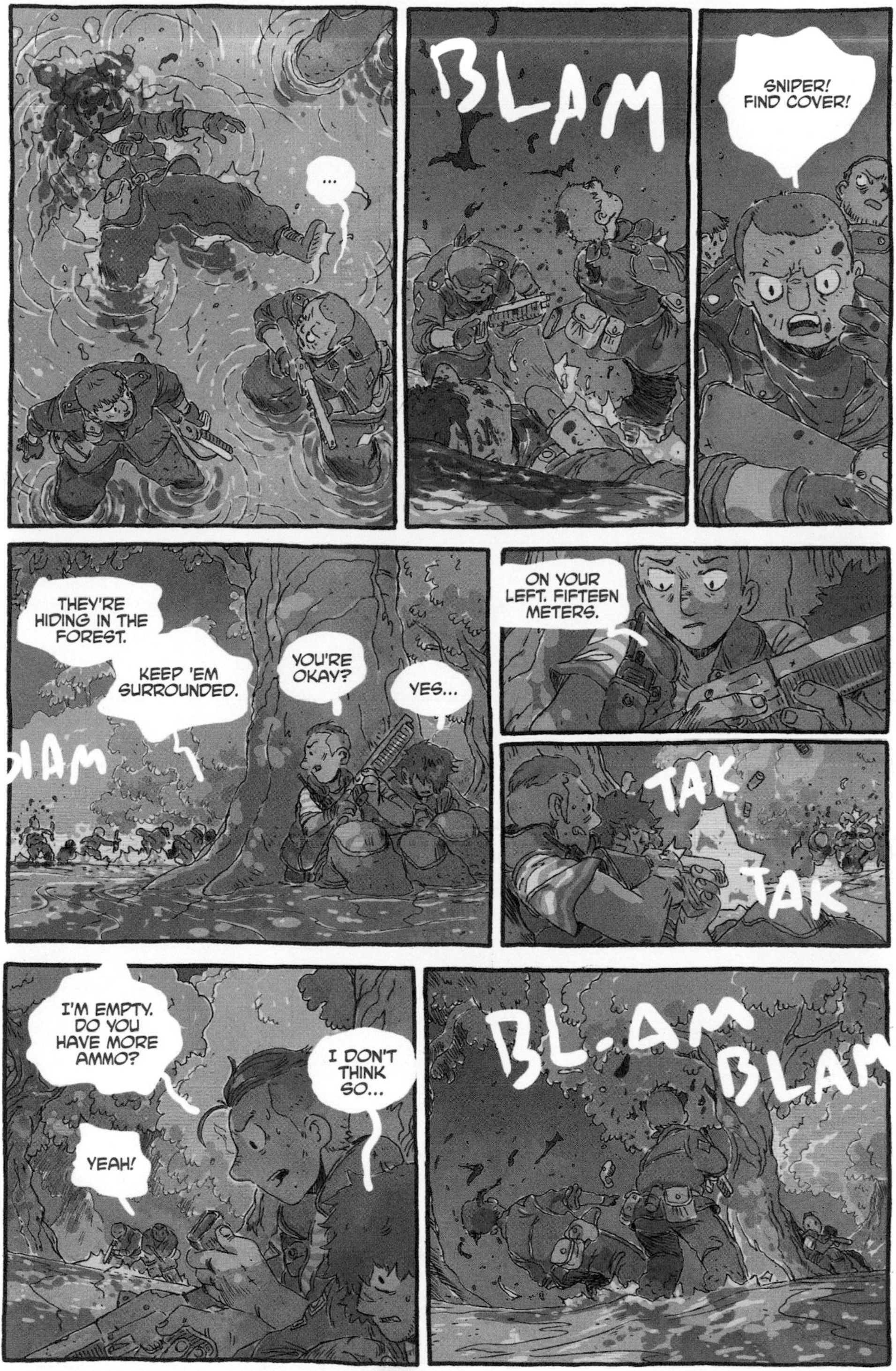
...
BLAM
SNIPER! FIND COVER!
THEY'RE HIDING IN THE FOREST.
KEEP 'EM SURROUNDED.
YOU'RE OKAY?
YES...
ON YOUR LEFT. FIFTEEN METERS.
TAK
TAK
I'M EMPTY. DO YOU HAVE MORE AMMO?
I DON'T THINK SO...
YEAH!
BLAM

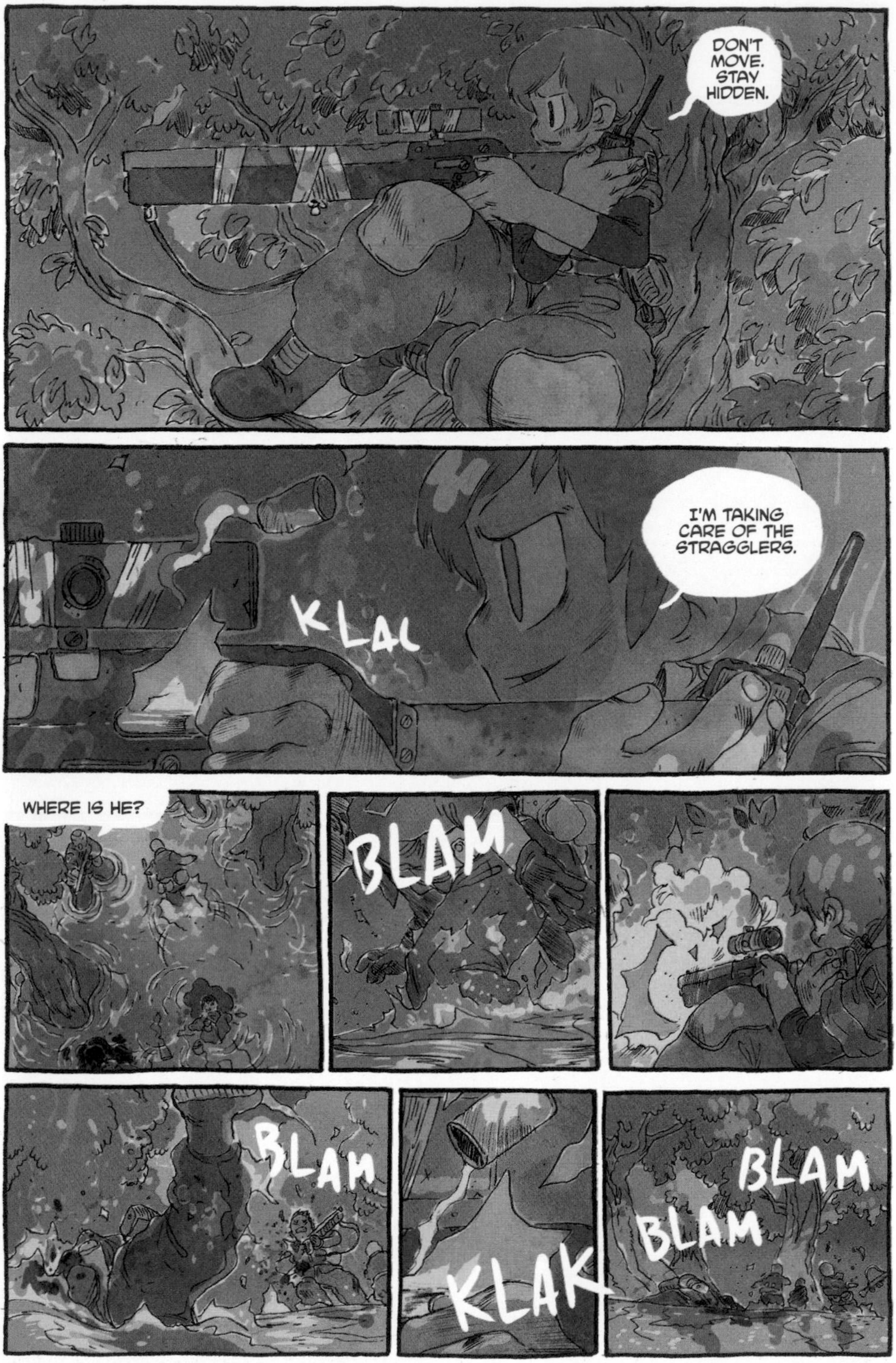
DON'T MOVE. STAY HIDDEN.
I'M TAKING CARE OF THE STRAGGLERS.
KLAK
WHERE IS HE?
BLAM
BLAM
KLAK
BLAM
BLAM

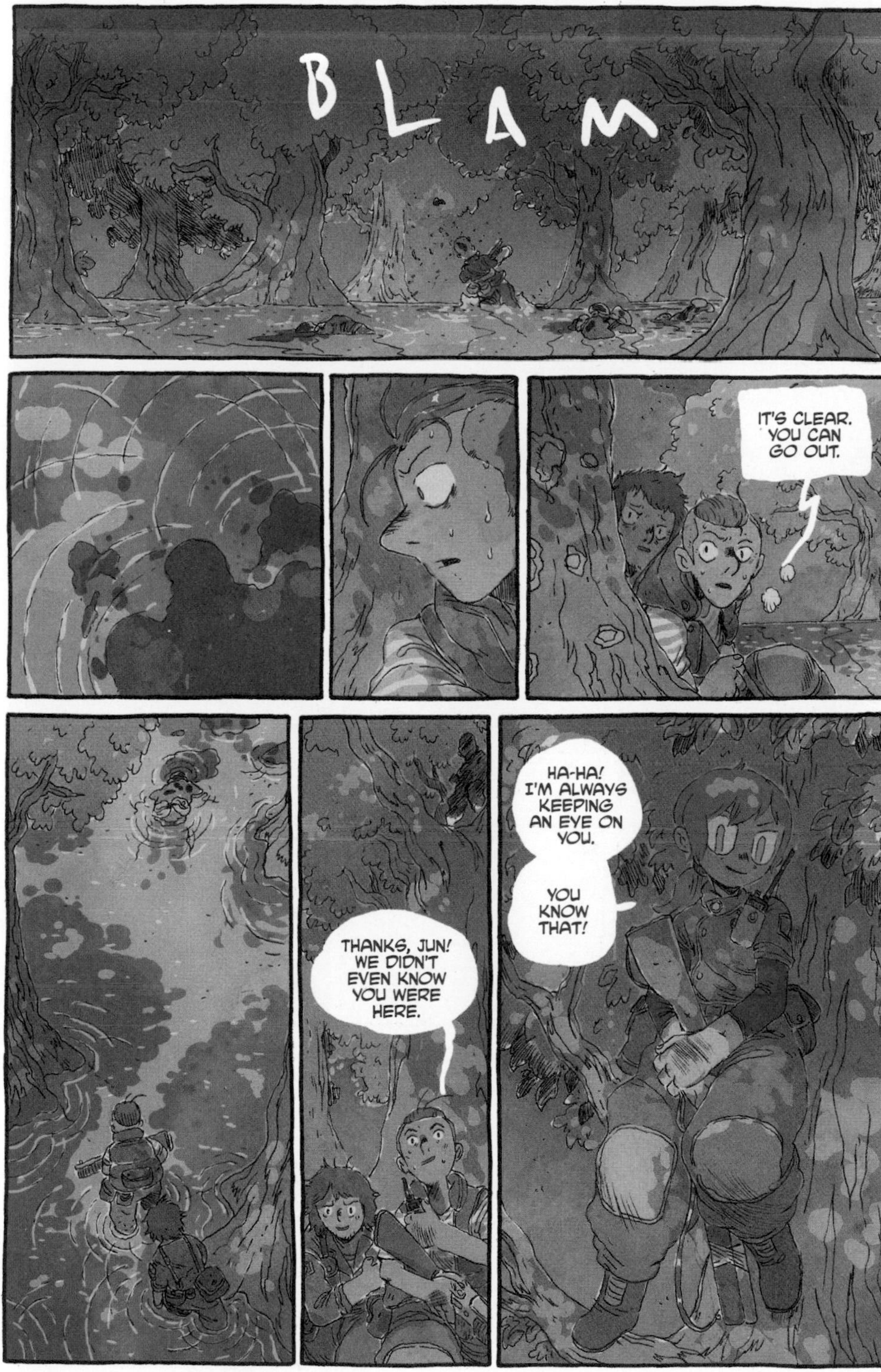
BLAM
IT'S CLEAR. YOU CAN GO OUT.
THANKS, JUN! WE DIDN'T EVEN KNOW YOU WERE HERE.
HA-HA! I'M ALWAYS KEEPING AN EYE ON YOU.
YOU KNOW THAT!

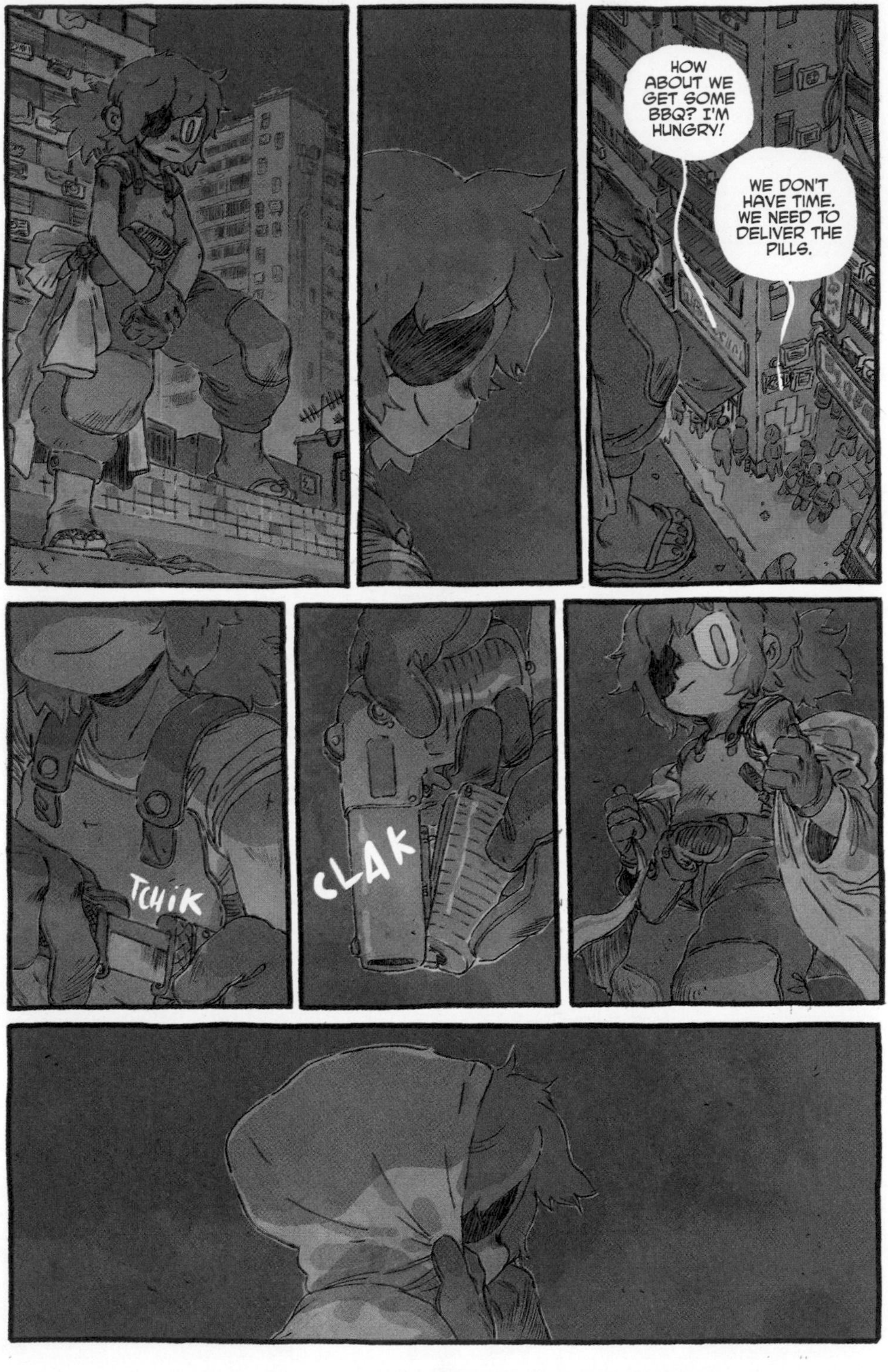
HOW ABOUT WE GET SOME BBQ? I'M HUNGRY!
WE DON'T HAVE TIME. WE NEED TO DELIVER THE PILLS.
TCHIK
CLAK

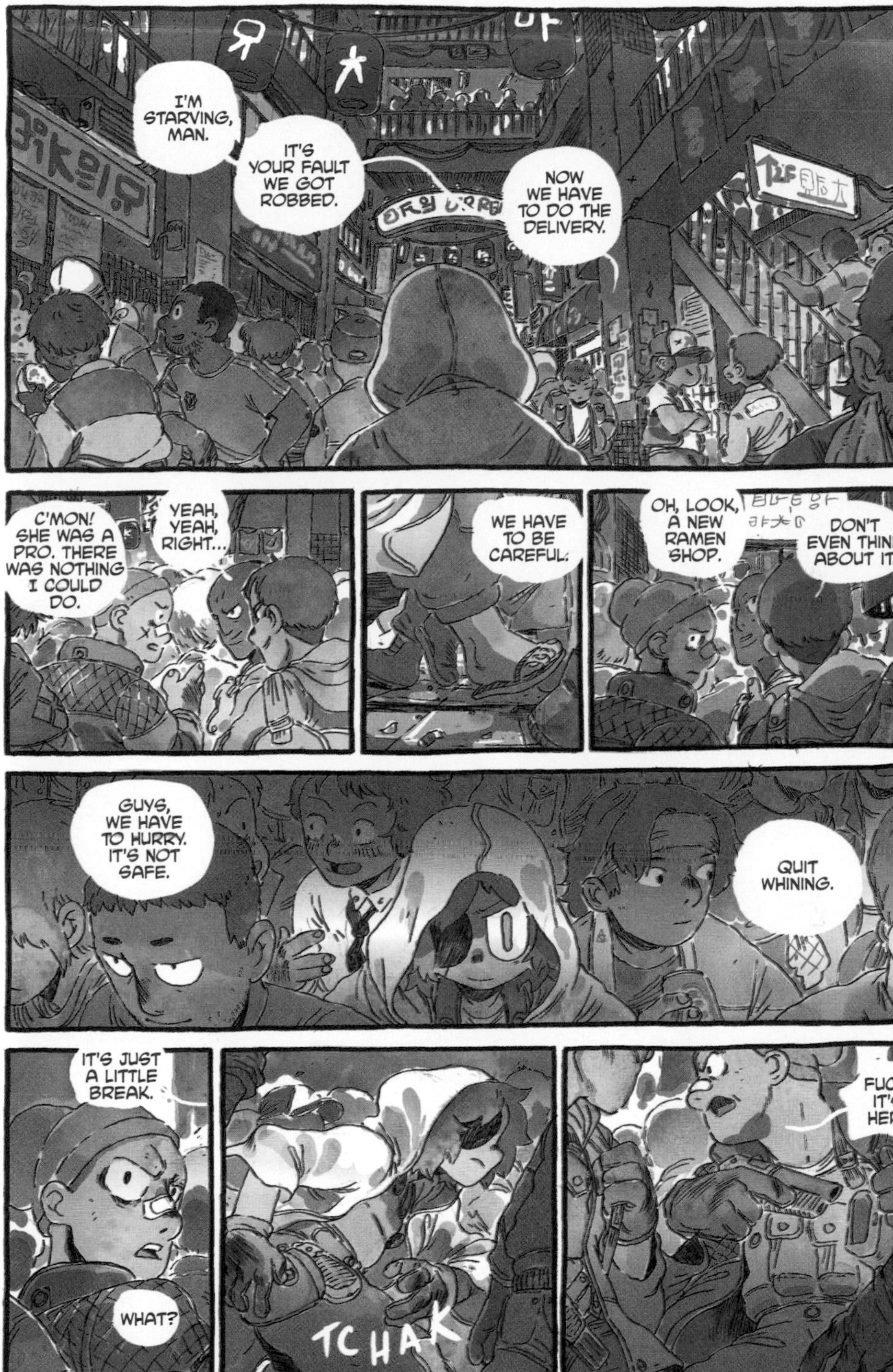
I'M STARVING, MAN.
IT'S YOUR FAULT WE GOT ROBBED.
NOW WE HAVE TO DO THE DELIVERY.
C'MON! SHE WAS A PRO. THERE WAS NOTHING I COULD DO.
YEAH, YEAH, RIGHT...
WE HAVE TO BE CAREFUL.
OH, LOOK, A NEW RAMEN SHOP.
DON'T EVEN THINK ABOUT IT.
GUYS, WE HAVE TO HURRY. IT'S NOT SAFE.
QUIT WHINING.
IT'S JUST A LITTLE BREAK.
WHAT?
TCHAK
FUCK, IT'S HER!

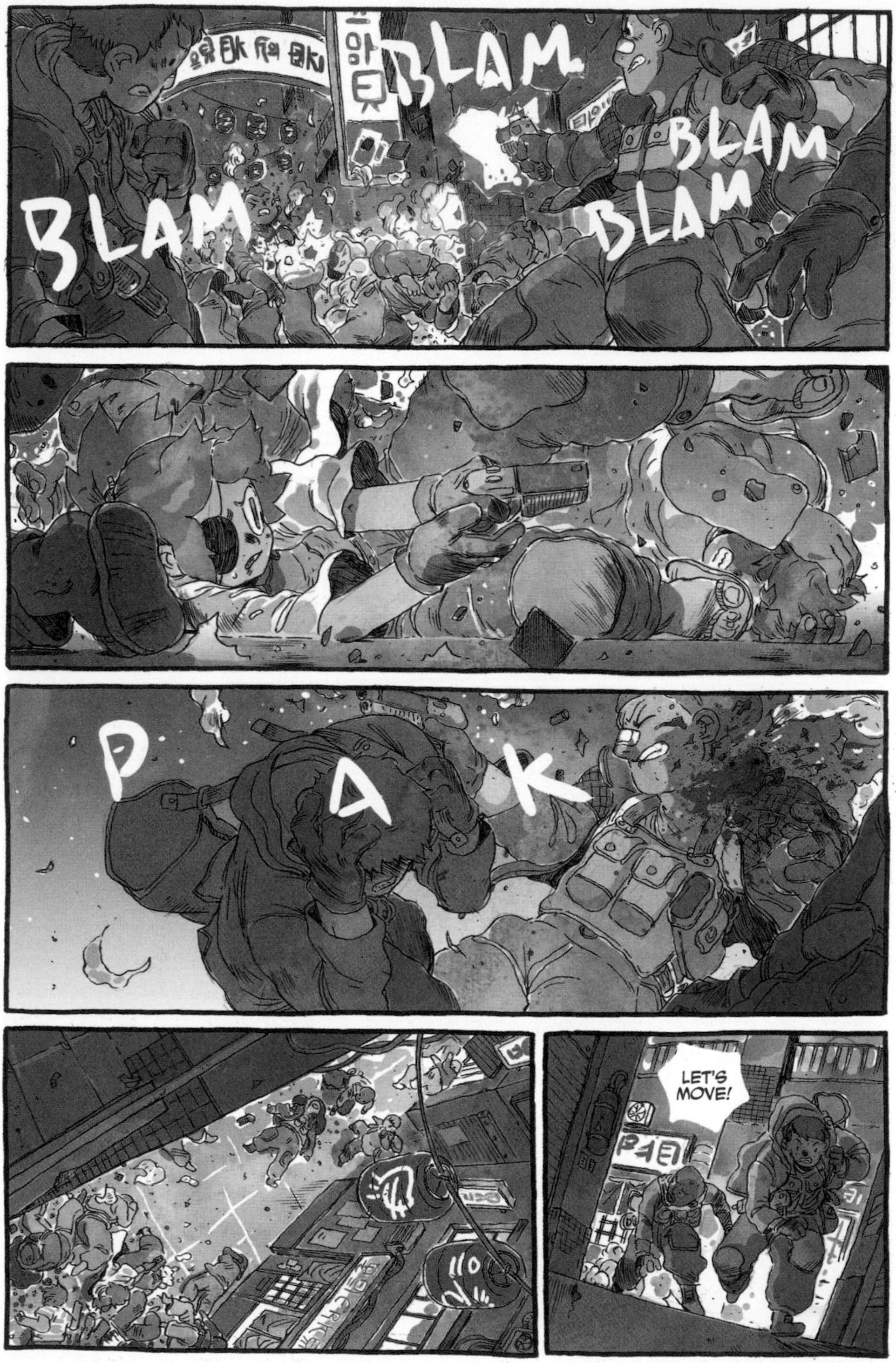
BLAM
BLAM
BLAM
BLAM
BLAM
P A K
LET'S MOVE!

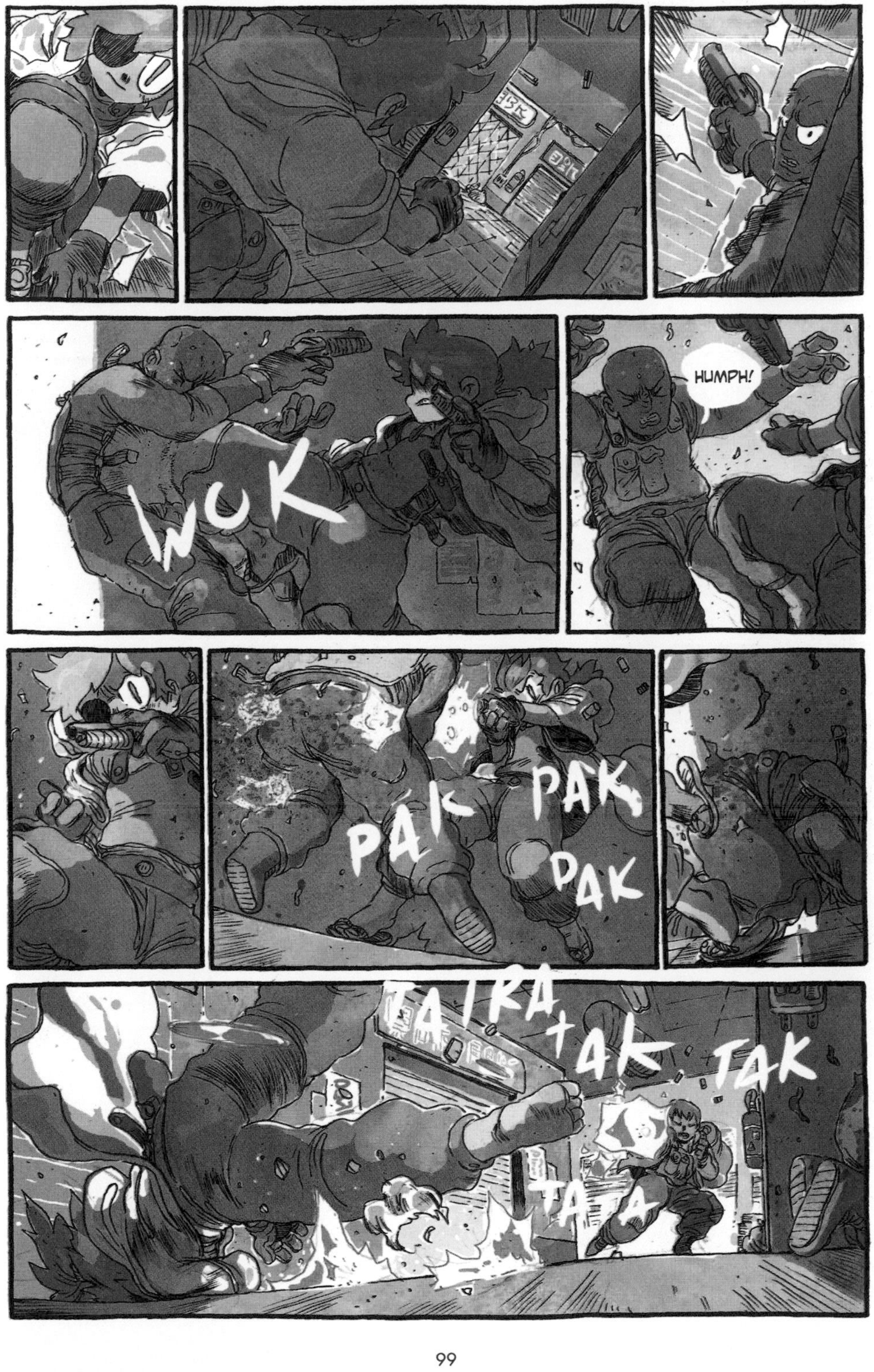
HUMPH!
WUK
PAK PAK
PAK
TA TRA
TAK TAK
TA TA

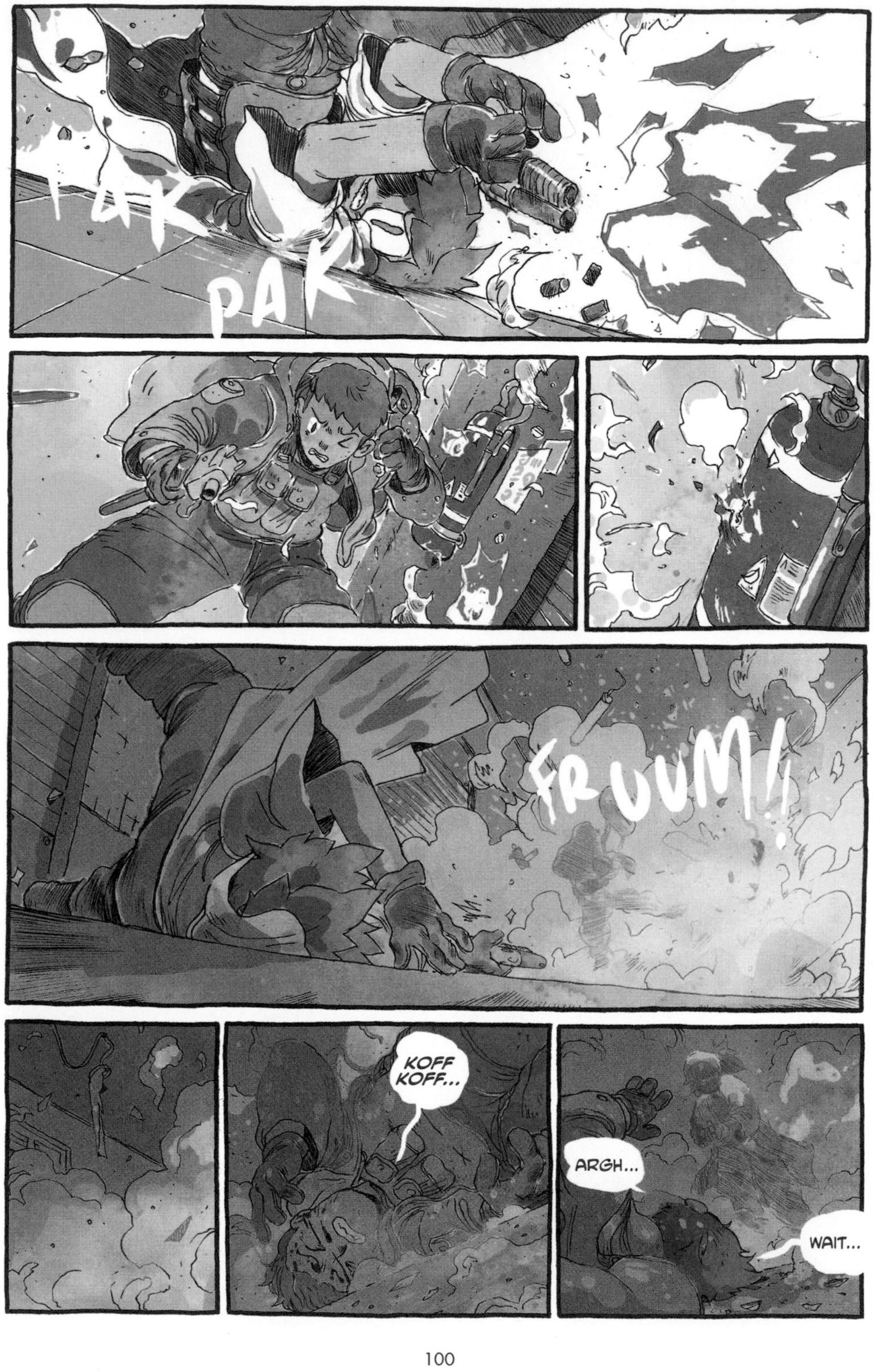
PAK
FRUUM!
KOFF KOFF...
ARGH...
WAIT...

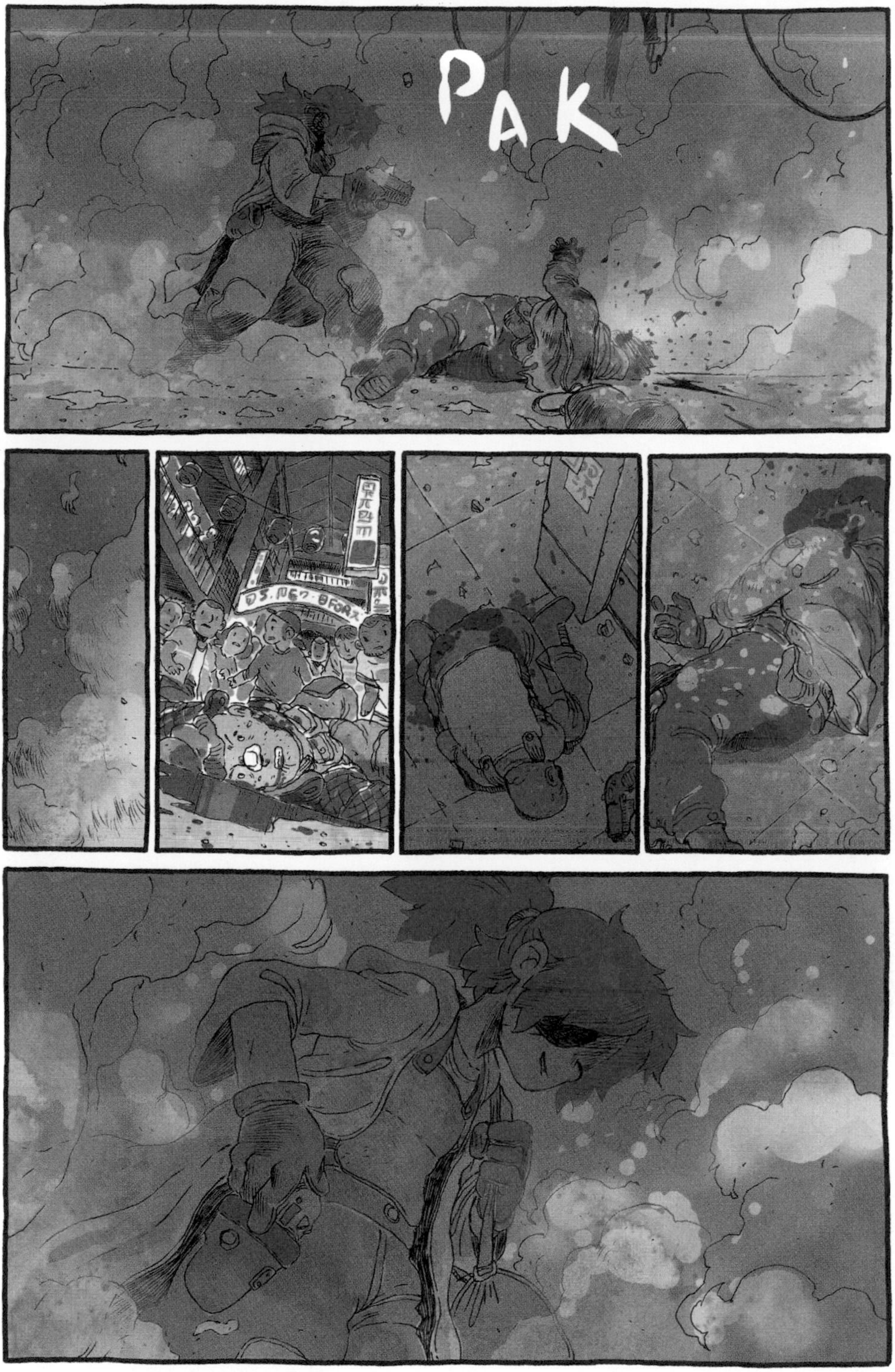
PAK

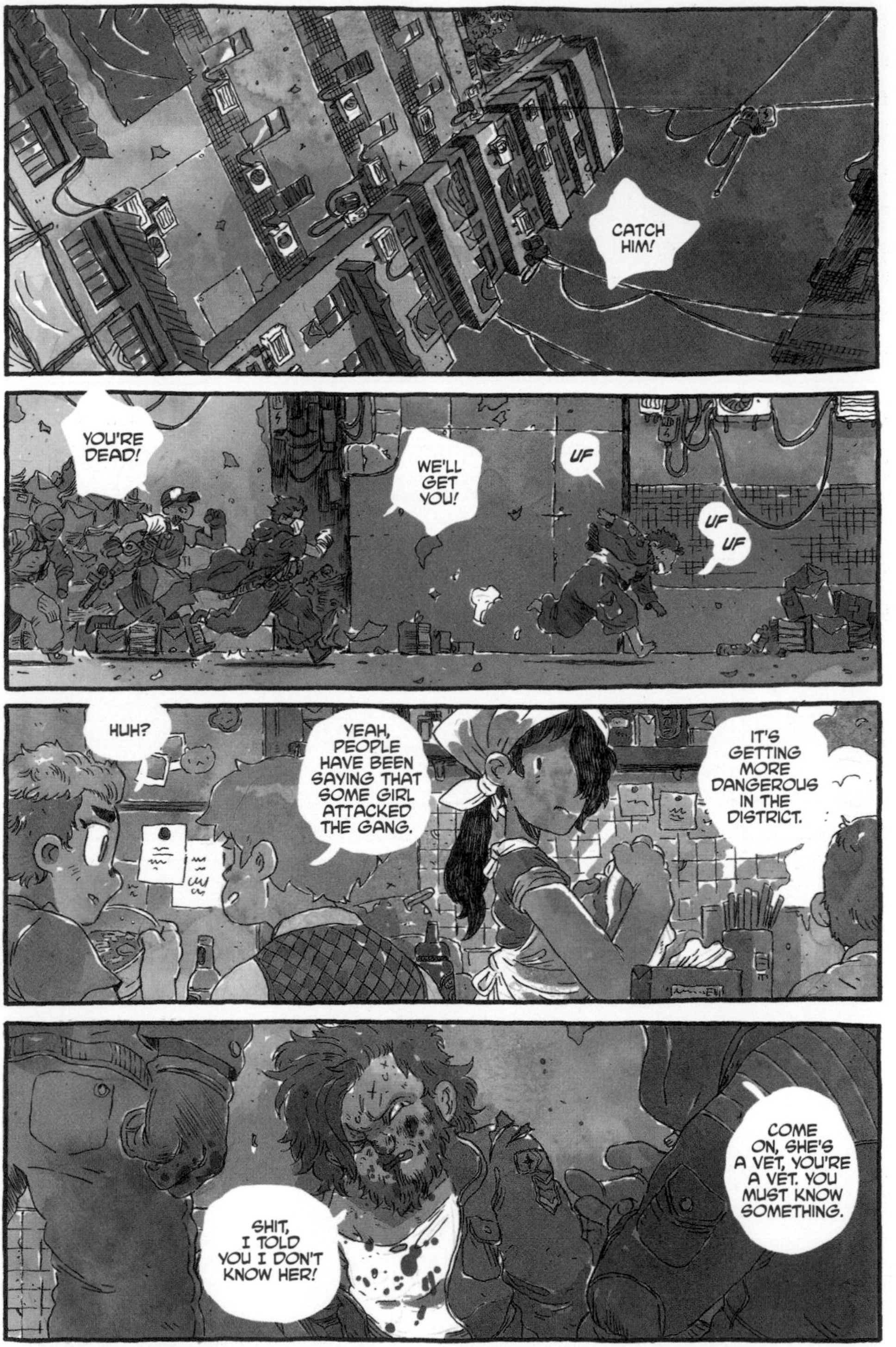
CATCH HIM!
YOU'RE DEAD!
WE'LL GET YOU!
UF
UF UF
HUH?
YEAH, PEOPLE HAVE BEEN SAYING THAT SOME GIRL ATTACKED THE GANG.
IT'S GETTING MORE DANGEROUS IN THE DISTRICT.
COME ON, SHE'S A VET, YOU'RE A VET. YOU MUST KNOW SOMETHING.
SHIT, I TOLD YOU I DON'T KNOW HER!

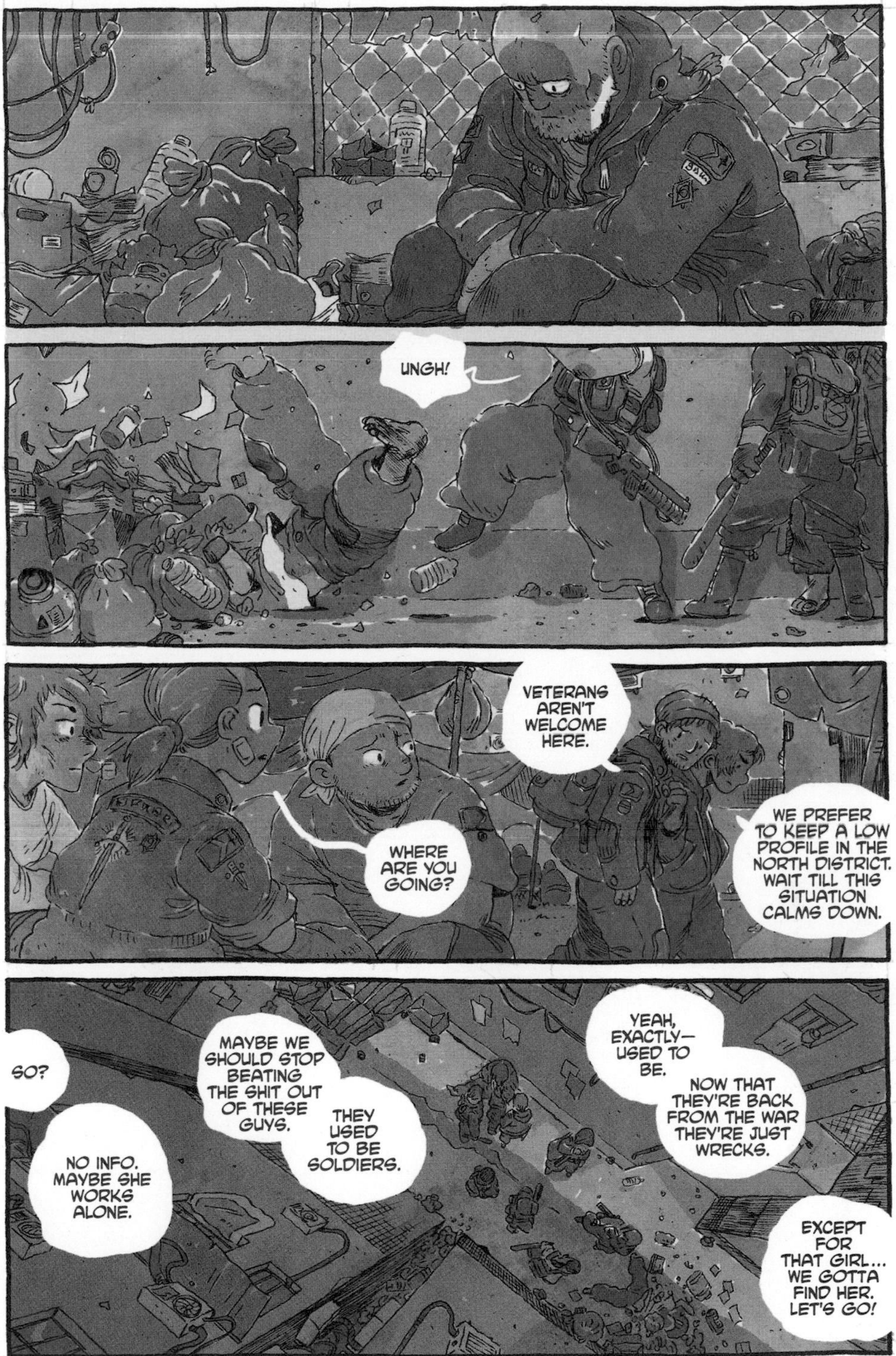
UNGH!
VETERANS AREN'T WELCOME HERE.
WHERE ARE YOU GOING?
WE PREFER TO KEEP A LOW PROFILE IN THE NORTH DISTRICT. WAIT TILL THIS SITUATION CALMS DOWN.
SO?
NO INFO. MAYBE SHE WORKS ALONE.
MAYBE WE SHOULD STOP BEATING THE SHIT OUT OF THESE GUYS.
THEY USED TO BE SOLDIERS.
YEAH, EXACTLY— USED TO BE.
NOW THAT THEY'RE BACK FROM THE WAR THEY'RE JUST WRECKS.
EXCEPT FOR THAT GIRL... WE GOTTA FIND HER. LET'S GO!

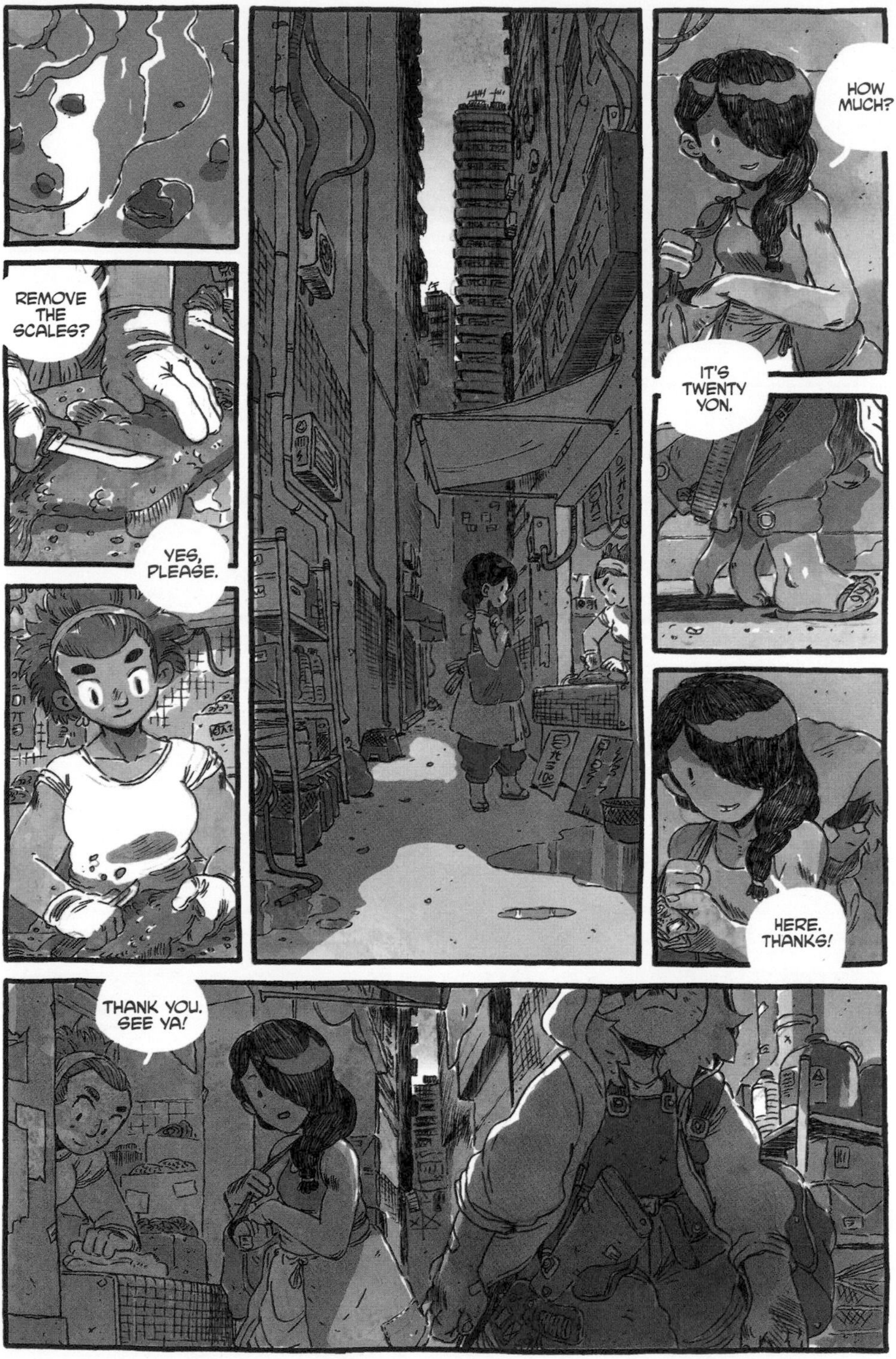
REMOVE THE SCALES?
YES, PLEASE.
HOW MUCH?
IT'S TWENTY YON.
HERE. THANKS!
THANK YOU. SEE YA!

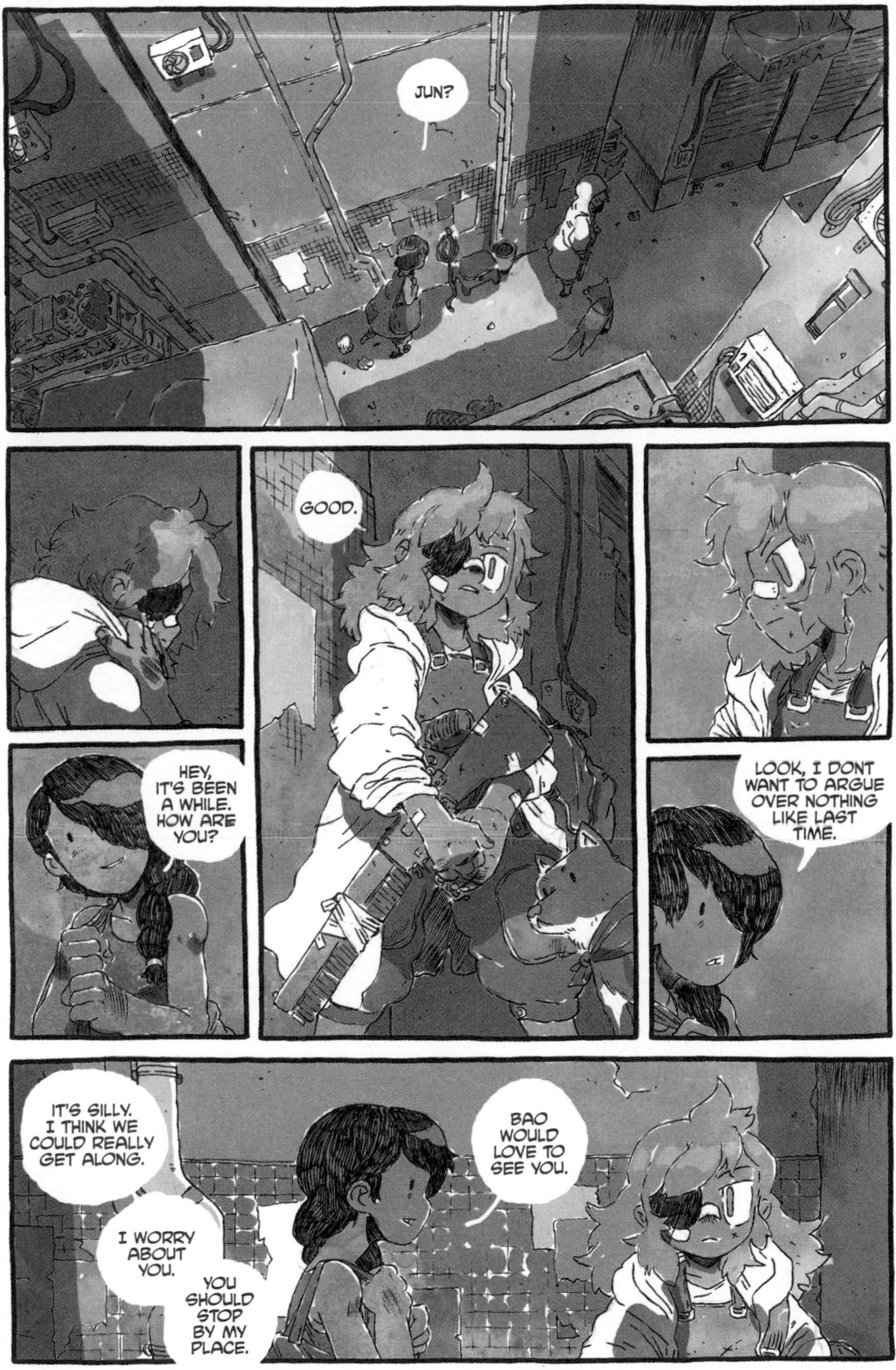
JUN?
GOOD.
HEY, IT'S BEEN A WHILE. HOW ARE YOU?
LOOK, I DONT WANT TO ARGUE OVER NOTHING LIKE LAST TIME.
IT'S SILLY. I THINK WE COULD REALLY GET ALONG.
I WORRY ABOUT YOU.
YOU SHOULD STOP BY MY PLACE.
BAO WOULD LOVE TO SEE YOU.

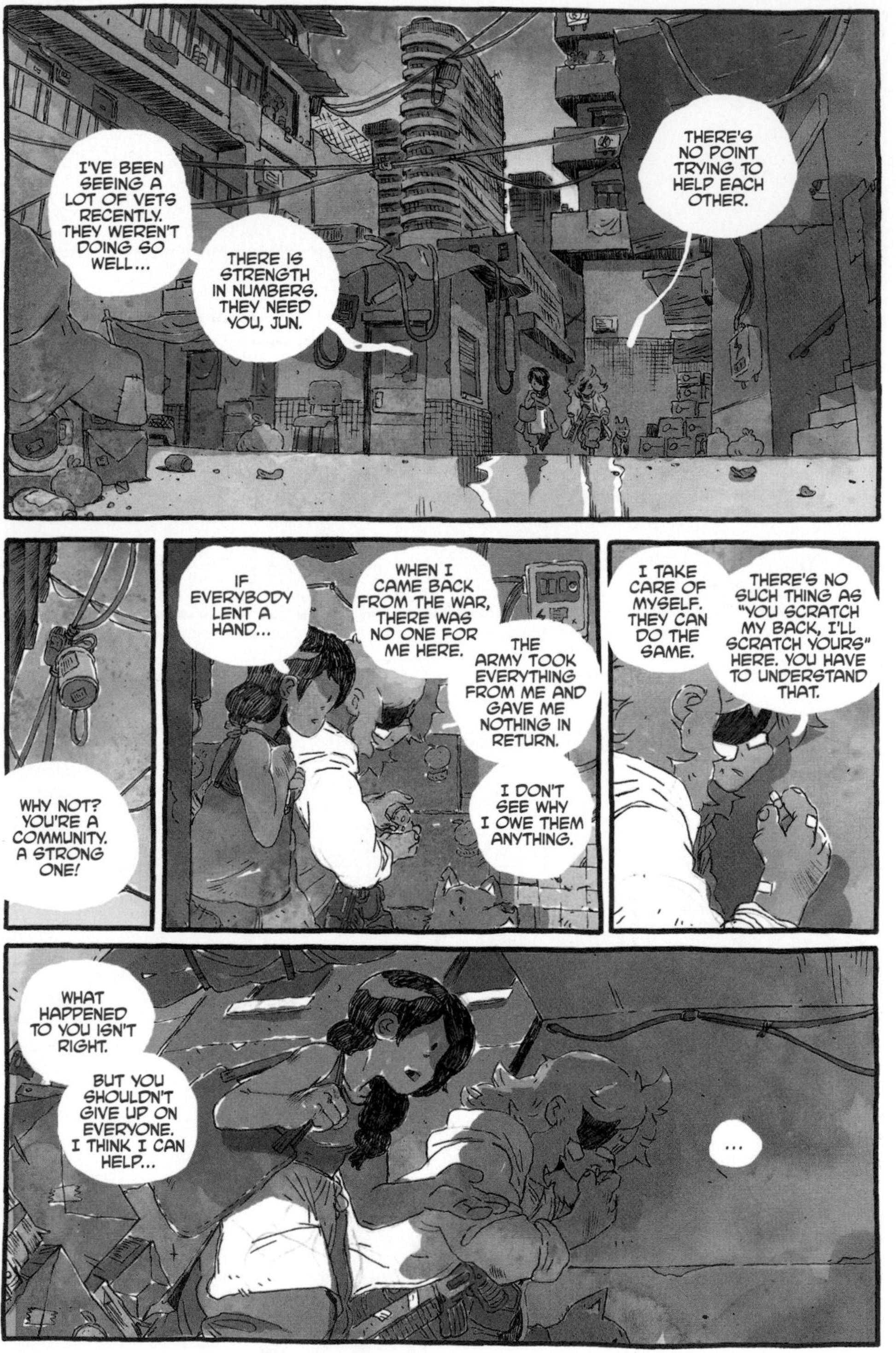
I'VE BEEN SEEING A LOT OF VETS RECENTLY. THEY WEREN'T DOING SO WELL...
THERE IS STRENGTH IN NUMBERS. THEY NEED YOU, JUN.
THERE'S NO POINT TRYING TO HELP EACH OTHER.
WHY NOT? YOU'RE A COMMUNITY. A STRONG ONE!
IF EVERYBODY LENT A HAND...
WHEN I CAME BACK FROM THE WAR, THERE WAS NO ONE FOR ME HERE.
THE ARMY TOOK EVERYTHING FROM ME AND GAVE ME NOTHING IN RETURN.
I DON'T SEE WHY I OWE THEM ANYTHING.
I TAKE CARE OF MYSELF. THEY CAN DO THE SAME.
THERE'S NO SUCH THING AS "YOU SCRATCH MY BACK, I'LL SCRATCH YOURS" HERE. YOU HAVE TO UNDERSTAND THAT.
WHAT HAPPENED TO YOU ISN'T RIGHT.
BUT YOU SHOULDN'T GIVE UP ON EVERYONE. I THINK I CAN HELP...
...

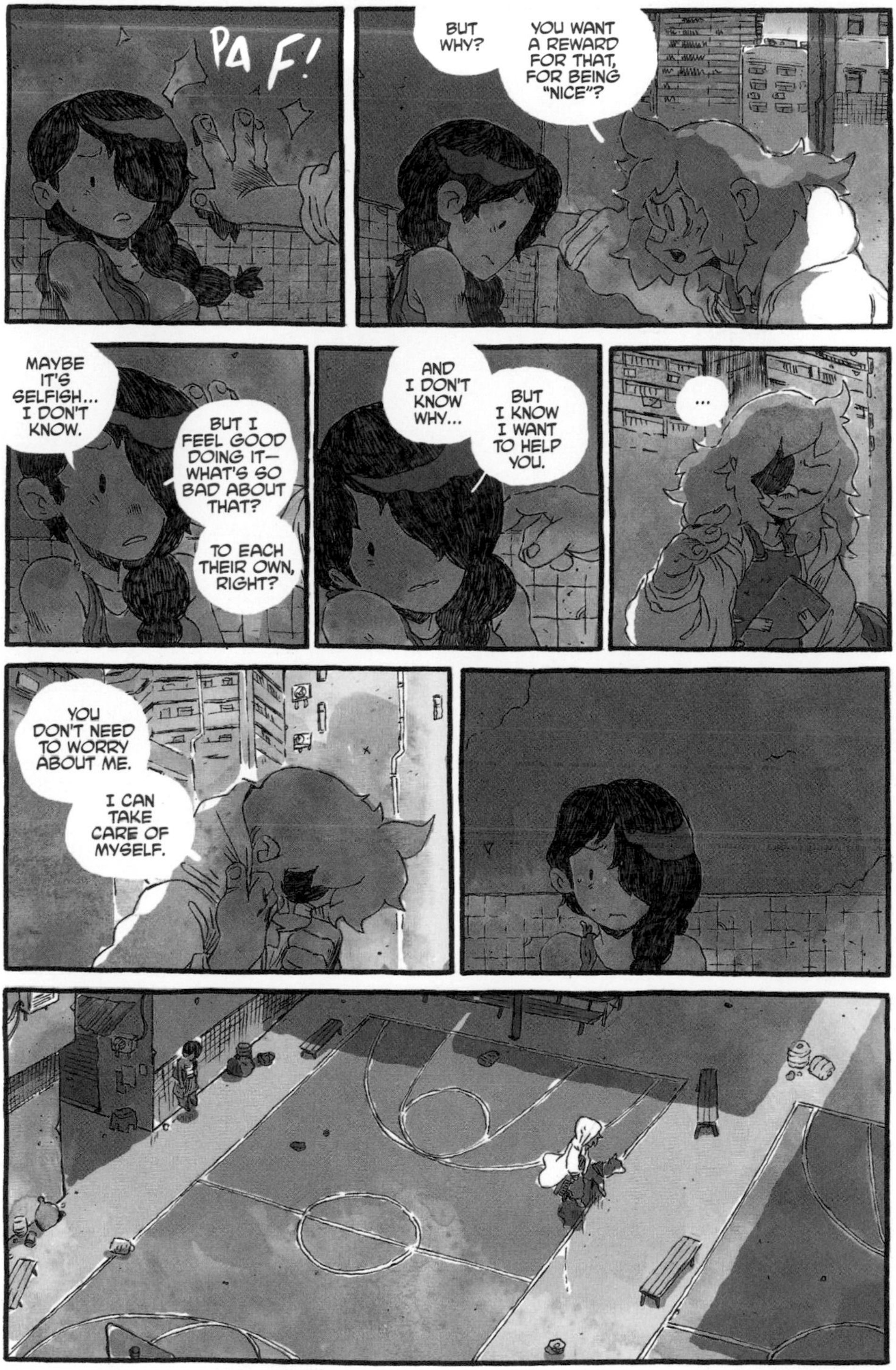
PAF!
BUT WHY?
YOU WANT A REWARD FOR THAT, FOR BEING "NICE"?
MAYBE IT'S SELFISH... I DON'T KNOW.
BUT I FEEL GOOD DOING IT— WHAT'S SO BAD ABOUT THAT?
TO EACH THEIR OWN, RIGHT?
AND I DON'T KNOW WHY...
BUT I KNOW I WANT TO HELP YOU.
...
YOU DON'T NEED TO WORRY ABOUT ME.
I CAN TAKE CARE OF MYSELF.

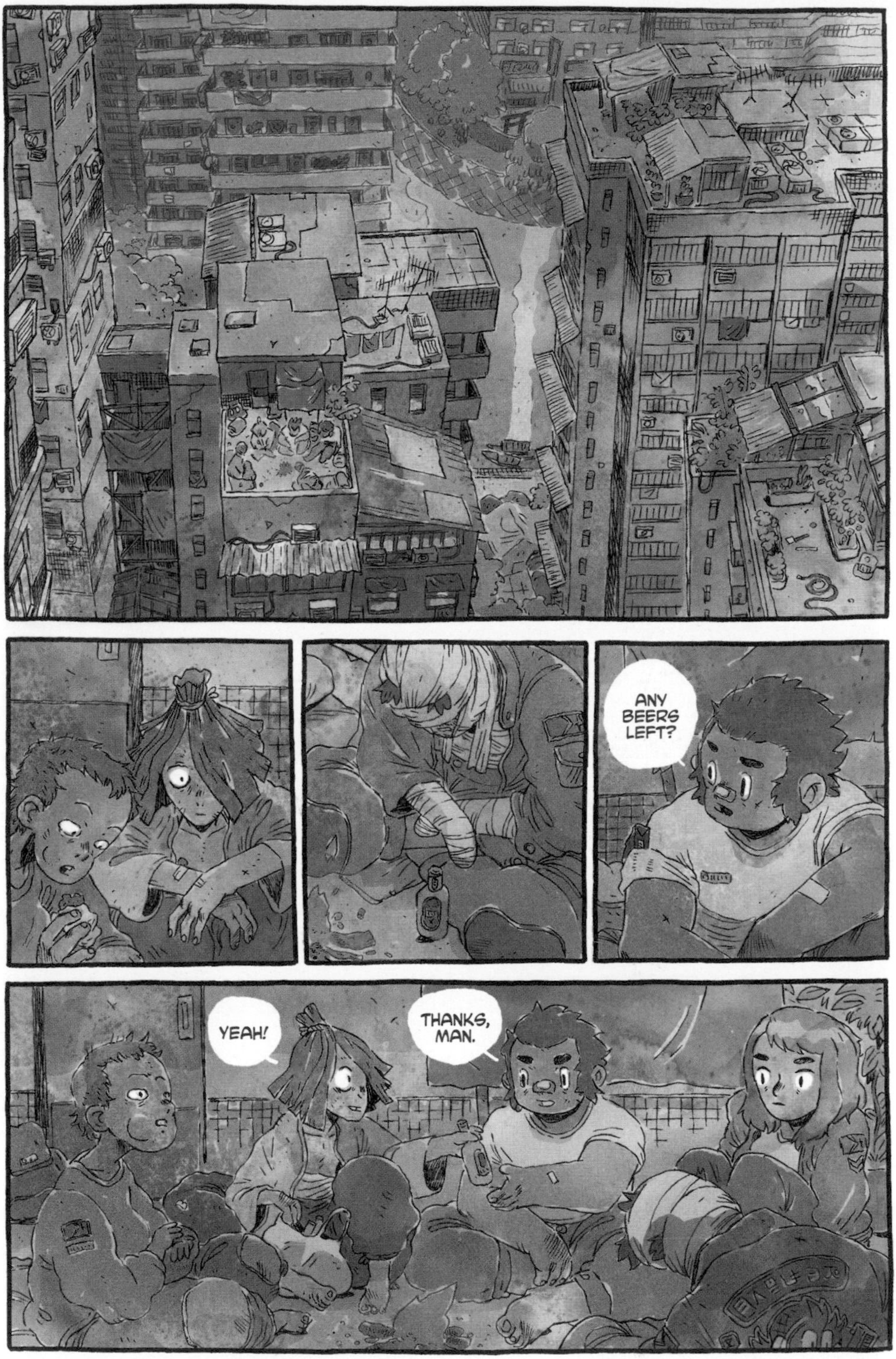
ANY BEERS LEFT?
YEAH!
THANKS, MAN.

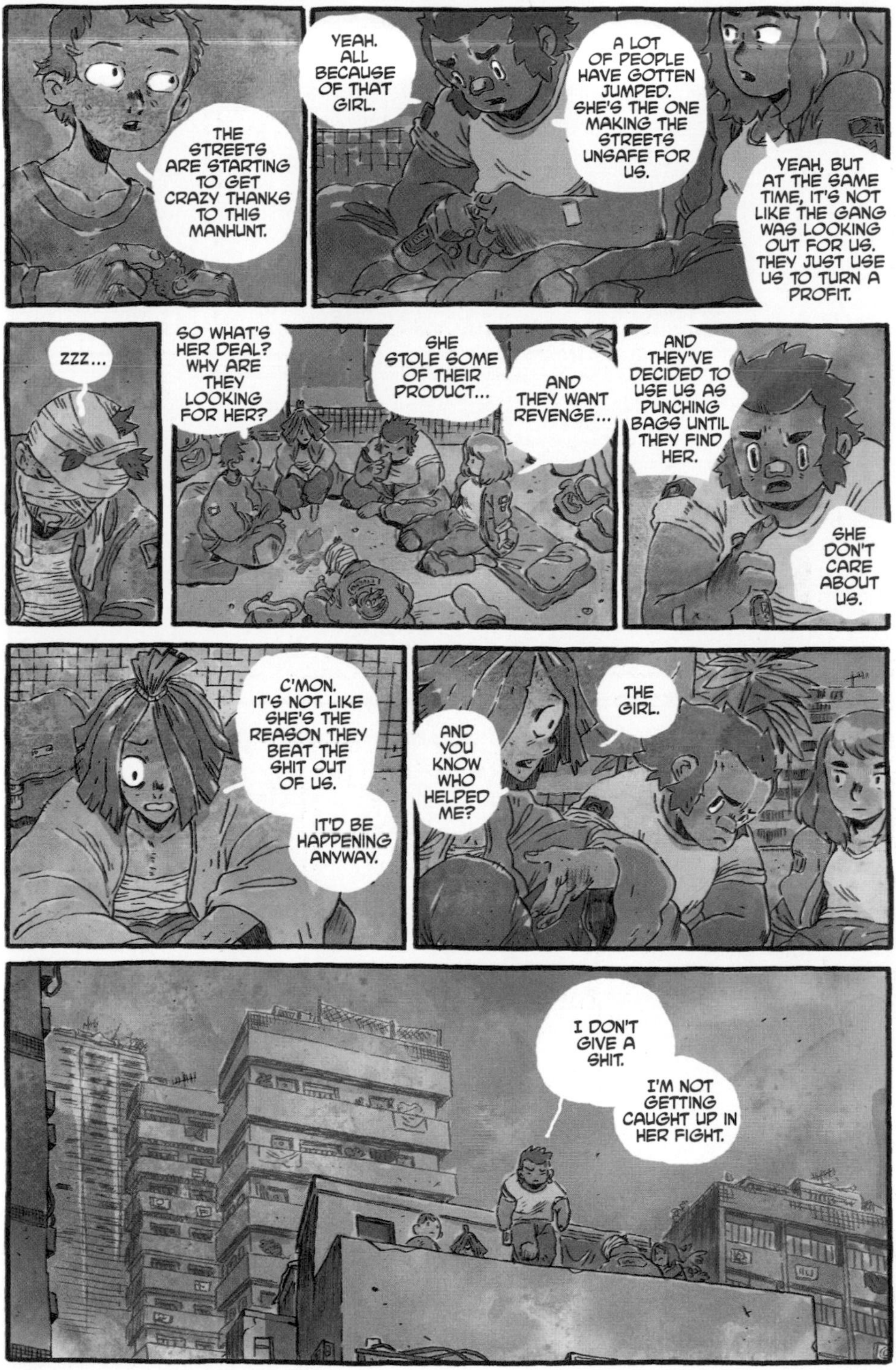
THE STREETS ARE STARTING TO GET CRAZY THANKS TO THIS MANHUNT.
YEAH. ALL BECAUSE OF THAT GIRL.
A LOT OF PEOPLE HAVE GOTTEN JUMPED. SHE'S THE ONE MAKING THE STREETS UNSAFE FOR US.
YEAH, BUT AT THE SAME TIME, IT'S NOT LIKE THE GANG WAS LOOKING OUT FOR US. THEY JUST USE US TO TURN A PROFIT.
ZZZ...
SO WHAT'S HER DEAL? WHY ARE THEY LOOKING FOR HER?
SHE STOLE SOME OF THEIR PRODUCT...
AND THEY WANT REVENGE...
AND THEY'VE DECIDED TO USE US AS PUNCHING BAGS UNTIL THEY FIND HER.
SHE DON'T CARE ABOUT US.
C'MON. IT'S NOT LIKE SHE'S THE REASON THEY BEAT THE SHIT OUT OF US.
IT'D BE HAPPENING ANYWAY.
THE GIRL.
AND YOU KNOW WHO HELPED ME?
I DON'T GIVE A SHIT.
I'M NOT GETTING CAUGHT UP IN HER FIGHT.

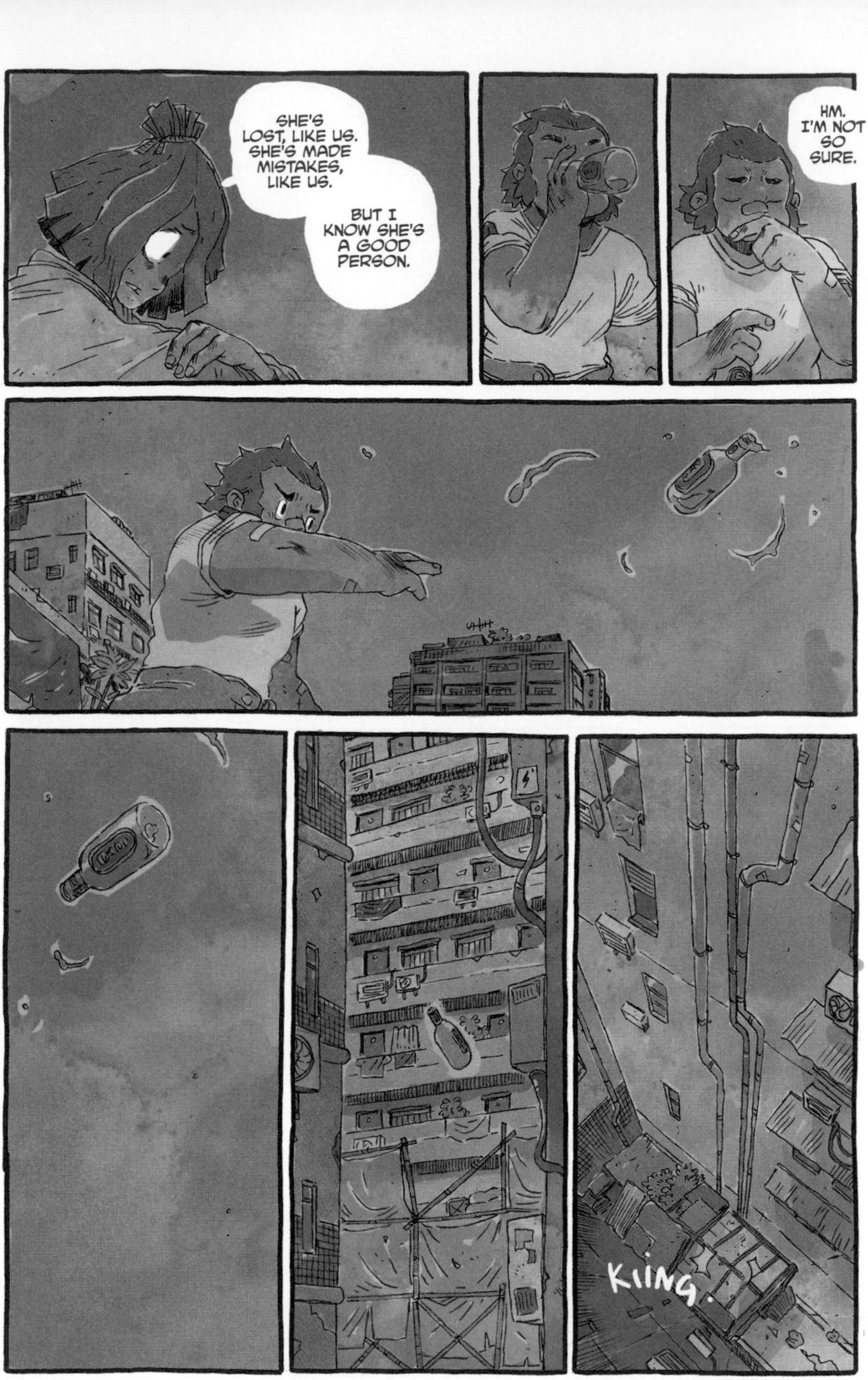
SHE'S LOST, LIKE US. SHE'S MADE MISTAKES, LIKE US.
BUT I KNOW SHE'S A GOOD PERSON.
HM. I'M NOT SO SURE.
KLING.

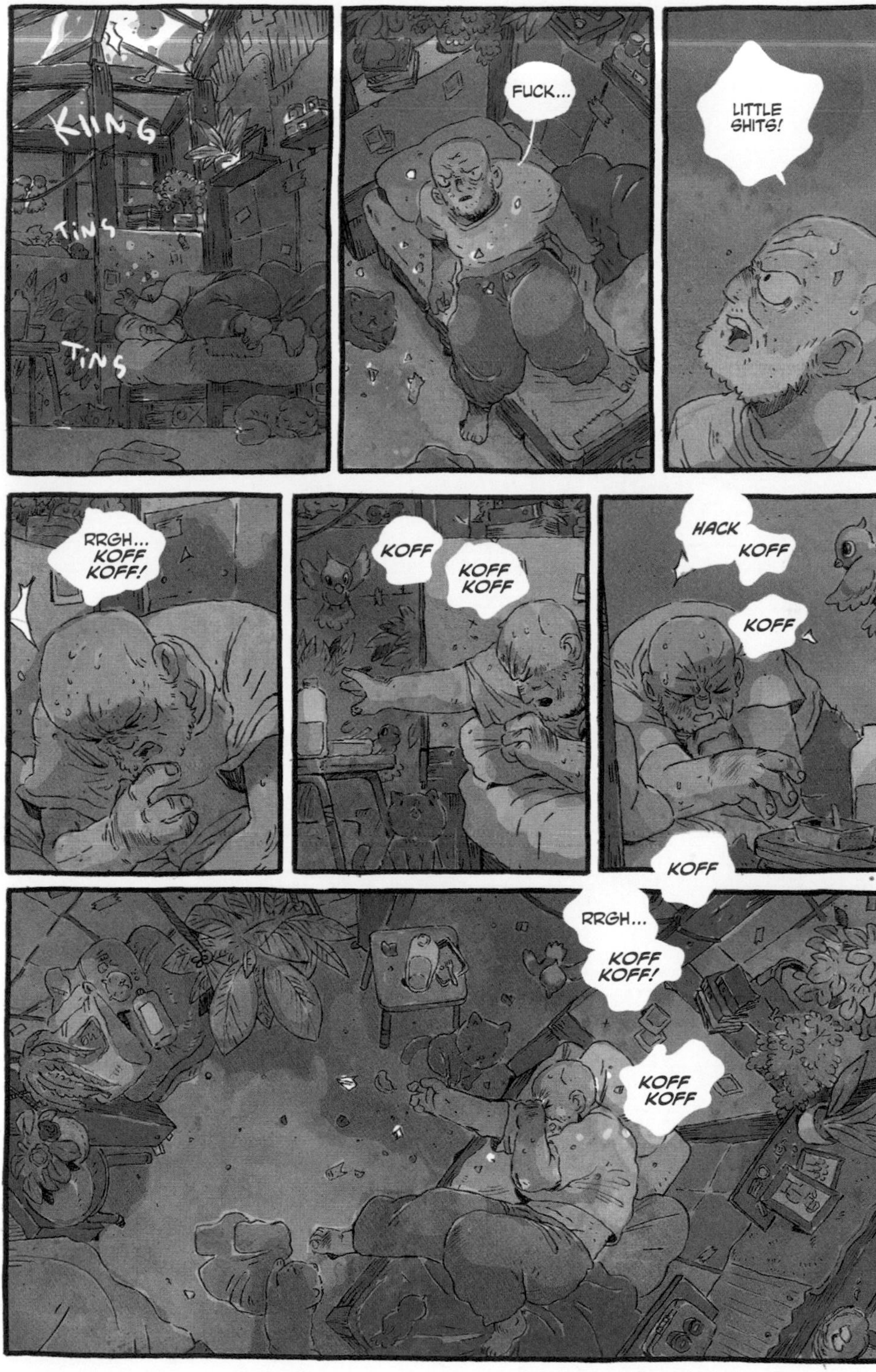
KLING
TING
TING
FUCK...
LITTLE SHITS!
RRGH... KOFF KOFF!
KOFF
KOFF KOFF
HACK
KOFF
KOFF
KOFF
RRGH...
KOFF KOFF!
KOFF KOFF

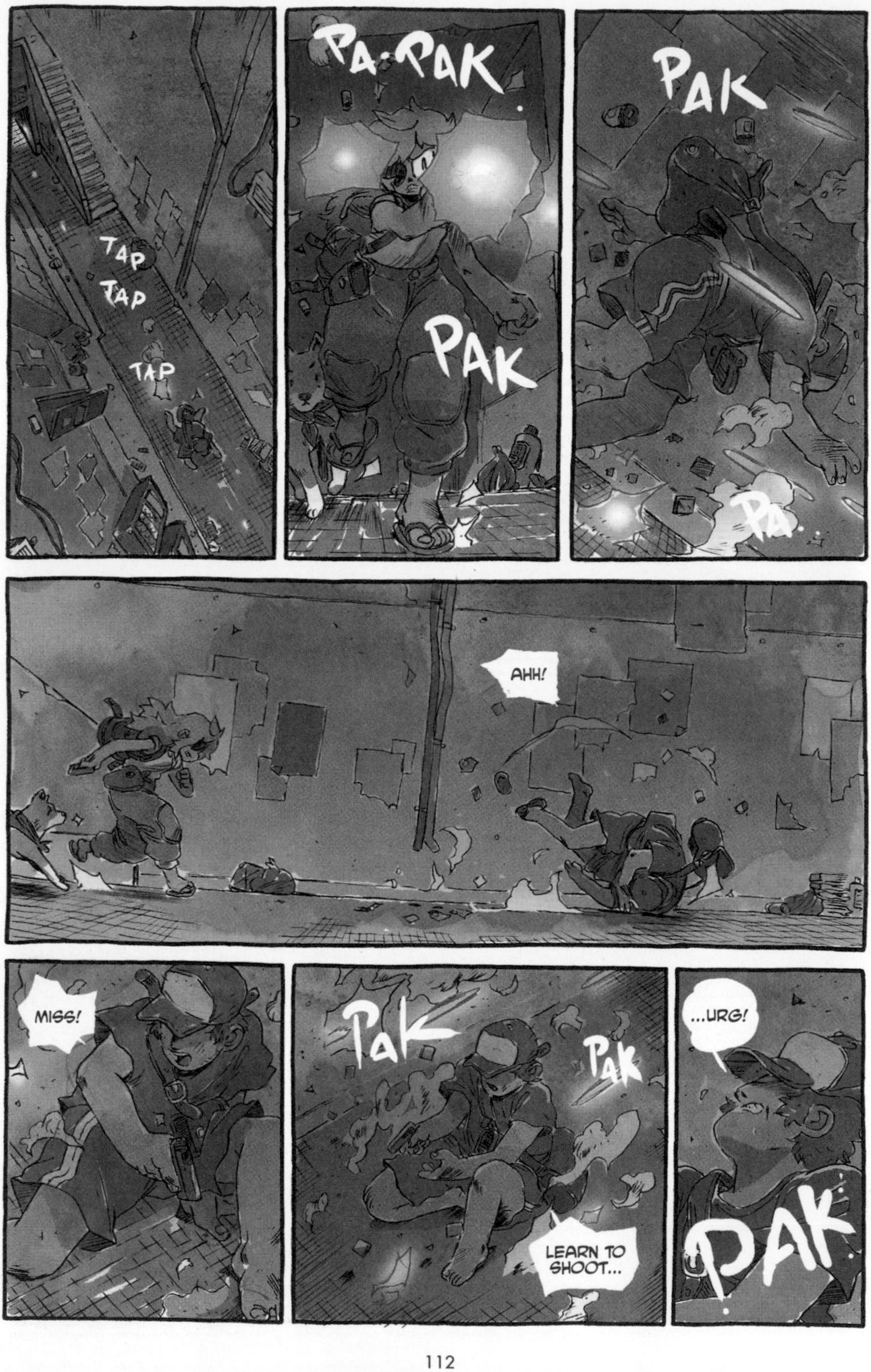
TAP
TAP
TAP
PA-PAK
PAK
PAK
PA
AHH!
MISS!
PAK
PAK
LEARN TO SHOOT...
...URG!
PAK

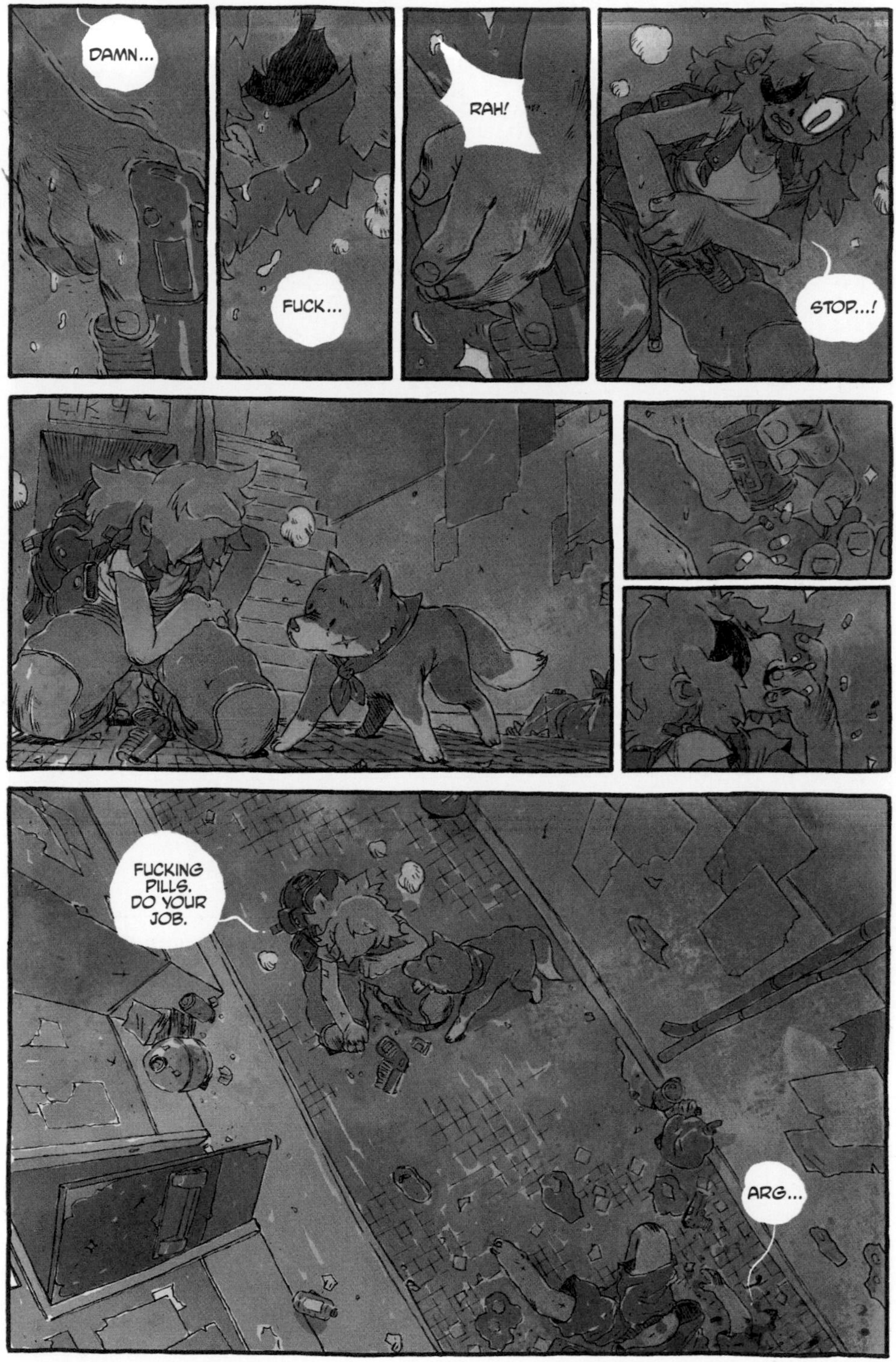
DAMN...
FUCK...
RAH!
STOP...!
FUCKING PILLS. DO YOUR JOB.
ARG...

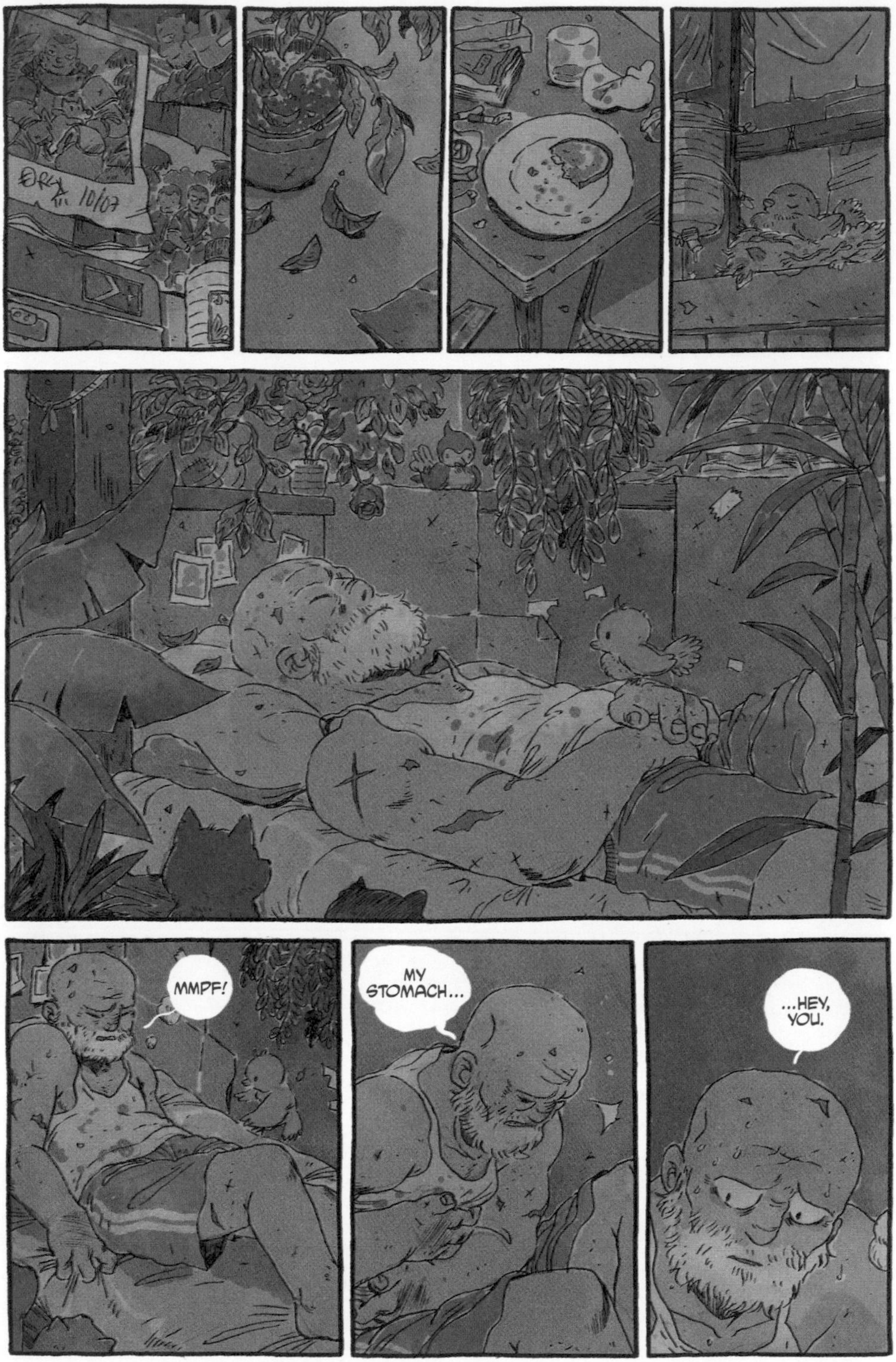
MMPF!
MY STOMACH...
...HEY, YOU.

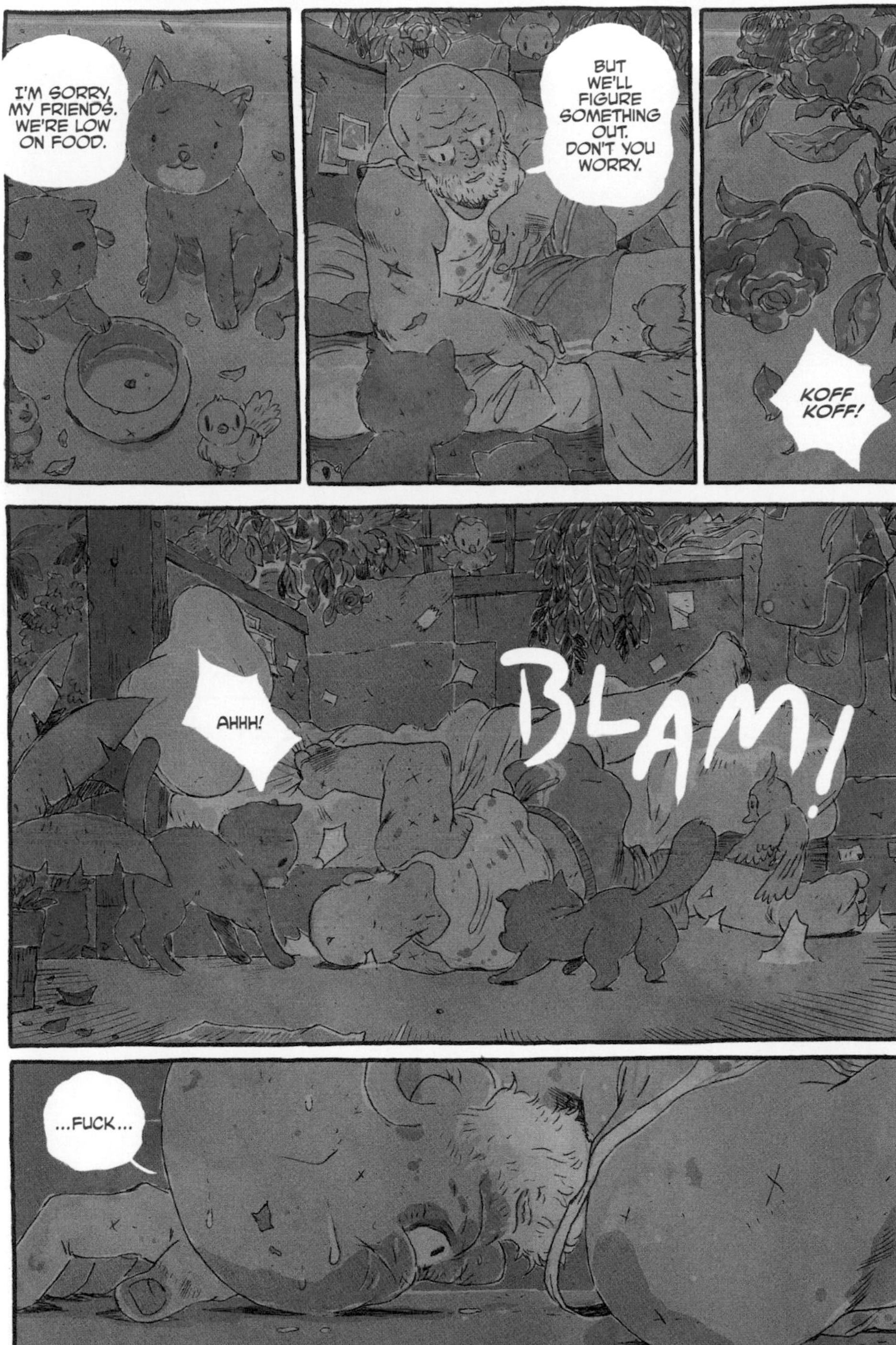
I'M SORRY, MY FRIENDS. WE'RE LOW ON FOOD.
BUT WE'LL FIGURE SOMETHING OUT. DON'T YOU WORRY.
KOFF KOFF!
AHHH!
BLAM!
...FUCK...

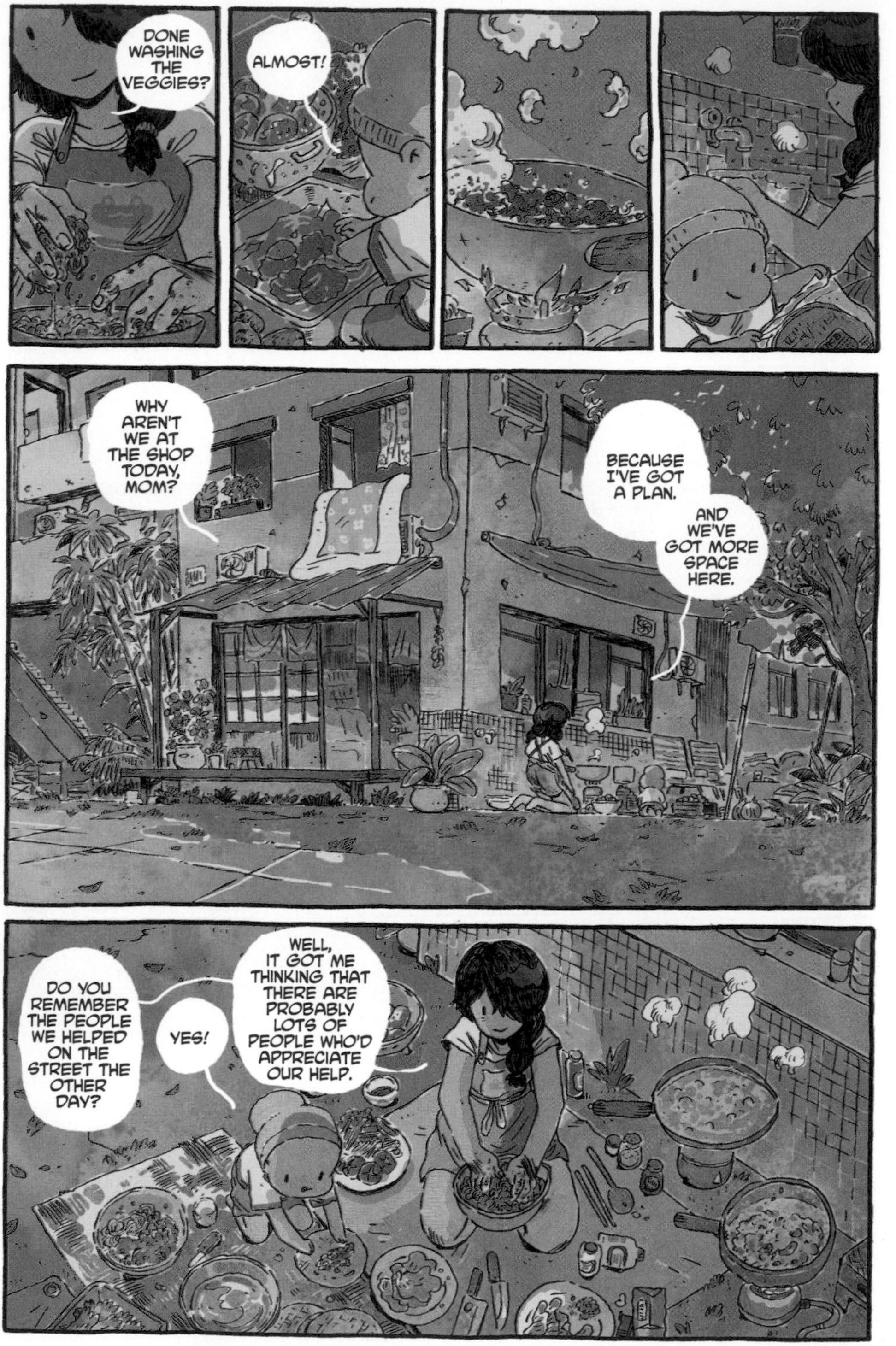
DONE WASHING THE VEGGIES?
ALMOST!
WHY AREN'T WE AT THE SHOP TODAY, MOM?
BECAUSE I'VE GOT A PLAN.
AND WE'VE GOT MORE SPACE HERE.
DO YOU REMEMBER THE PEOPLE WE HELPED ON THE STREET THE OTHER DAY?
YES!
WELL, IT GOT ME THINKING THAT THERE ARE PROBABLY LOTS OF PEOPLE WHO'D APPRECIATE OUR HELP.

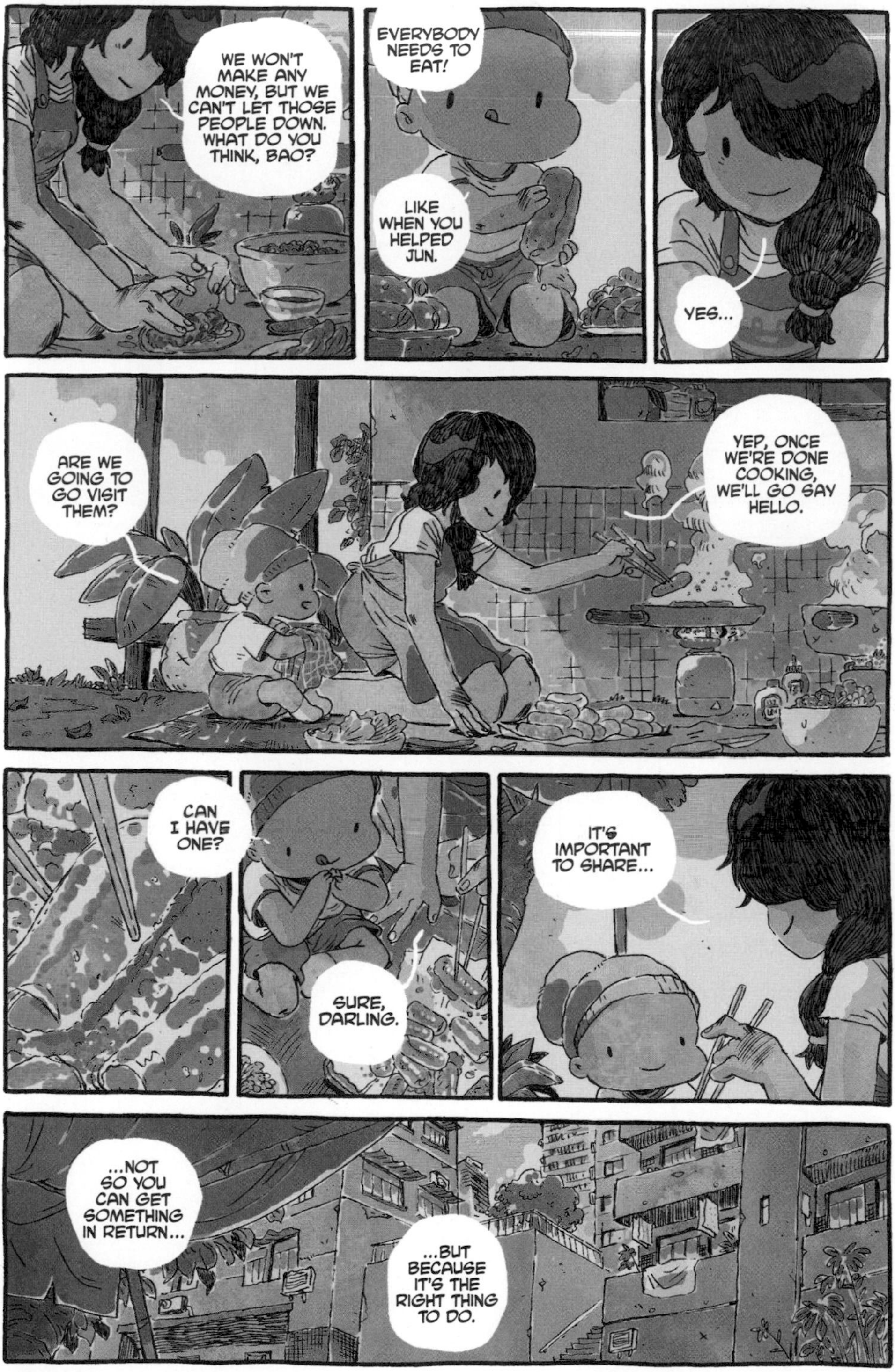
WE WON'T MAKE ANY MONEY, BUT WE CAN'T LET THOSE PEOPLE DOWN. WHAT DO YOU THINK, BAO?
EVERYBODY NEEDS TO EAT!
LIKE WHEN YOU HELPED JUN.
YES...
ARE WE GOING TO GO VISIT THEM?
YEP, ONCE WE'RE DONE COOKING, WE'LL GO SAY HELLO.
CAN I HAVE ONE?
SURE, DARLING.
IT'S IMPORTANT TO SHARE...
...NOT SO YOU CAN GET SOMETHING IN RETURN...
...BUT BECAUSE IT'S THE RIGHT THING TO DO.

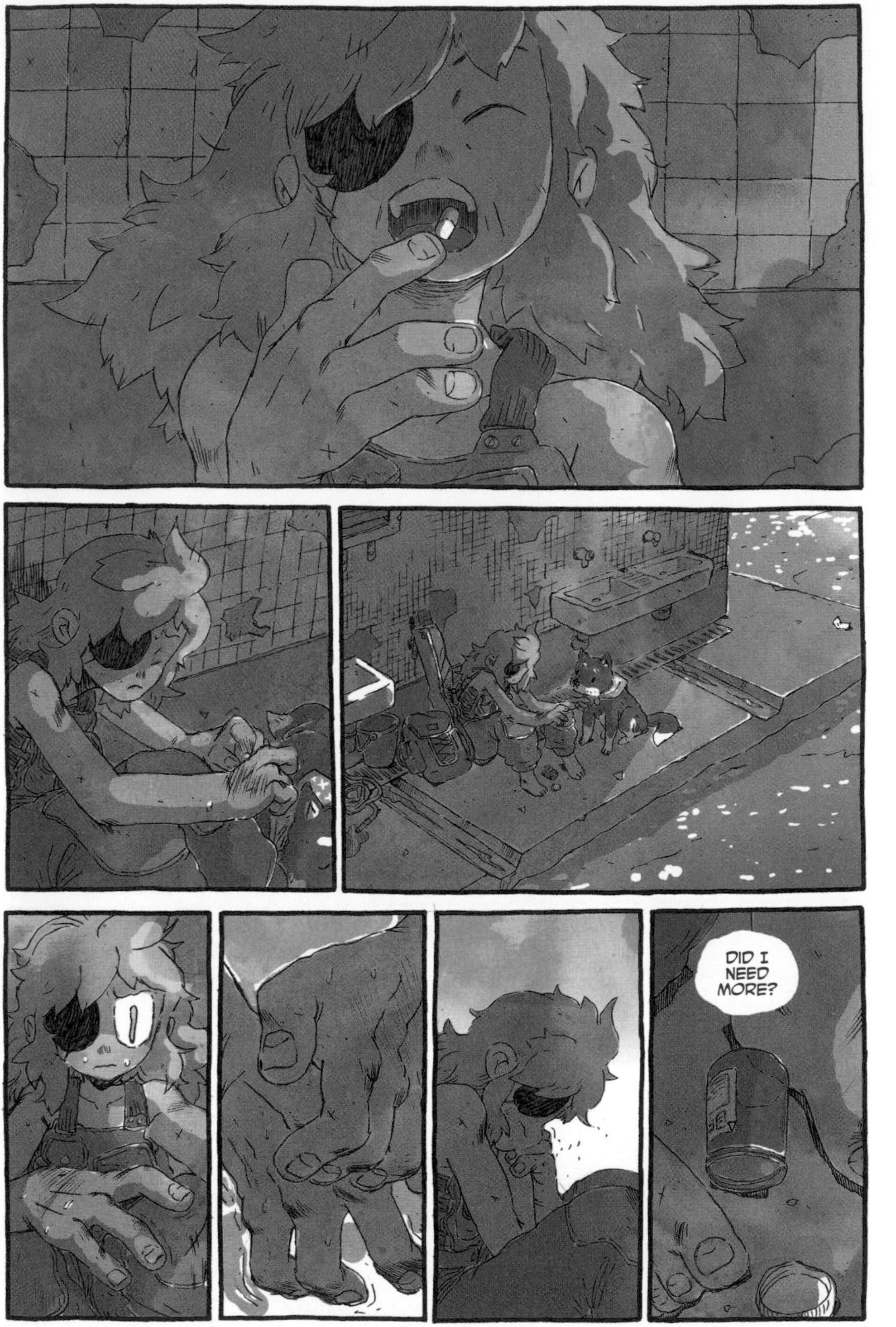
DID I NEED MORE?

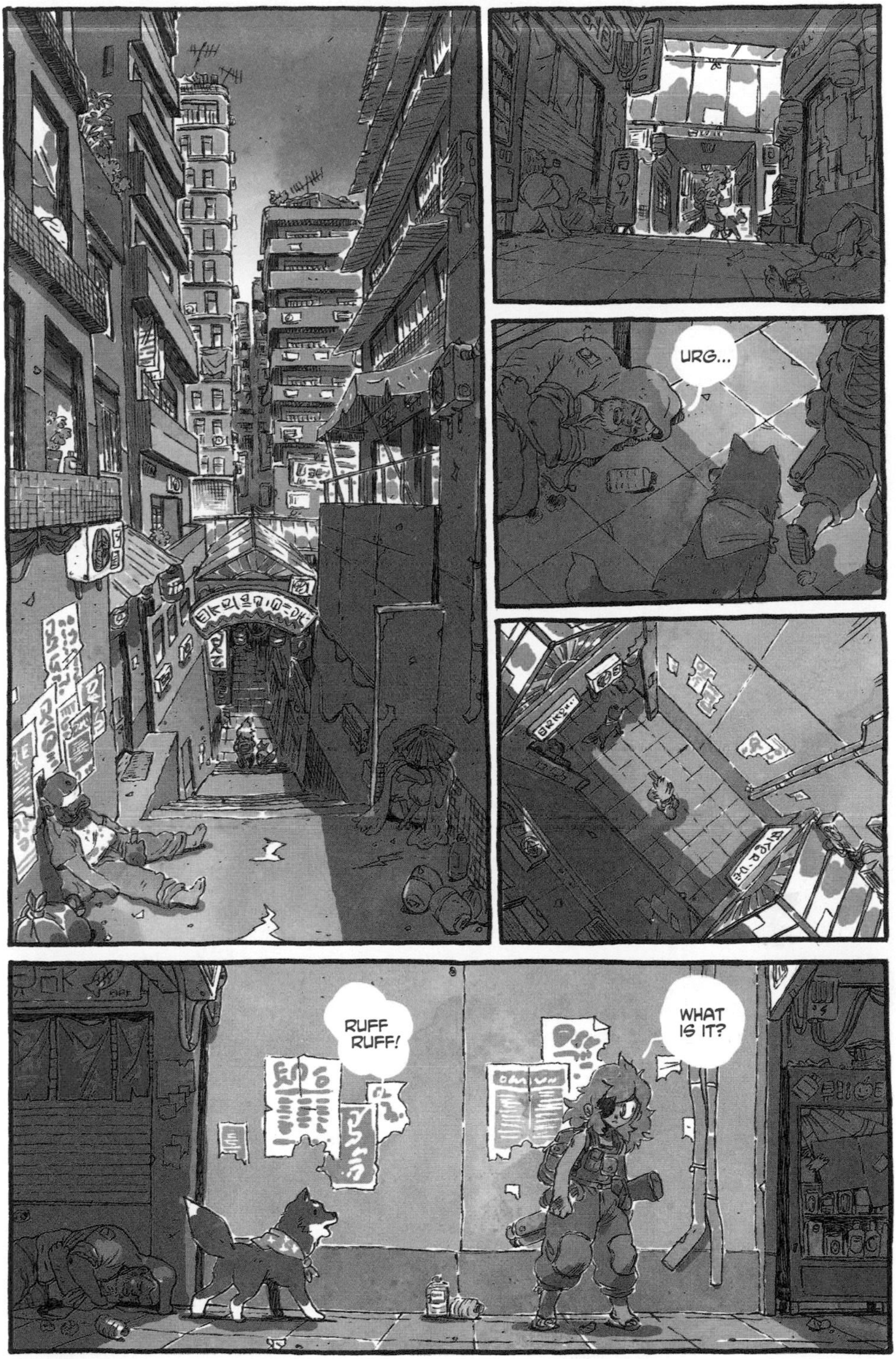
URG...
RUFF RUFF!
WHAT IS IT?

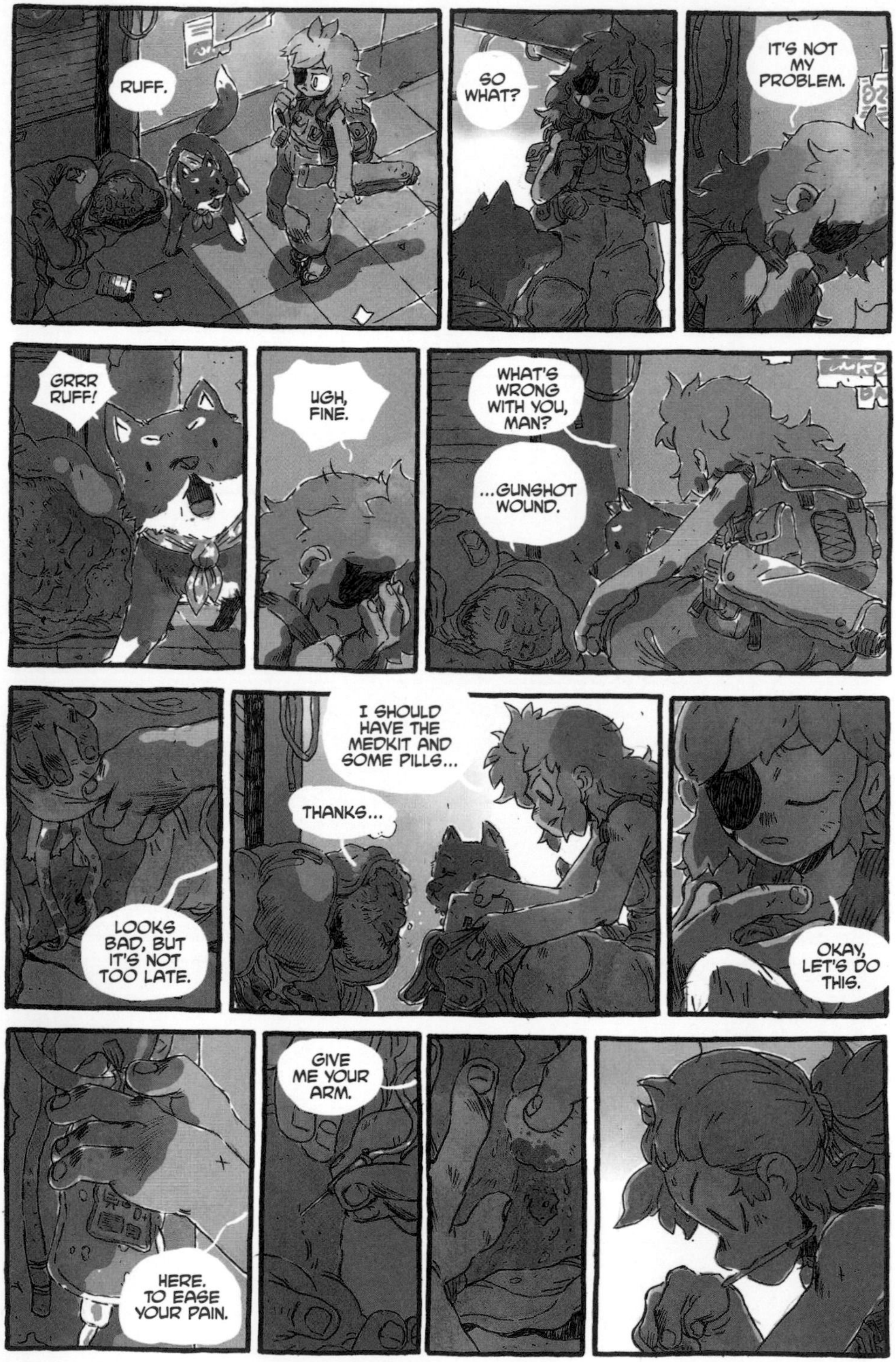
RUFF.
SO WHAT?
IT'S NOT MY PROBLEM.
GRRR RUFF!
UGH, FINE.
WHAT'S WRONG WITH YOU, MAN?
...GUNSHOT WOUND.
LOOKS BAD, BUT IT'S NOT TOO LATE.
I SHOULD HAVE THE MEDKIT AND SOME PILLS...
THANKS...
OKAY, LET'S DO THIS.
HERE. TO EASE YOUR PAIN.
GIVE ME YOUR ARM.

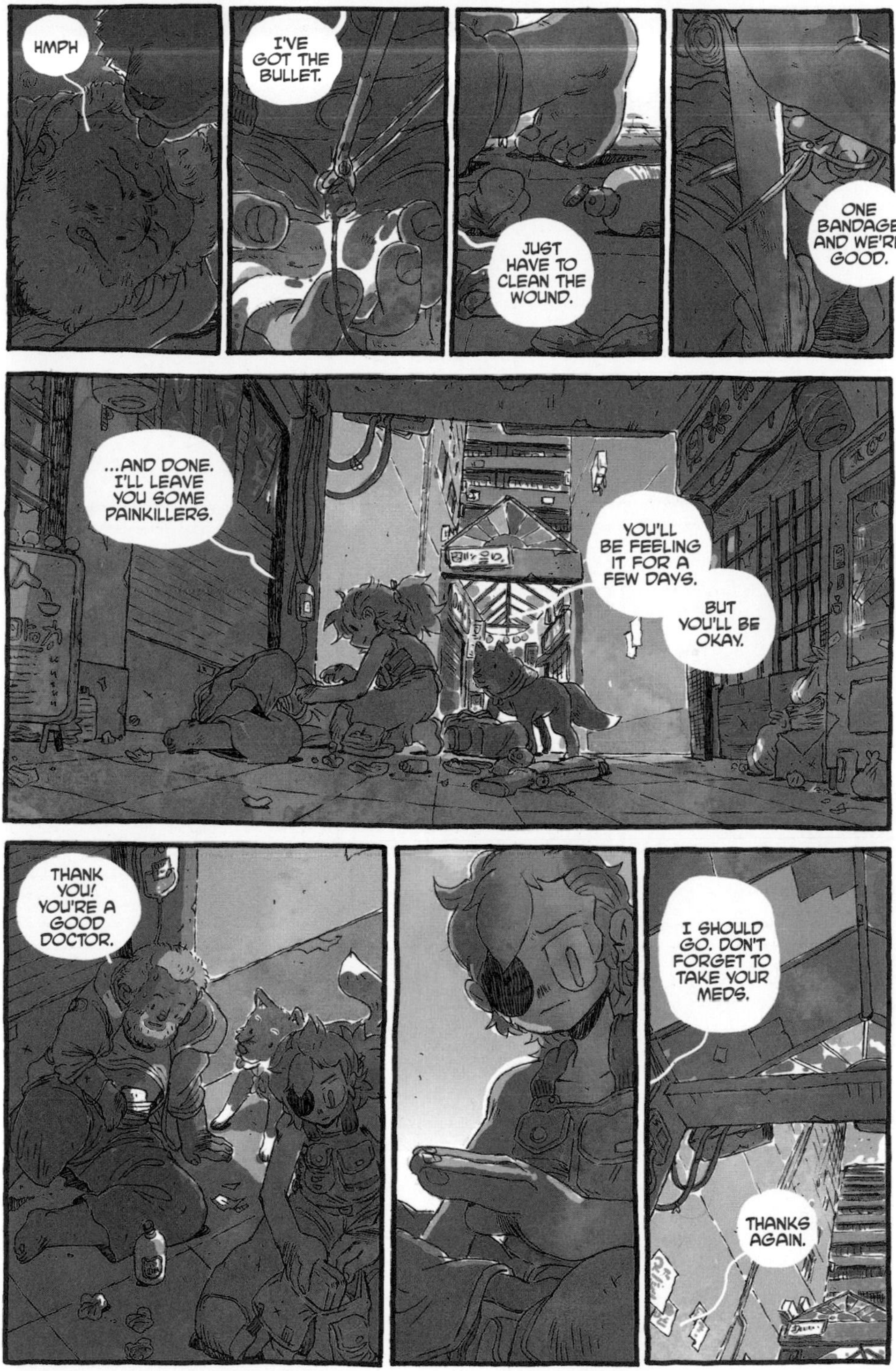
HMPH
I'VE GOT THE BULLET.
JUST HAVE TO CLEAN THE WOUND.
ONE BANDAGE AND WE'RE GOOD.
...AND DONE. I'LL LEAVE YOU SOME PAINKILLERS.
YOU'LL BE FEELING IT FOR A FEW DAYS.
BUT YOU'LL BE OKAY.
THANK YOU! YOU'RE A GOOD DOCTOR.
I SHOULD GO. DON'T FORGET TO TAKE YOUR MEDS.
THANKS AGAIN.

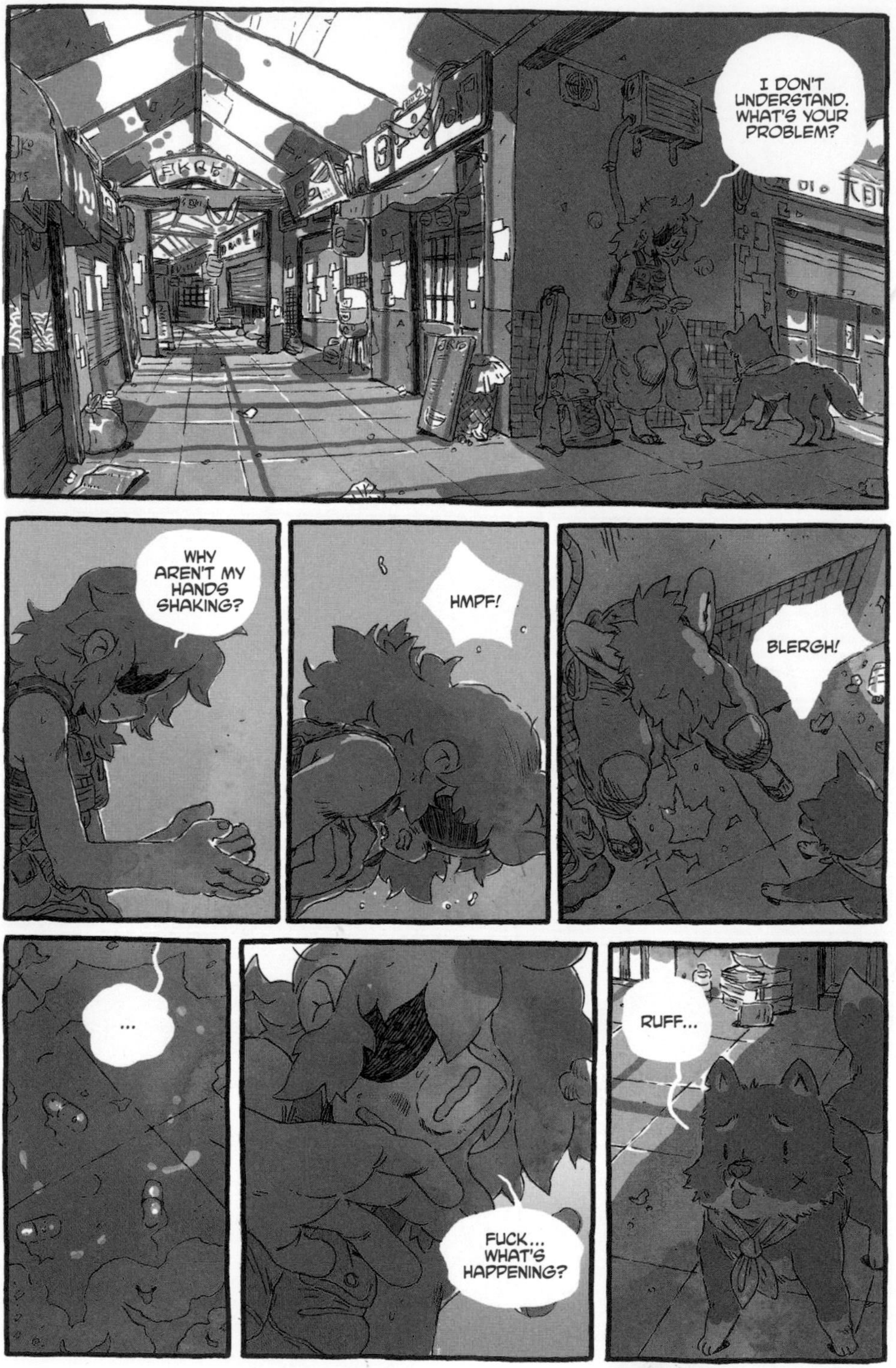
I DON'T UNDERSTAND. WHAT'S YOUR PROBLEM?
WHY AREN'T MY HANDS SHAKING?
HMPF!
BLERGH!
...
FUCK... WHAT'S HAPPENING?
RUFF...

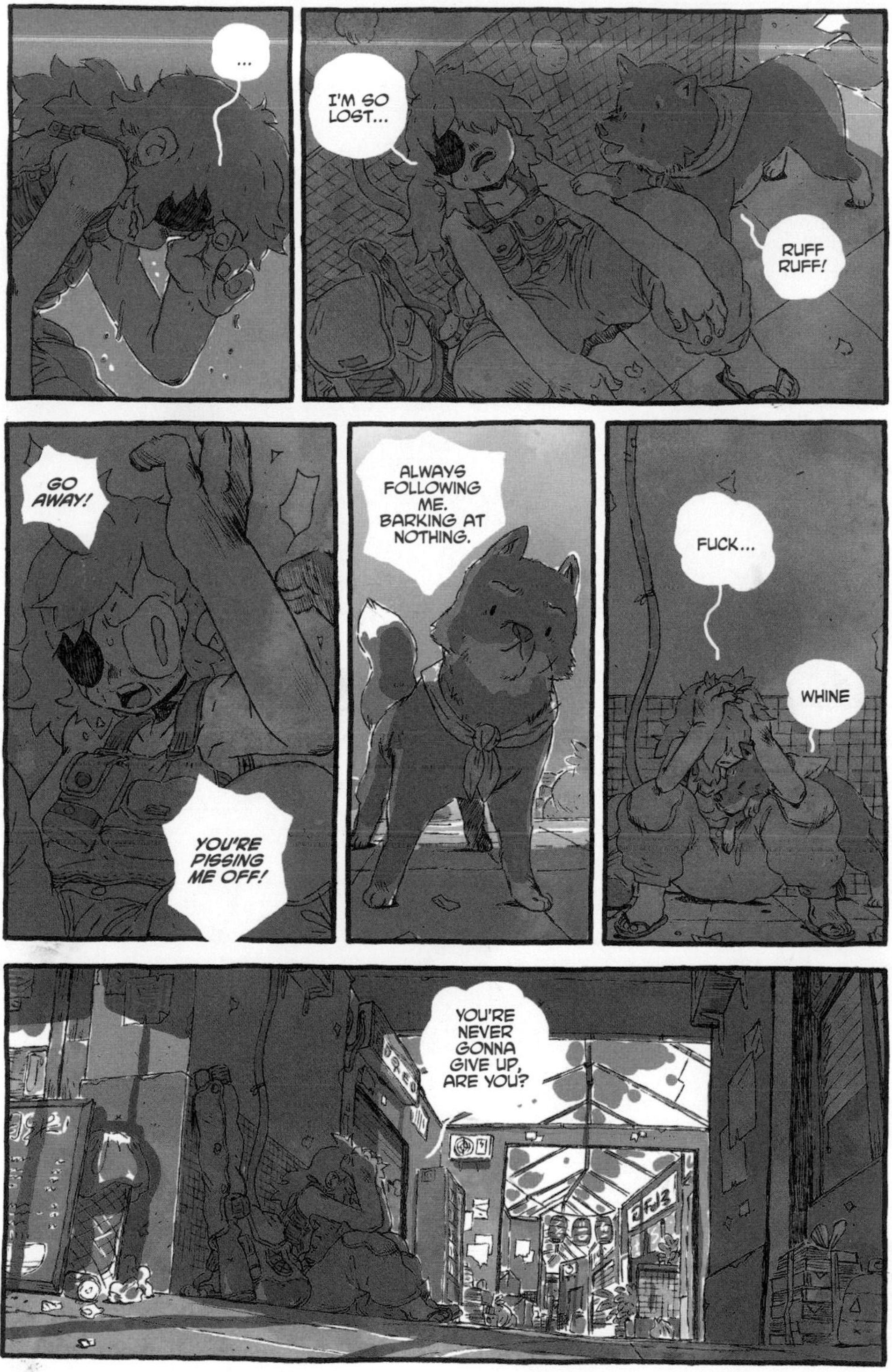
...
I'M SO LOST...
RUFF RUFF!
GO AWAY!
YOU'RE PISSING ME OFF!
ALWAYS FOLLOWING ME. BARKING AT NOTHING.
FUCK...
WHINE
YOU'RE NEVER GONNA GIVE UP, ARE YOU?

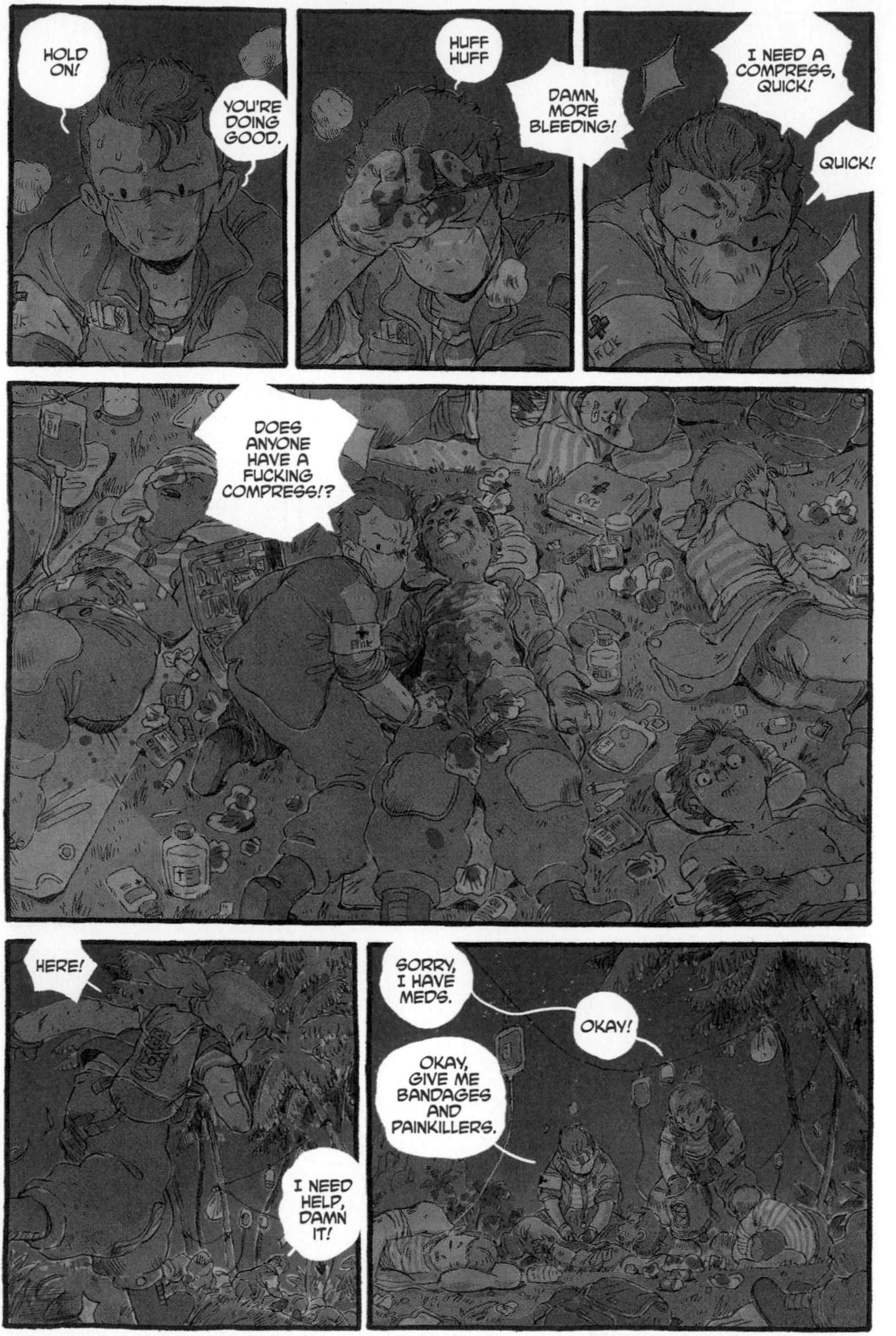
HOLD ON!
YOU'RE DOING GOOD.
HUFF HUFF
DAMN, MORE BLEEDING!
I NEED A COMPRESS, QUICK!
QUICK!
DOES ANYONE HAVE A FUCKING COMPRESS!?
HERE!
I NEED HELP, DAMN IT!
SORRY, I HAVE MEDS.
OKAY!
OKAY, GIVE ME BANDAGES AND PAINKILLERS.

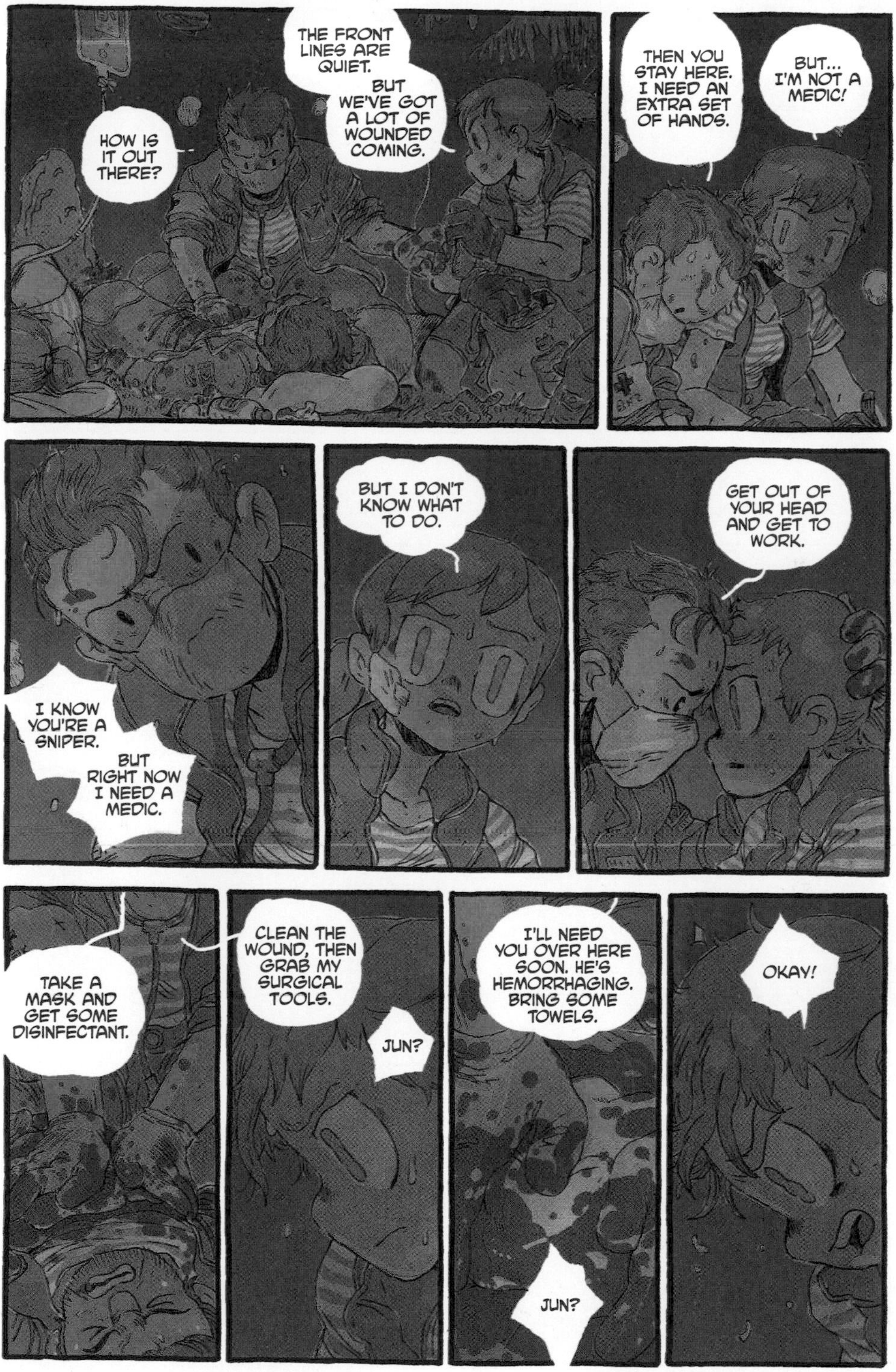
HOW IS IT OUT THERE?
THE FRONT LINES ARE QUIET.
BUT WE'VE GOT A LOT OF WOUNDED COMING.
THEN YOU STAY HERE. I NEED AN EXTRA SET OF HANDS.
BUT... I'M NOT A MEDIC!
I KNOW YOU'RE A SNIPER.
BUT RIGHT NOW I NEED A MEDIC.
BUT I DON'T KNOW WHAT TO DO.
GET OUT OF YOUR HEAD AND GET TO WORK.
TAKE A MASK AND GET SOME DISINFECTANT.
CLEAN THE WOUND, THEN GRAB MY SURGICAL TOOLS.
JUN?
I'LL NEED YOU OVER HERE SOON. HE'S HEMORRHAGING. BRING SOME TOWELS.
JUN?
OKAY!

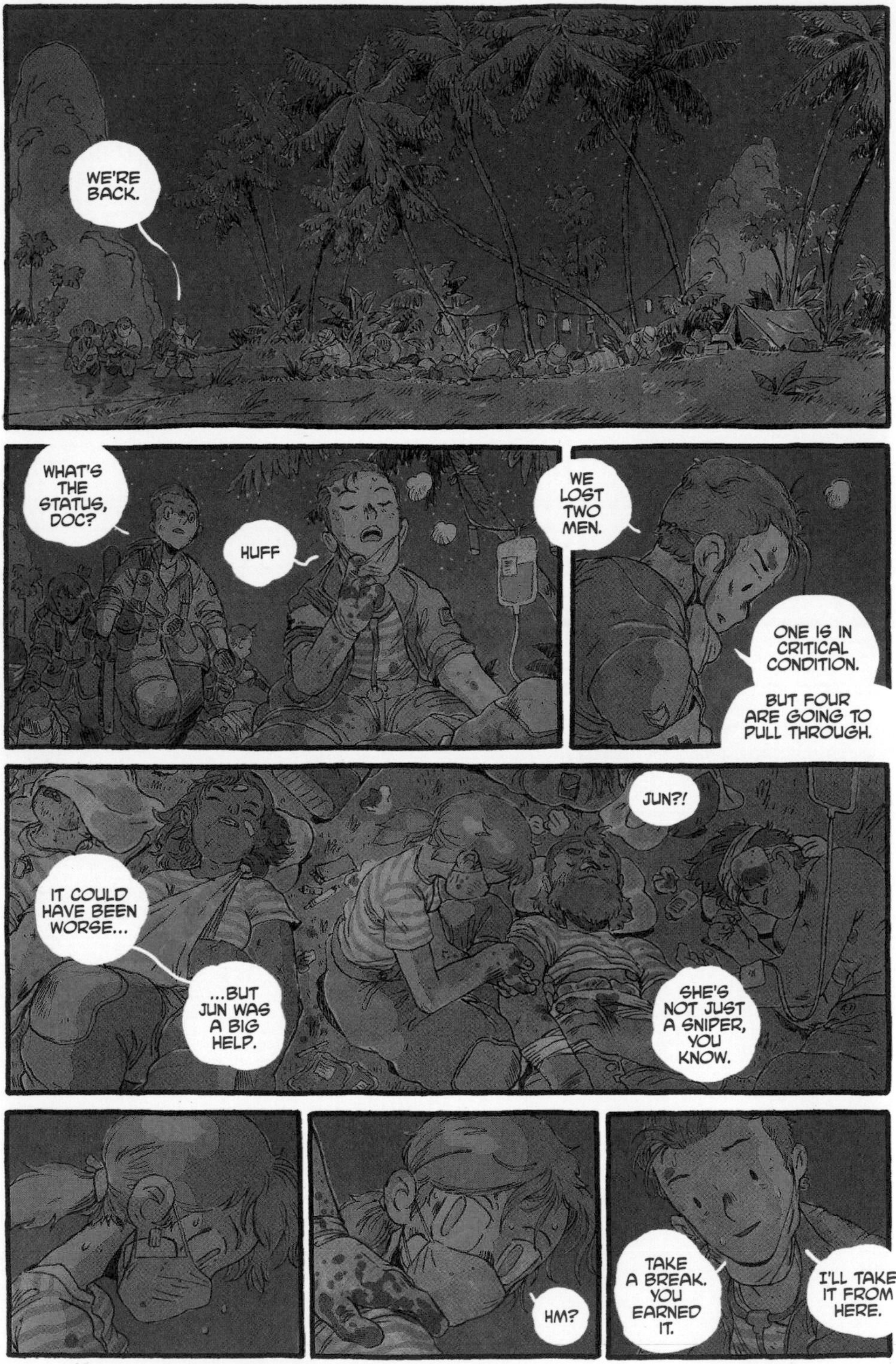
WE'RE BACK.
WHAT'S THE STATUS, DOC?
HUFF
WE LOST TWO MEN.
ONE IS IN CRITICAL CONDITION.
BUT FOUR ARE GOING TO PULL THROUGH.
JUN?!
IT COULD HAVE BEEN WORSE...
...BUT JUN WAS A BIG HELP.
SHE'S NOT JUST A SNIPER, YOU KNOW.
HM?
TAKE A BREAK. YOU EARNED IT.
I'LL TAKE IT FROM HERE.

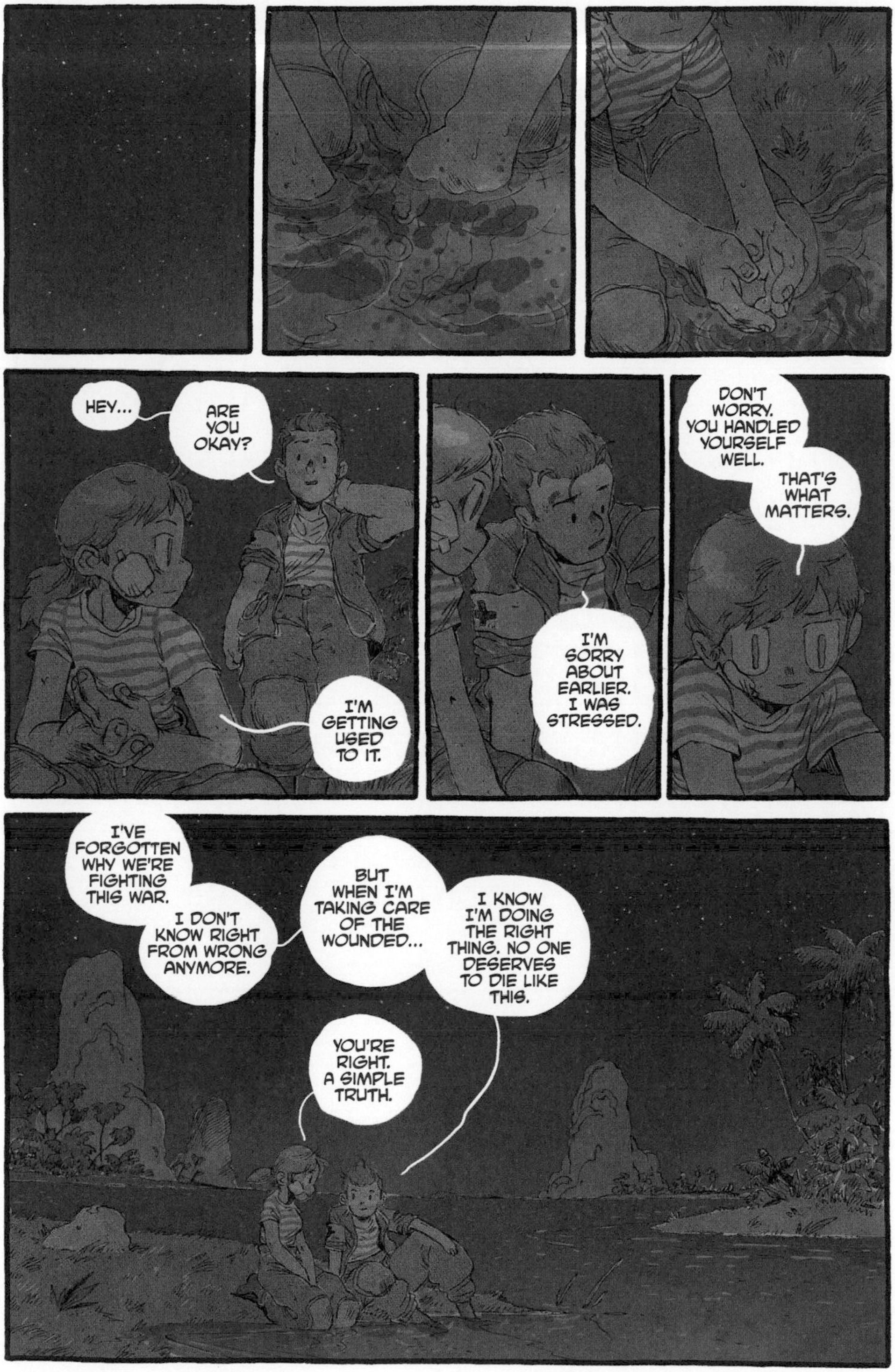
HEY...
ARE YOU OKAY?
I'M GETTING USED TO IT.
I'M SORRY ABOUT EARLIER. I WAS STRESSED.
DON'T WORRY. YOU HANDLED YOURSELF WELL.
THAT'S WHAT MATTERS.
I'VE FORGOTTEN WHY WE'RE FIGHTING THIS WAR.
I DON'T KNOW RIGHT FROM WRONG ANYMORE.
BUT WHEN I'M TAKING CARE OF THE WOUNDED...
I KNOW I'M DOING THE RIGHT THING. NO ONE DESERVES TO DIE LIKE THIS.
YOU'RE RIGHT. A SIMPLE TRUTH.

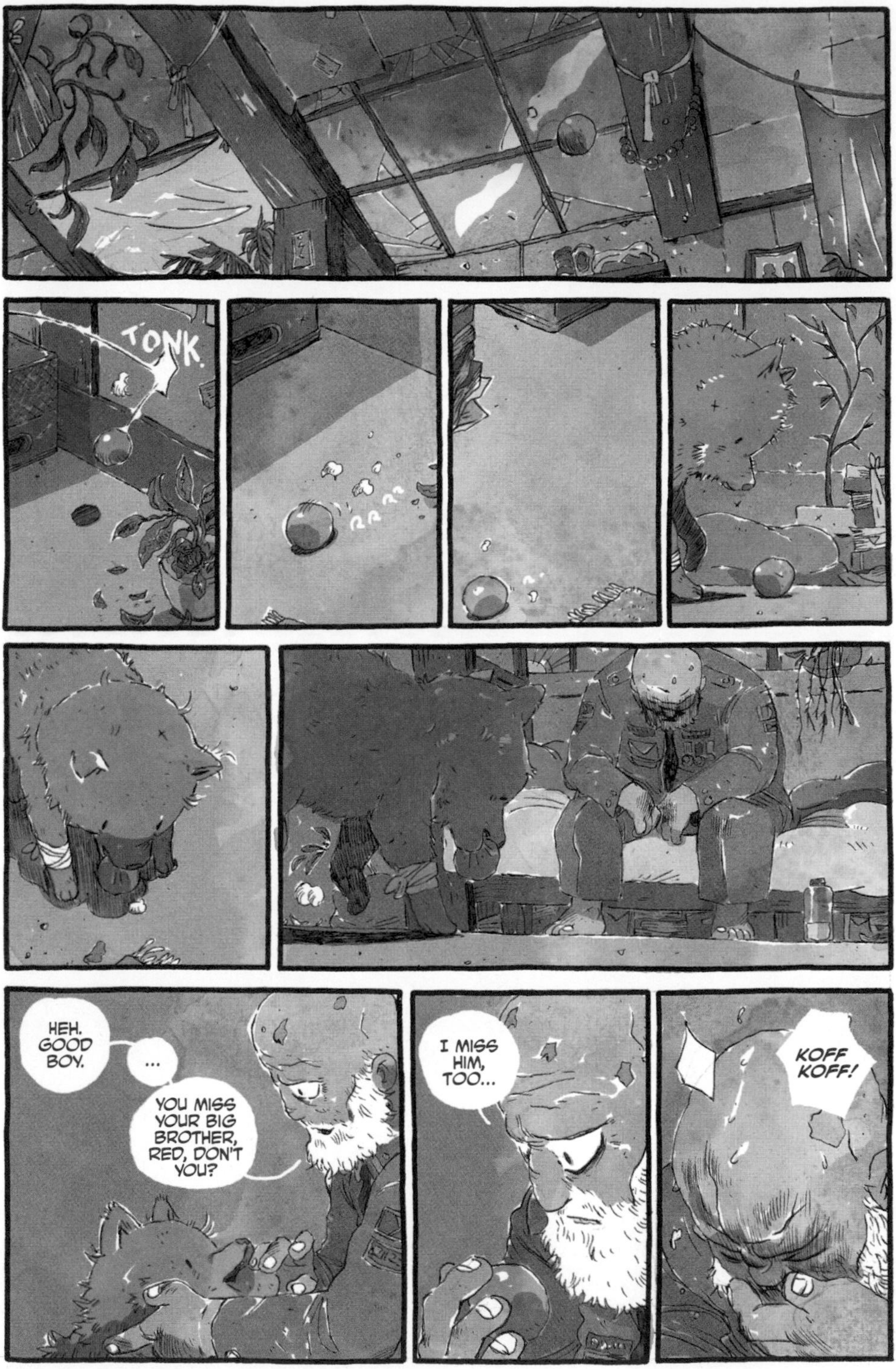
TONK.
RRR
HEH. GOOD BOY.
...
YOU MISS YOUR BIG BROTHER, RED, DON'T YOU?
I MISS HIM, TOO...
KOFF KOFF!

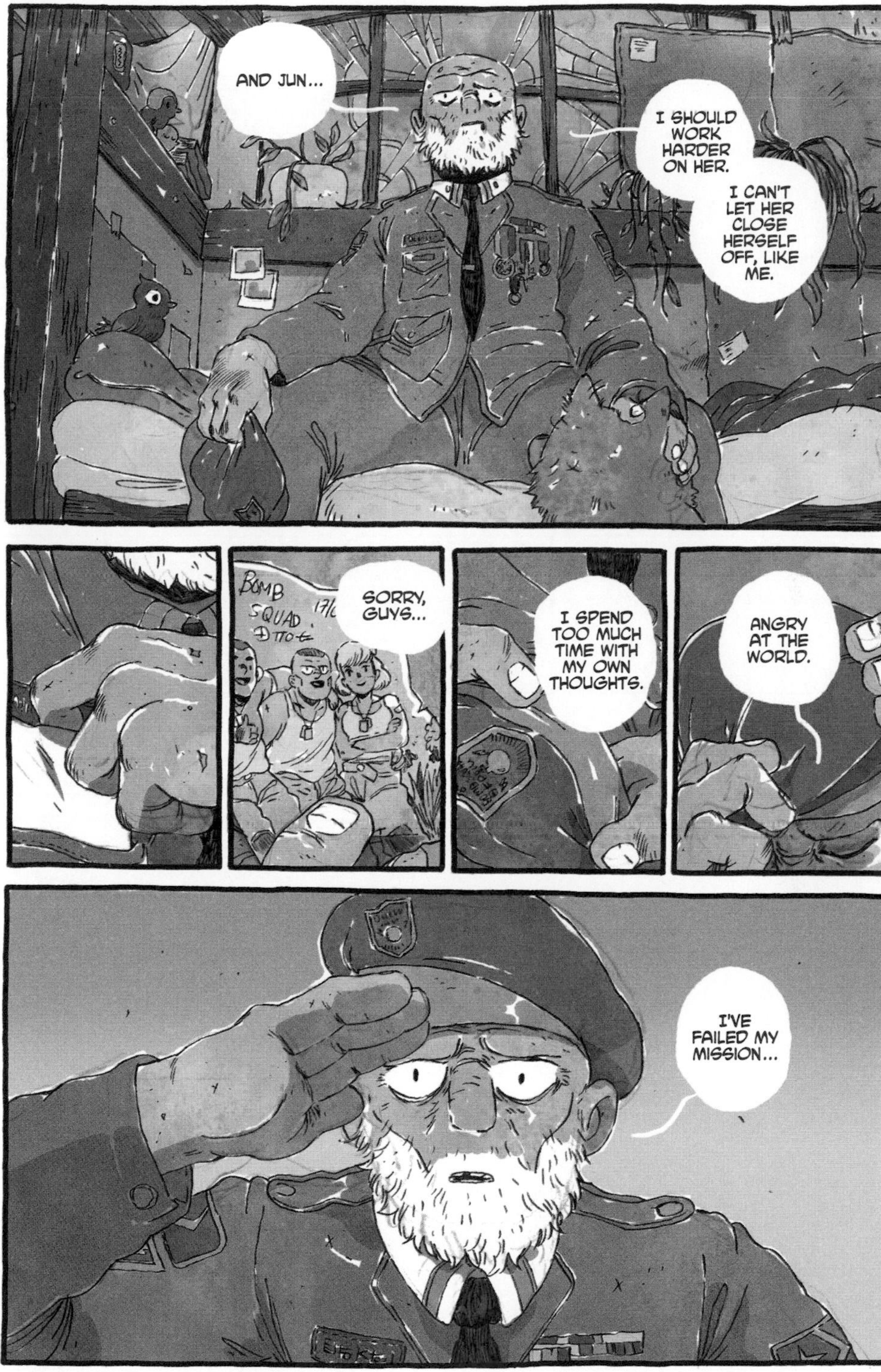
AND JUN...
I SHOULD WORK HARDER ON HER.
I CAN'T LET HER CLOSE HERSELF OFF, LIKE ME.
BOMB SQUAD
SORRY, GUYS...
I SPEND TOO MUCH TIME WITH MY OWN THOUGHTS.
ANGRY AT THE WORLD.
I'VE FAILED MY MISSION...

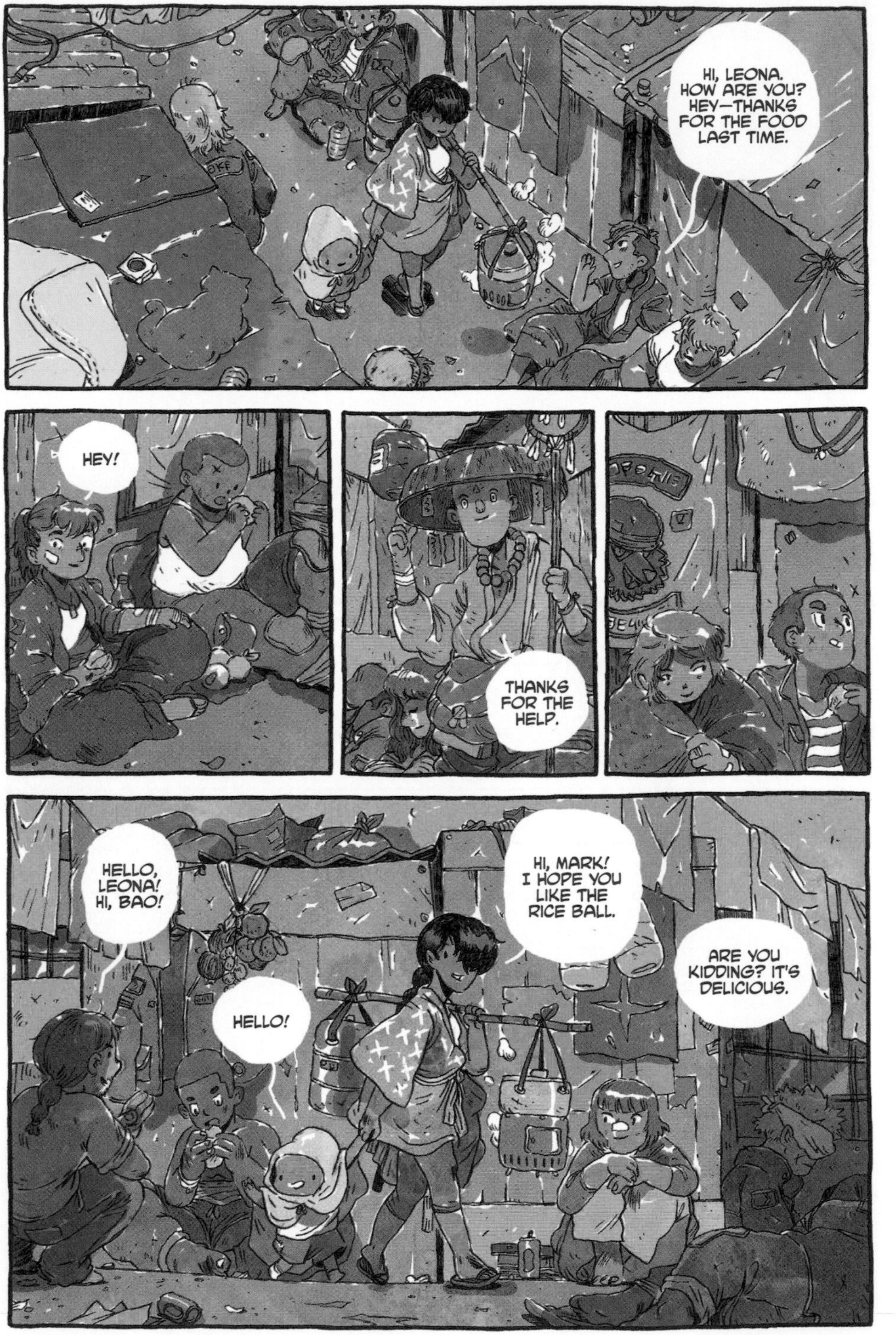
HI, LEONA. HOW ARE YOU? HEY—THANKS FOR THE FOOD LAST TIME.
HEY!
THANKS FOR THE HELP.
HELLO, LEONA! HI, BAO!
HELLO!
HI, MARK! I HOPE YOU LIKE THE RICE BALL.
ARE YOU KIDDING? IT'S DELICIOUS.

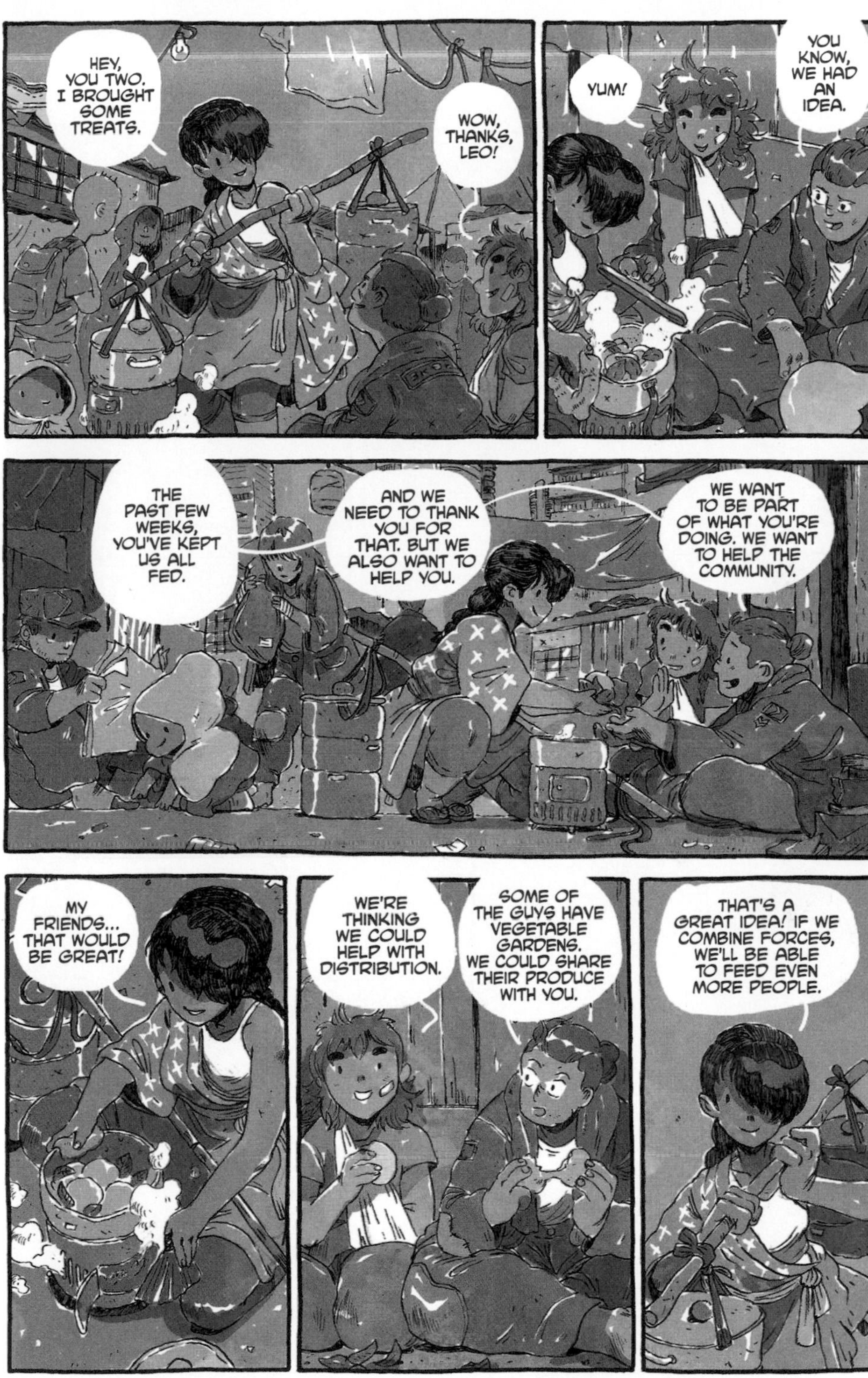
HEY, YOU TWO. I BROUGHT SOME TREATS.
WOW, THANKS, LEO!
YUM!
YOU KNOW, WE HAD AN IDEA.
THE PAST FEW WEEKS, YOU'VE KEPT US ALL FED.
AND WE NEED TO THANK YOU FOR THAT. BUT WE ALSO WANT TO HELP YOU.
WE WANT TO BE PART OF WHAT YOU'RE DOING. WE WANT TO HELP THE COMMUNITY.
MY FRIENDS... THAT WOULD BE GREAT!
WE'RE THINKING WE COULD HELP WITH DISTRIBUTION.
SOME OF THE GUYS HAVE VEGETABLE GARDENS. WE COULD SHARE THEIR PRODUCE WITH YOU.
THAT'S A GREAT IDEA! IF WE COMBINE FORCES, WE'LL BE ABLE TO FEED EVEN MORE PEOPLE.

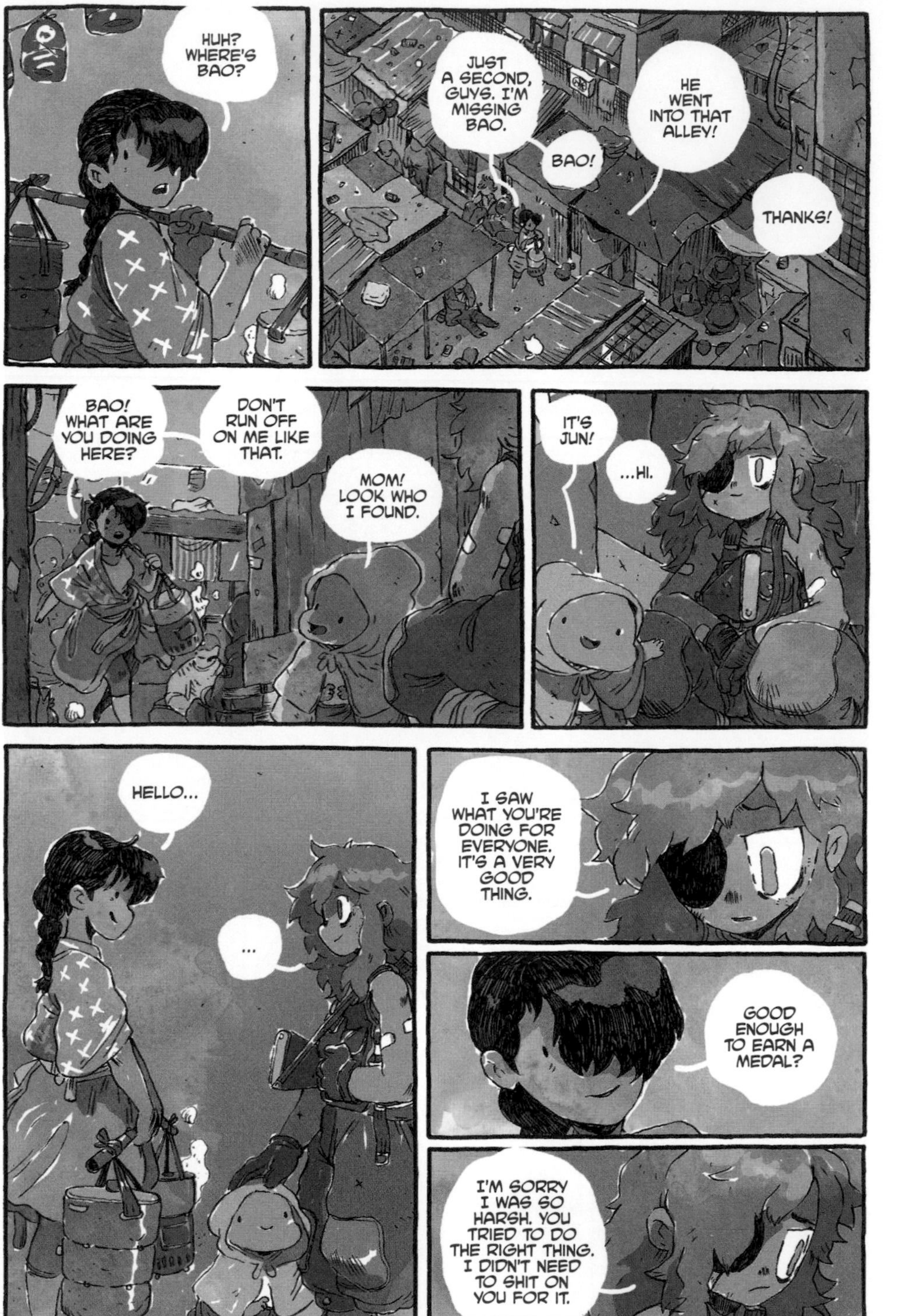
HUH? WHERE'S BAO?
JUST A SECOND, GUYS. I'M MISSING BAO.
BAO!
HE WENT INTO THAT ALLEY!
THANKS!
BAO! WHAT ARE YOU DOING HERE?
DON'T RUN OFF ON ME LIKE THAT.
MOM! LOOK WHO I FOUND.
IT'S JUN!
...HI.
HELLO...
...
I SAW WHAT YOU'RE DOING FOR EVERYONE. IT'S A VERY GOOD THING.
GOOD ENOUGH TO EARN A MEDAL?
I'M SORRY I WAS SO HARSH. YOU TRIED TO DO THE RIGHT THING. I DIDN'T NEED TO SHIT ON YOU FOR IT.

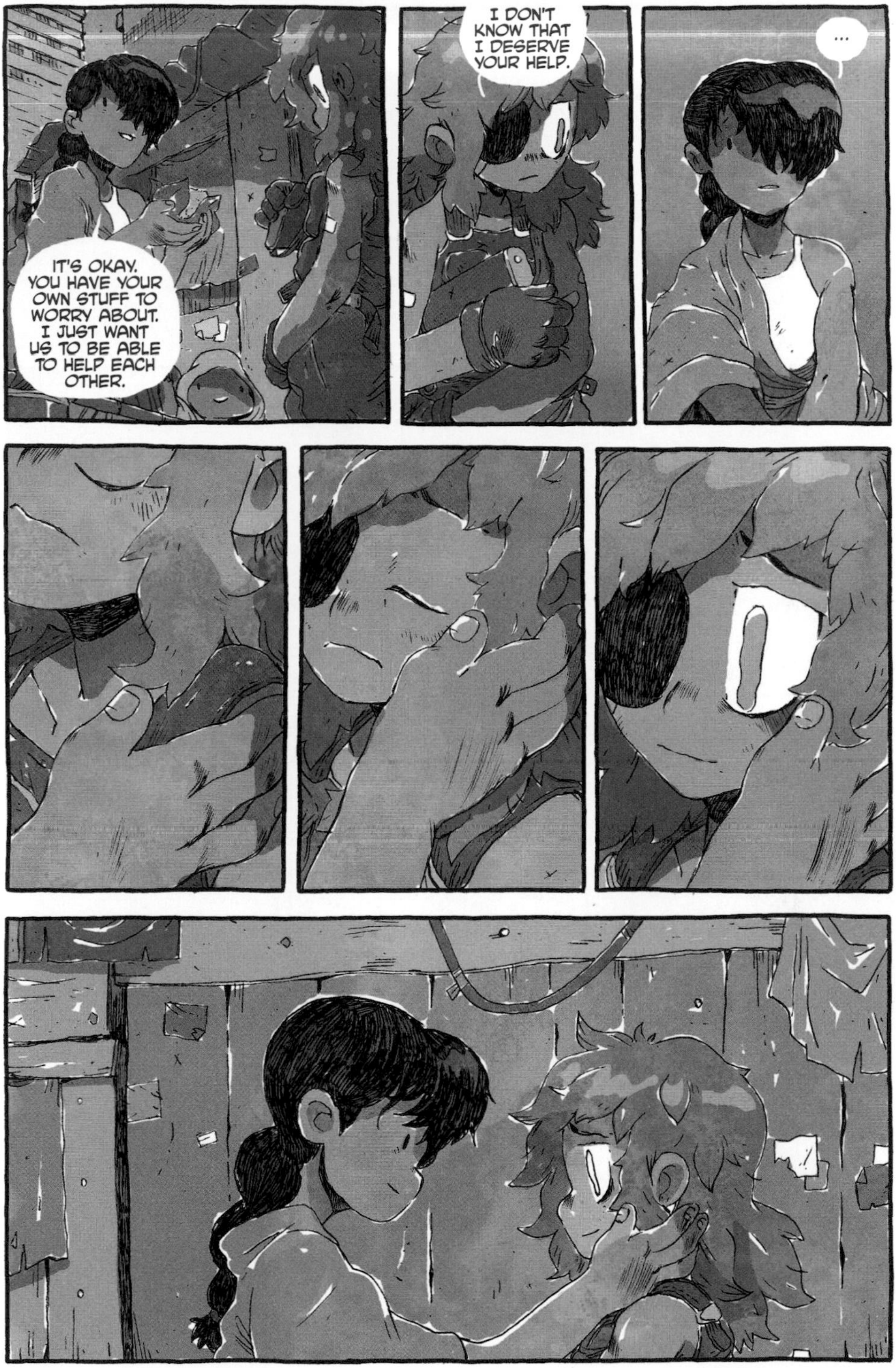
IT'S OKAY. YOU HAVE YOUR OWN STUFF TO WORRY ABOUT. I JUST WANT US TO BE ABLE TO HELP EACH OTHER.
I DON'T KNOW THAT I DESERVE YOUR HELP.
...

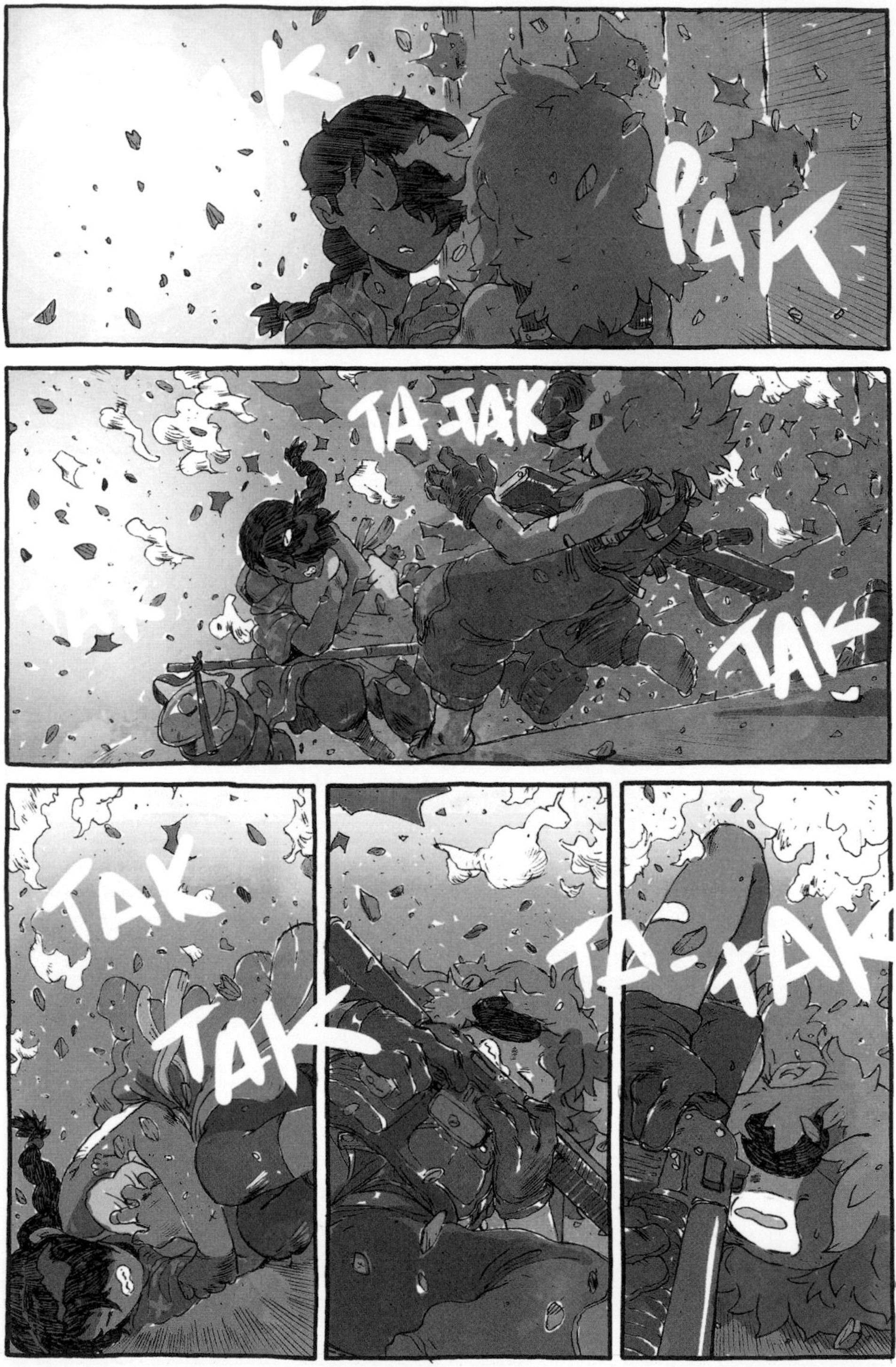
PAK
TA-TAK
TAK
TAK
TAK
TA-TAK

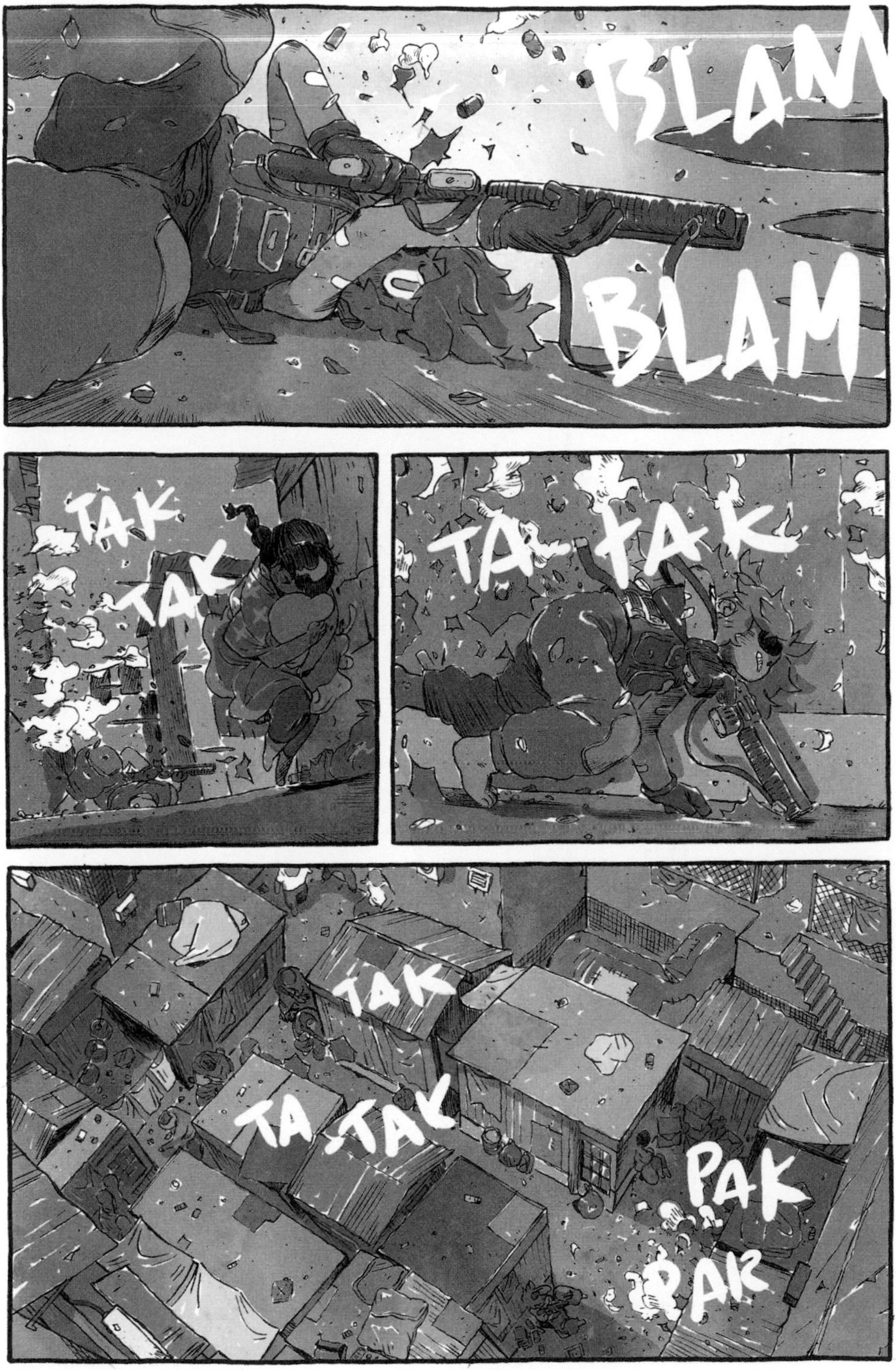
BLAM
BLAM
TAK
TAK
TA-TAK
TAK
TA-TAK
PAK
PAK

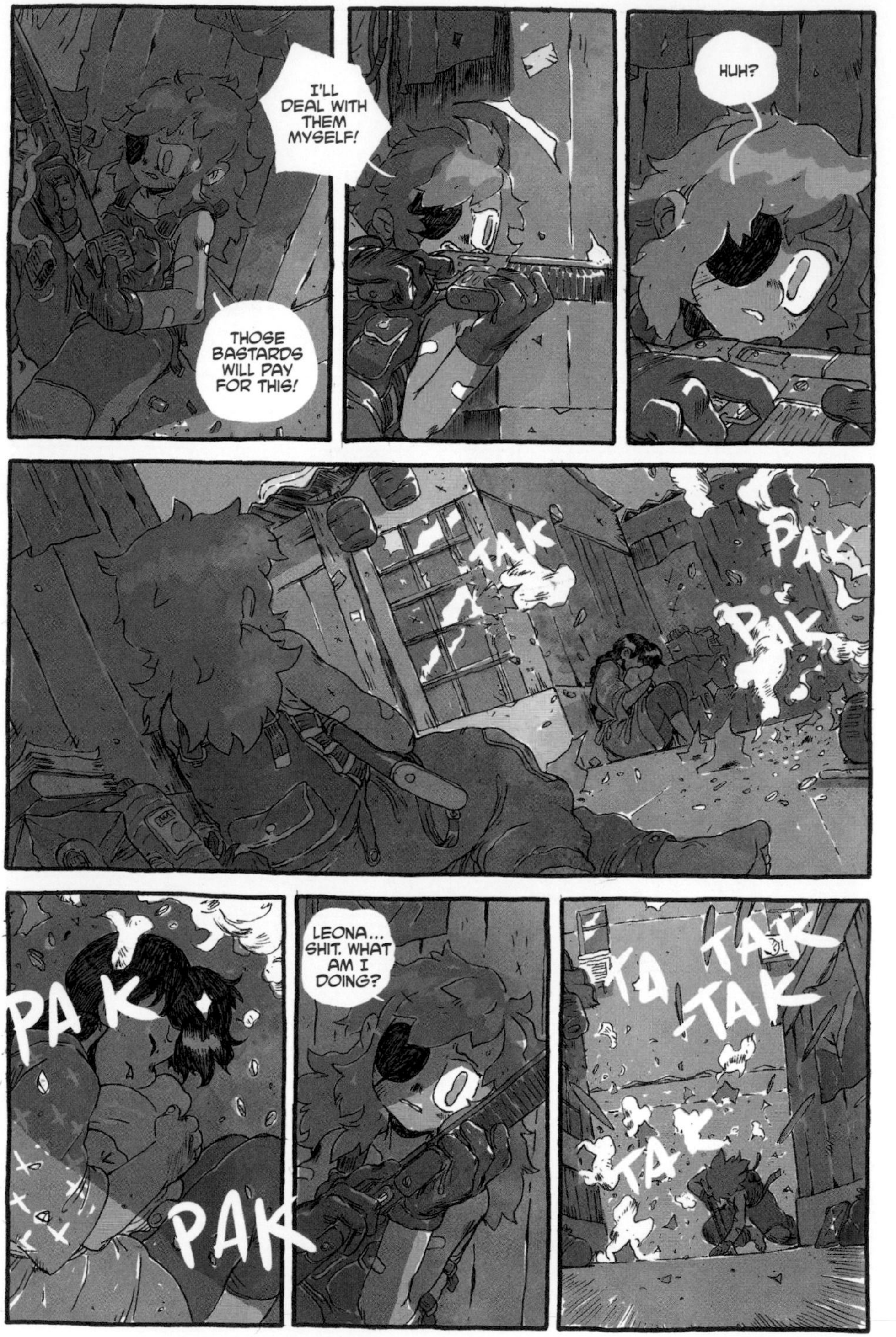
I'LL DEAL WITH THEM MYSELF!
THOSE BASTARDS WILL PAY FOR THIS!
HUH?
TAK
PAK
PAK
PAK
PAK
LEONA... SHIT. WHAT AM I DOING?
TA TAK
TAK
TAK

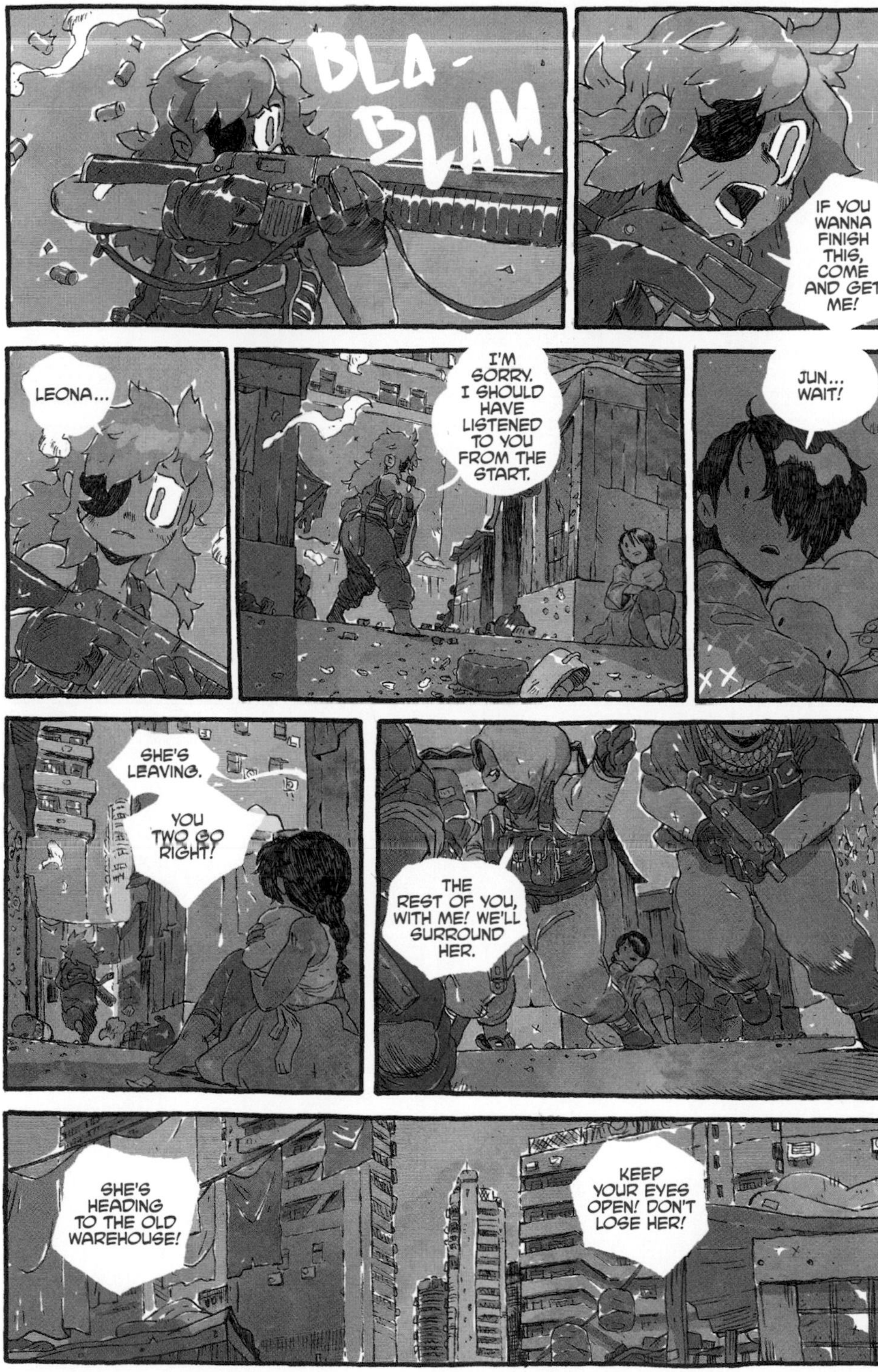
BLA-
BLAM
IF YOU WANNA FINISH THIS, COME AND GET ME!
LEONA...
I'M SORRY. I SHOULD HAVE LISTENED TO YOU FROM THE START.
JUN... WAIT!
SHE'S LEAVING.
YOU TWO GO RIGHT!
THE REST OF YOU, WITH ME! WE'LL SURROUND HER.
SHE'S HEADING TO THE OLD WAREHOUSE!
KEEP YOUR EYES OPEN! DON'T LOSE HER!

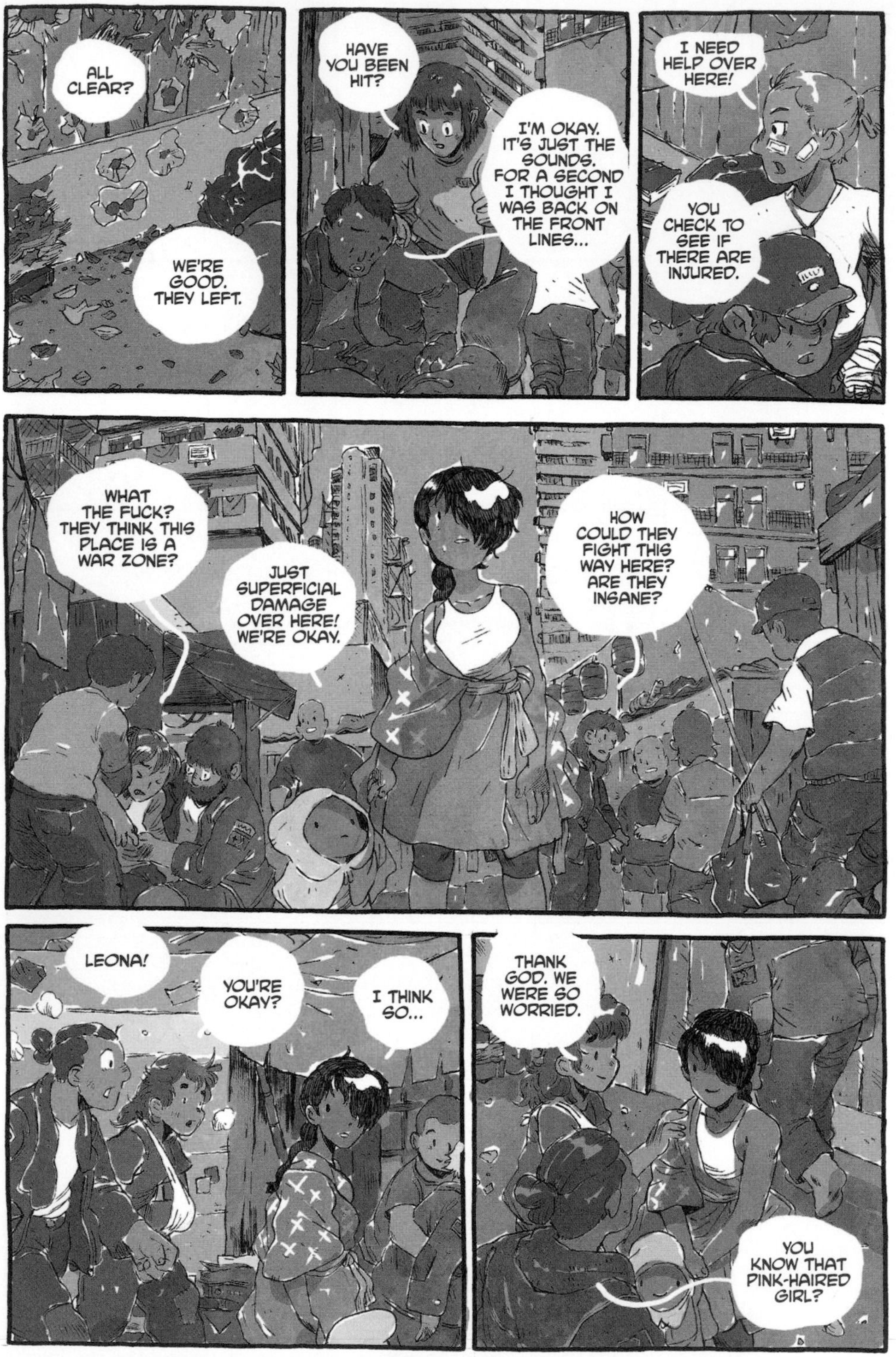
ALL CLEAR?
WE'RE GOOD. THEY LEFT.
HAVE YOU BEEN HIT?
I'M OKAY. IT'S JUST THE SOUNDS. FOR A SECOND I THOUGHT I WAS BACK ON THE FRONT LINES...
I NEED HELP OVER HERE!
YOU CHECK TO SEE IF THERE ARE INJURED.
WHAT THE FUCK? THEY THINK THIS PLACE IS A WAR ZONE?
JUST SUPERFICIAL DAMAGE OVER HERE! WE'RE OKAY.
HOW COULD THEY FIGHT THIS WAY HERE? ARE THEY INSANE?
LEONA!
YOU'RE OKAY?
I THINK SO...
THANK GOD. WE WERE SO WORRIED.
YOU KNOW THAT PINK-HAIRED GIRL?

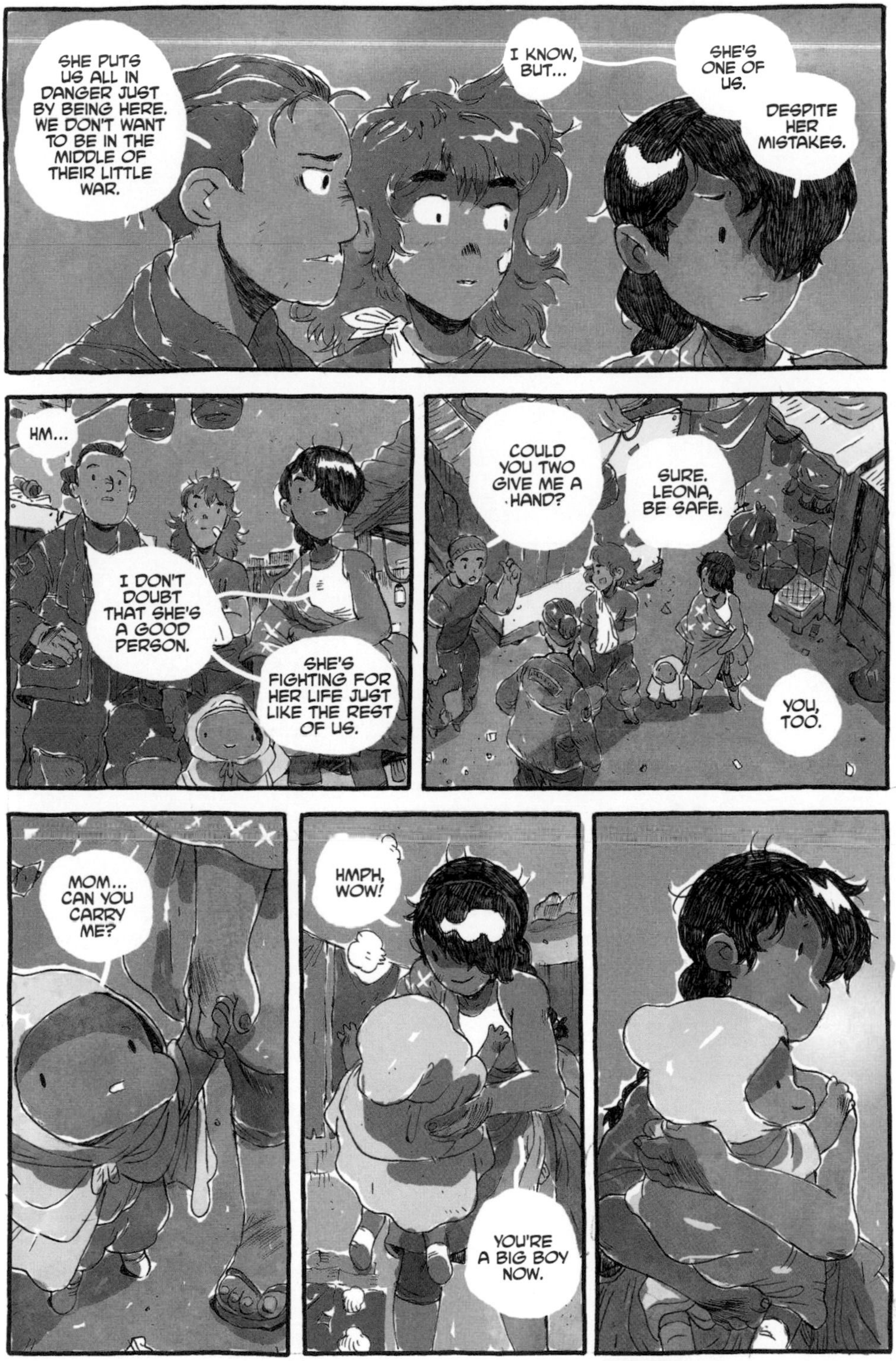
SHE PUTS US ALL IN DANGER JUST BY BEING HERE. WE DON'T WANT TO BE IN THE MIDDLE OF THEIR LITTLE WAR.
I KNOW, BUT...
SHE'S ONE OF US.
DESPITE HER MISTAKES.
HM...
I DON'T DOUBT THAT SHE'S A GOOD PERSON.
SHE'S FIGHTING FOR HER LIFE JUST LIKE THE REST OF US.
COULD YOU TWO GIVE ME A HAND?
SURE. LEONA, BE SAFE.
YOU, TOO.
MOM... CAN YOU CARRY ME?
HMPH, WOW!
YOU'RE A BIG BOY NOW.

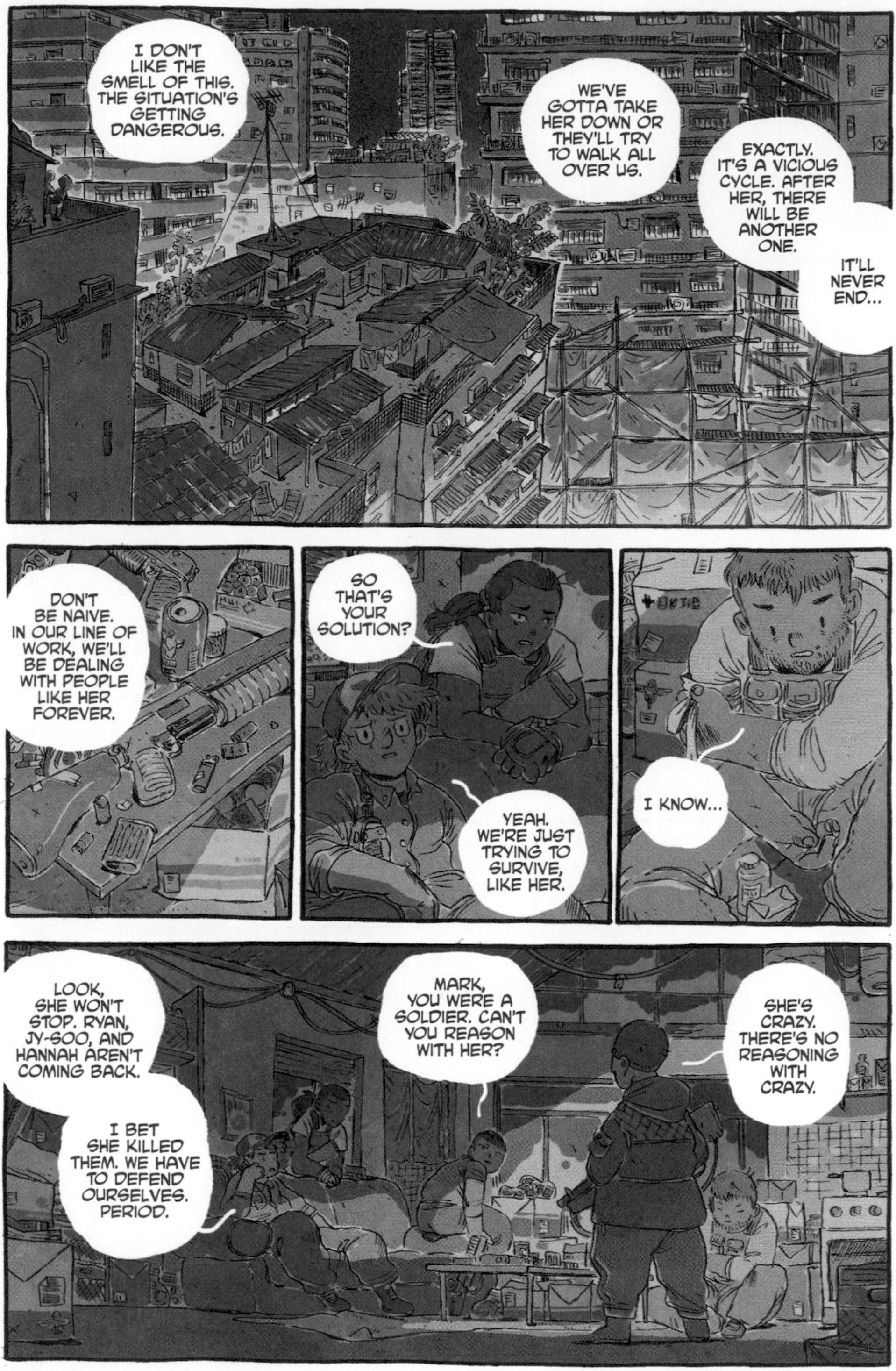
I DON'T LIKE THE SMELL OF THIS. THE SITUATION'S GETTING DANGEROUS.
WE'VE GOTTA TAKE HER DOWN OR THEY'LL TRY TO WALK ALL OVER US.
EXACTLY. IT'S A VICIOUS CYCLE. AFTER HER, THERE WILL BE ANOTHER ONE.
IT'LL NEVER END...
DON'T BE NAIVE. IN OUR LINE OF WORK, WE'LL BE DEALING WITH PEOPLE LIKE HER FOREVER.
SO THAT'S YOUR SOLUTION?
YEAH. WE'RE JUST TRYING TO SURVIVE, LIKE HER.
I KNOW...
LOOK, SHE WON'T STOP. RYAN, JY-SOO, AND HANNAH AREN'T COMING BACK.
I BET SHE KILLED THEM. WE HAVE TO DEFEND OURSELVES. PERIOD.
MARK, YOU WERE A SOLDIER. CAN'T YOU REASON WITH HER?
SHE'S CRAZY. THERE'S NO REASONING WITH CRAZY.

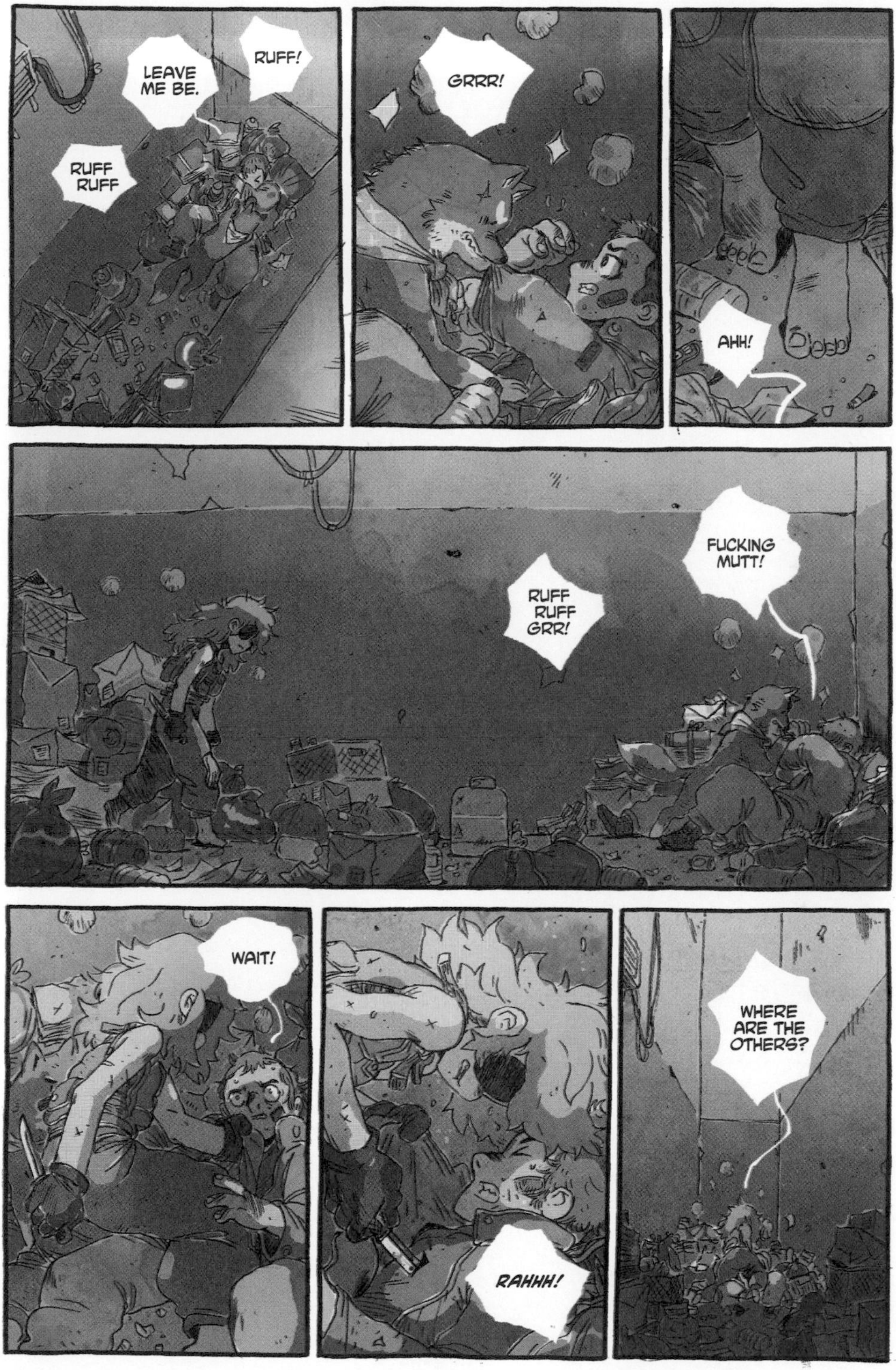
LEAVE ME BE.
RUFF!
RUFF RUFF
GRRR!
AHH!
RUFF RUFF GRR!
FUCKING MUTT!
WAIT!
RAHHH!
WHERE ARE THE OTHERS?

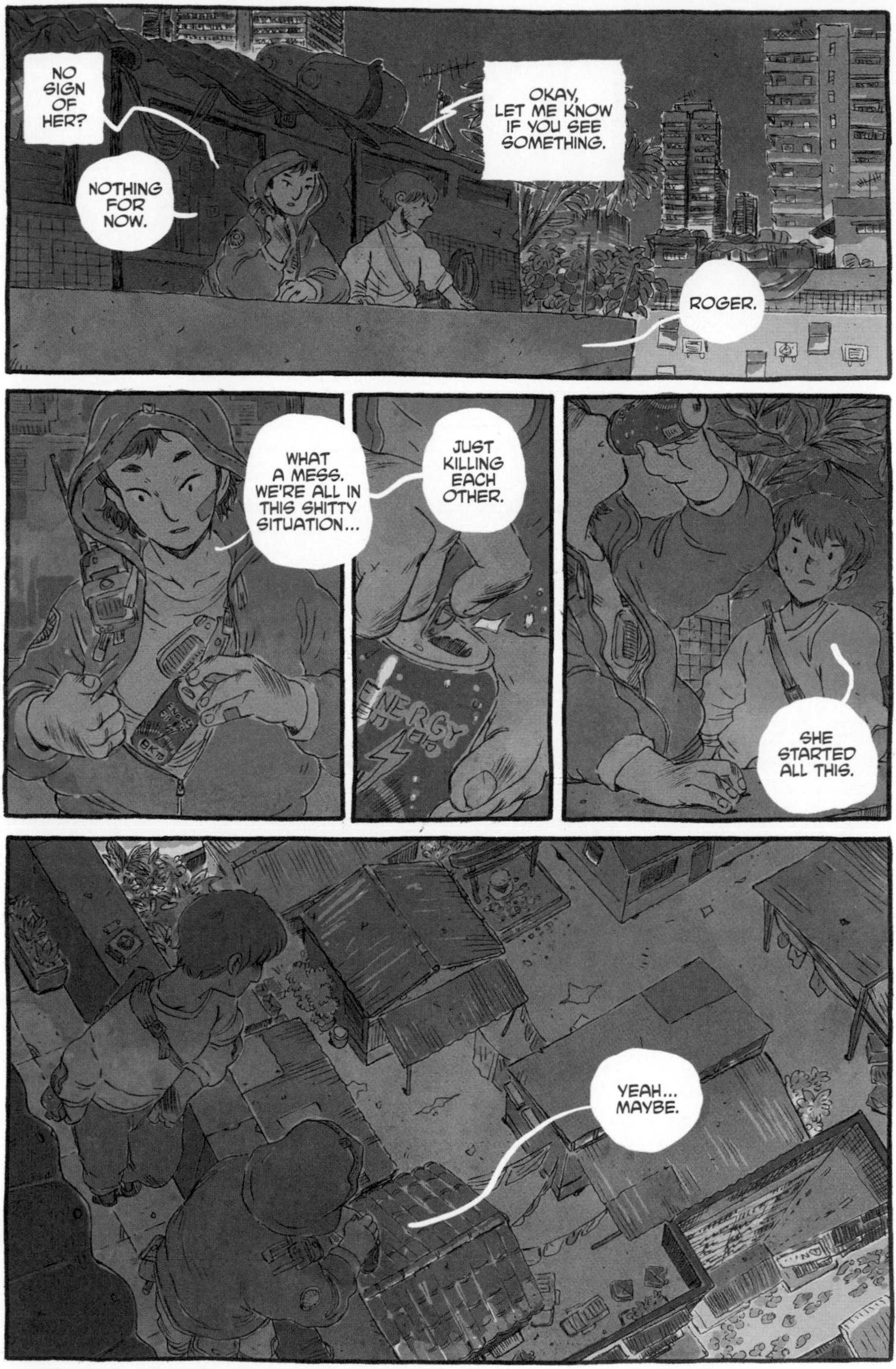
NO SIGN OF HER?
NOTHING FOR NOW.
OKAY, LET ME KNOW IF YOU SEE SOMETHING.
ROGER.
WHAT A MESS. WE'RE ALL IN THIS SHITTY SITUATION...
JUST KILLING EACH OTHER.
SHE STARTED ALL THIS.
YEAH... MAYBE.

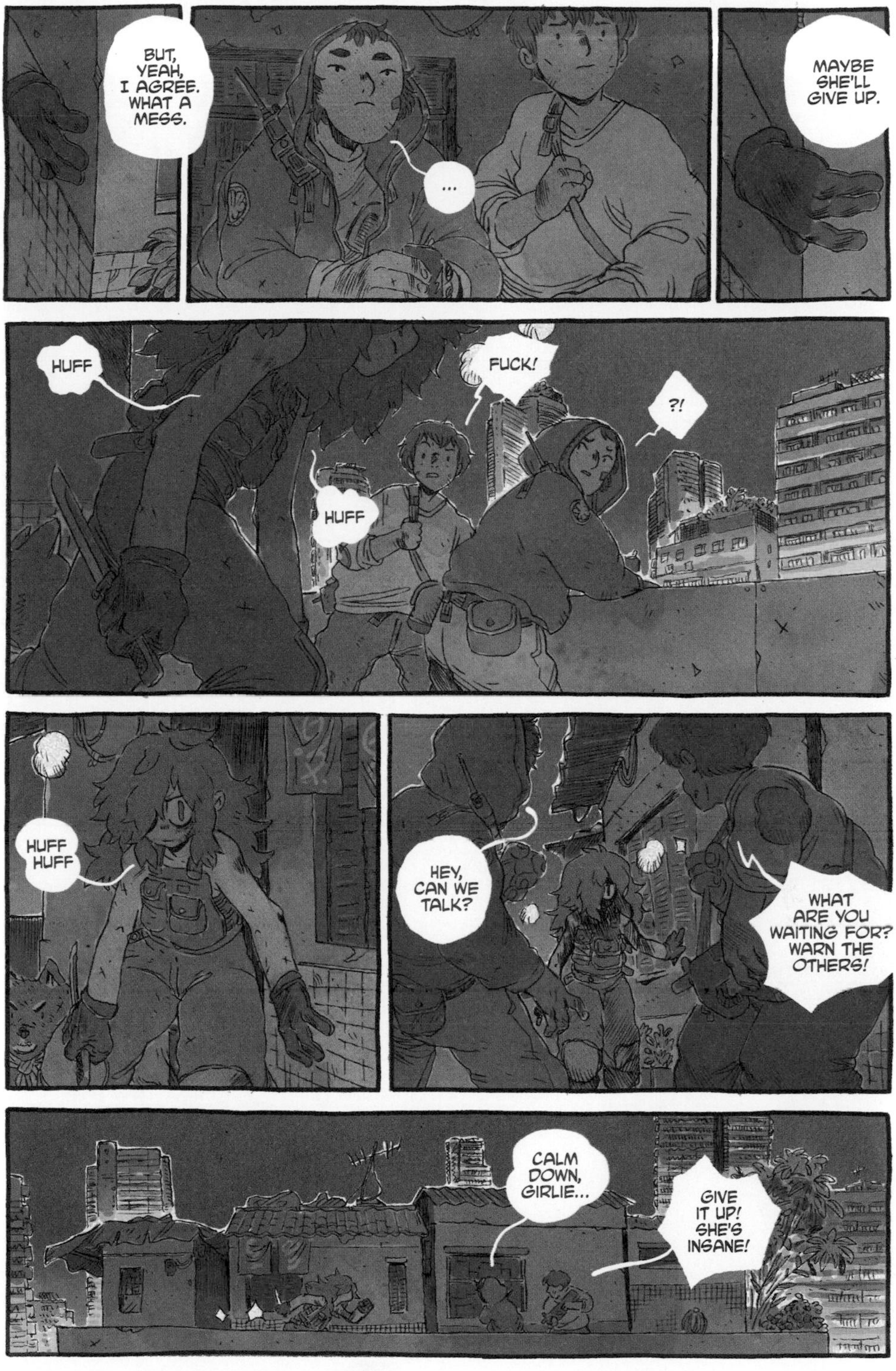
BUT, YEAH, I AGREE. WHAT A MESS.
...
MAYBE SHE'LL GIVE UP.
HUFF
FUCK!
?!
HUFF
HUFF HUFF
HEY, CAN WE TALK?
WHAT ARE YOU WAITING FOR? WARN THE OTHERS!
CALM DOWN, GIRLIE...
GIVE IT UP! SHE'S INSANE!

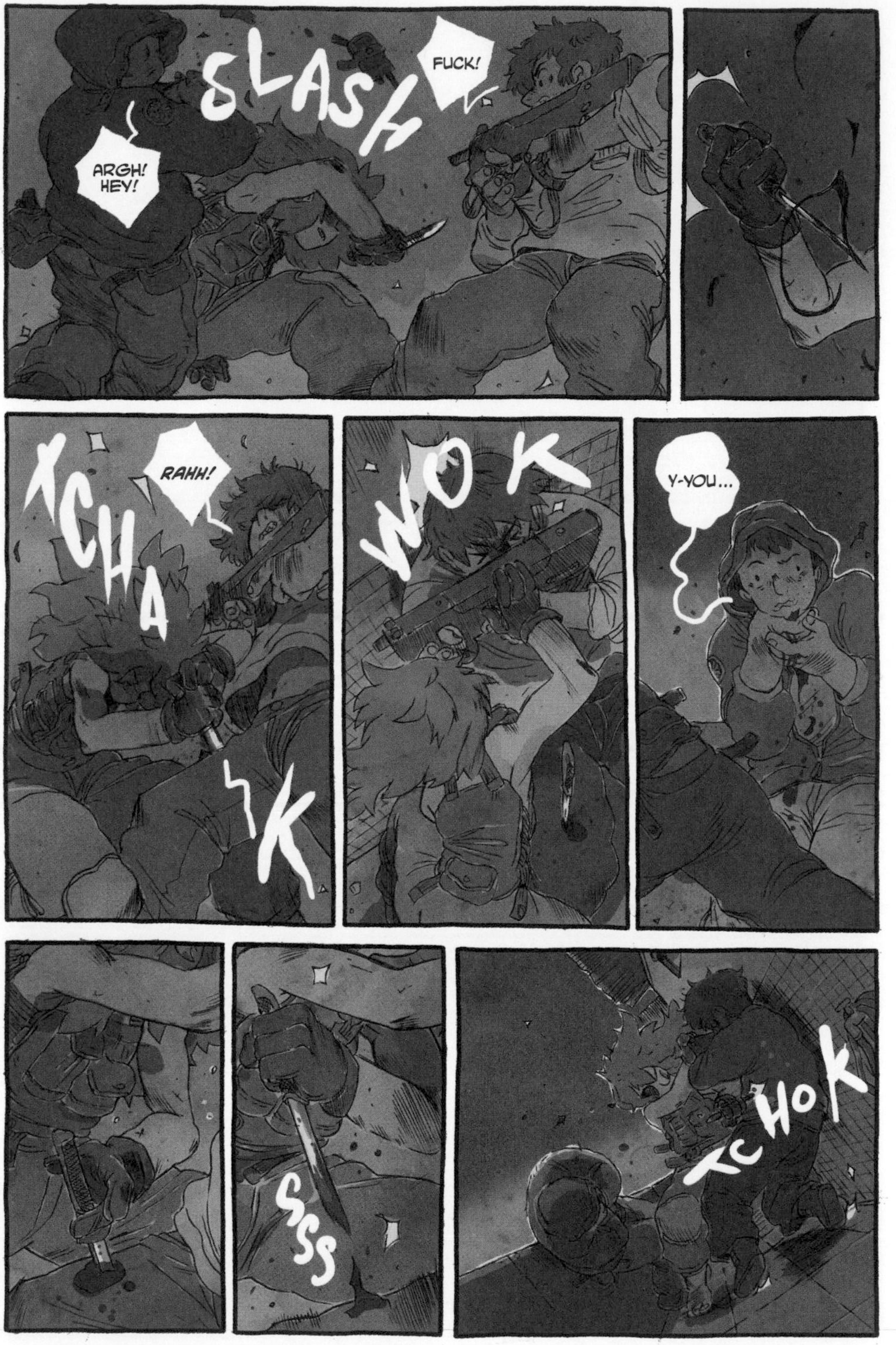
ARGH! HEY!
SLASH
FUCK!
RAHH!
XCHA
SHK
WOK
Y-YOU...
SSS
TCHOK

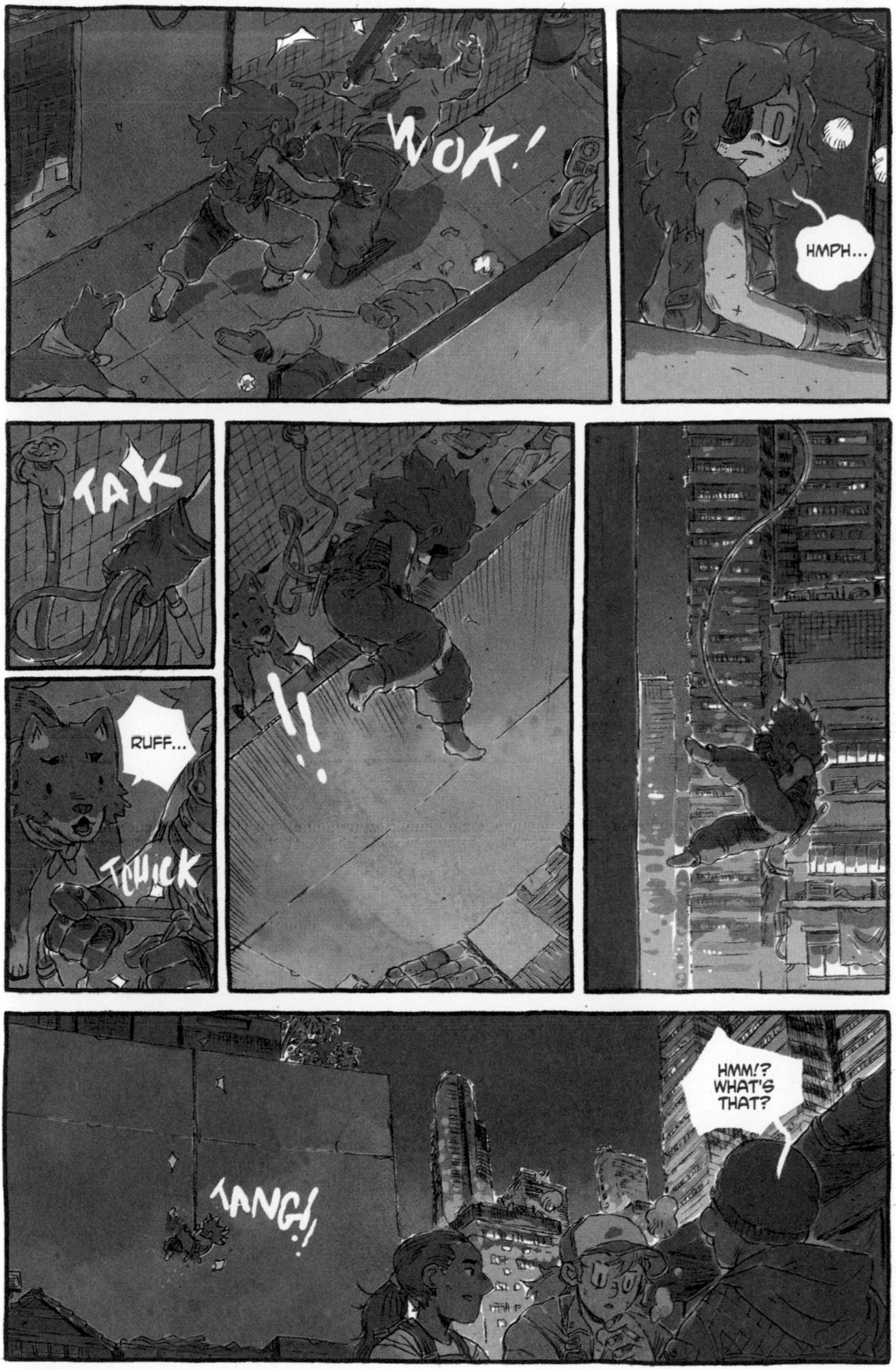
WOK!
HMPH...
TAK
RUFF...
TCHICK
!!
TANG!!
HMM!? WHAT'S THAT?

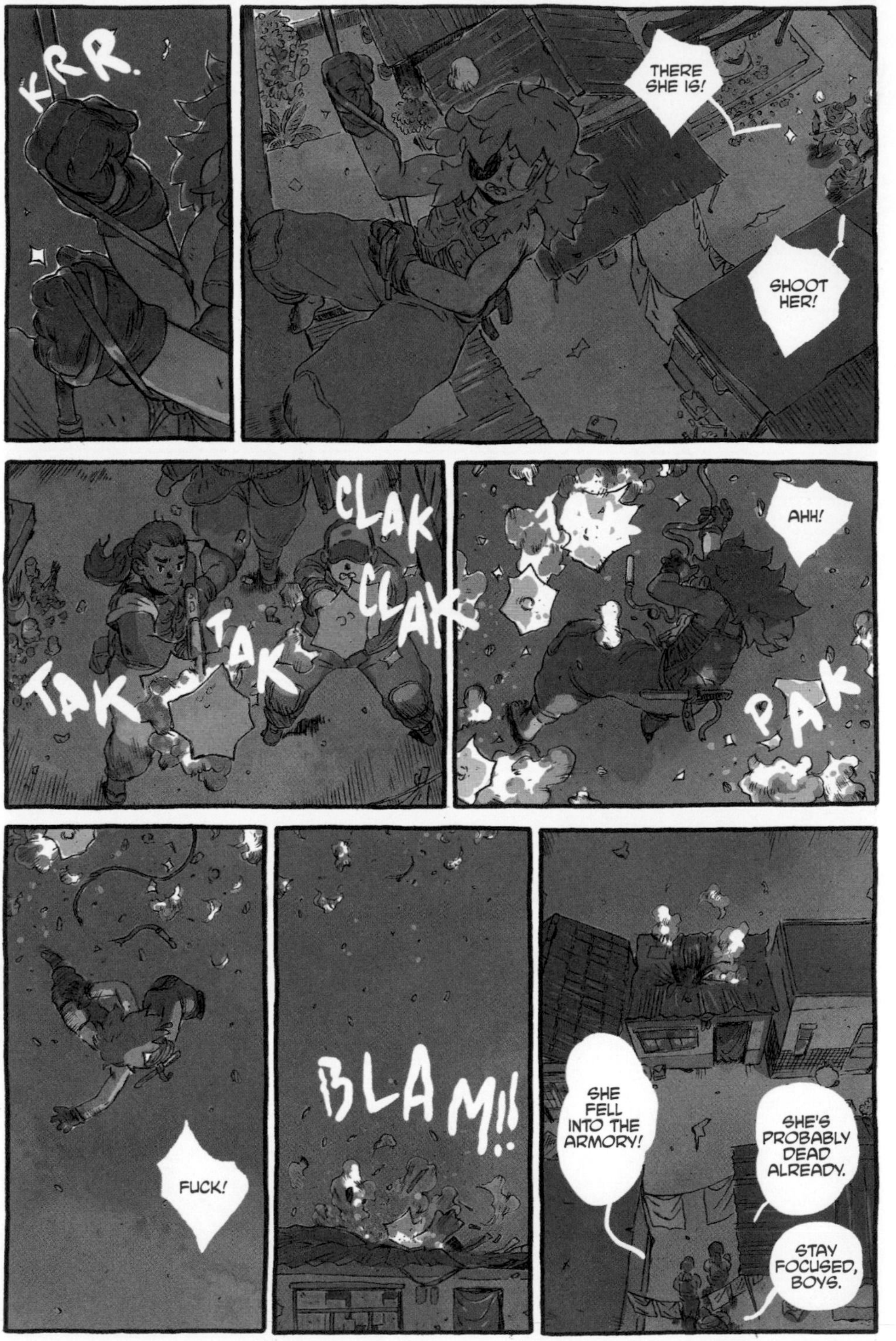

KRR.
THERE SHE IS!
SHOOT HER!
CLAK
CLAK
TAK
TAK
AHH!
PAK
FUCK!
BLAM!!
SHE FELL INTO THE ARMORY!
SHE'S PROBABLY DEAD ALREADY.
STAY FOCUSED, BOYS.

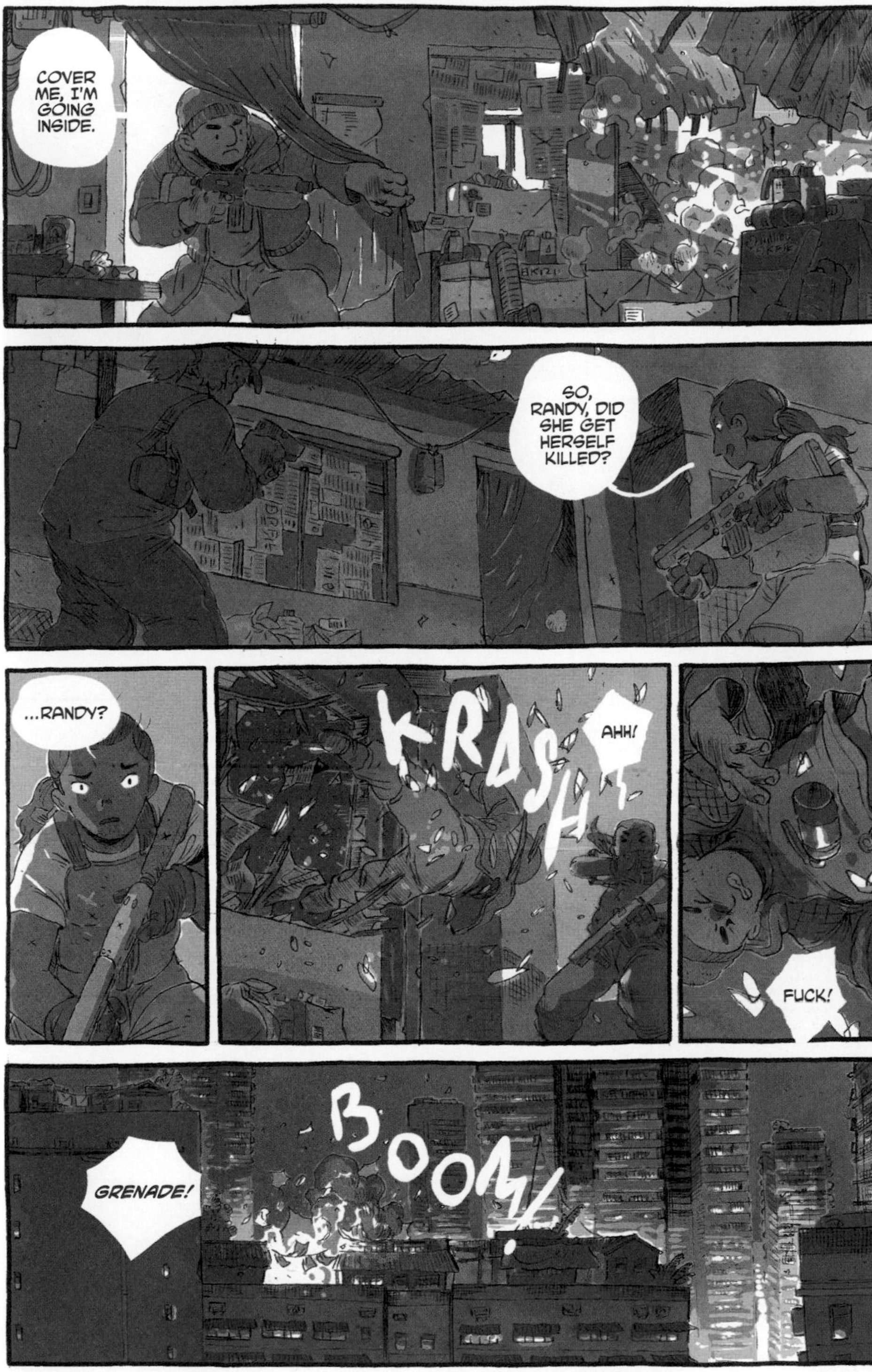
COVER ME, I'M GOING INSIDE.
SO, RANDY, DID SHE GET HERSELF KILLED?
...RANDY?
KRASH!
AHH!
FUCK!
GRENADE!
BOOM!

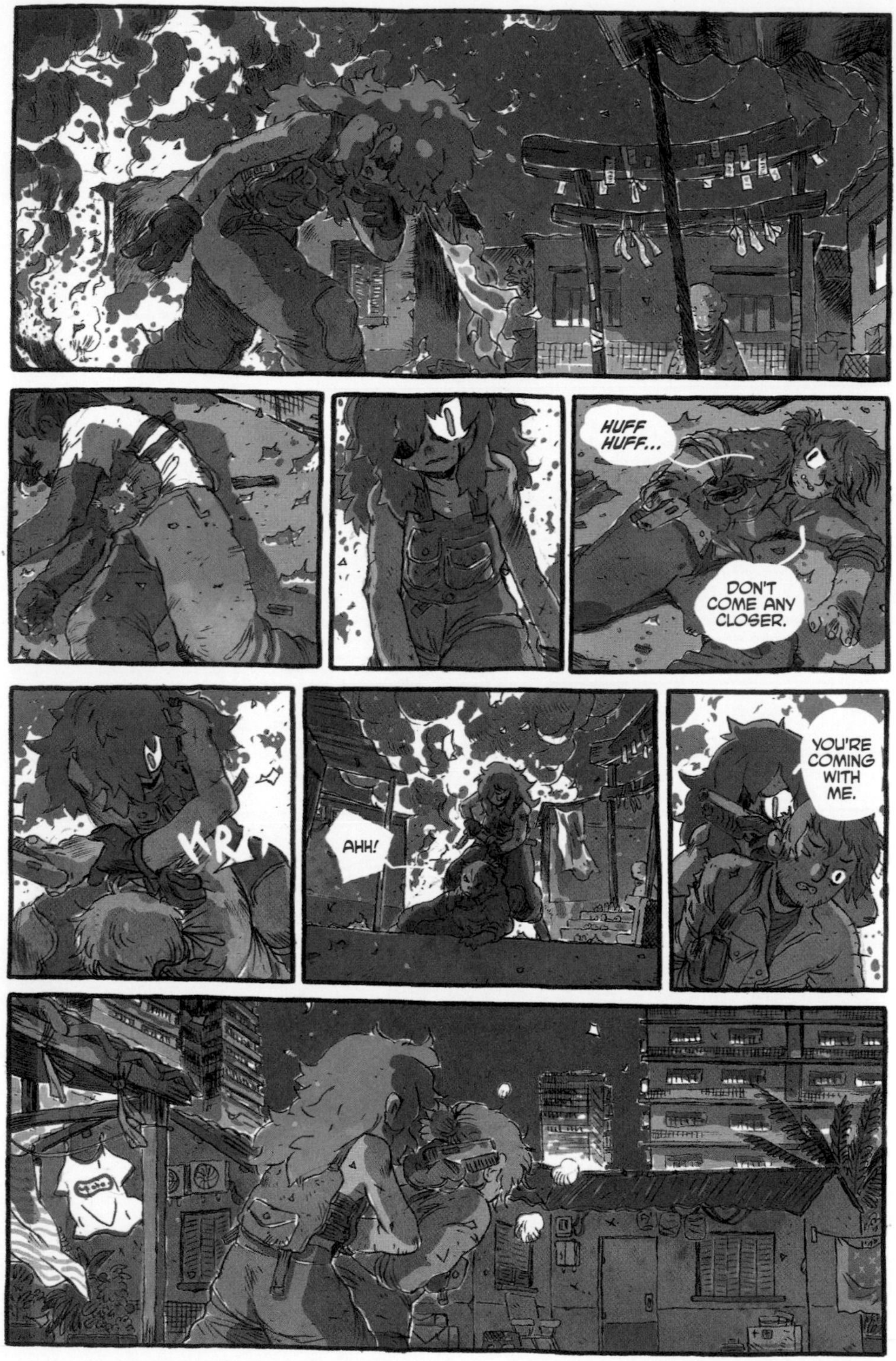
HUFF HUFF...
DON'T COME ANY CLOSER.
KR
AHH!
YOU'RE COMING WITH ME.

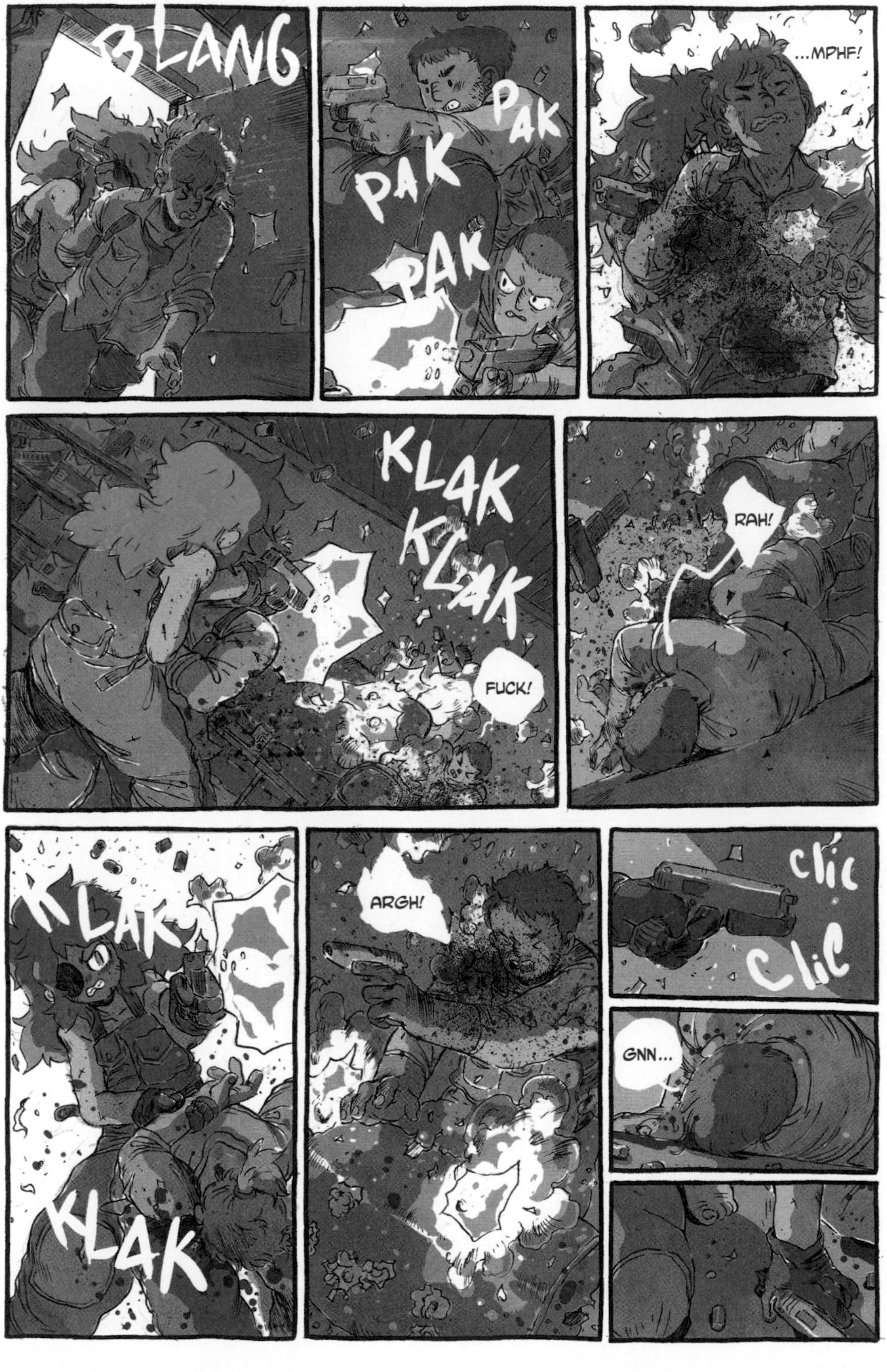
BLANG
PAK
PAK
PAK
PAK
...MPHF!
KLAK
KLAK
KLAK
FUCK!
RAH!
KLAK
KLAK
ARGH!
CLIC
CLIC
GNN...

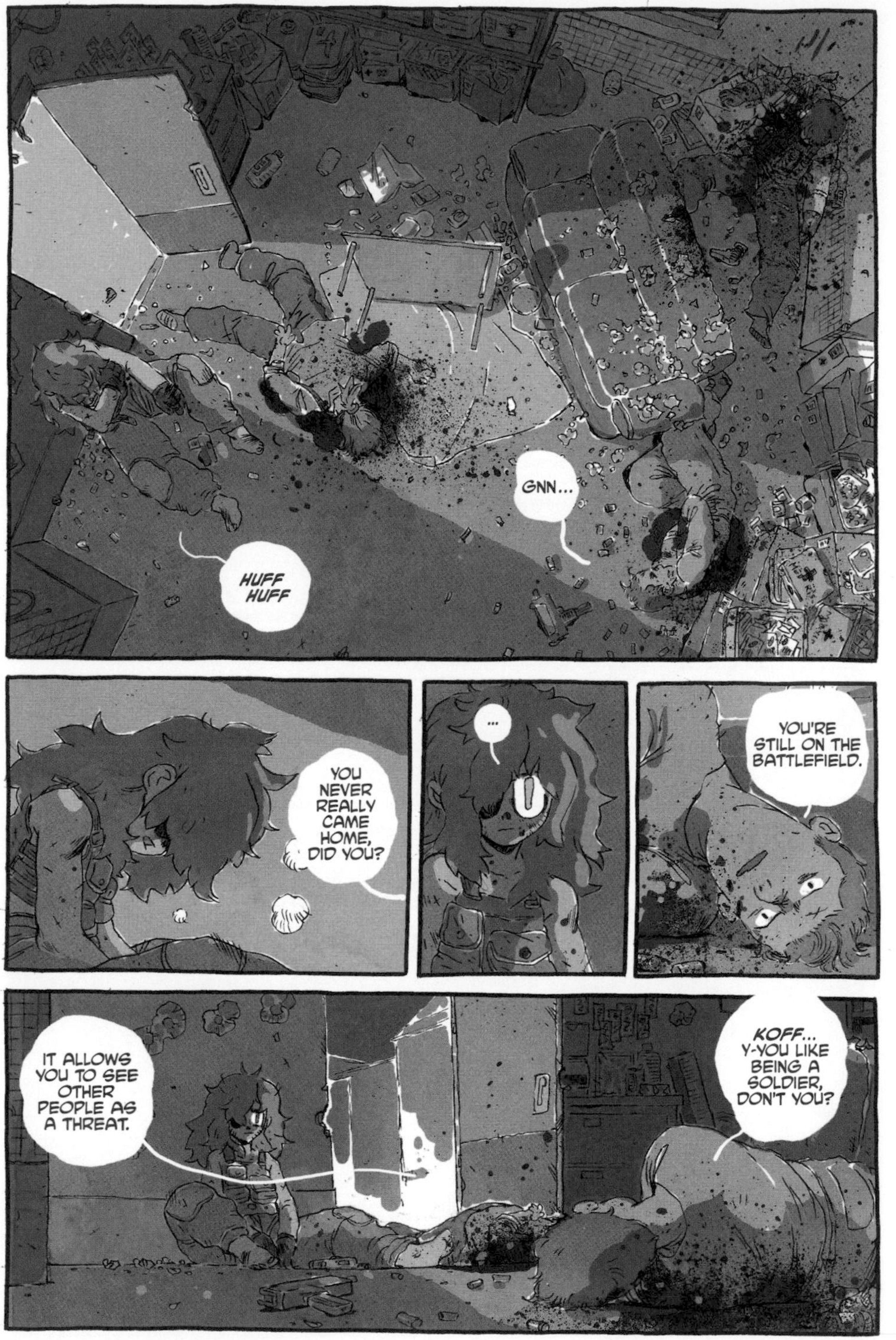
GNN...
HUFF HUFF
...
YOU NEVER REALLY CAME HOME, DID YOU?
YOU'RE STILL ON THE BATTLEFIELD.
KOFF... Y-YOU LIKE BEING A SOLDIER, DON'T YOU?
IT ALLOWS YOU TO SEE OTHER PEOPLE AS A THREAT.

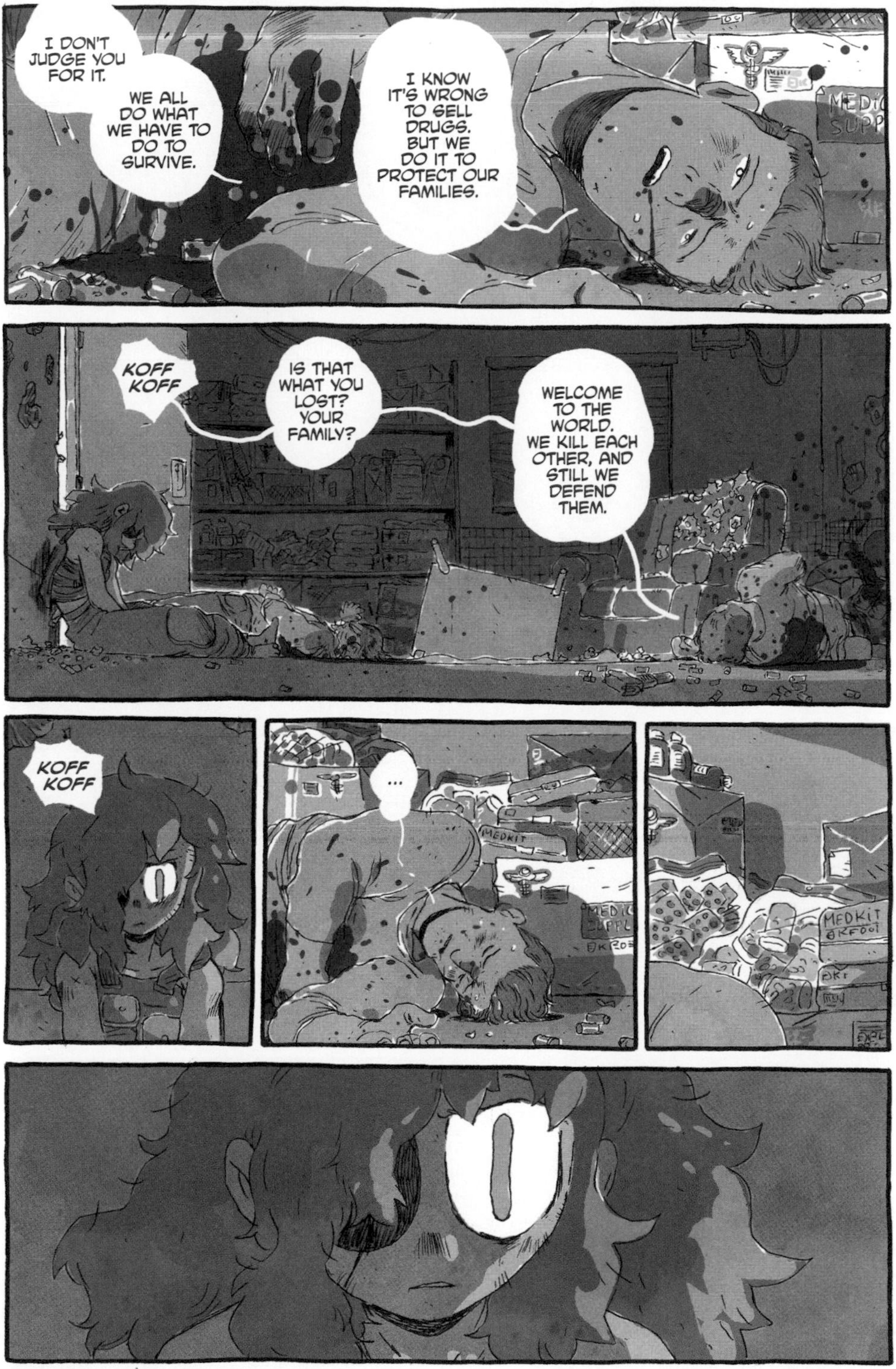
I DON'T JUDGE YOU FOR IT.
WE ALL DO WHAT WE HAVE TO DO TO SURVIVE.
I KNOW IT'S WRONG TO SELL DRUGS. BUT WE DO IT TO PROTECT OUR FAMILIES.
KOFF KOFF
IS THAT WHAT YOU LOST? YOUR FAMILY?
WELCOME TO THE WORLD. WE KILL EACH OTHER, AND STILL WE DEFEND THEM.
KOFF KOFF
...
MEDKIT
MEDKIT

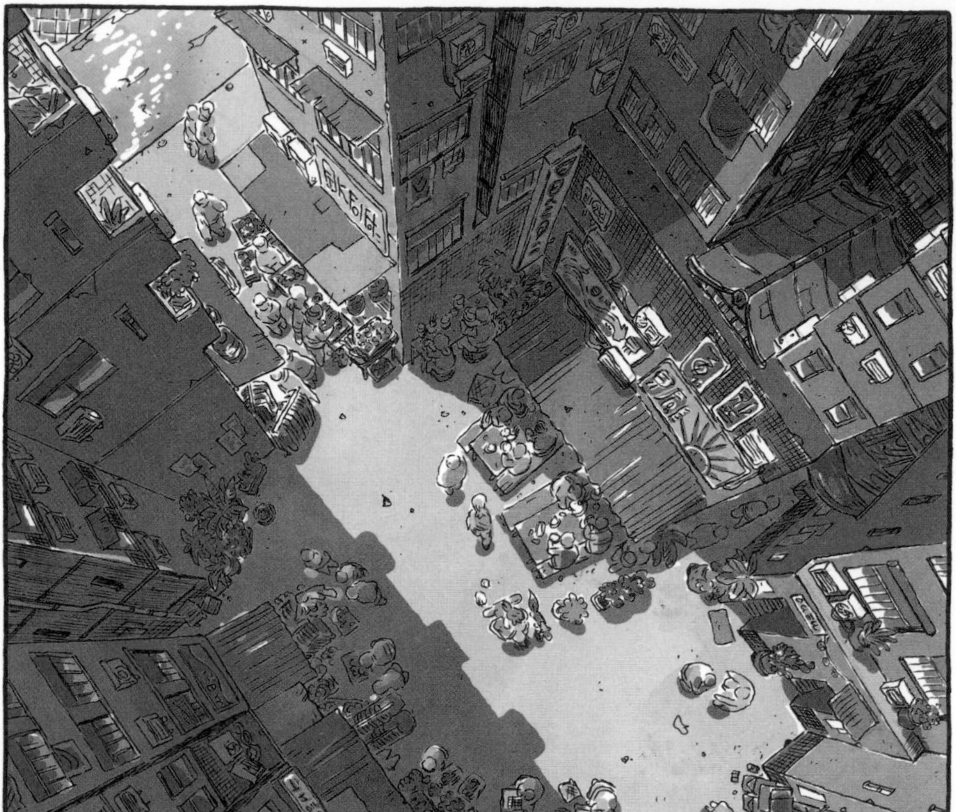

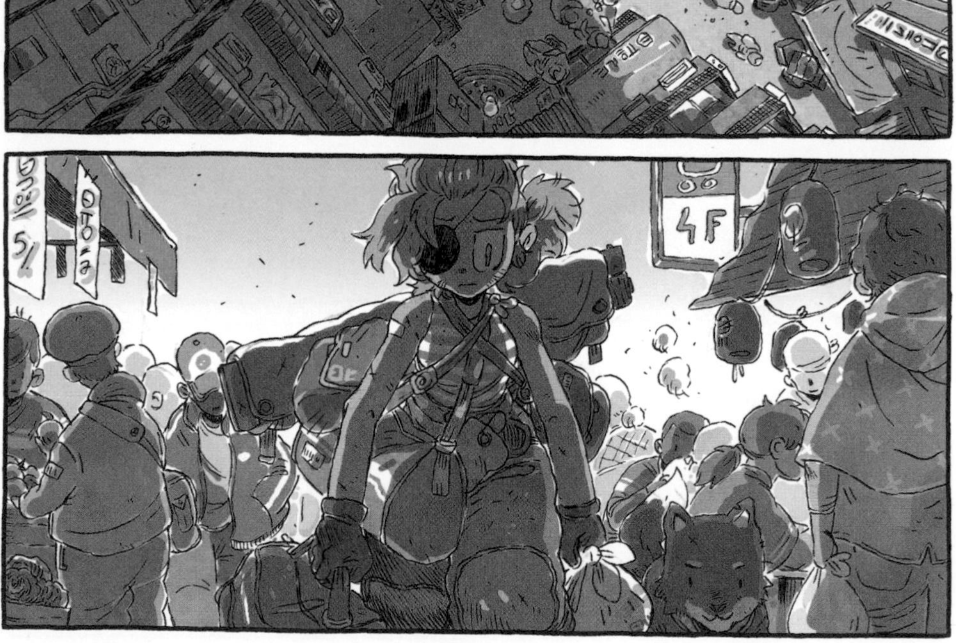
4F

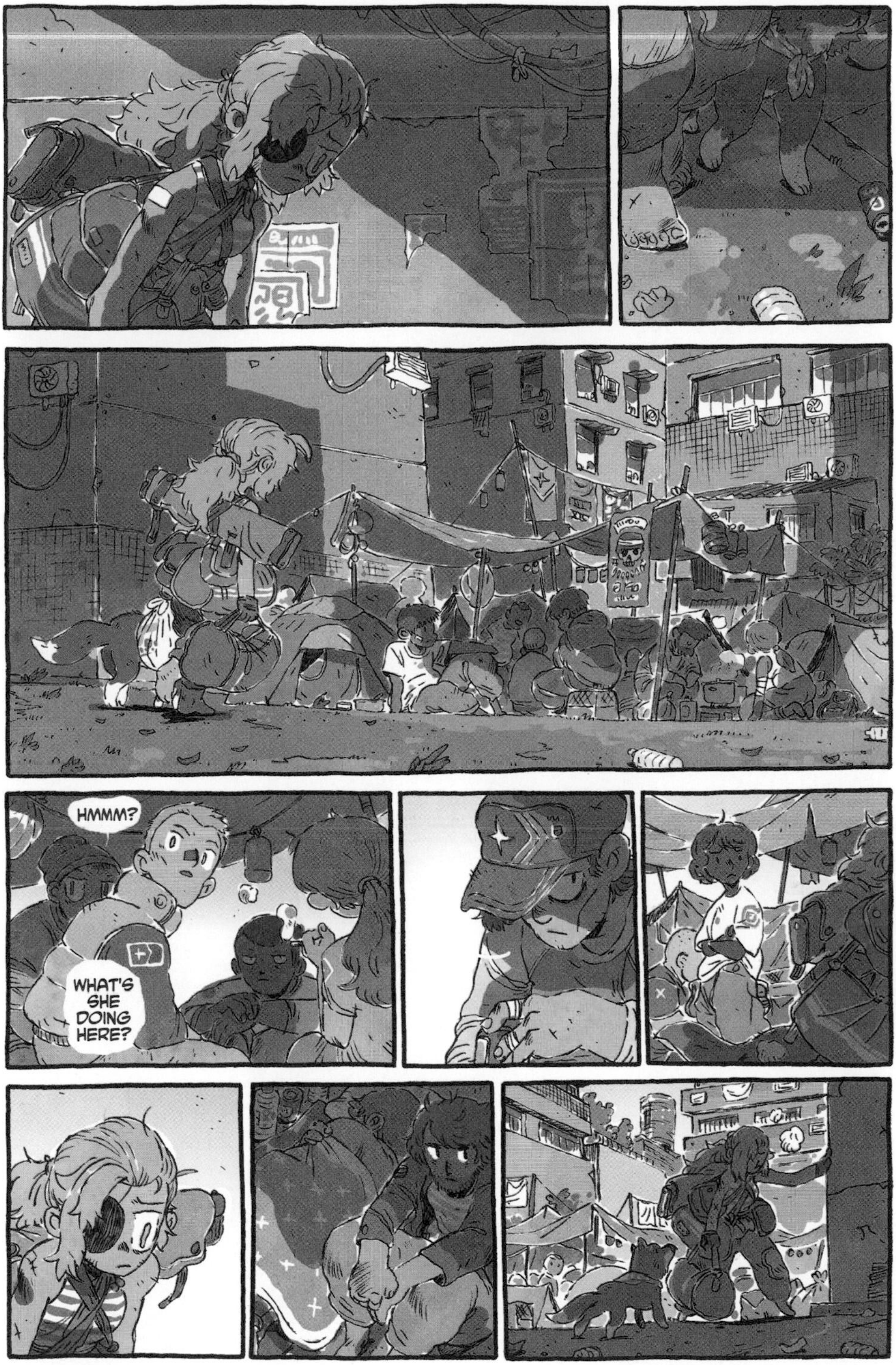
HMMM?
WHAT'S SHE DOING HERE?

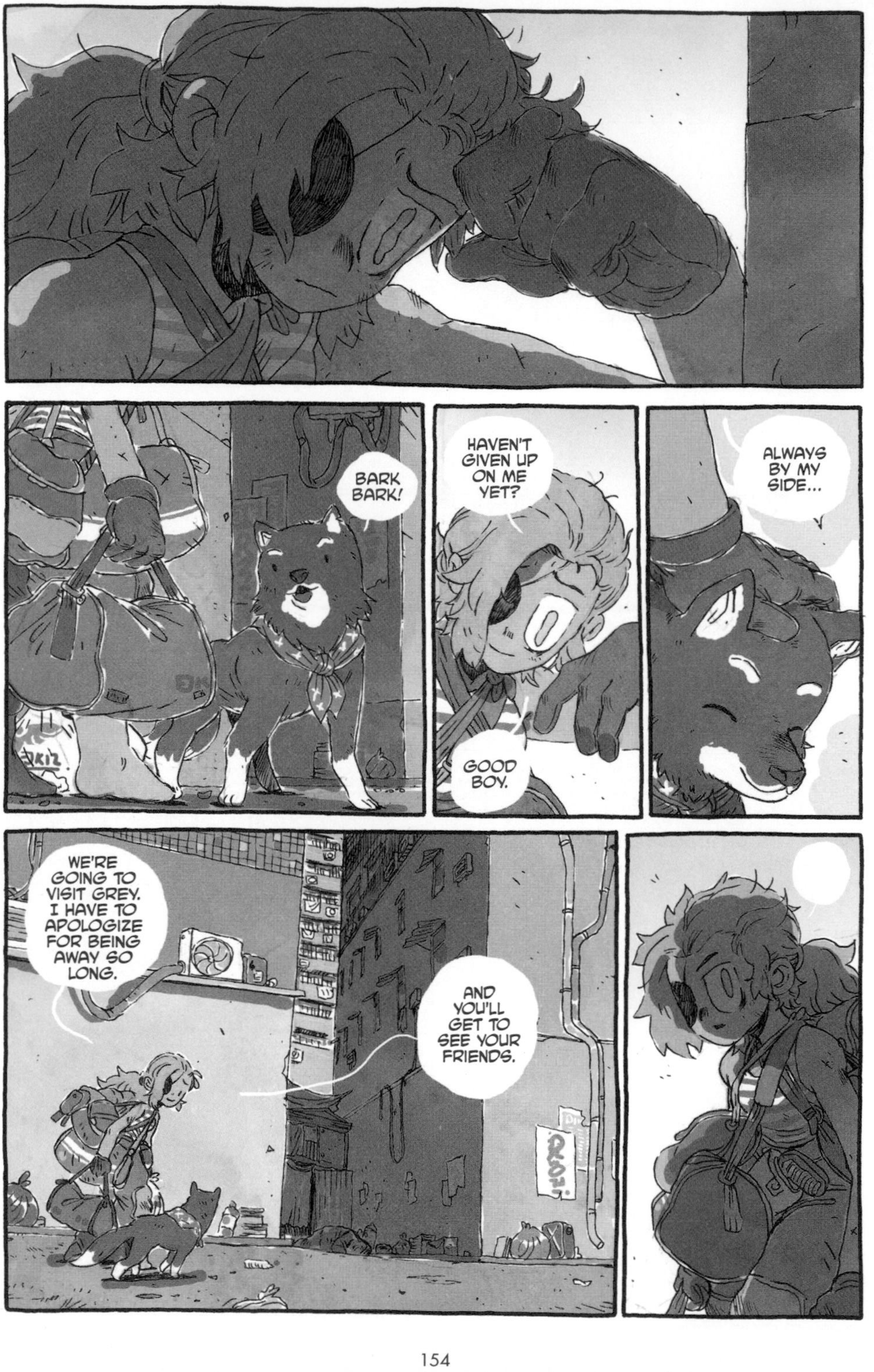

BARK BARK!
HAVEN'T GIVEN UP ON ME YET?
GOOD BOY.
ALWAYS BY MY SIDE...
WE'RE GOING TO VISIT GREY. I HAVE TO APOLOGIZE FOR BEING AWAY SO LONG.
AND YOU'LL GET TO SEE YOUR FRIENDS.

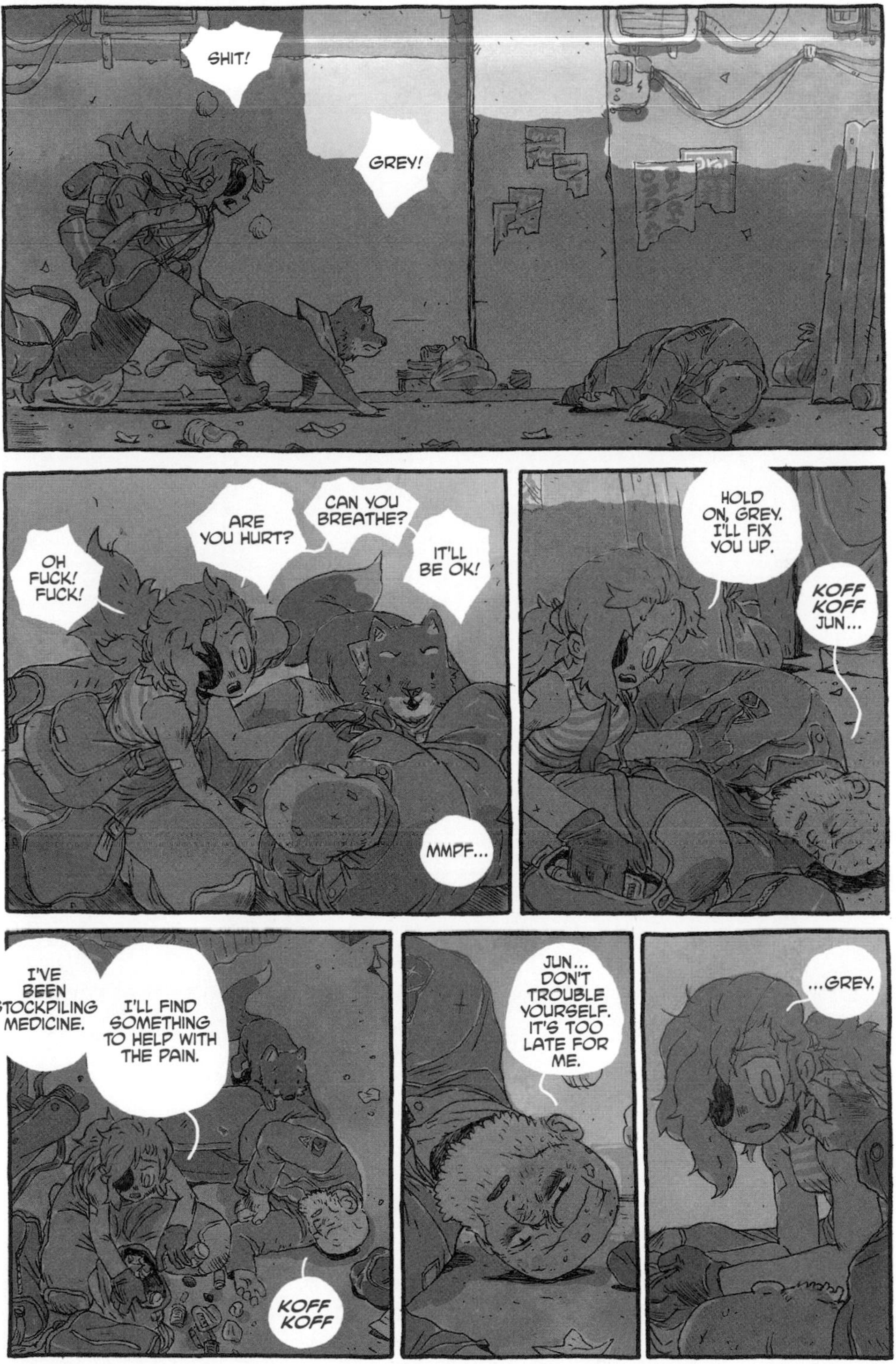
SHIT!
GREY!
OH FUCK! FUCK!
ARE YOU HURT?
CAN YOU BREATHE?
IT'LL BE OK!
MMPF...
HOLD ON, GREY. I'LL FIX YOU UP.
KOFF KOFF JUN...
I'VE BEEN STOCKPILING MEDICINE.
I'LL FIND SOMETHING TO HELP WITH THE PAIN.
KOFF KOFF
JUN... DON'T TROUBLE YOURSELF. IT'S TOO LATE FOR ME.
...GREY.

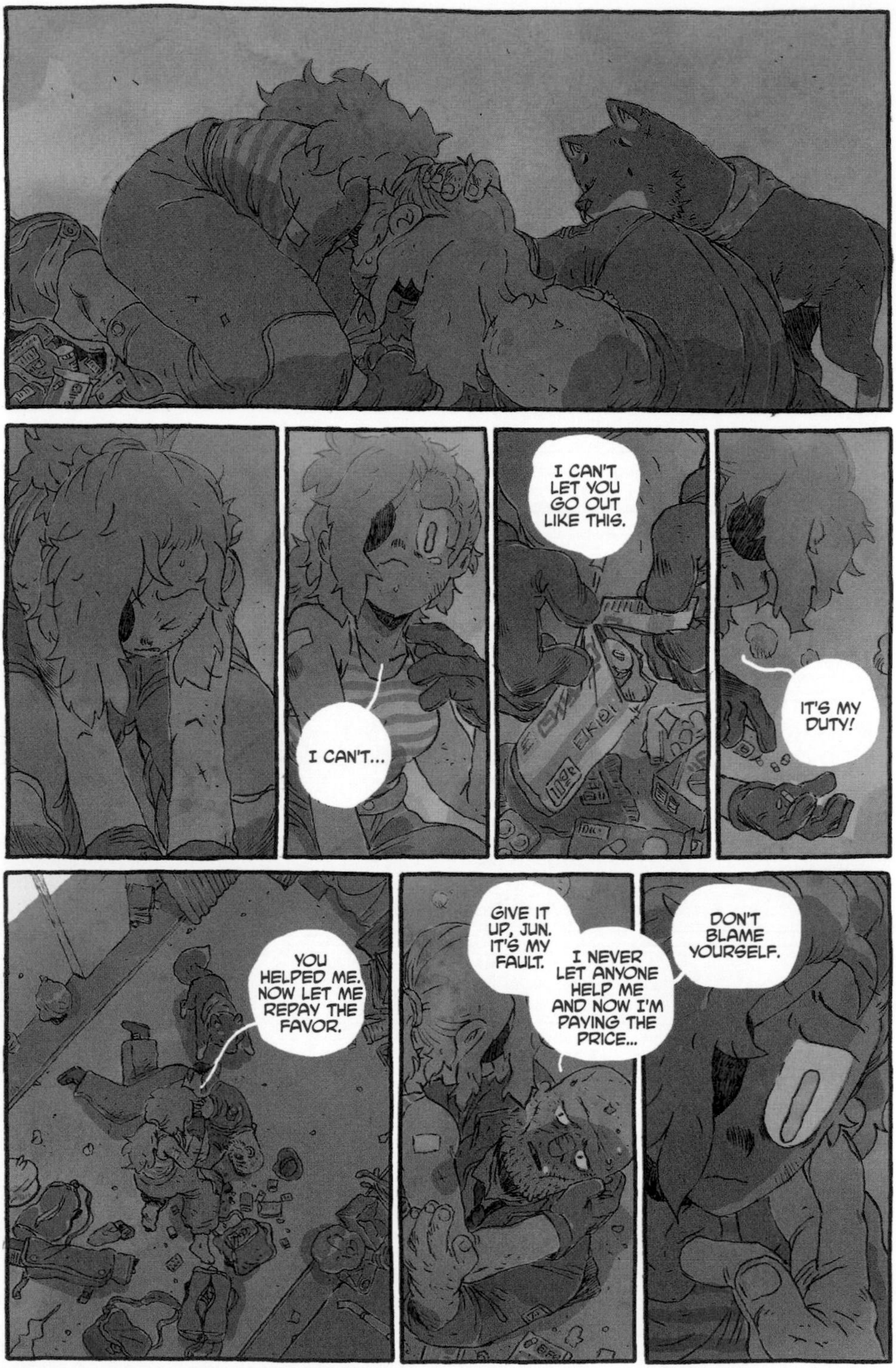
I CAN'T...
I CAN'T LET YOU GO OUT LIKE THIS.
IT'S MY DUTY!
YOU HELPED ME. NOW LET ME REPAY THE FAVOR.
GIVE IT UP, JUN. IT'S MY FAULT.
I NEVER LET ANYONE HELP ME AND NOW I'M PAYING THE PRICE...
DON'T BLAME YOURSELF.

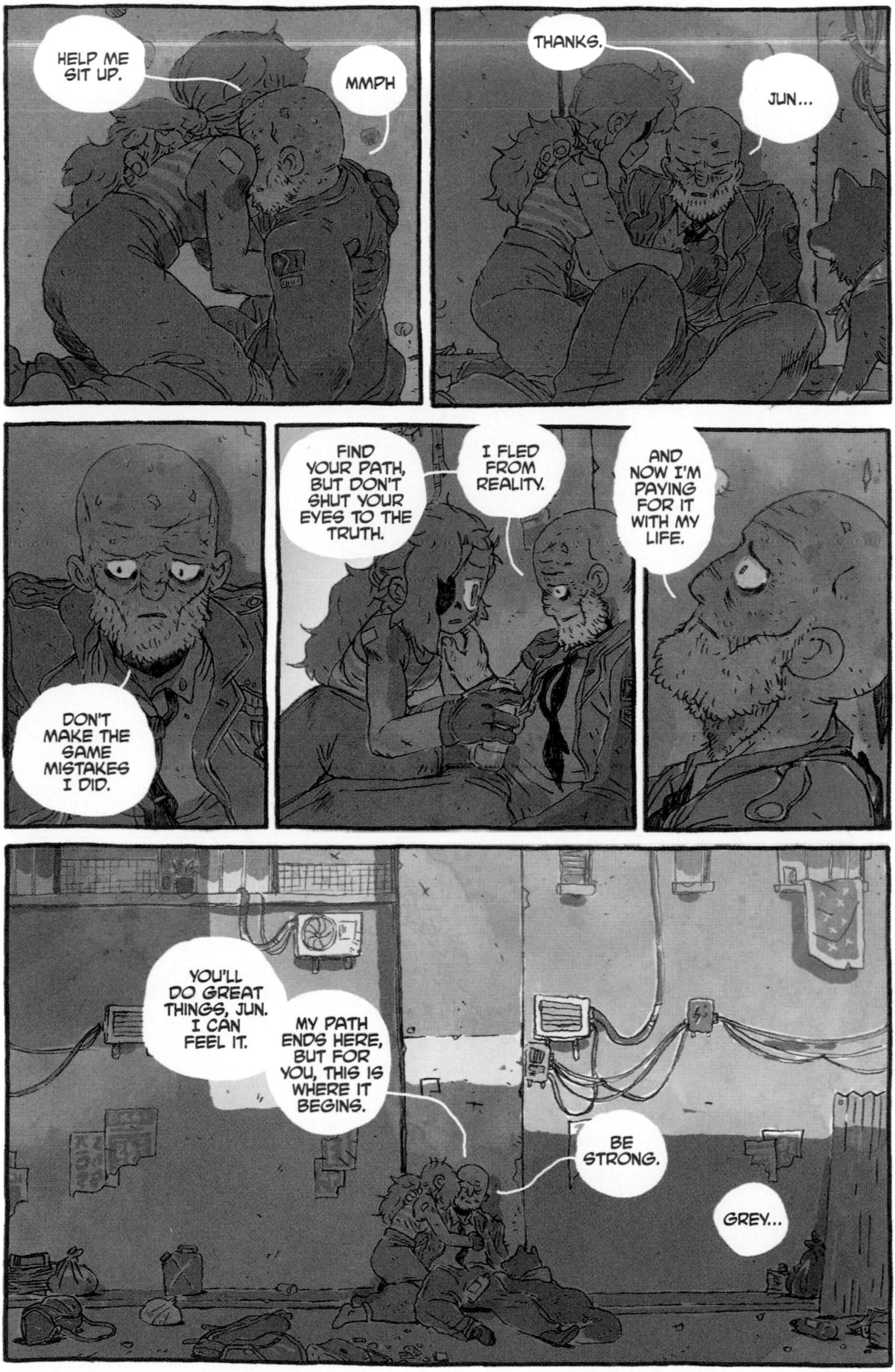
HELP ME SIT UP.
MMPH
THANKS.
JUN...
DON'T MAKE THE SAME MISTAKES I DID.
FIND YOUR PATH, BUT DON'T SHUT YOUR EYES TO THE TRUTH.
I FLED FROM REALITY.
AND NOW I'M PAYING FOR IT WITH MY LIFE.
YOU'LL DO GREAT THINGS, JUN. I CAN FEEL IT.
MY PATH ENDS HERE, BUT FOR YOU, THIS IS WHERE IT BEGINS.
BE STRONG.
GREY...

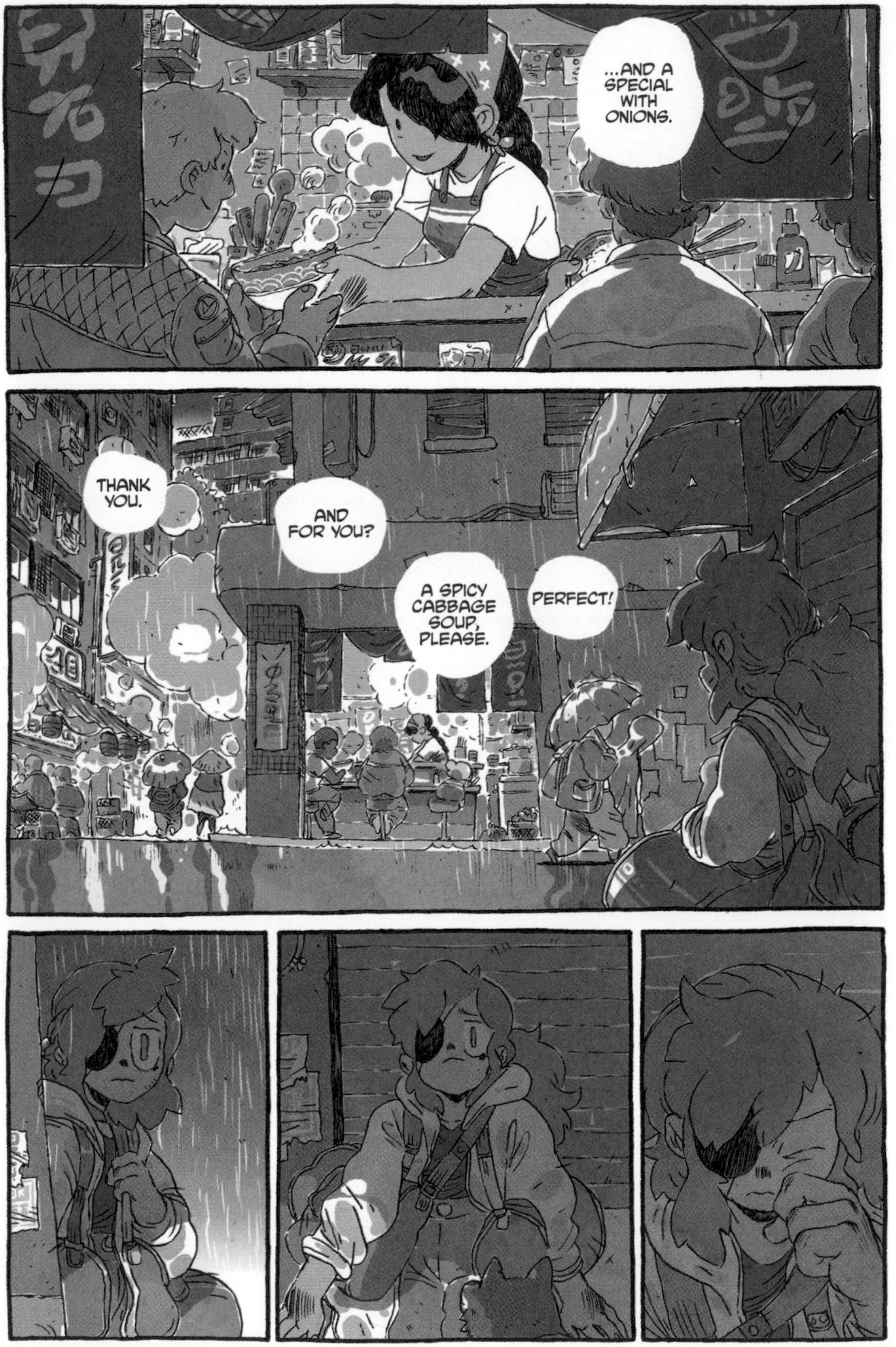
...AND A SPECIAL WITH ONIONS.
THANK YOU.
AND FOR YOU?
A SPICY CABBAGE SOUP, PLEASE.
PERFECT!

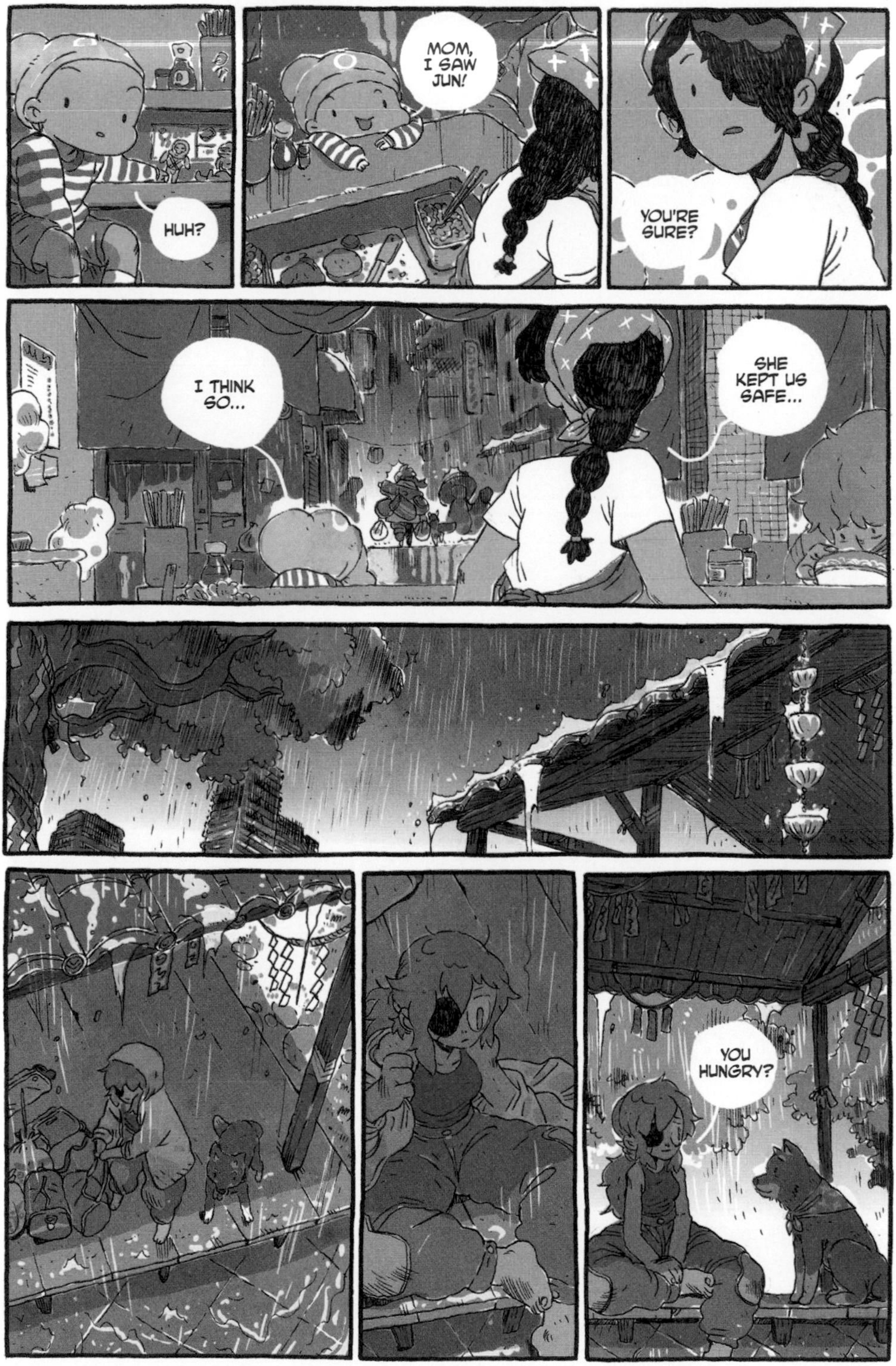
HUH?
MOM, I SAW JUN!
YOU'RE SURE?
I THINK SO...
SHE KEPT US SAFE...
YOU HUNGRY?

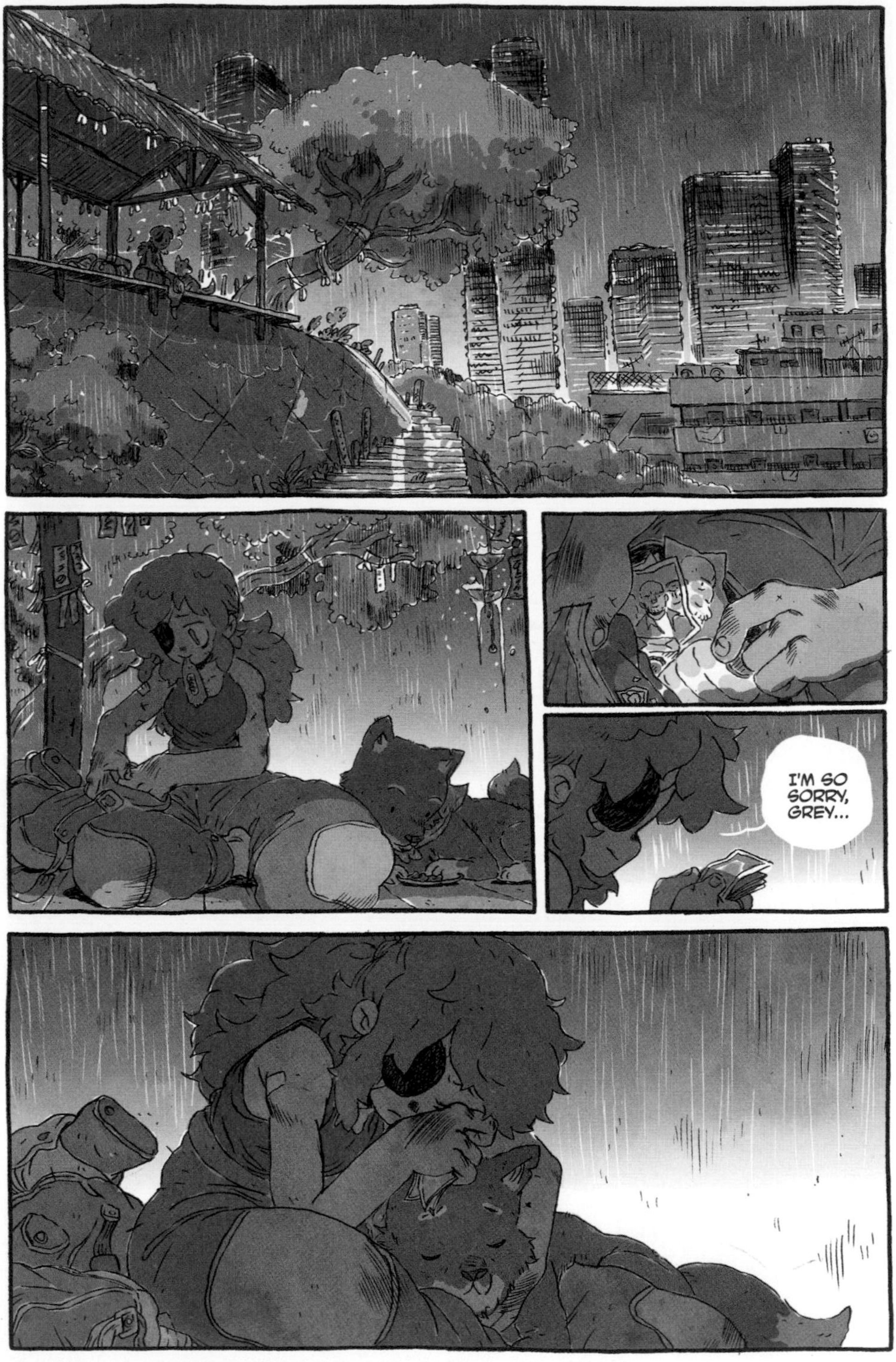
I'M SO SORRY, GREY...

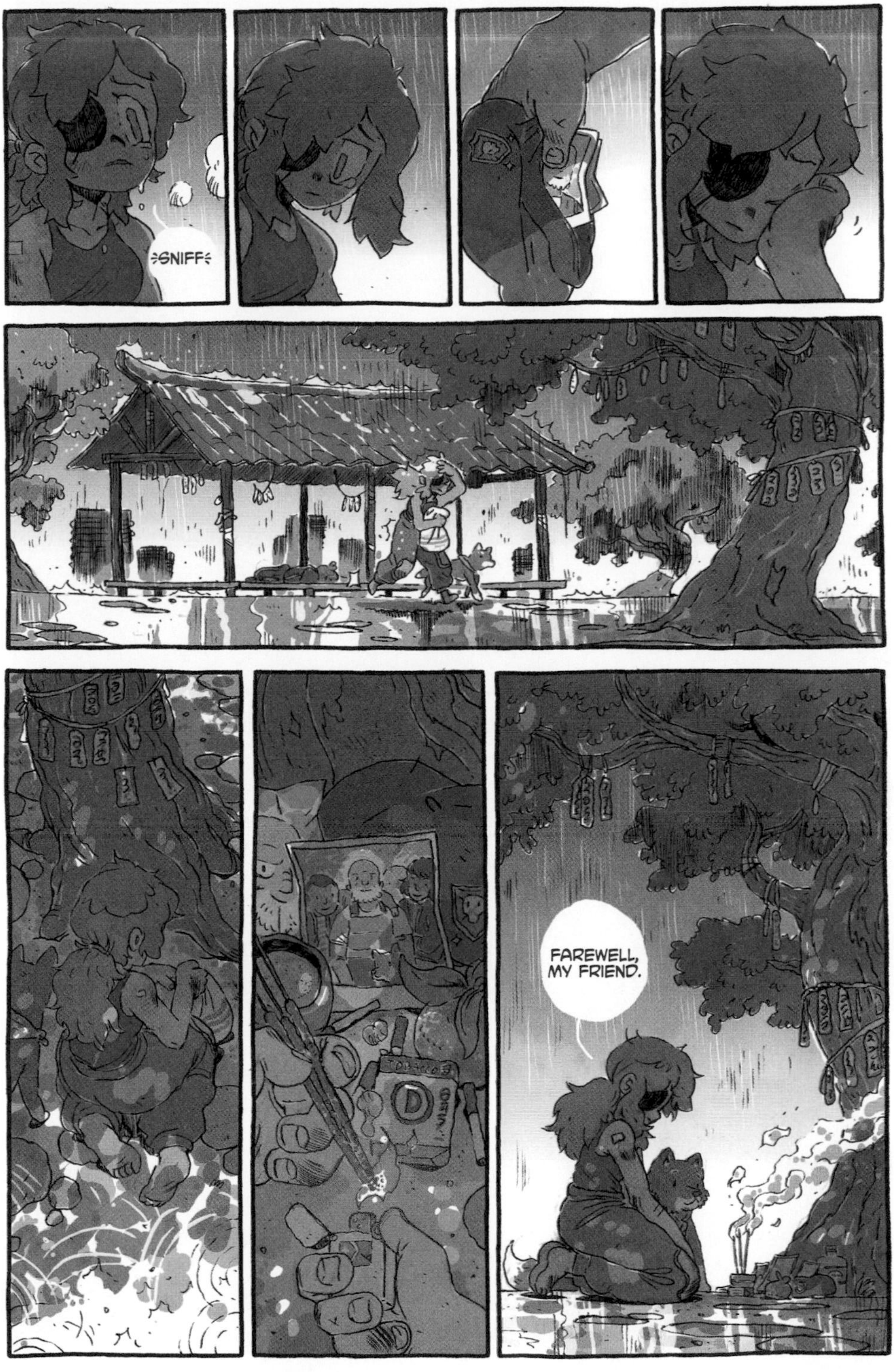
SNIFF
FAREWELL, MY FRIEND.

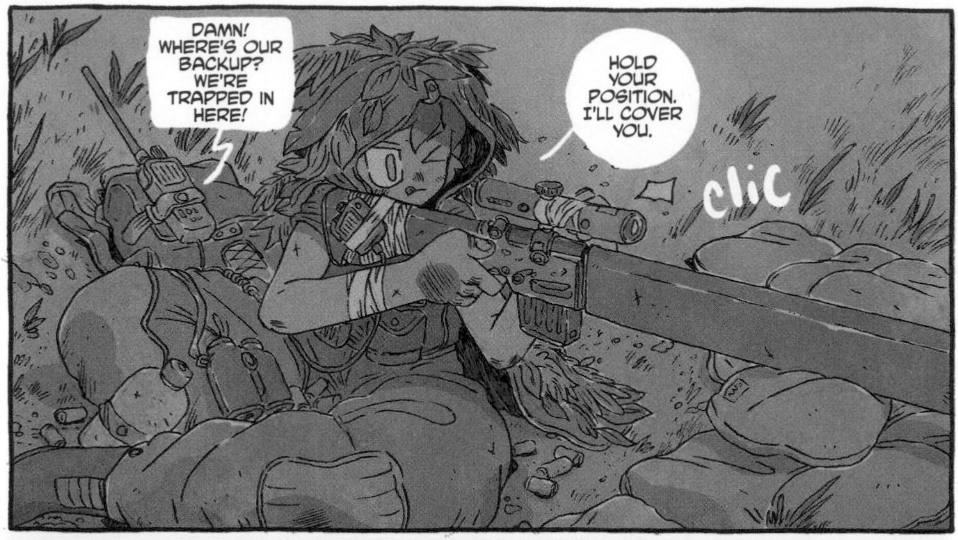
DAMN! WHERE'S OUR BACKUP? WE'RE TRAPPED IN HERE!
HOLD YOUR POSITION. I'LL COVER YOU.
CLIC

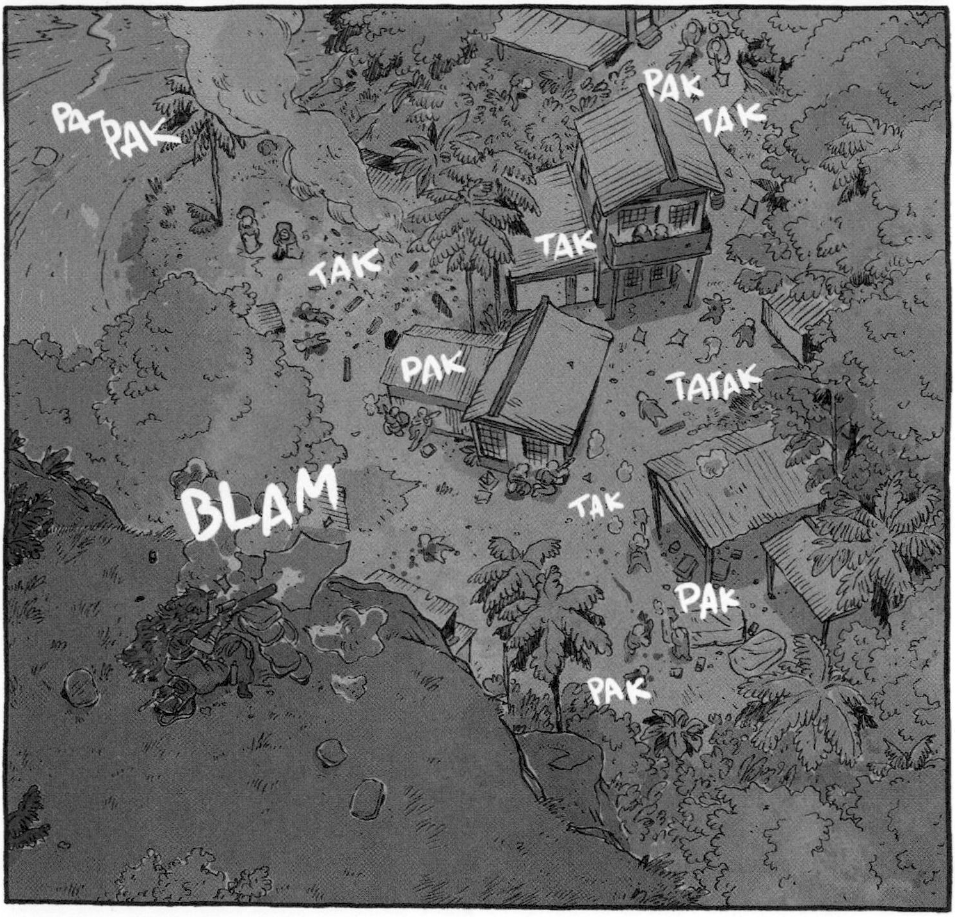
PA-PAK
PAK
TAK
TAK
TAK
PAK
TATAK
BLAM
TAK
PAK
PAK

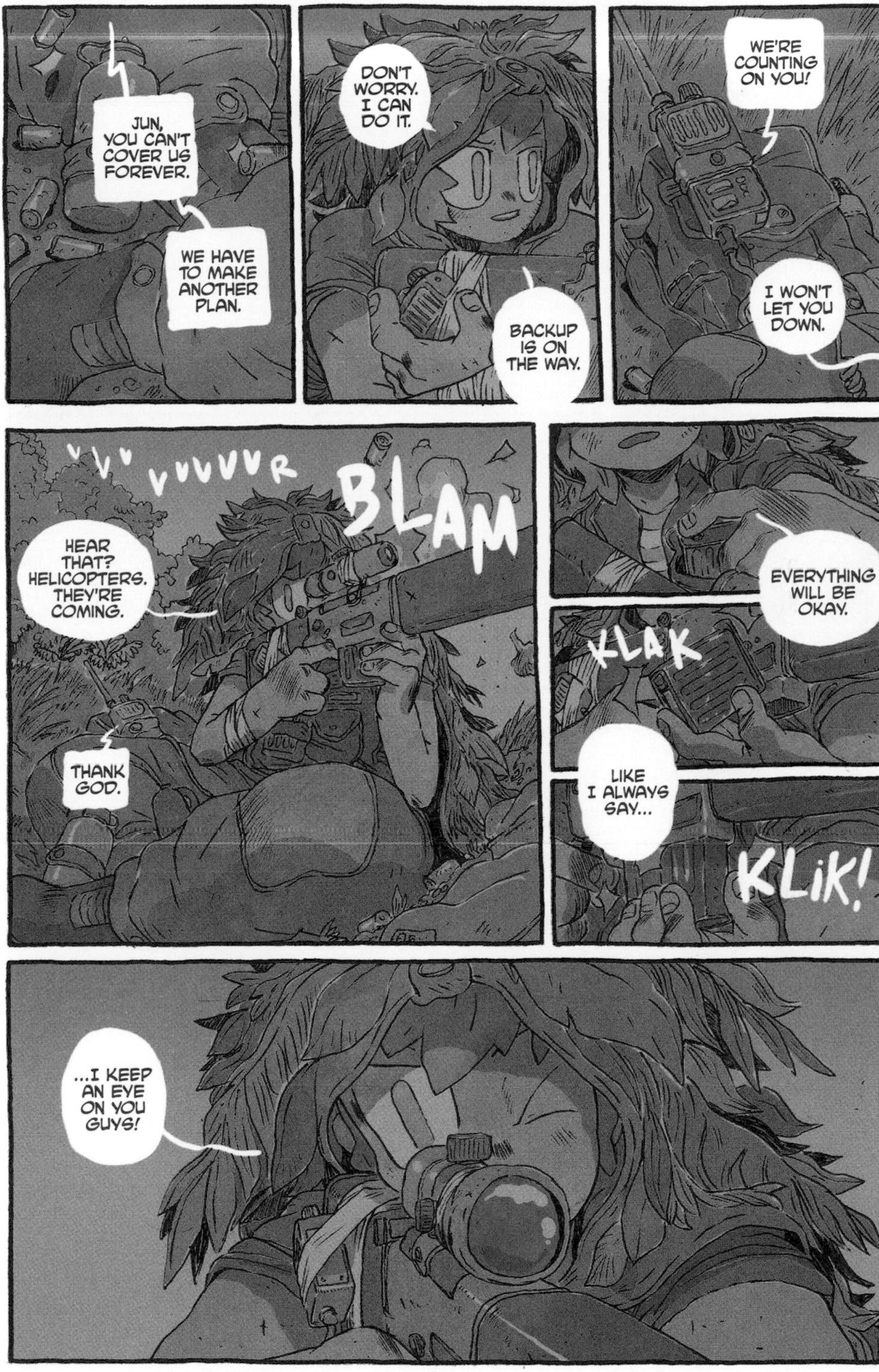
JUN, YOU CAN'T COVER US FOREVER.
WE HAVE TO MAKE ANOTHER PLAN.
DON'T WORRY. I CAN DO IT.
BACKUP IS ON THE WAY.
WE'RE COUNTING ON YOU!
I WON'T LET YOU DOWN.
VVV VUUUVR
BLAM
HEAR THAT? HELICOPTERS. THEY'RE COMING.
THANK GOD.
EVERYTHING WILL BE OKAY.
KLAK
LIKE I ALWAYS SAY...
KLIK!
...I KEEP AN EYE ON YOU GUYS!

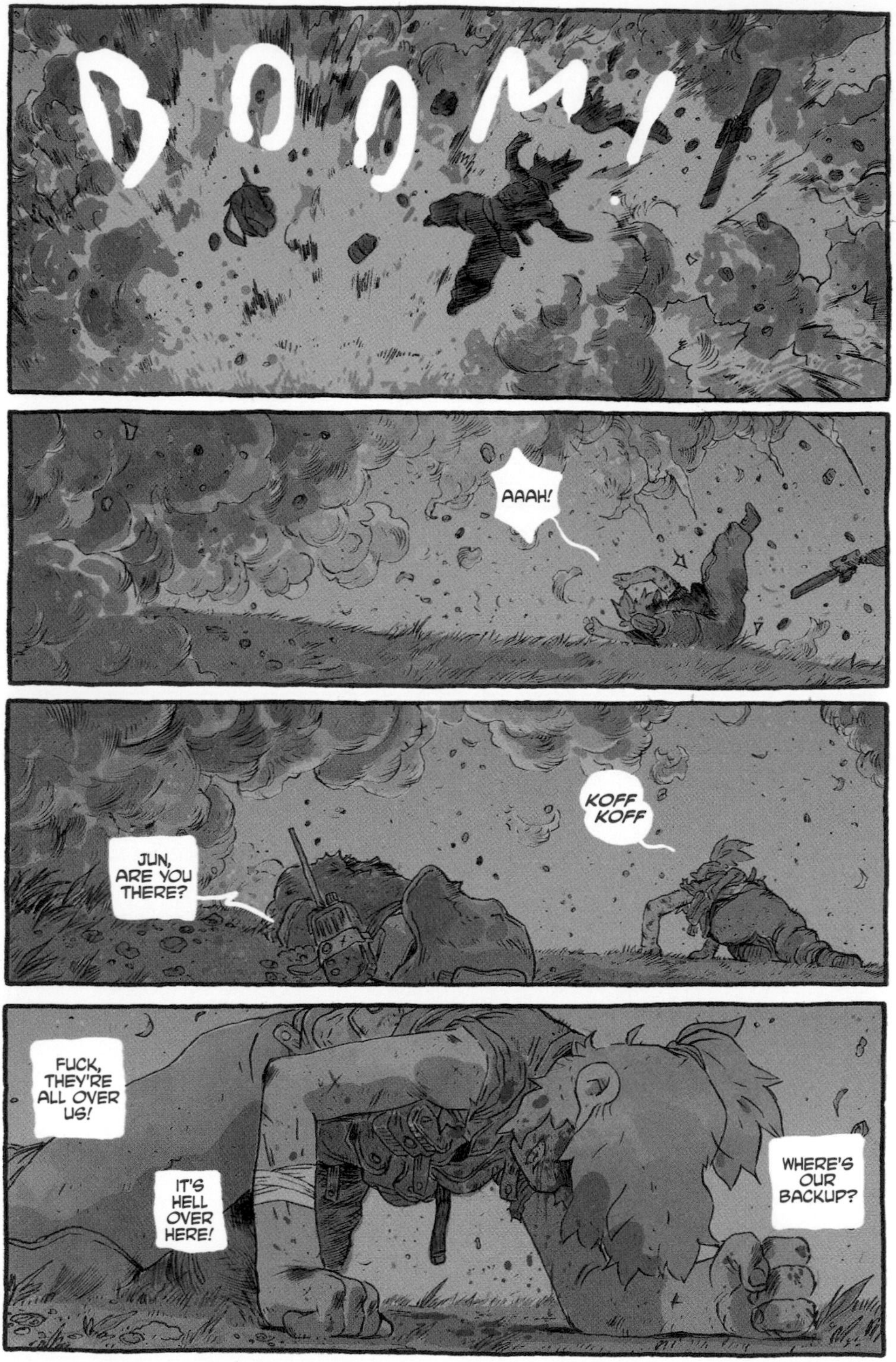
BOOM!
AAAH!
JUN, ARE YOU THERE?
KOFF KOFF
FUCK, THEY'RE ALL OVER US!
IT'S HELL OVER HERE!
WHERE'S OUR BACKUP?

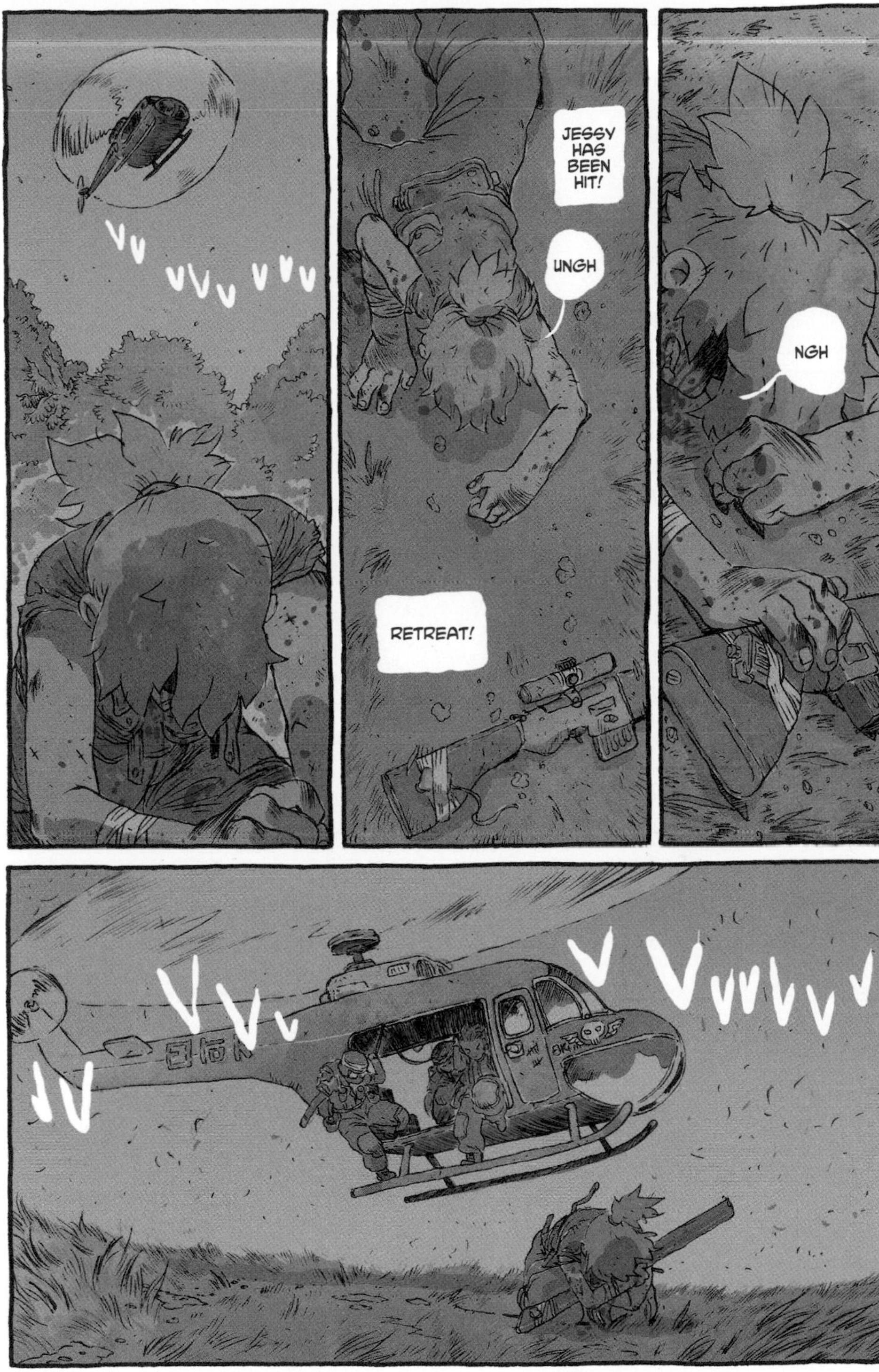
VVVVVVVV
JESSY HAS BEEN HIT!
UNGH
RETREAT!
NGH
VVVVVVVVVVVV

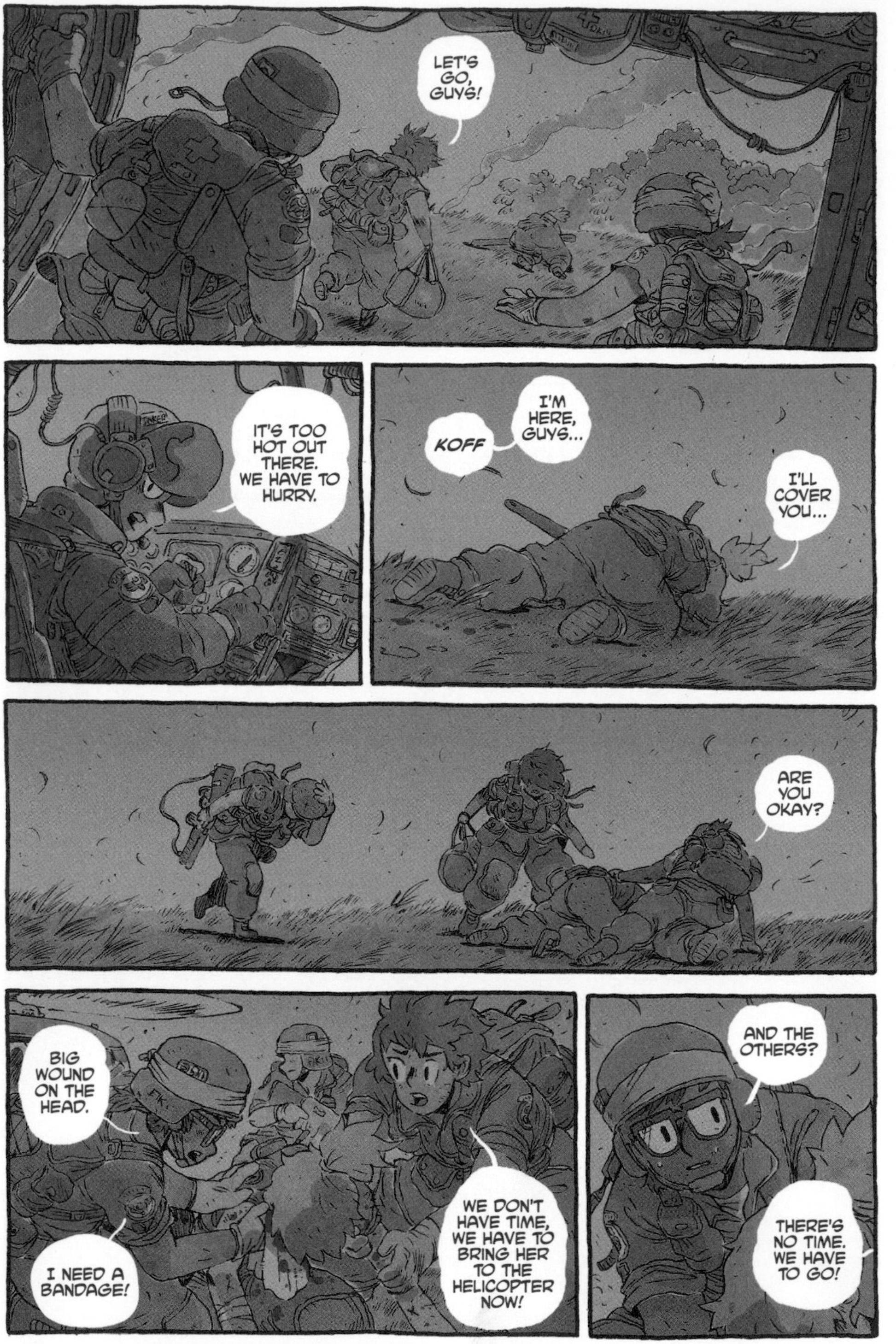
LET'S GO, GUYS!
IT'S TOO HOT OUT THERE. WE HAVE TO HURRY.
I'M HERE, GUYS...
KOFF
I'LL COVER YOU...
ARE YOU OKAY?
BIG WOUND ON THE HEAD.
I NEED A BANDAGE!
WE DON'T HAVE TIME, WE HAVE TO BRING HER TO THE HELICOPTER NOW!
AND THE OTHERS?
THERE'S NO TIME. WE HAVE TO GO!

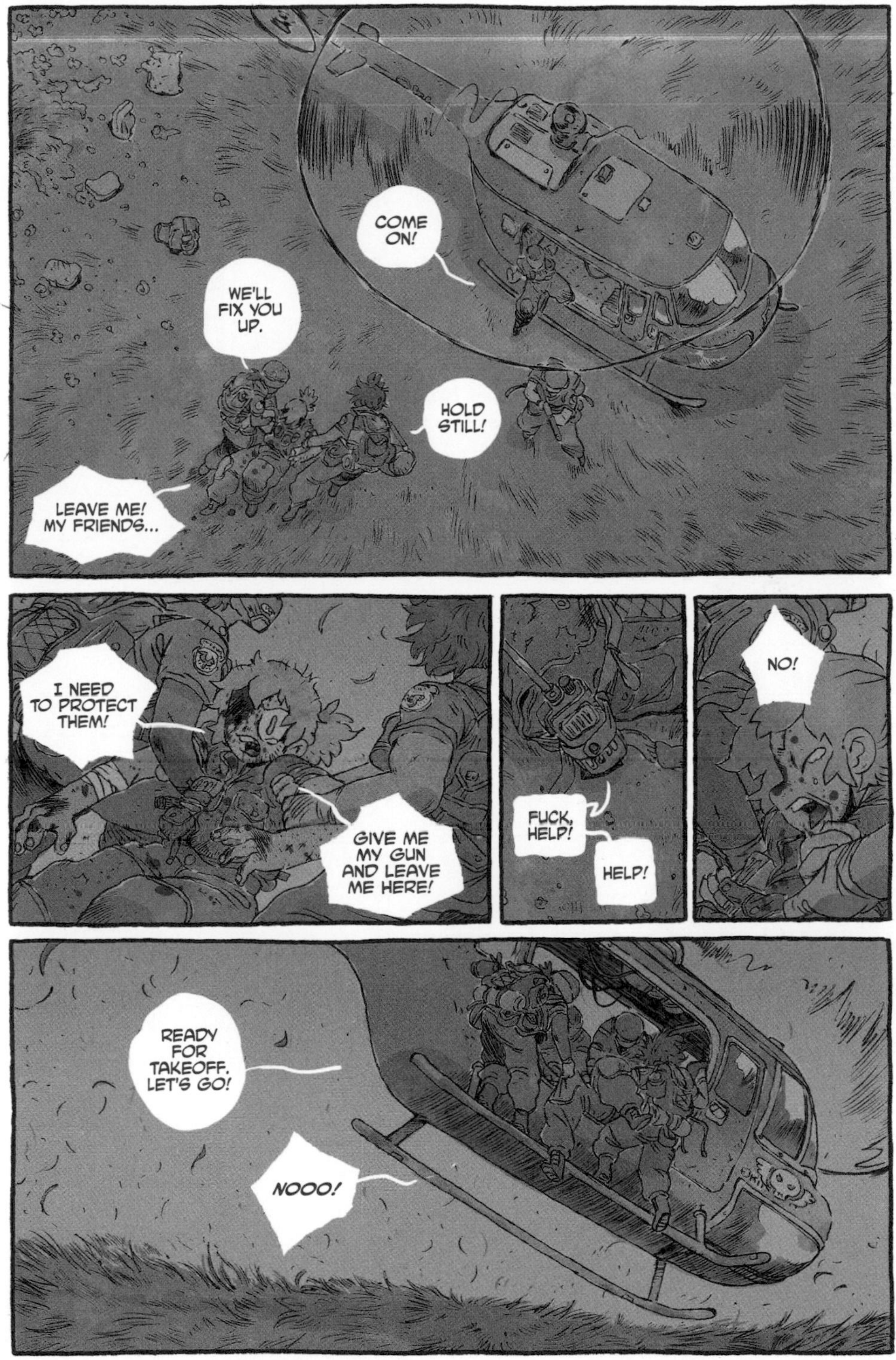
COME ON!
WE'LL FIX YOU UP.
HOLD STILL!
LEAVE ME! MY FRIENDS...
I NEED TO PROTECT THEM!
GIVE ME MY GUN AND LEAVE ME HERE!
FUCK, HELP!
HELP!
NO!
READY FOR TAKEOFF. LET'S GO!
NOOO!

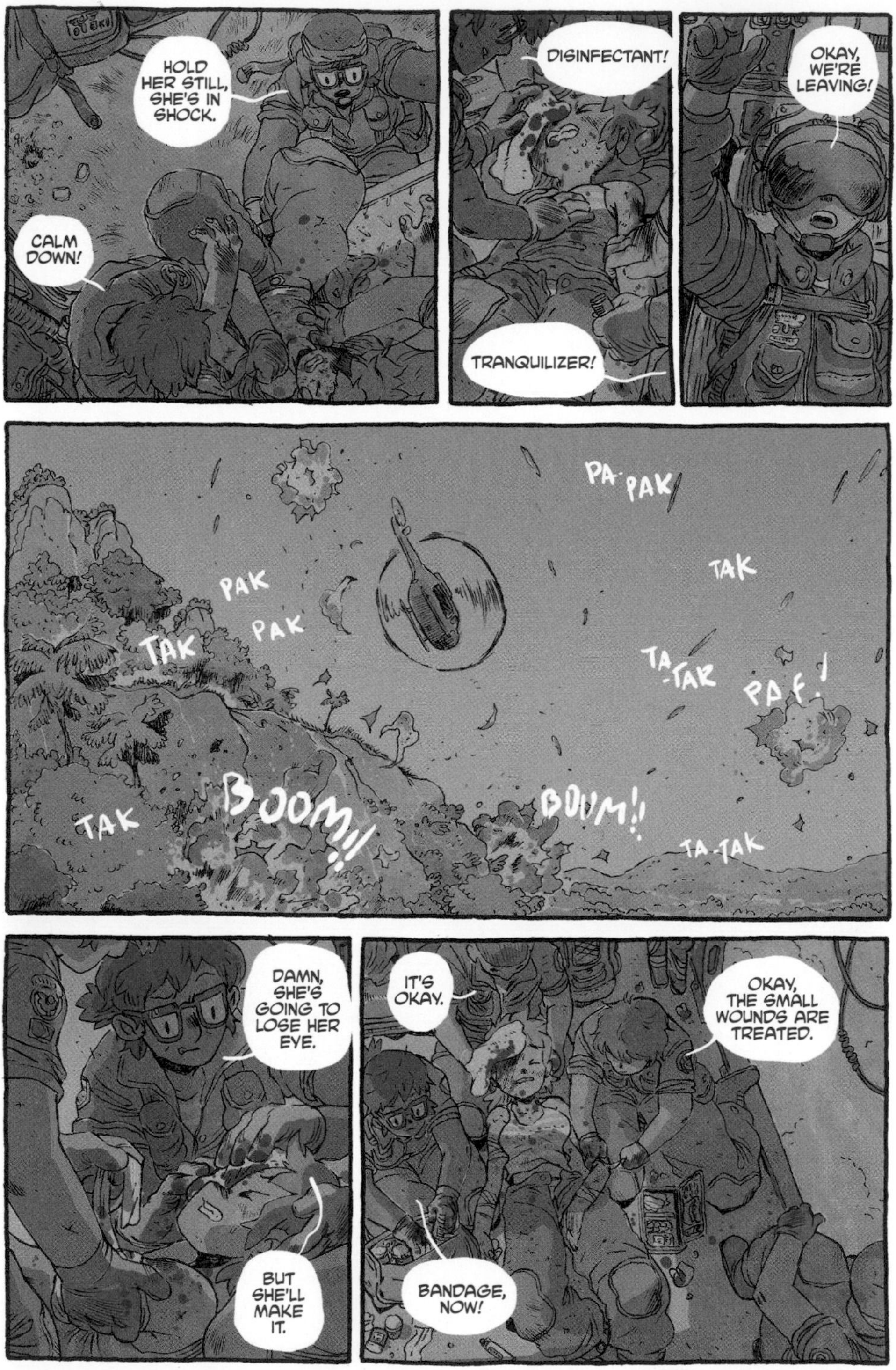
HOLD HER STILL, SHE'S IN SHOCK.
CALM DOWN!
DISINFECTANT!
TRANQUILIZER!
OKAY, WE'RE LEAVING!
PA-PAK
PAK
PAK
TAK
TAK
TA-TAK
PAF!
TAK
BOOM!!
BOUM!!
TA-TAK
DAMN, SHE'S GOING TO LOSE HER EYE.
BUT SHE'LL MAKE IT.
IT'S OKAY.
OKAY, THE SMALL WOUNDS ARE TREATED.
BANDAGE, NOW!

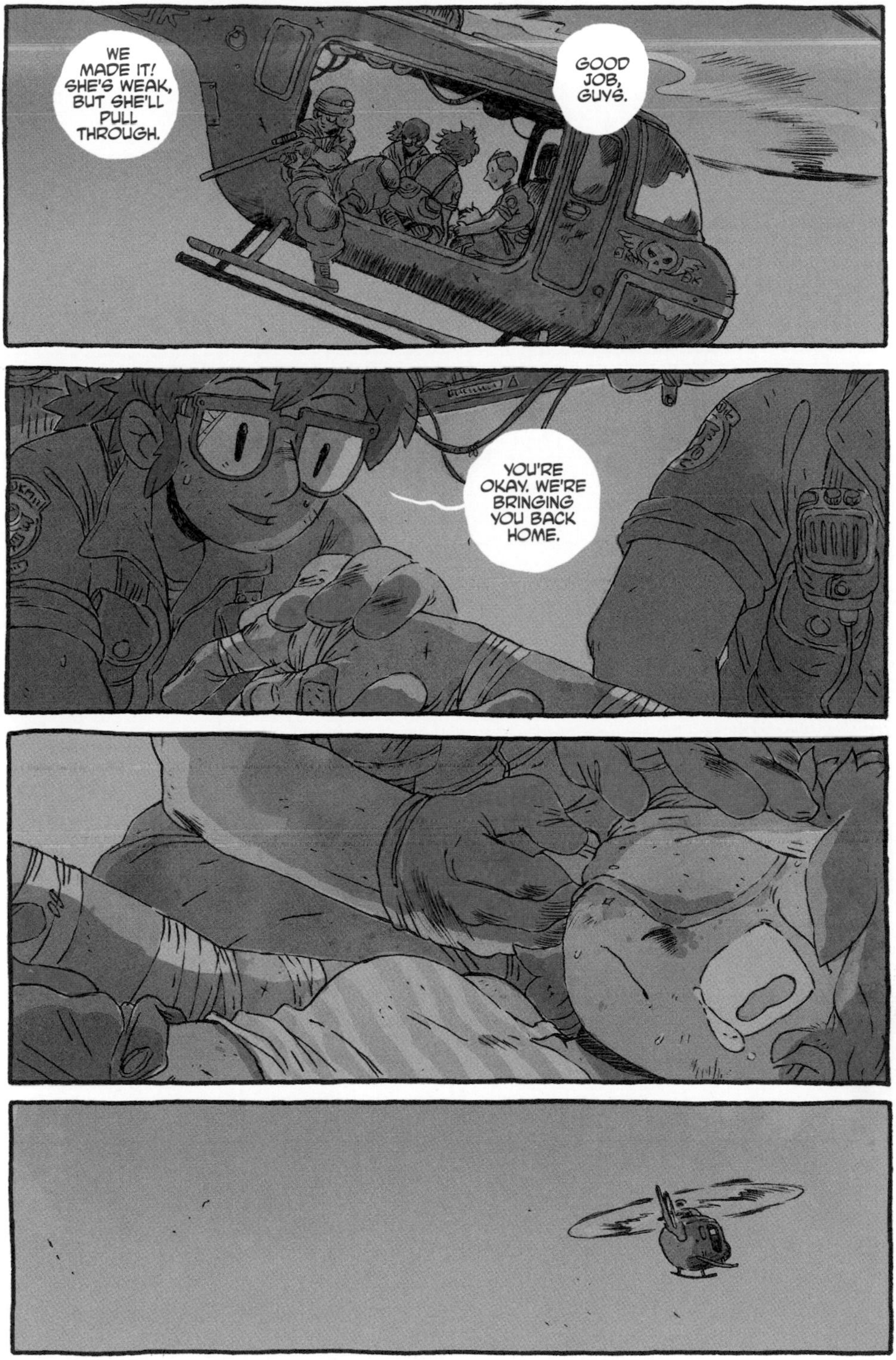
WE MADE IT! SHE'S WEAK, BUT SHE'LL PULL THROUGH.
GOOD JOB, GUYS.
YOU'RE OKAY. WE'RE BRINGING YOU BACK HOME.

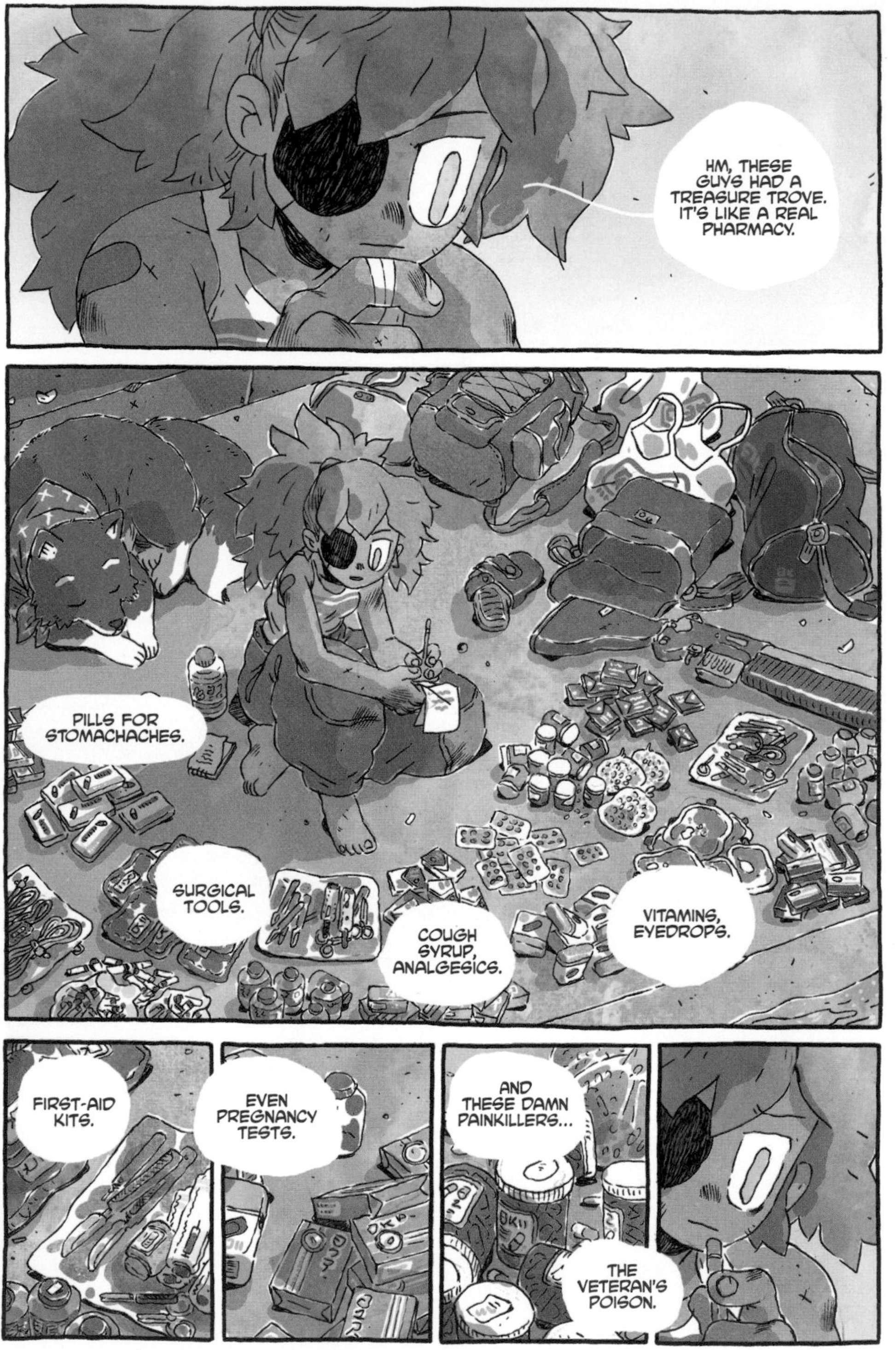
HM, THESE GUYS HAD A TREASURE TROVE. IT'S LIKE A REAL PHARMACY.
PILLS FOR STOMACHACHES.
SURGICAL TOOLS.
COUGH SYRUP, ANALGESICS.
VITAMINS, EYEDROPS.
FIRST-AID KITS.
EVEN PREGNANCY TESTS.
AND THESE DAMN PAINKILLERS...
THE VETERAN'S POISON.

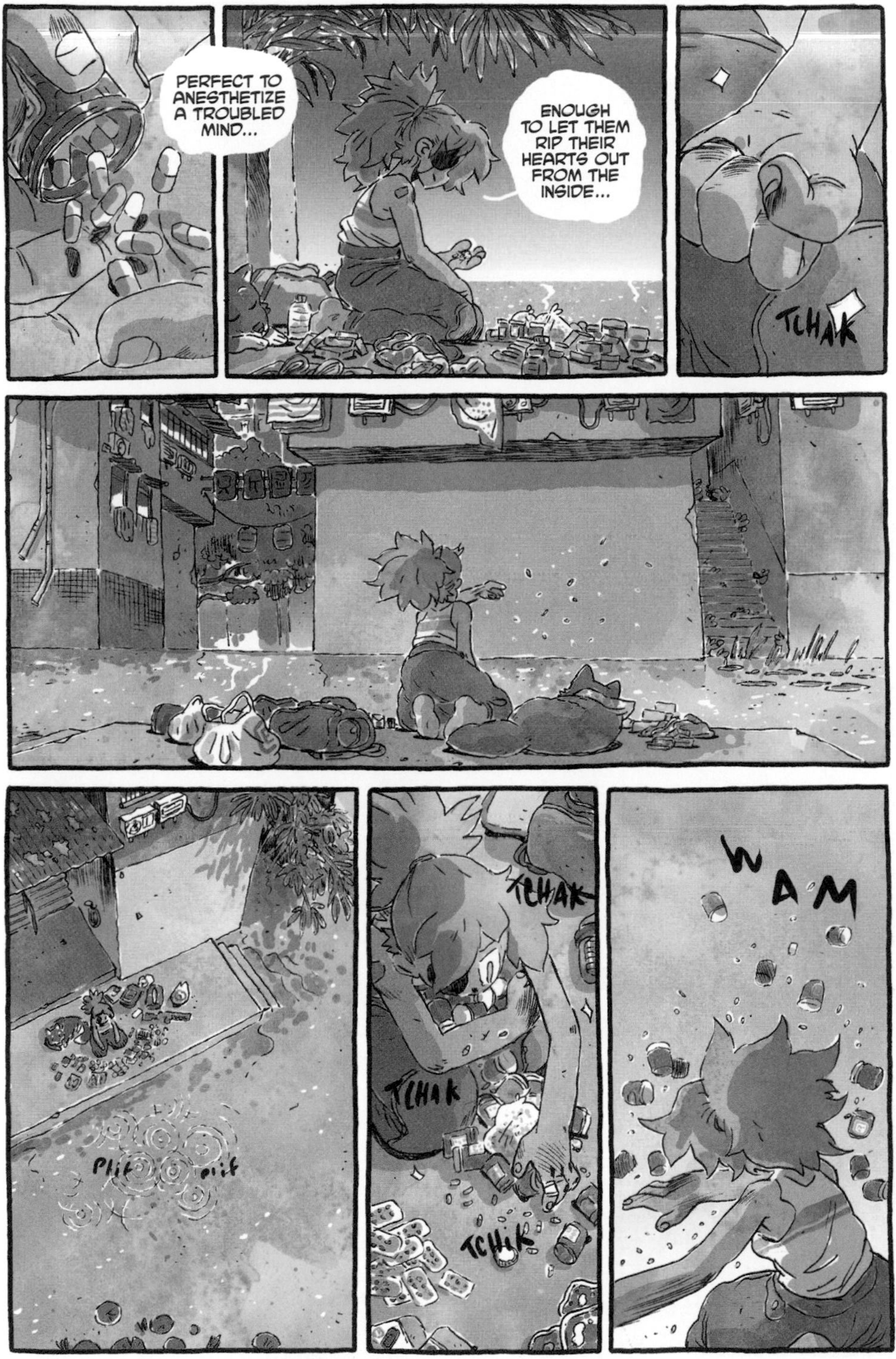
PERFECT TO ANESTHETIZE A TROUBLED MIND...
ENOUGH TO LET THEM RIP THEIR HEARTS OUT FROM THE INSIDE...
TCHAK
Plik plik
TCHAK
TCHAK
TCHIK
WAM

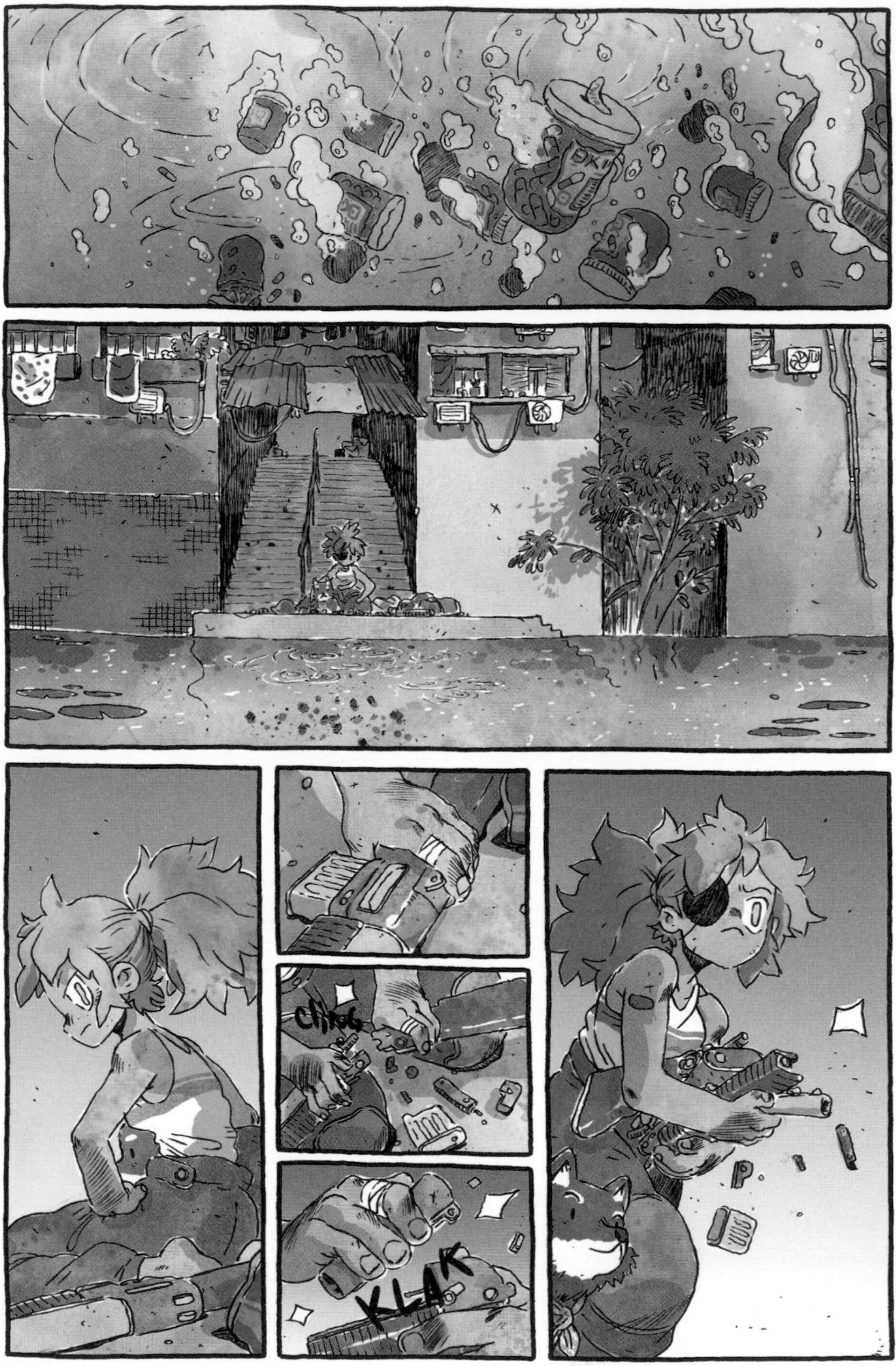
CLING
KLAK

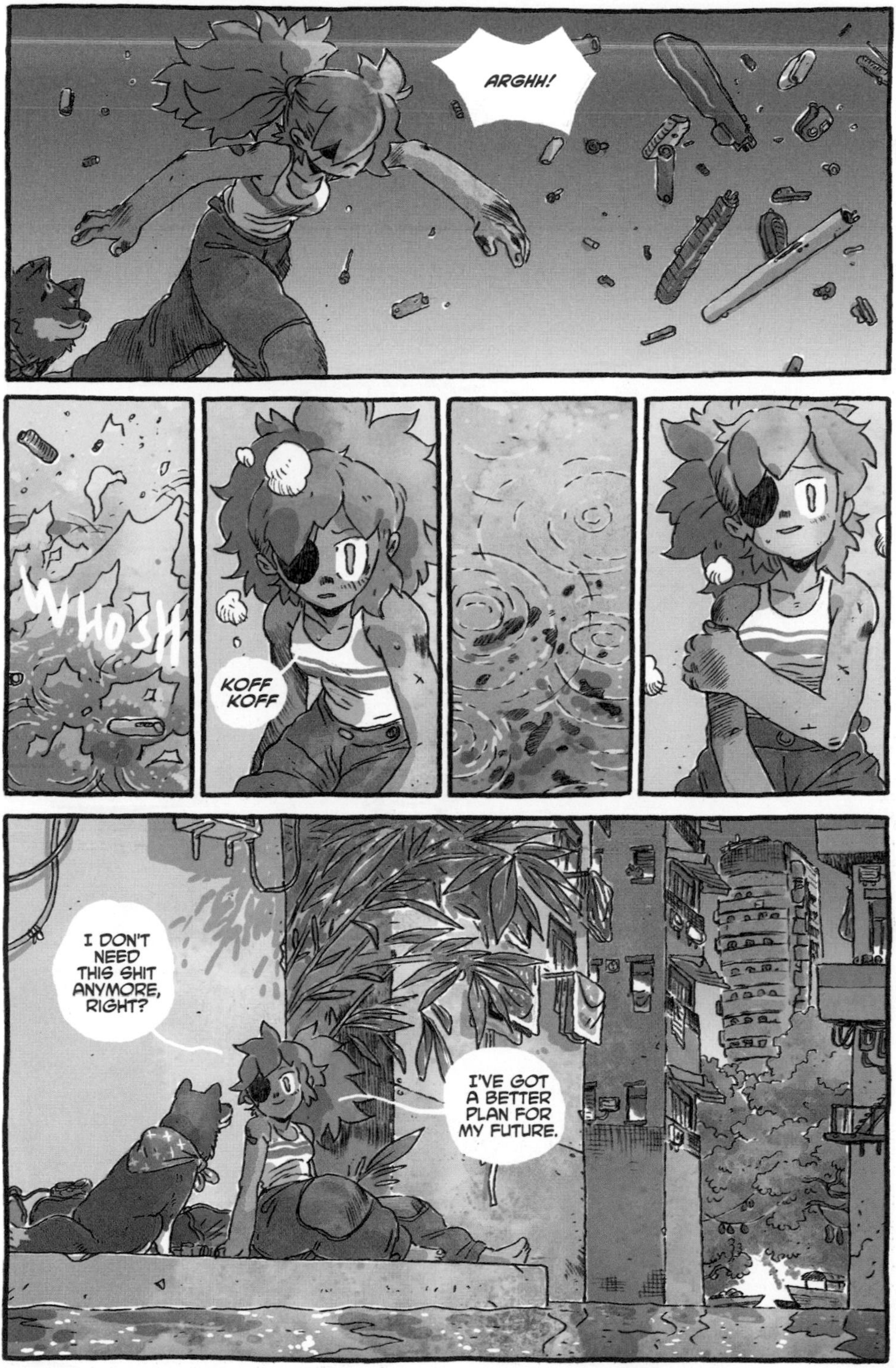
ARGHH!
WHOSH
KOFF KOFF
I DON'T NEED THIS SHIT ANYMORE, RIGHT?
I'VE GOT A BETTER PLAN FOR MY FUTURE.

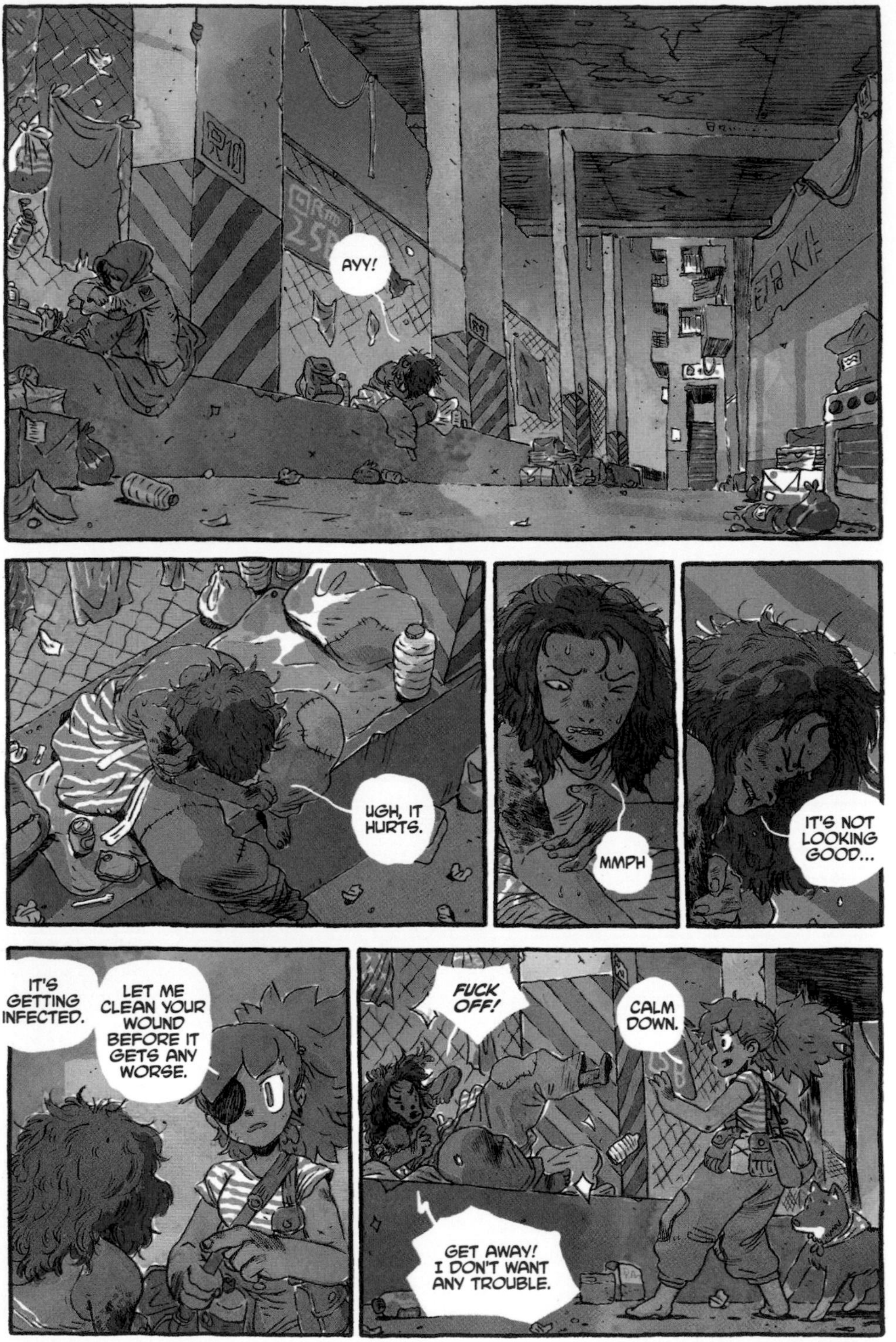
AYY!
UGH, IT HURTS.
MMPH
IT'S NOT LOOKING GOOD...
IT'S GETTING INFECTED.
LET ME CLEAN YOUR WOUND BEFORE IT GETS ANY WORSE.
FUCK OFF!
CALM DOWN.
GET AWAY! I DON'T WANT ANY TROUBLE.

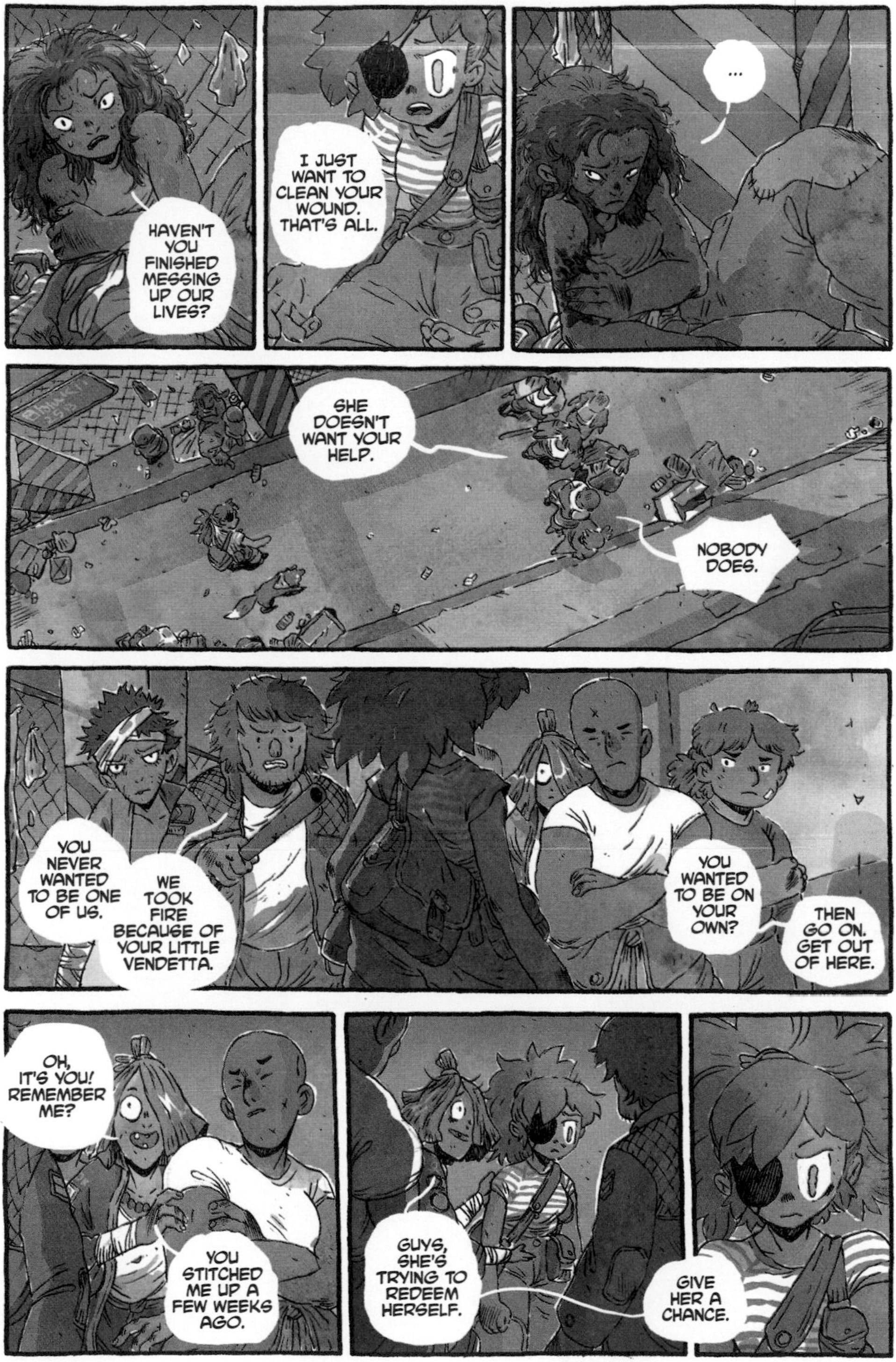
HAVEN'T YOU FINISHED MESSING UP OUR LIVES?
I JUST WANT TO CLEAN YOUR WOUND. THAT'S ALL.
...
SHE DOESN'T WANT YOUR HELP.
NOBODY DOES.
YOU NEVER WANTED TO BE ONE OF US.
WE TOOK FIRE BECAUSE OF YOUR LITTLE VENDETTA.
YOU WANTED TO BE ON YOUR OWN?
THEN GO ON. GET OUT OF HERE.
OH, IT'S YOU! REMEMBER ME?
YOU STITCHED ME UP A FEW WEEKS AGO.
GUYS, SHE'S TRYING TO REDEEM HERSELF.
GIVE HER A CHANCE.

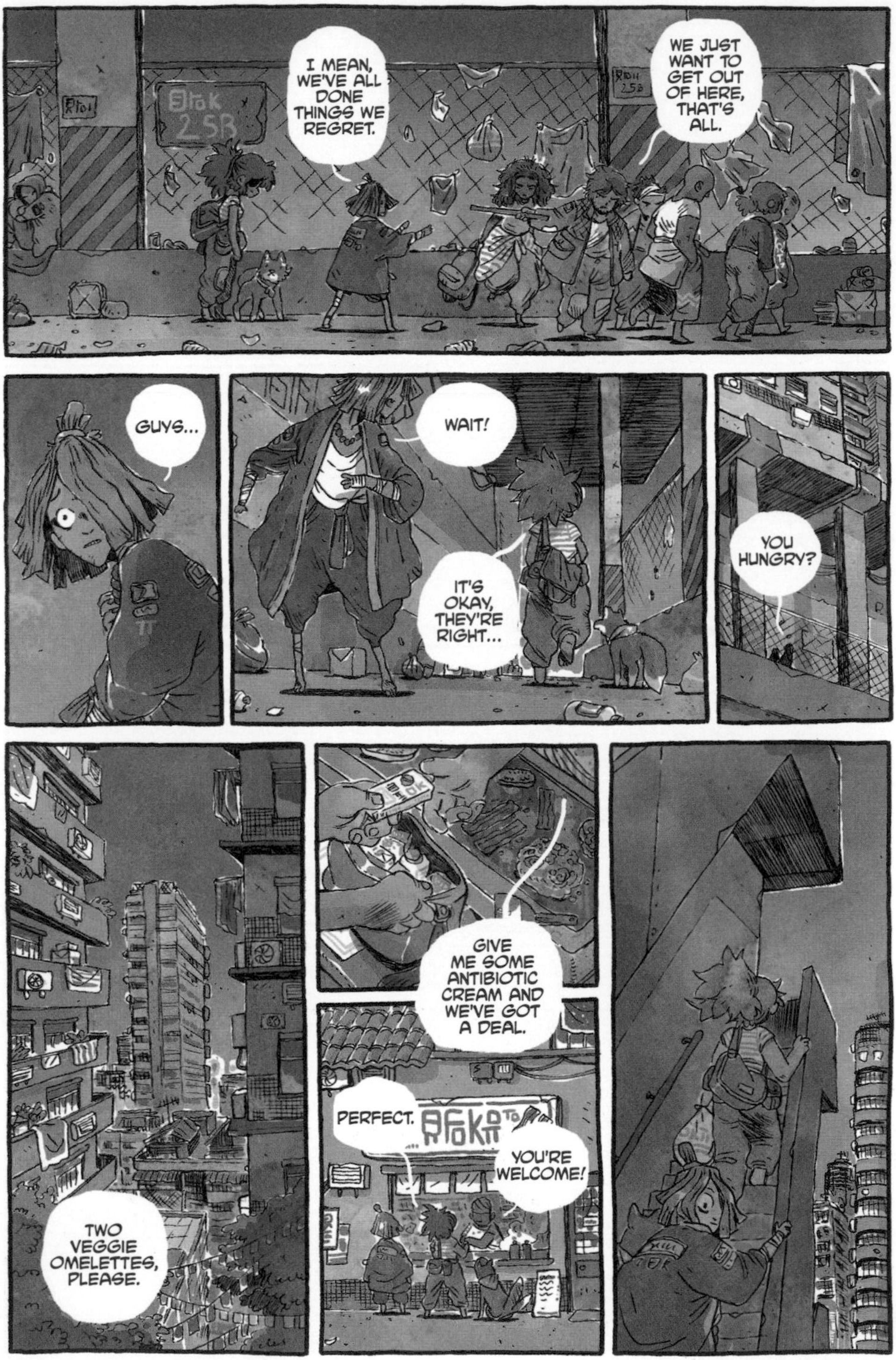
I MEAN, WE'VE ALL DONE THINGS WE REGRET.
WE JUST WANT TO GET OUT OF HERE, THAT'S ALL.
GUYS...
WAIT!
IT'S OKAY, THEY'RE RIGHT...
YOU HUNGRY?
TWO VEGGIE OMELETTES, PLEASE.
GIVE ME SOME ANTIBIOTIC CREAM AND WE'VE GOT A DEAL.
PERFECT.
YOU'RE WELCOME!

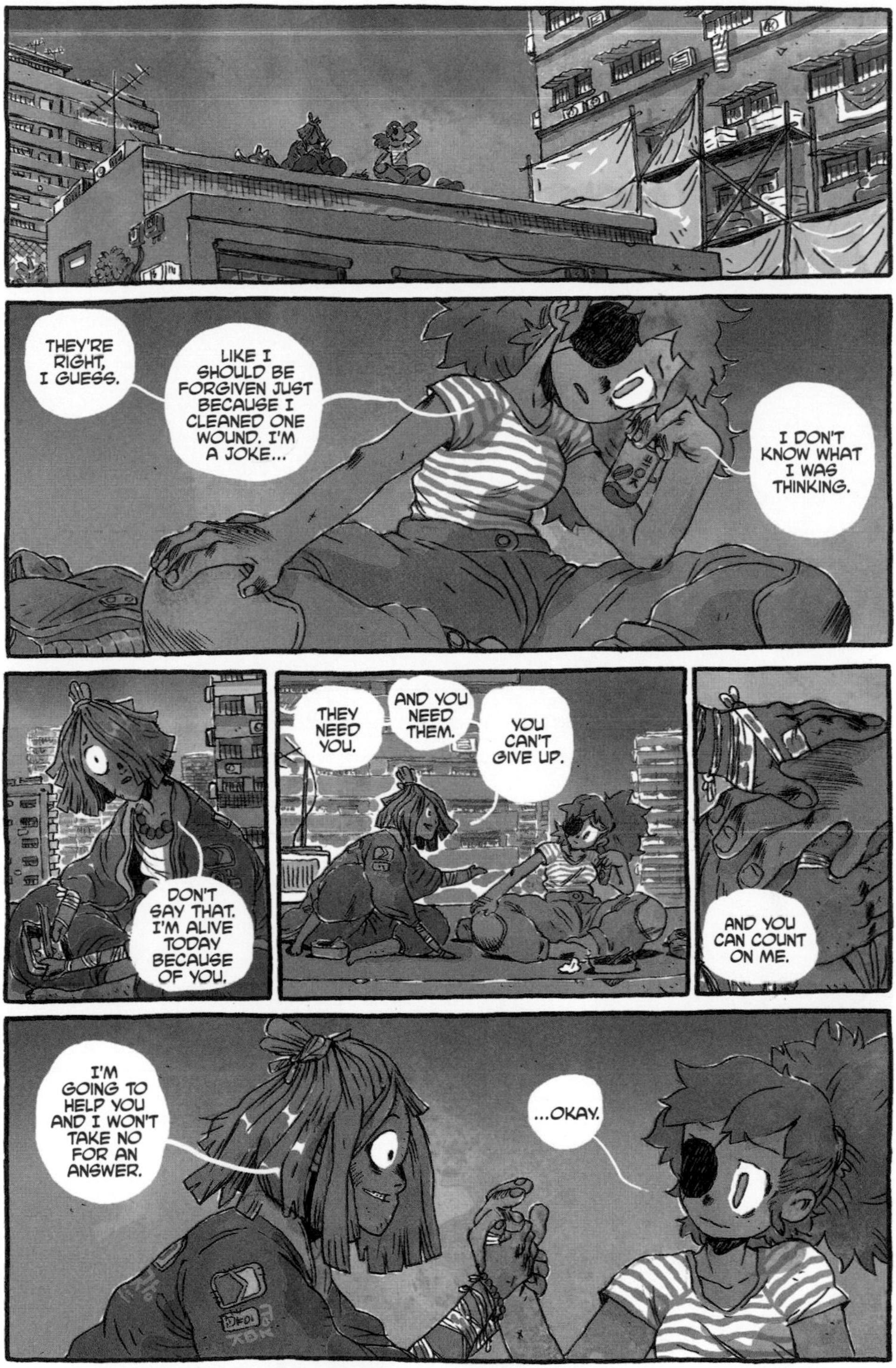

THEY'RE RIGHT, I GUESS.
LIKE I SHOULD BE FORGIVEN JUST BECAUSE I CLEANED ONE WOUND. I'M A JOKE...
I DON'T KNOW WHAT I WAS THINKING.
DON'T SAY THAT. I'M ALIVE TODAY BECAUSE OF YOU.
THEY NEED YOU.
AND YOU NEED THEM.
YOU CAN'T GIVE UP.
AND YOU CAN COUNT ON ME.
I'M GOING TO HELP YOU AND I WON'T TAKE NO FOR AN ANSWER.
...OKAY.

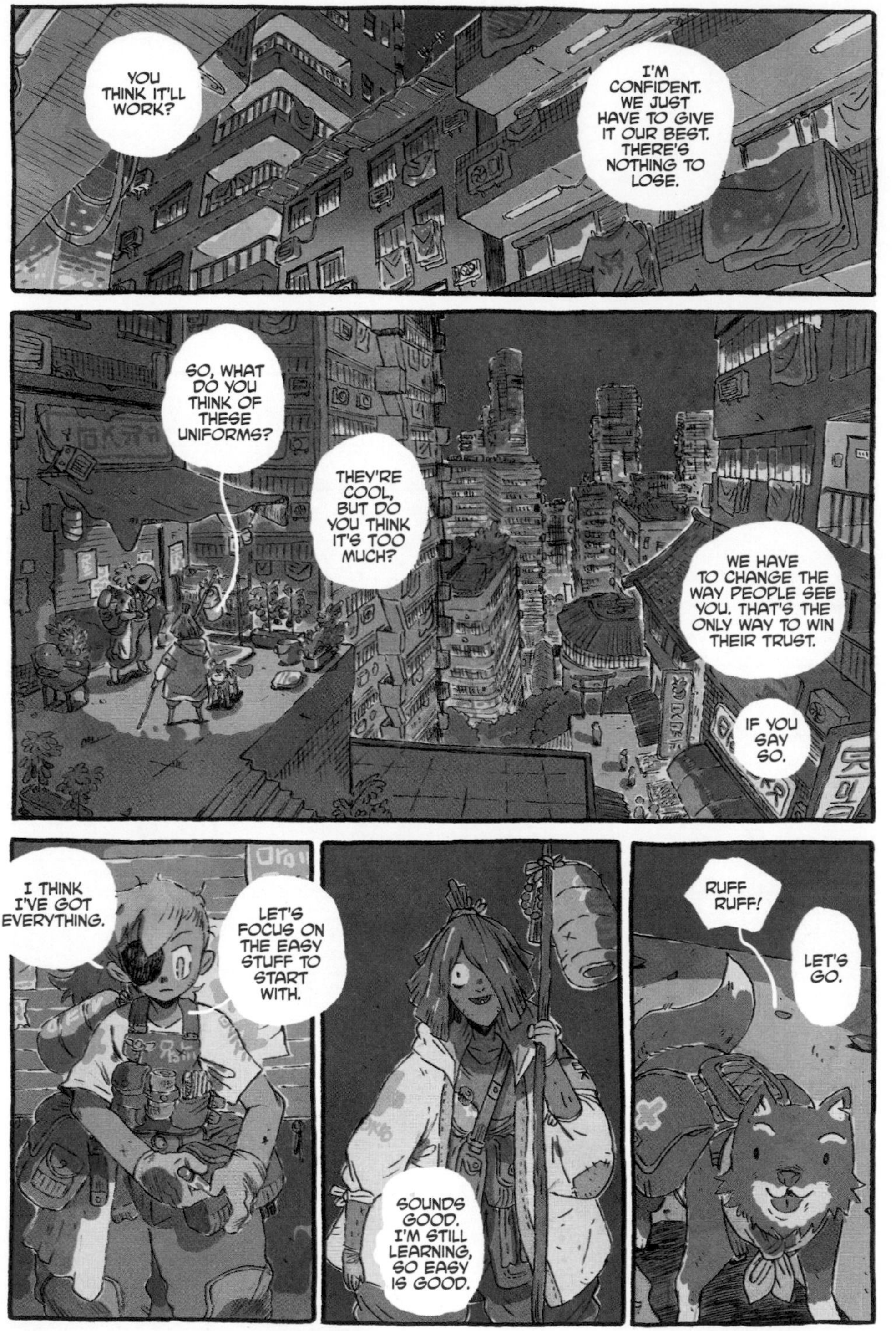
YOU THINK IT'LL WORK?
I'M CONFIDENT. WE JUST HAVE TO GIVE IT OUR BEST. THERE'S NOTHING TO LOSE.
SO, WHAT DO YOU THINK OF THESE UNIFORMS?
THEY'RE COOL, BUT DO YOU THINK IT'S TOO MUCH?
WE HAVE TO CHANGE THE WAY PEOPLE SEE YOU. THAT'S THE ONLY WAY TO WIN THEIR TRUST.
IF YOU SAY SO.
I THINK I'VE GOT EVERYTHING.
LET'S FOCUS ON THE EASY STUFF TO START WITH.
SOUNDS GOOD. I'M STILL LEARNING, SO EASY IS GOOD.
RUFF RUFF!
LET'S GO.

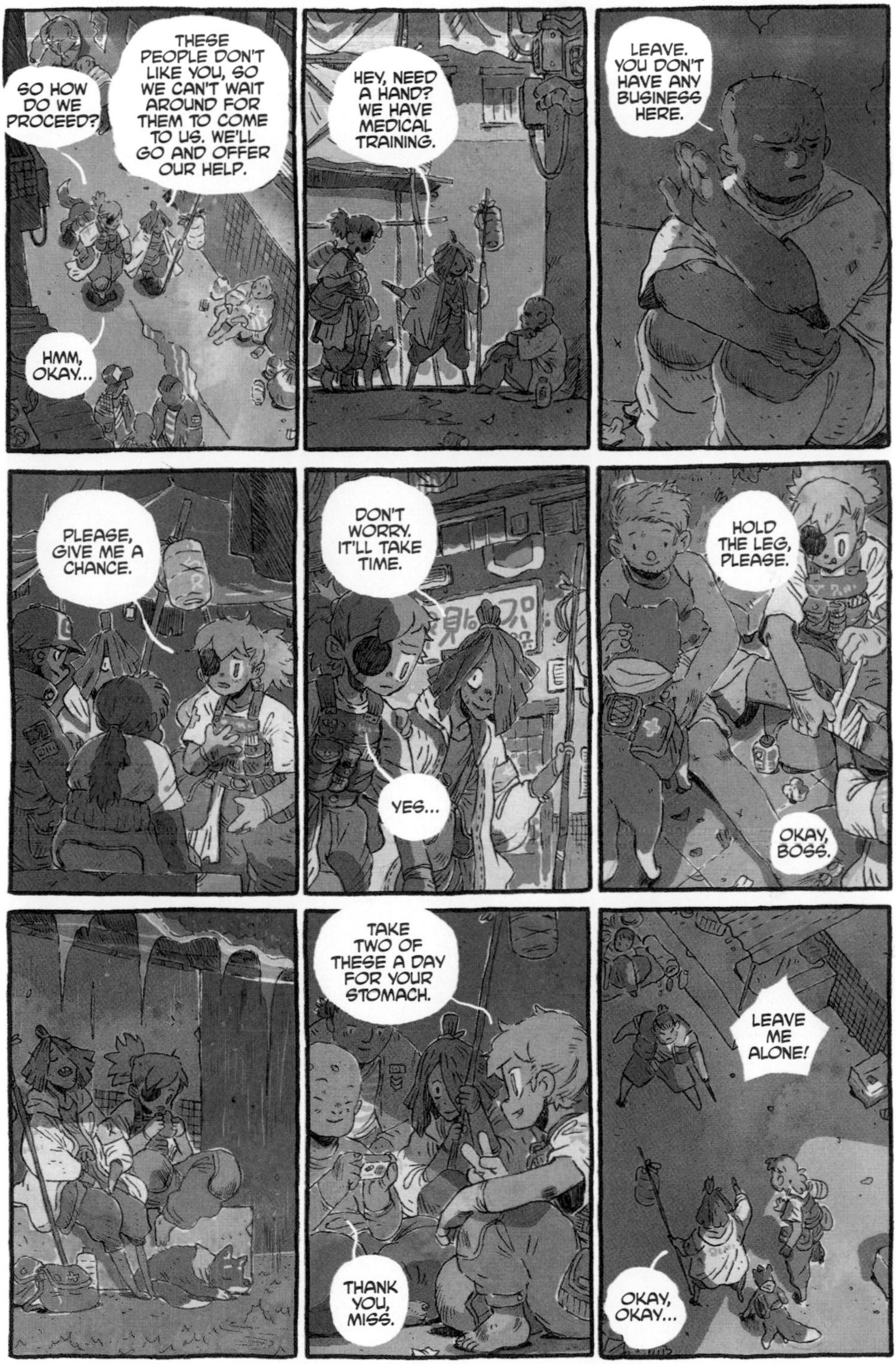
SO HOW DO WE PROCEED?
THESE PEOPLE DON'T LIKE YOU, SO WE CAN'T WAIT AROUND FOR THEM TO COME TO US. WE'LL GO AND OFFER OUR HELP.
HMM, OKAY...
HEY, NEED A HAND? WE HAVE MEDICAL TRAINING.
LEAVE. YOU DON'T HAVE ANY BUSINESS HERE.
PLEASE, GIVE ME A CHANCE.
DON'T WORRY. IT'LL TAKE TIME.
YES...
HOLD THE LEG, PLEASE.
OKAY, BOSS.
TAKE TWO OF THESE A DAY FOR YOUR STOMACH.
THANK YOU, MISS.
LEAVE ME ALONE!
OKAY, OKAY...

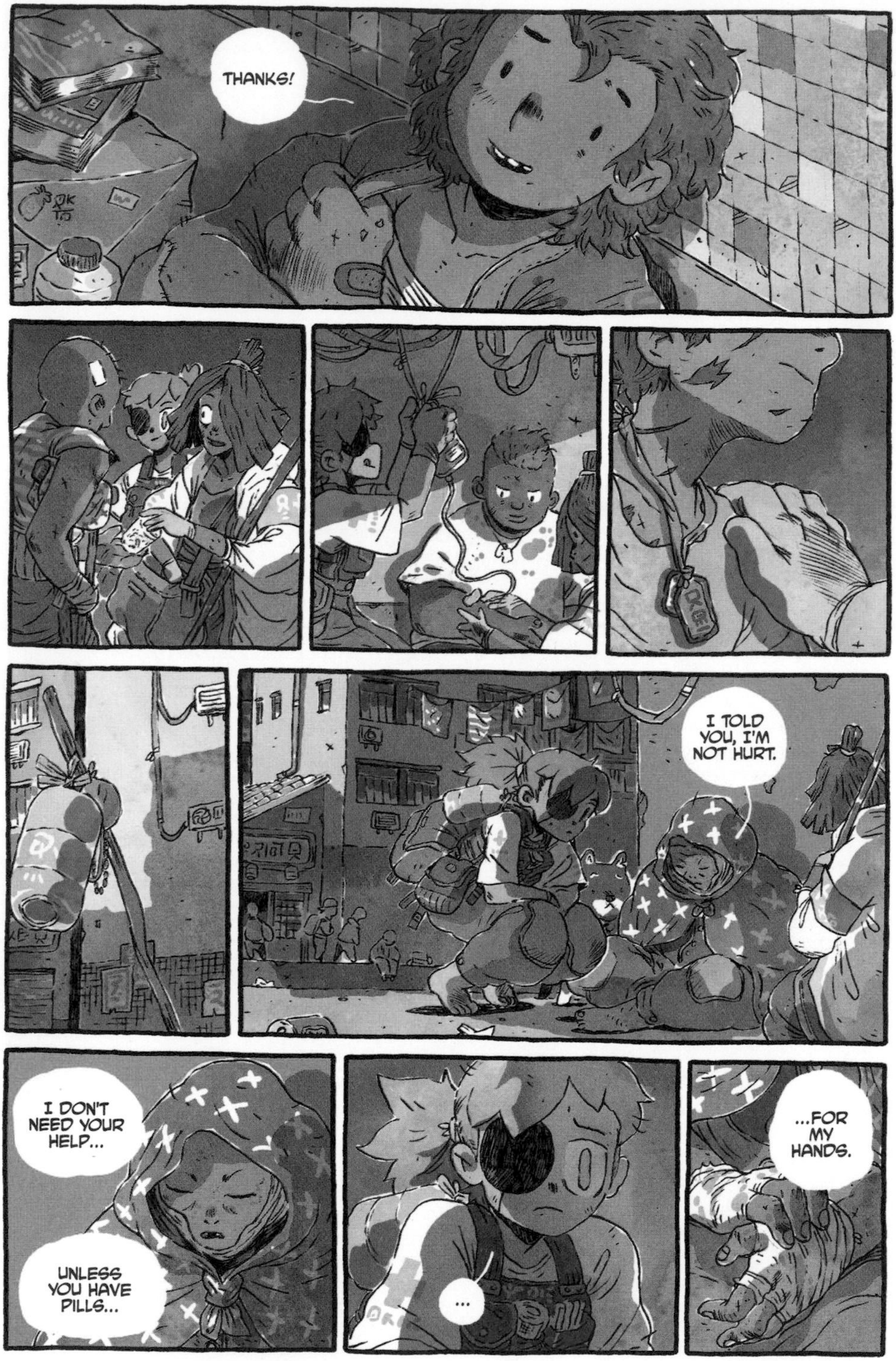
THANKS!
I TOLD YOU, I'M NOT HURT.
I DON'T NEED YOUR HELP...
UNLESS YOU HAVE PILLS...
...
...FOR MY HANDS.

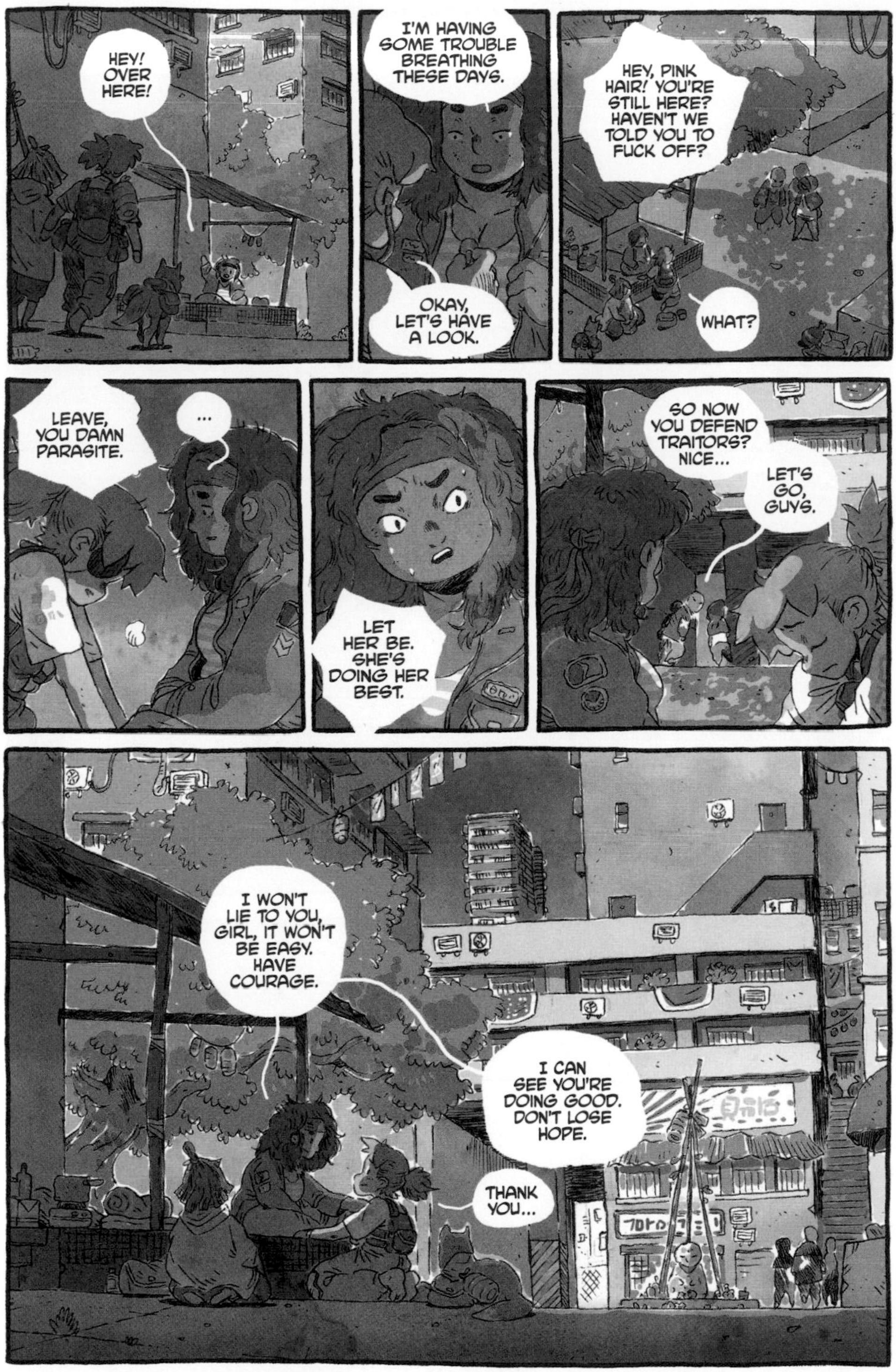
HEY! OVER HERE!
I'M HAVING SOME TROUBLE BREATHING THESE DAYS.
OKAY, LET'S HAVE A LOOK.
HEY, PINK HAIR! YOU'RE STILL HERE? HAVEN'T WE TOLD YOU TO FUCK OFF?
WHAT?
LEAVE, YOU DAMN PARASITE.
...
LET HER BE. SHE'S DOING HER BEST.
SO NOW YOU DEFEND TRAITORS? NICE...
LET'S GO, GUYS.
I WON'T LIE TO YOU, GIRL, IT WON'T BE EASY. HAVE COURAGE.
I CAN SEE YOU'RE DOING GOOD. DON'T LOSE HOPE.
THANK YOU...

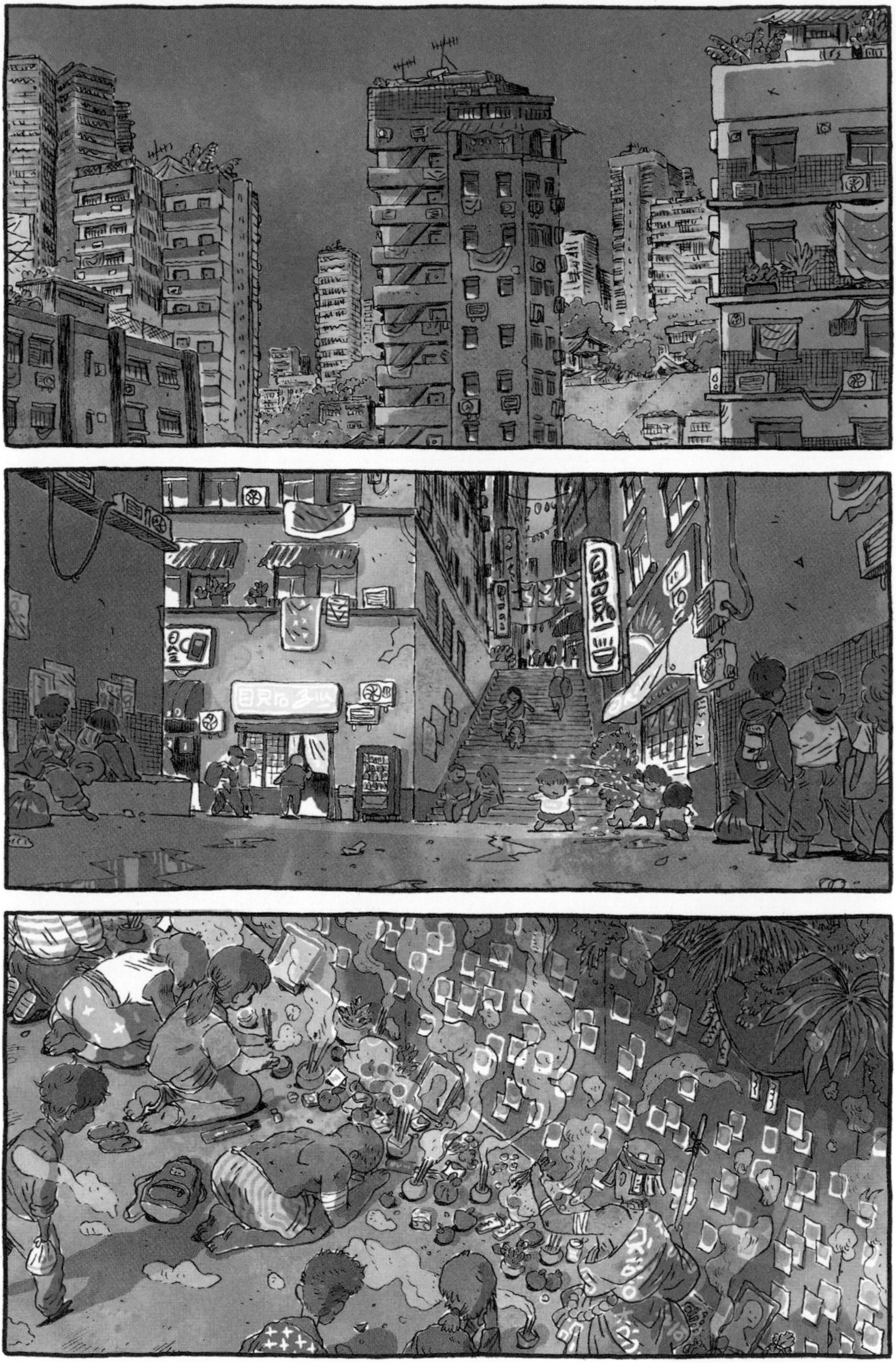

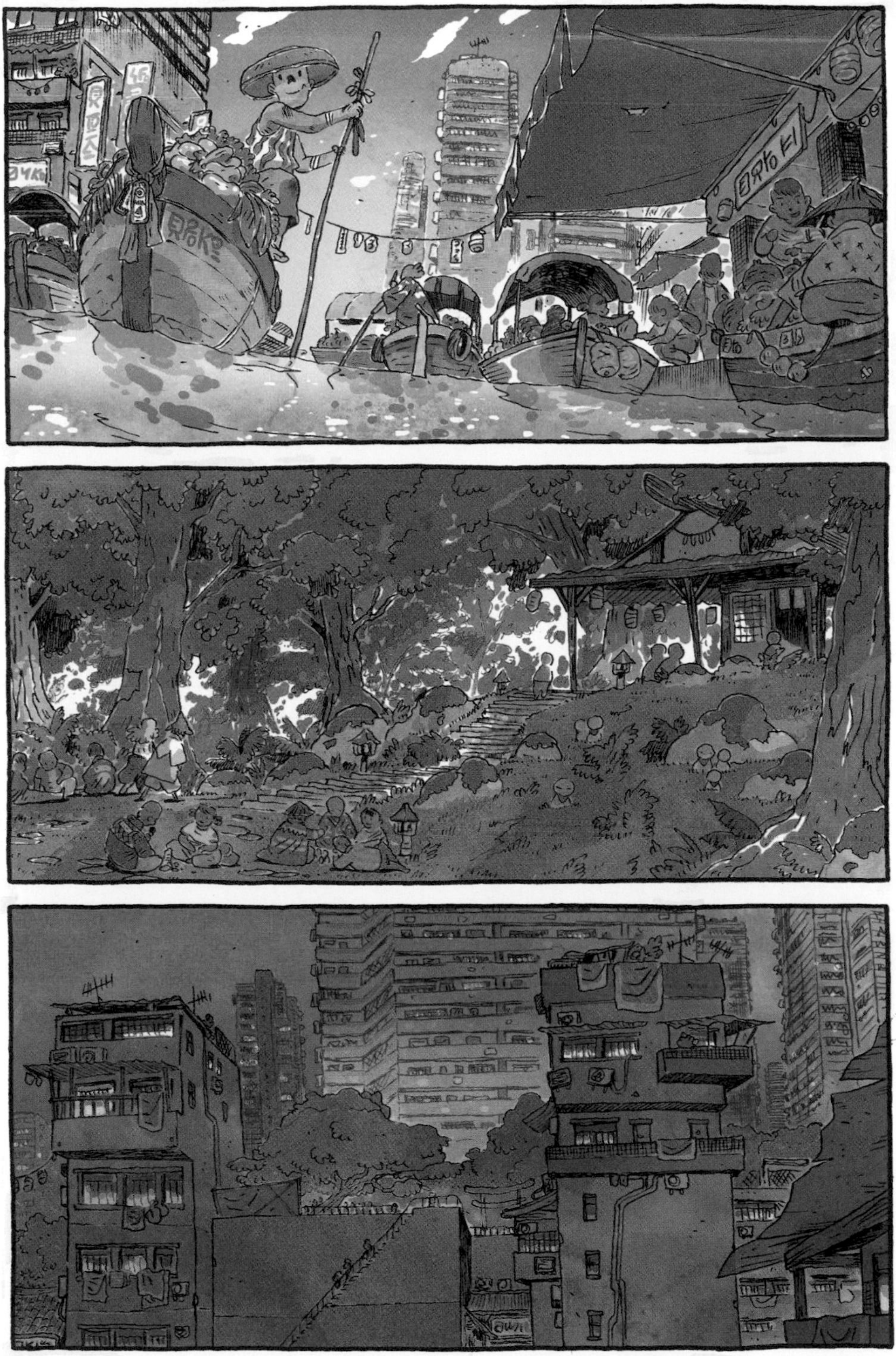

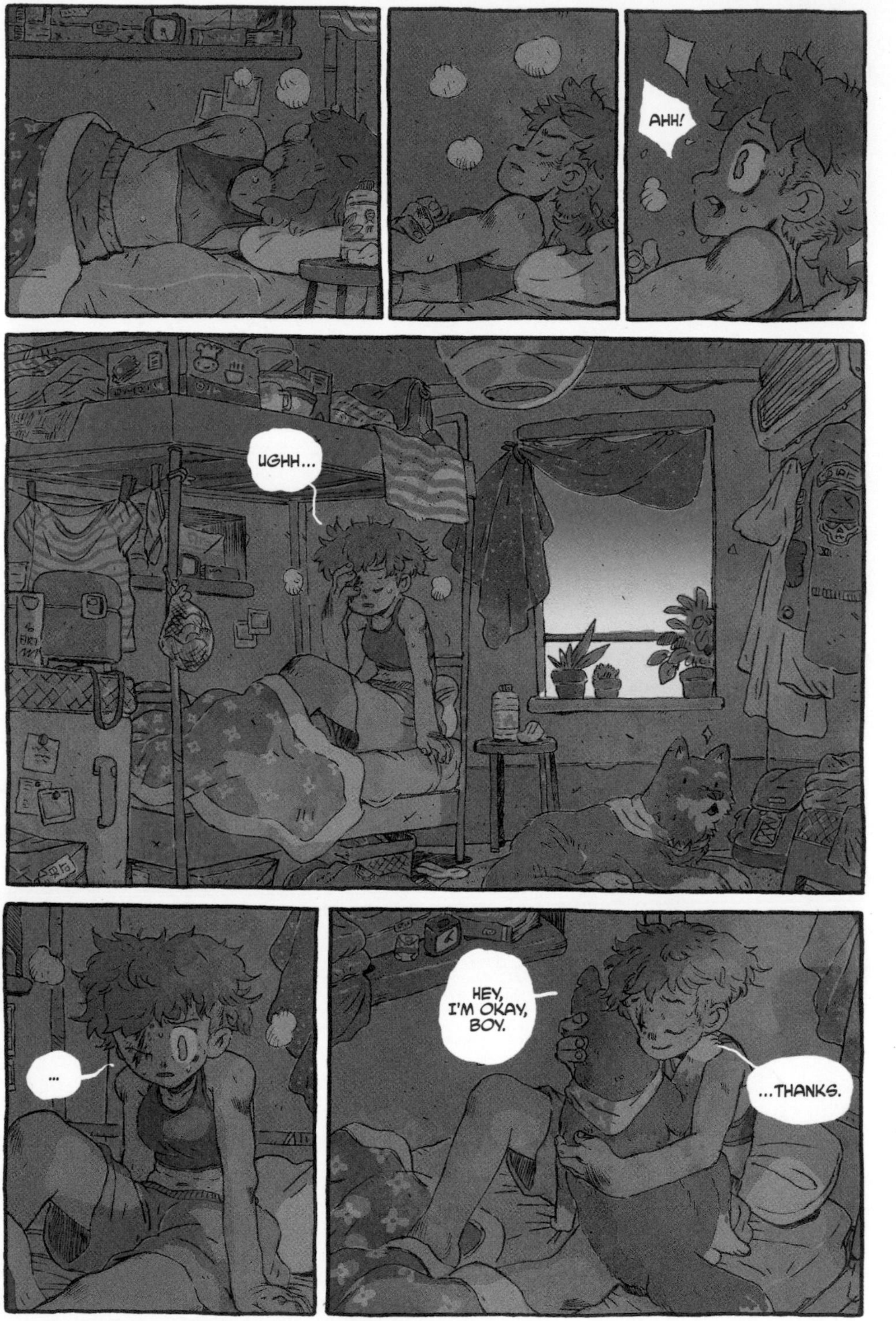
AHH!
UGHH...
...
HEY, I'M OKAY, BOY.
...THANKS.

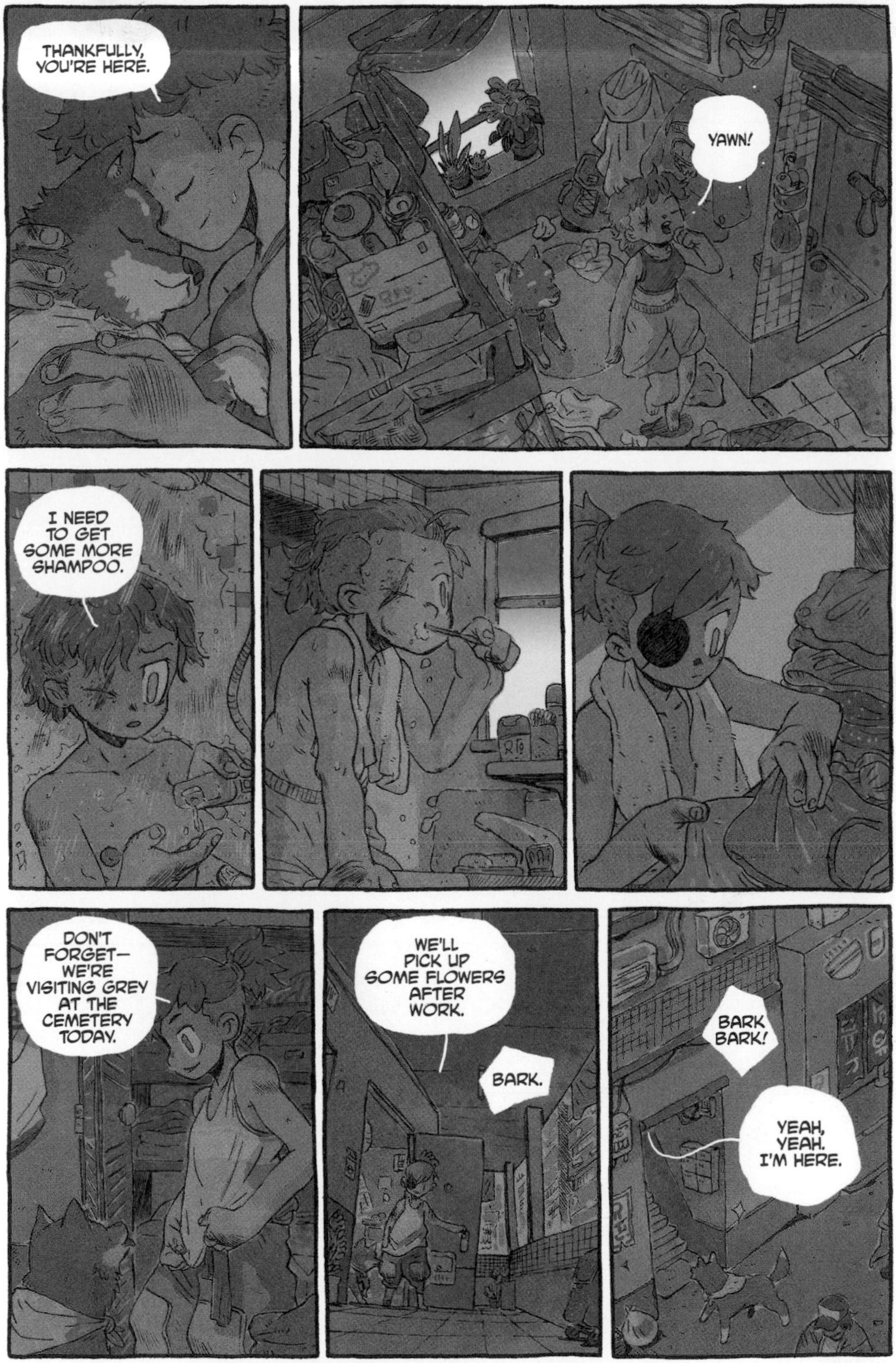
THANKFULLY, YOU'RE HERE.
YAWN!
I NEED TO GET SOME MORE SHAMPOO.
DON'T FORGET— WE'RE VISITING GREY AT THE CEMETERY TODAY.
WE'LL PICK UP SOME FLOWERS AFTER WORK.
BARK.
BARK BARK!
YEAH, YEAH. I'M HERE.

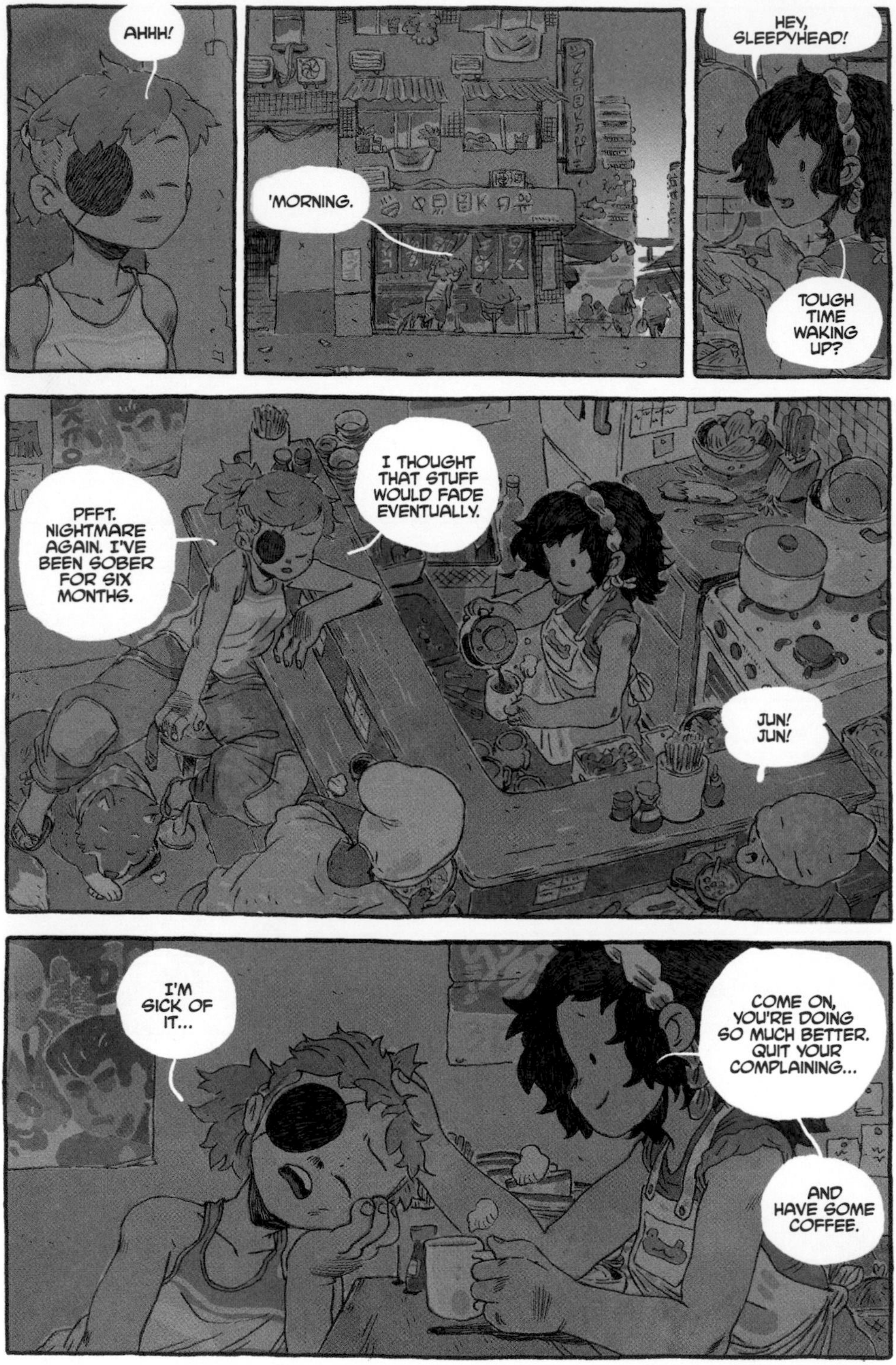
AHHH!
'MORNING.
HEY, SLEEPYHEAD!
TOUGH TIME WAKING UP?
PFFT. NIGHTMARE AGAIN. I'VE BEEN SOBER FOR SIX MONTHS.
I THOUGHT THAT STUFF WOULD FADE EVENTUALLY.
JUN! JUN!
I'M SICK OF IT...
COME ON, YOU'RE DOING SO MUCH BETTER. QUIT YOUR COMPLAINING...
AND HAVE SOME COFFEE.

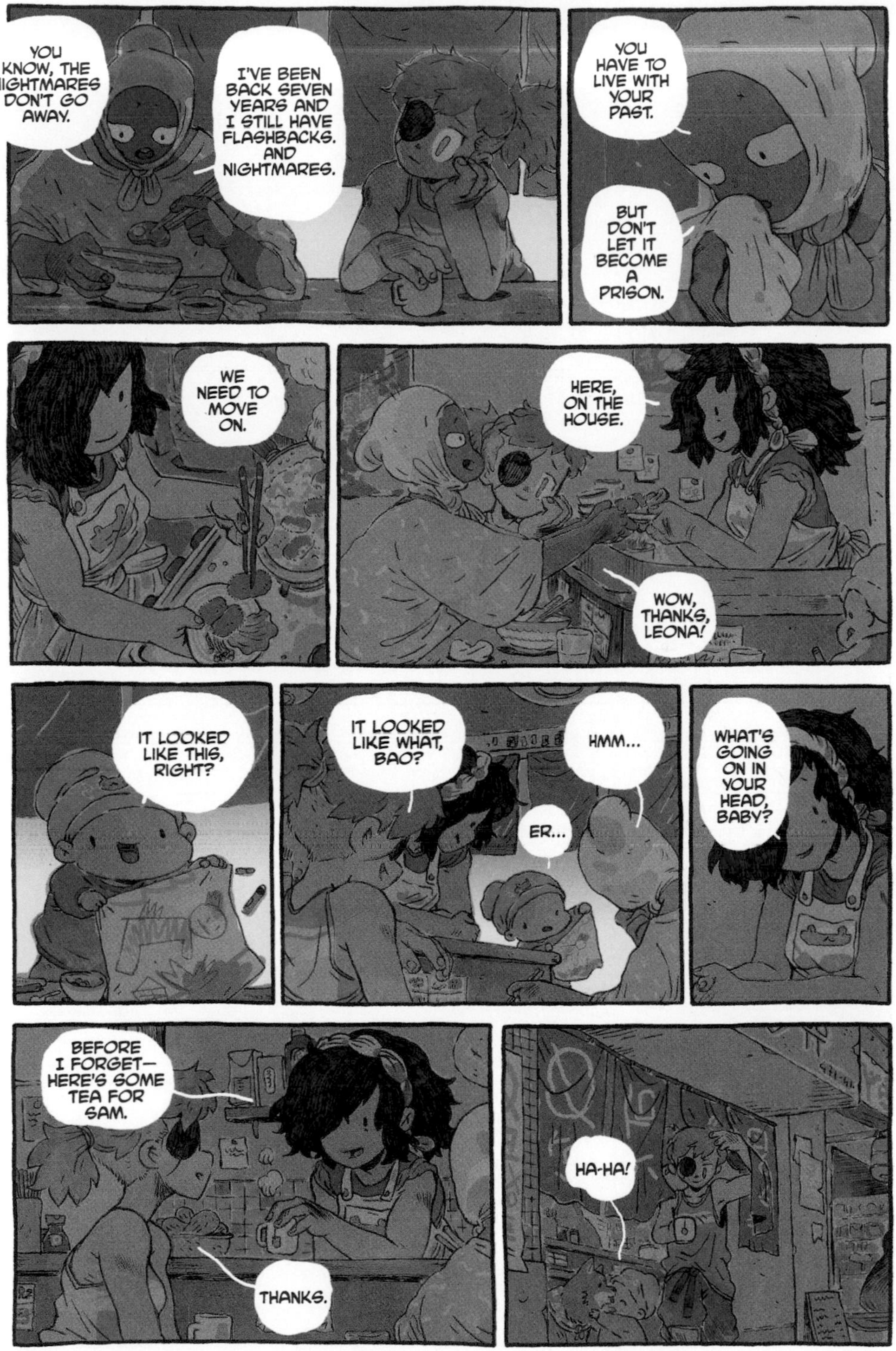
YOU KNOW, THE NIGHTMARES DON'T GO AWAY.
I'VE BEEN BACK SEVEN YEARS AND I STILL HAVE FLASHBACKS. AND NIGHTMARES.
YOU HAVE TO LIVE WITH YOUR PAST.
BUT DON'T LET IT BECOME A PRISON.
WE NEED TO MOVE ON.
HERE, ON THE HOUSE.
WOW, THANKS, LEONA!
IT LOOKED LIKE THIS, RIGHT?
IT LOOKED LIKE WHAT, BAO?
HMM...
ER...
WHAT'S GOING ON IN YOUR HEAD, BABY?
BEFORE I FORGET— HERE'S SOME TEA FOR SAM.
THANKS.
HA-HA!

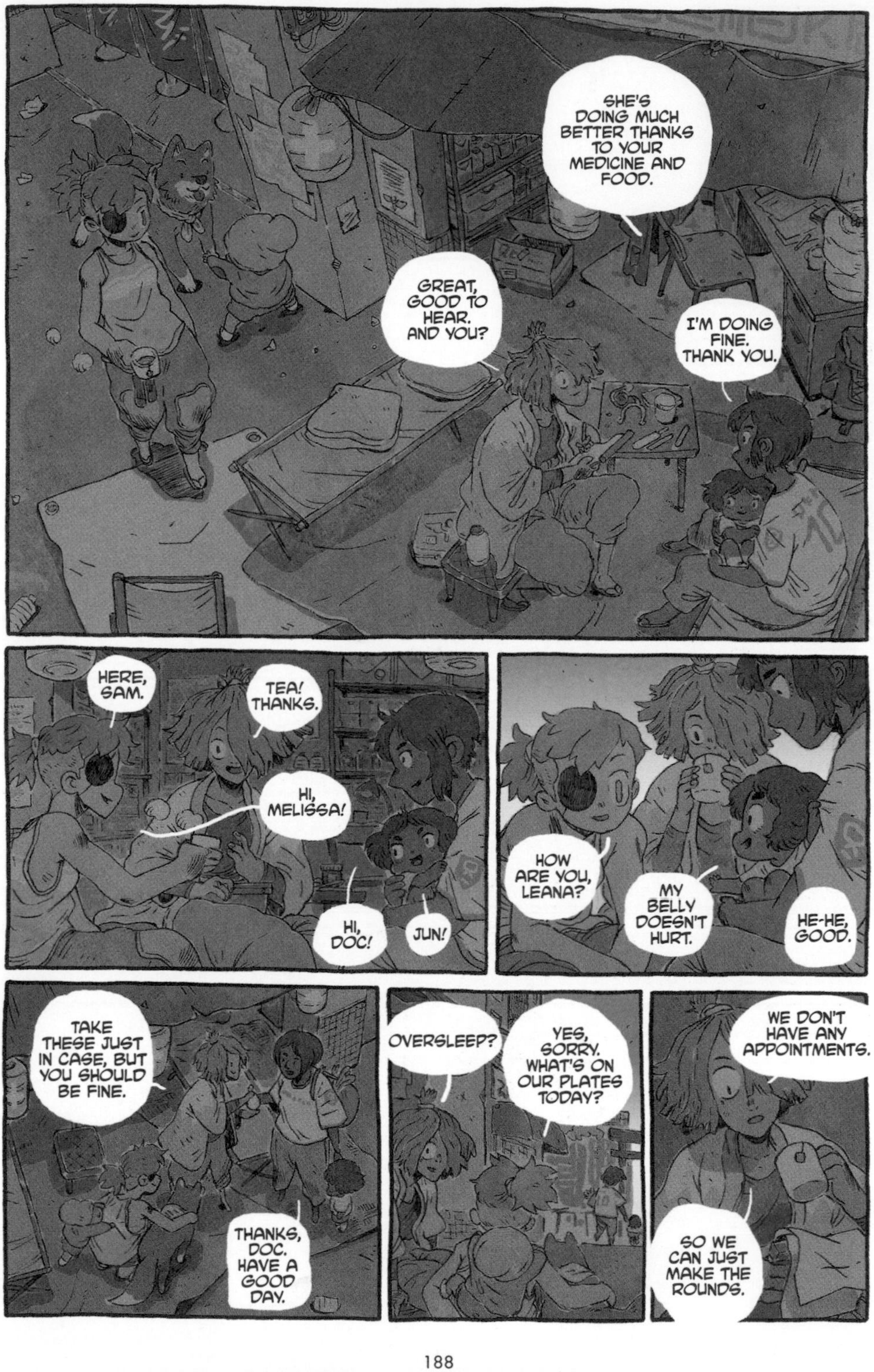
SHE'S DOING MUCH BETTER THANKS TO YOUR MEDICINE AND FOOD.
GREAT, GOOD TO HEAR. AND YOU?
I'M DOING FINE. THANK YOU.
HERE, SAM.
TEA! THANKS.
HI, MELISSA!
HI, DOC!
JUN!
HOW ARE YOU, LEANA?
MY BELLY DOESN'T HURT.
HE-HE, GOOD.
TAKE THESE JUST IN CASE, BUT YOU SHOULD BE FINE.
THANKS, DOC. HAVE A GOOD DAY.
OVERSLEEP?
YES, SORRY. WHAT'S ON OUR PLATES TODAY?
WE DON'T HAVE ANY APPOINTMENTS.
SO WE CAN JUST MAKE THE ROUNDS.

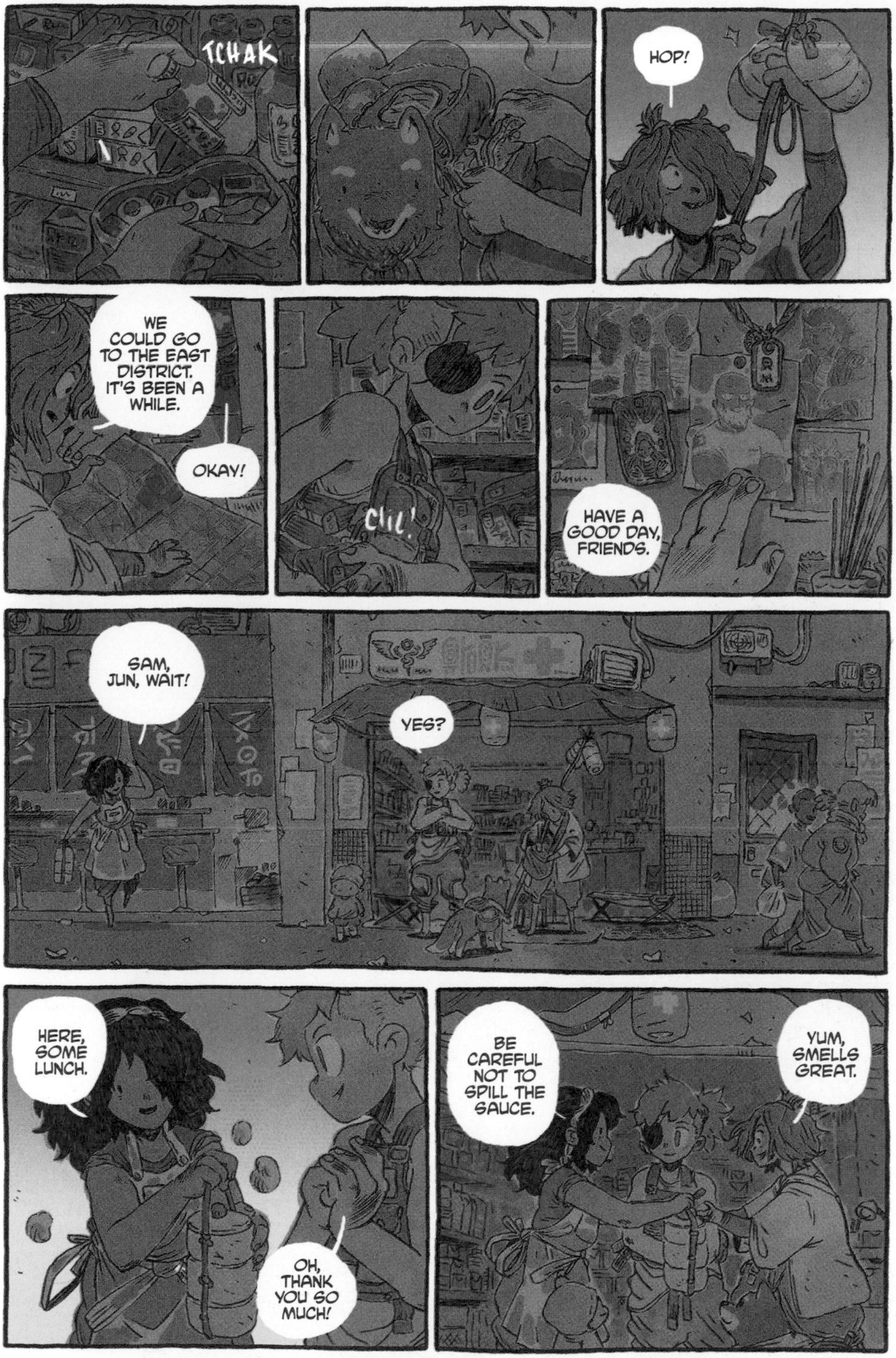
TCHAK
HOP!
WE COULD GO TO THE EAST DISTRICT. IT'S BEEN A WHILE.
OKAY!
CLIC!
HAVE A GOOD DAY, FRIENDS.
SAM, JUN, WAIT!
YES?
HERE, SOME LUNCH.
OH, THANK YOU SO MUCH!
BE CAREFUL NOT TO SPILL THE SAUCE.
YUM, SMELLS GREAT.

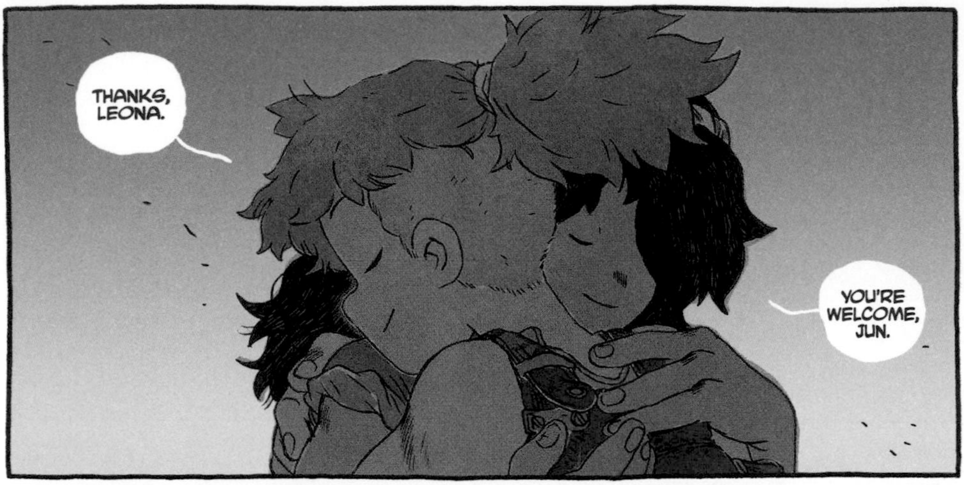
THANKS, LEONA.
YOU'RE WELCOME, JUN.

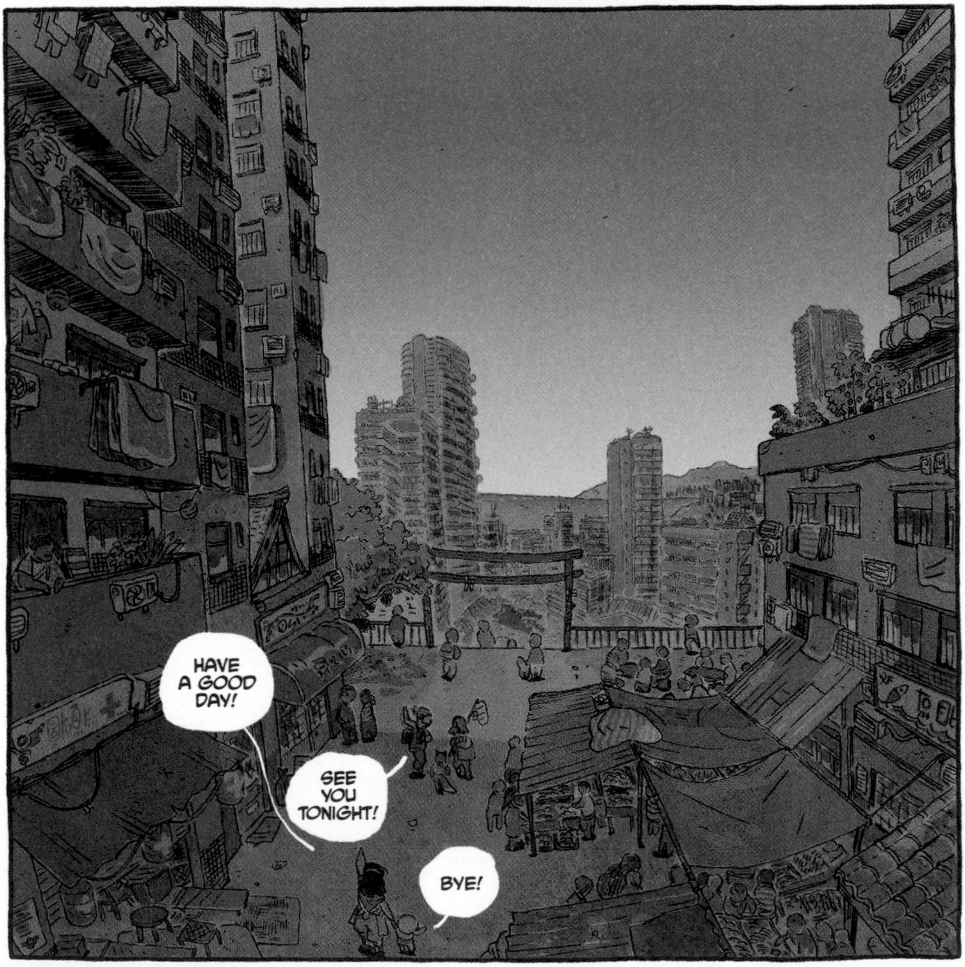
HAVE A GOOD DAY!
SEE YOU TONIGHT!
BYE!

AUTHOR'S NOTE

I became interested in the subject of PTSD while doing research for another project. It became obvious that the subject is very complex, and that it had played a significant role in many of the books and movies that were important touchstones for me. One thing I noticed right away was that PTSD wasn't always recognized as a real, diagnosable condition. As a result, people suffered without resources or support. I'm interested in how we treat and talk about "invisible" diseases like PTSD.

In my research, I learned that many veterans benefit from animal therapy. The presence of an animal gives them a sense of security and nonjudgmental, unconditional love. This was part of my inspiration for Red.

—G.S.

THE MAKING OF **PTSD**

I was living in Tokyo when I started working on *PTSD*. Tokyo is an inspiring city, a city that combines modern skyscrapers with traditional shops, the austerity of urban landscapes with an incredibly rich history. I knew that I wanted *PTSD* to take place in a lushly detailed, full-color world much like Tokyo.

PTSD started with just a few sketches. That's my process—in the early stages, I don't even put words down on paper; I focus on creating an atmosphere and visual style. I let the flow of my early sketches lead me to the story I want to tell.

I also drew inspiration for *PTSD* from some of my favorite movies from childhood. I watched hours and hours of kung fu movies—everything from Jackie Chan to Johnnie To and John Woo, as well as animated movies like *Akira* (Katsuhiro Otomo) and *Ghost in the Shell* (Masamune Shirow). The multicultural cities depicted in those movies always impressed me—I was drawn to their diversity, and also to the feeling of being surrounded by humanity, while being isolated at the same time.

But it wasn't just movies that inspired me. I found inspiration in my own family, too. I'm steeped in French culture thanks to my dad and Lao culture thanks to my mom, so capturing that multiculturalism in the story was important to me. I believe that really beautiful things can come from the merging of two cultures.

Food and cooking also take up a lot of real estate in the story thanks to my parents. They've taught my brother and me about the importance of making food and sharing meals with loved ones. It's a way of communicating with one another. Jûzô Itami's *Tampopo* and the cooking scene in *Breaking News* were touchstones for Leona's restaurant.

In my previous comic, *The Grocery*, writer Aurélien Ducoudray created a character who was a veteran. At the time, I was already ensconced in movies about war, like *The Deer Hunter* (Michael Cimino), *Full Metal Jacket* (Stanley Kubrick), and *First Blood*, or *Rambo* (Ted Kotcheff). I was also interested in the idea of discovering the person behind the uniform, and used movies like *Generation Kill* (David Simons, Evan Wright, and Ed Burns), *Jarhead* (Sam Mendes), and *Hurt Locker* (Kathryn Bigelow) to inform this part of *PTSD*. The protagonist, Jun, became a sort of tribute to these other works.

Jun is the heart of *PTSD*. She's an archetype that I've played with for many years—a strong woman, but lost and lonely. She was inspired by more touchstones from my childhood—Deunan from *Appleseed* (Masamune Shirow) and Major Kusanagi from *Ghost in the Shell*. And, of course, much of Jun came from me. I think every author puts a lot of themselves into their characters, especially their protagonists. Jun's lonely side, her social anxiety, her will to find her place in society while also craving independence—these are things I feel strongly. They may be common feelings, and I wanted Jun to experience them. I find that characters that are informed by the author's real experiences are often more credible and interesting. It's one way of injecting some realism into a fictional world.

I didn't intend for *PTSD* to have a direct correlation with current events. The world of this book is fictional, as is its war. What I wanted to achieve in *PTSD* was to tell the story of a character fighting for inner peace. It's a simple story, but one that I felt was important to tell.

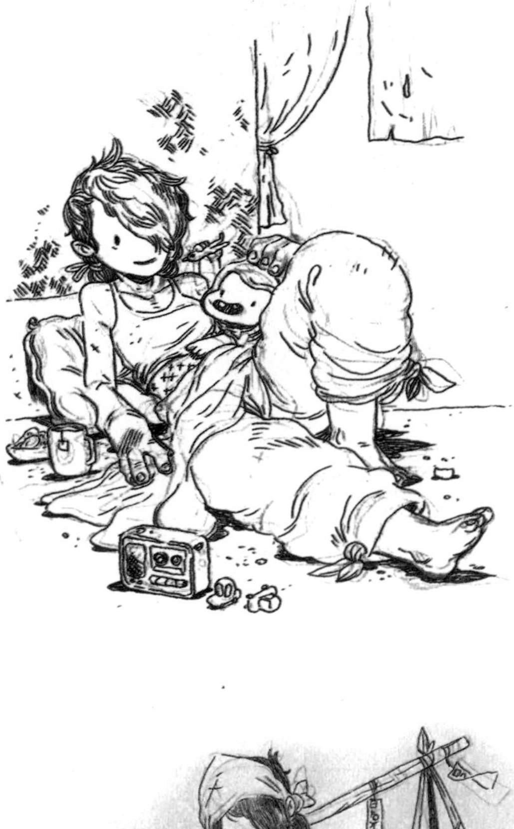

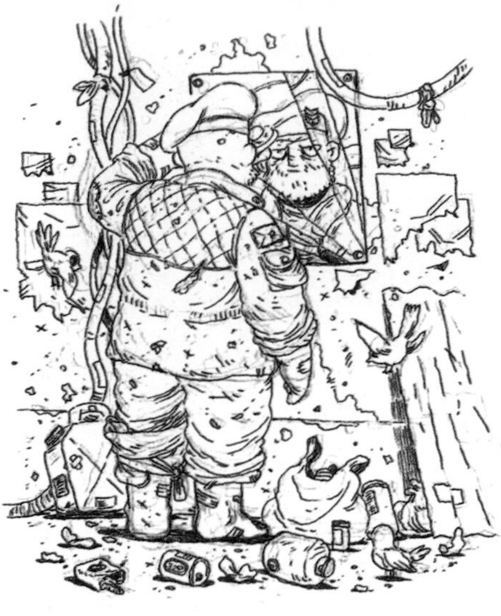

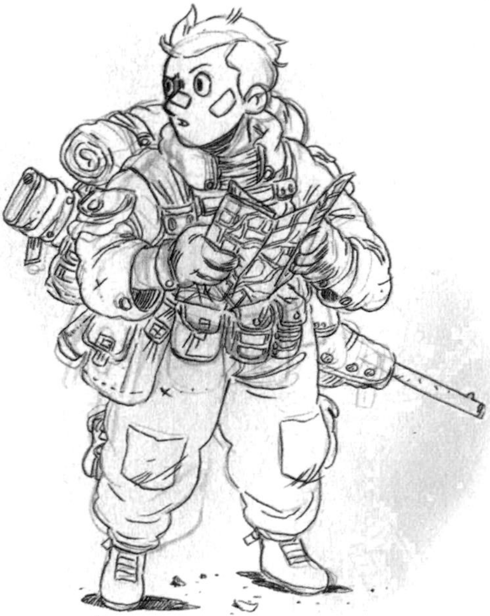

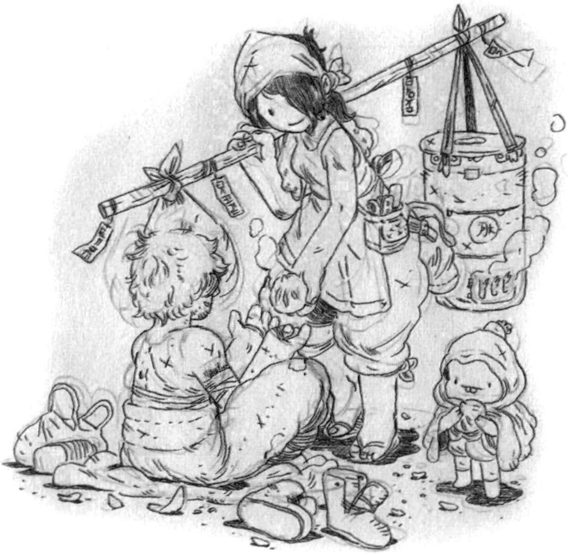

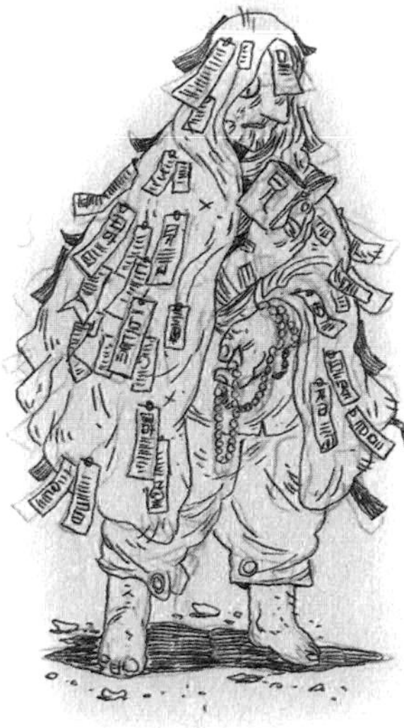

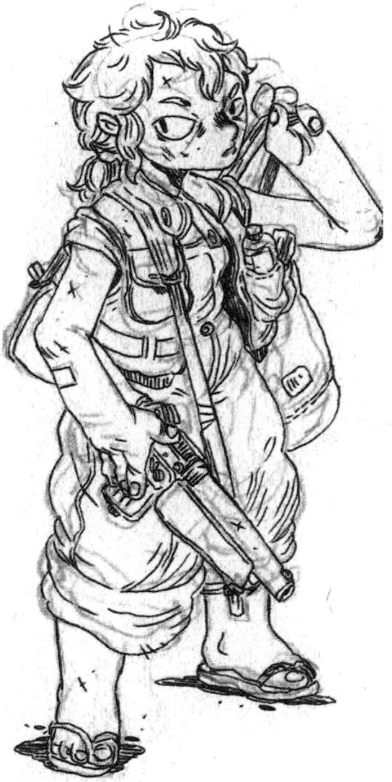

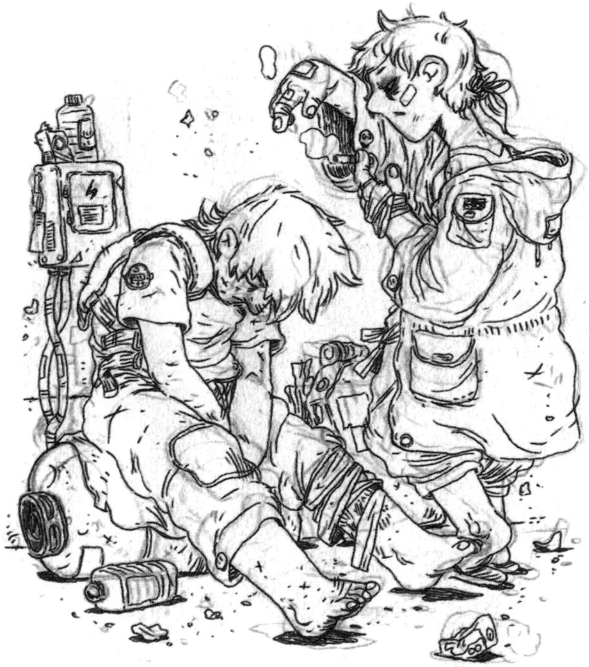

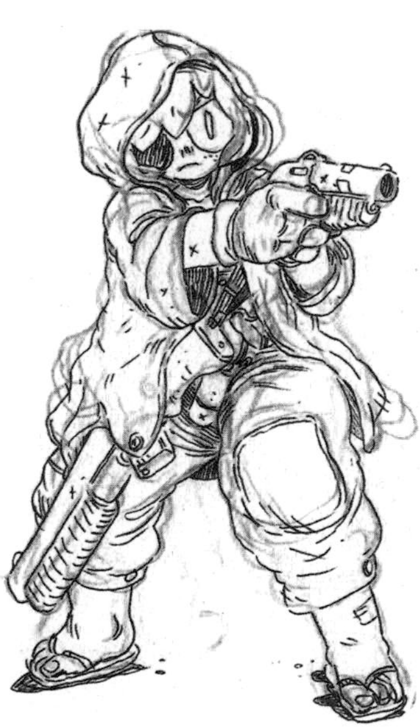

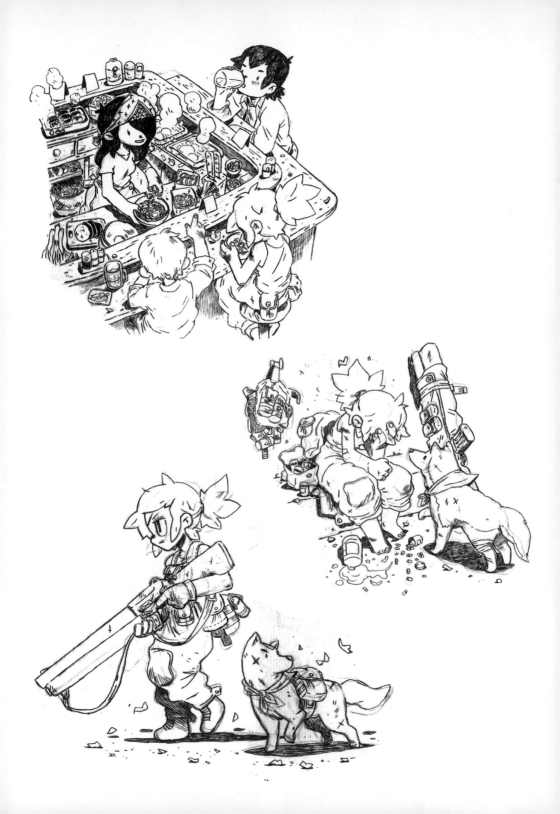

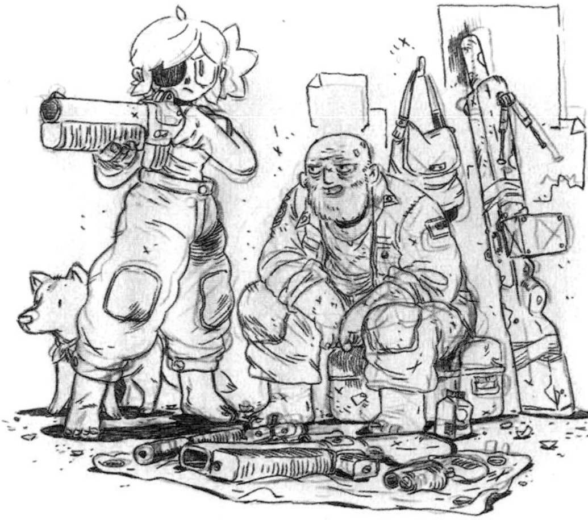

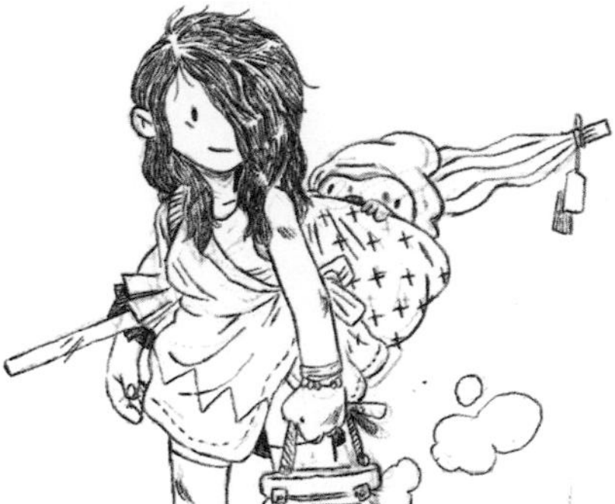

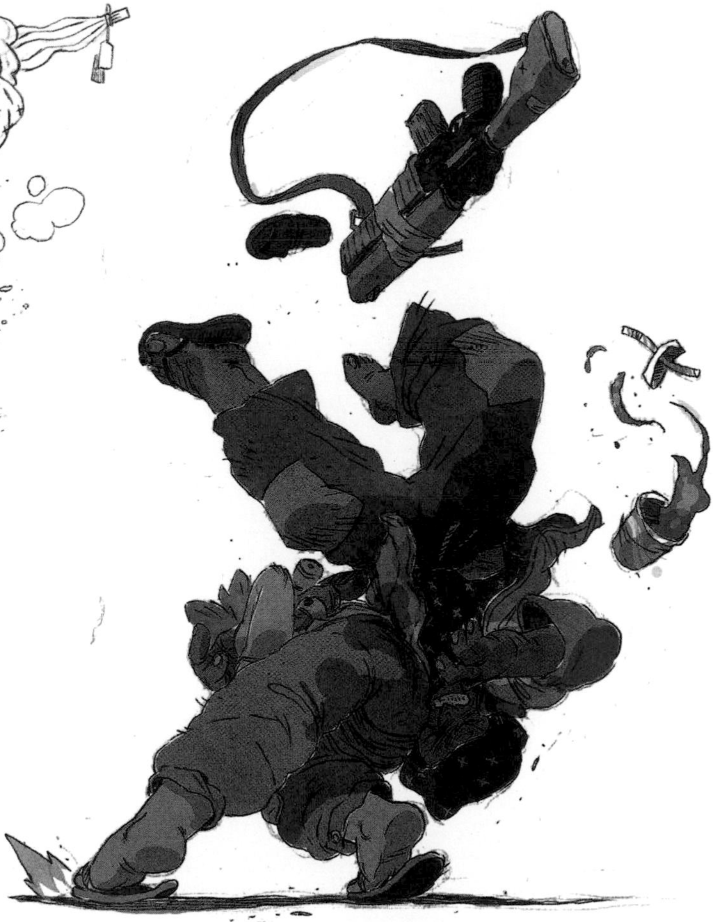

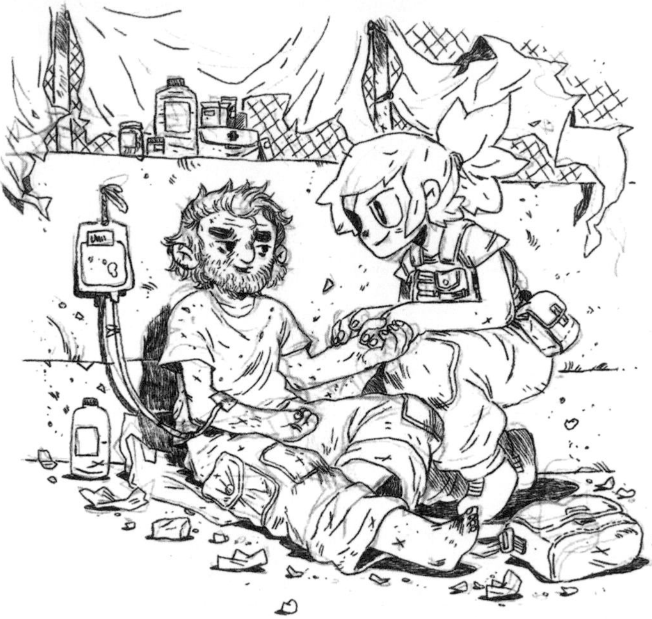

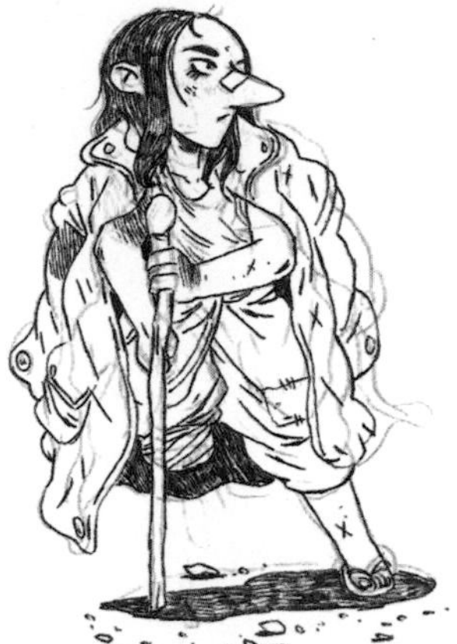

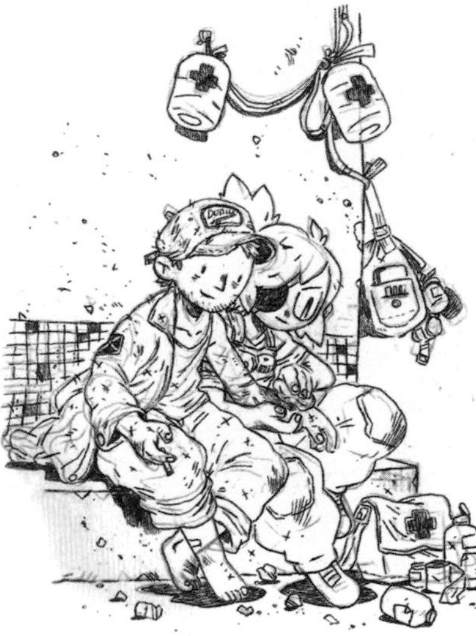

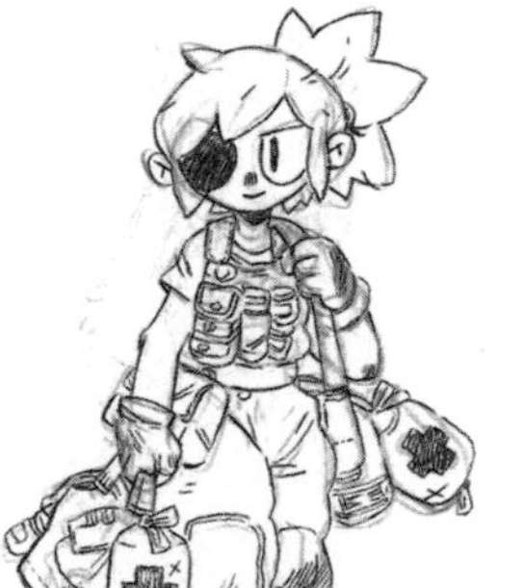

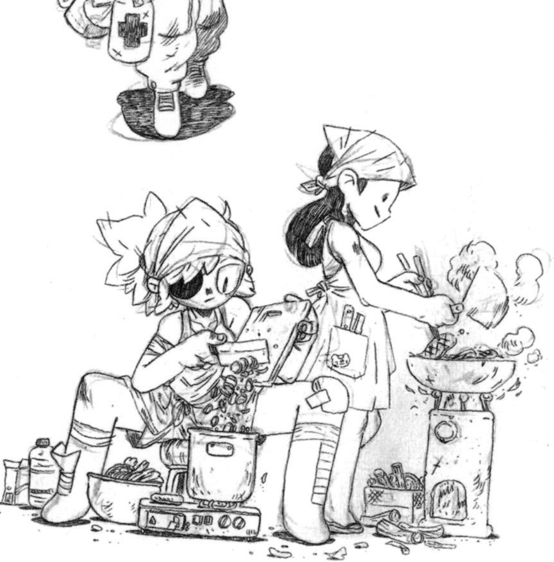

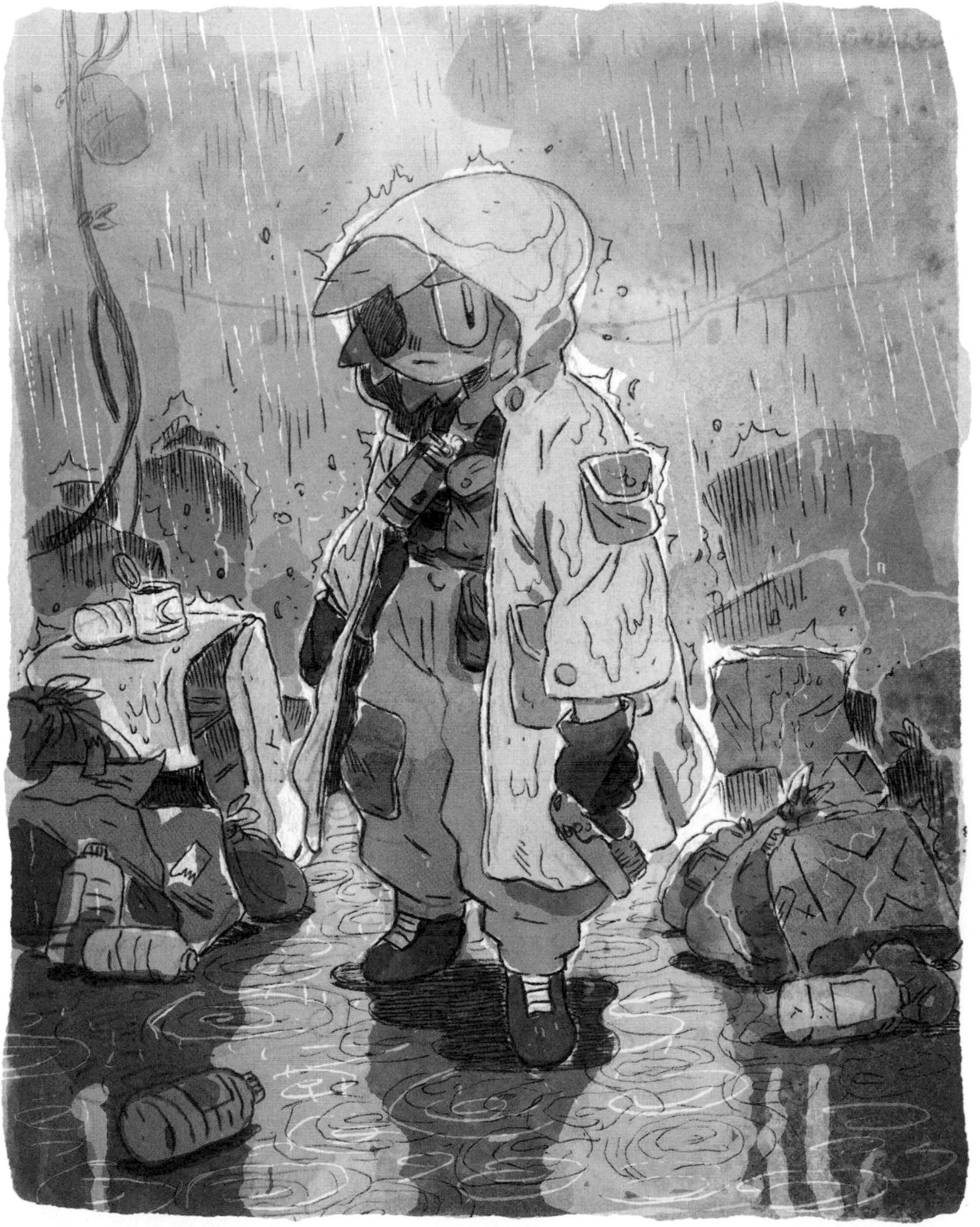

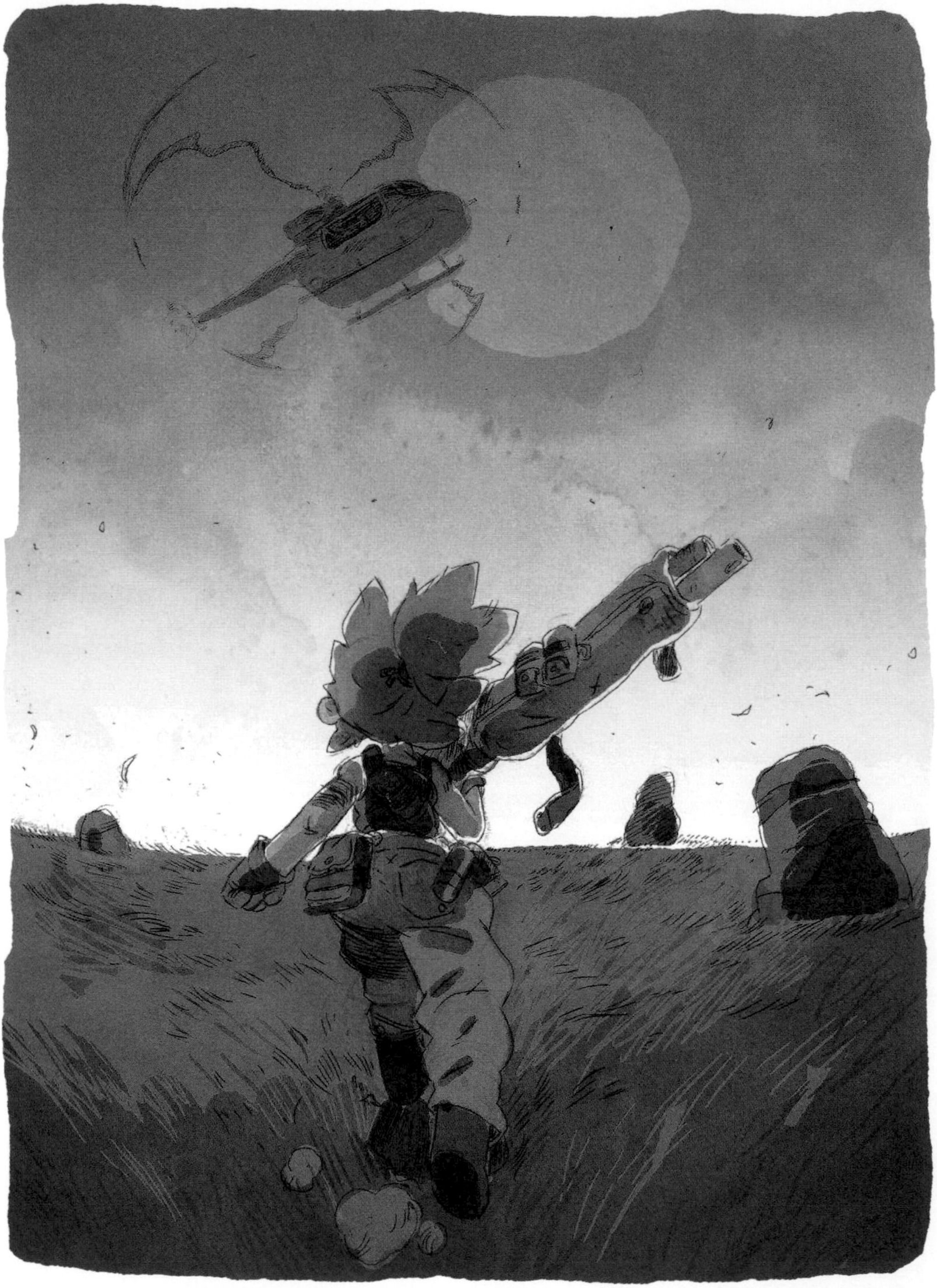

SPECIAL THANKS

to my family, Mark Siegel, and Elsa

ABOUT THE AUTHOR

Guillaume Singelin is a cartoonist and illustrator living in France. While studying graphic design in college, he created two graphic novels for the French publisher Casterman. After graduating, he did preproduction work for the animated film *Mutafukaz*, a collaboration between Ankama and Studio 4°C. He illustrated the graphic novel series The Grocery (written by Aurélien Ducoudray) and has contributed to the horror anthology DoggyBags, both of which are published by Ankama Editions. He also works as an illustrator for magazines, video games, and animated TV shows.

CUTTING-EDGE FICTION FROM :01 First Second

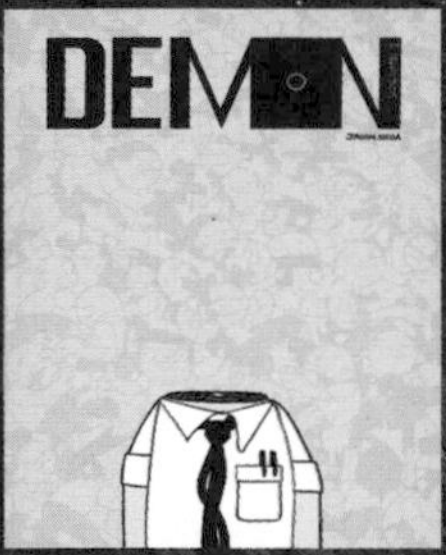
DEMON

Demon
by Jason Shiga

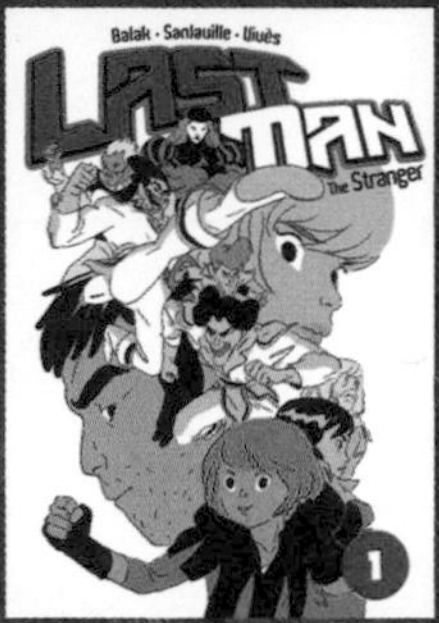
Balak · Sanlaville · Vivès
LAST MAN
The Stranger
1

Last Man
by Bastien Vivès,
Michaël Sanlaville & Balak

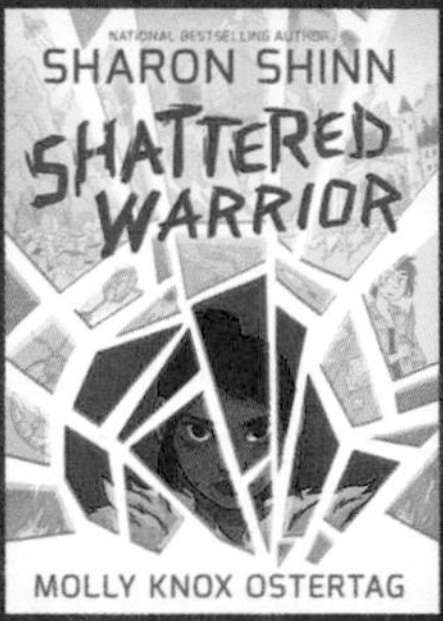
NATIONAL BESTSELLING AUTHOR
SHARON SHINN
SHATTERED WARRIOR
MOLLY KNOX OSTERTAG

Shattered Warrior
by Sharon Shinn
& Molly Knox Ostertag

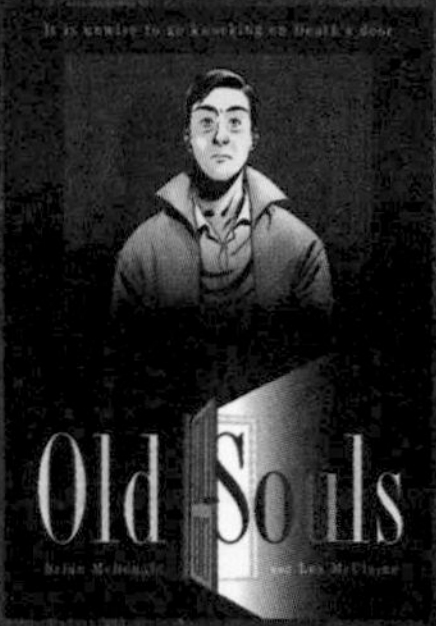
Old Souls

Old Souls
by Brian McDonald
& Les McClaine

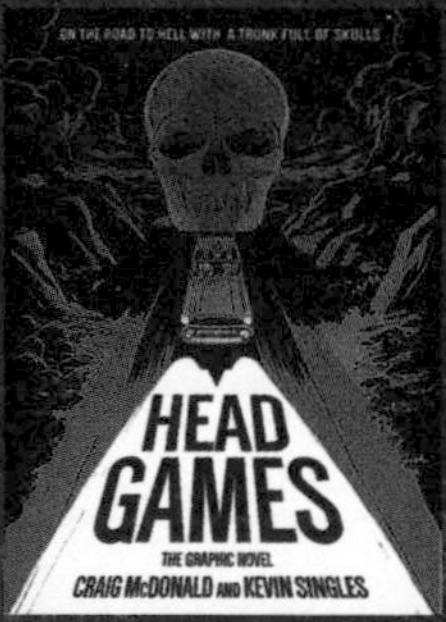
HEAD GAMES
THE GRAPHIC NOVEL
CRAIG McDONALD AND KEVIN SINGLES

Head Games:
The Graphic Novel
by Craig McDonald & Kevin Singles

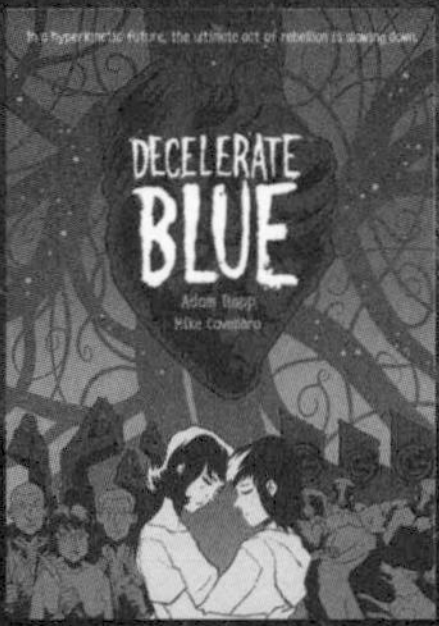
DECELERATE BLUE

Decelerate Blue
by Adam Rapp & Mike Cavallaro

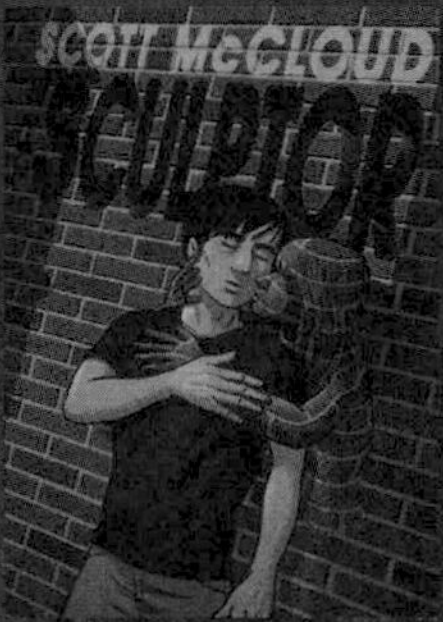
SCOTT McCLOUD
SCULPTOR

The Sculptor
by Scott McCloud

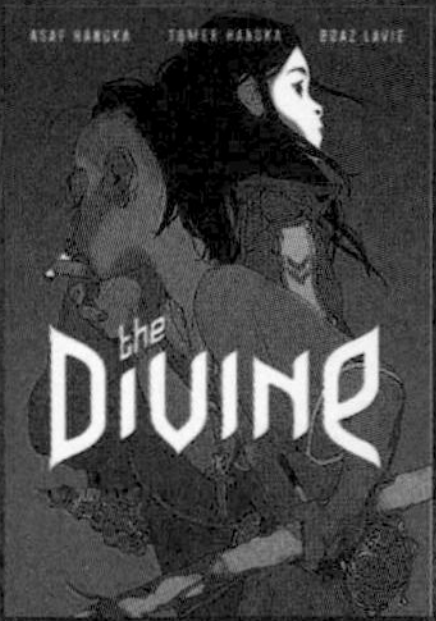
ASAF HANUKA TOMER HANUKA BOAZ LAVIE
the DIVINE

The Divine
by Boaz Lavie,
Asaf Hanuka & Tomer Hanuka

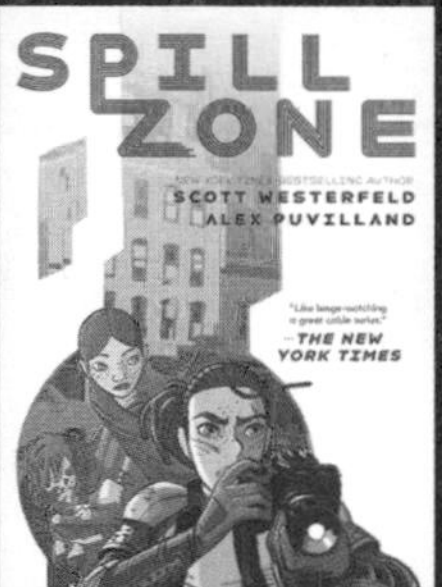
SPILL ZONE
SCOTT WESTERFELD
ALEX PUVILLAND
"Like binge-watching a great cable series." —THE NEW YORK TIMES

Spill Zone
by Scott Westerfeld
& Alex Puvilland

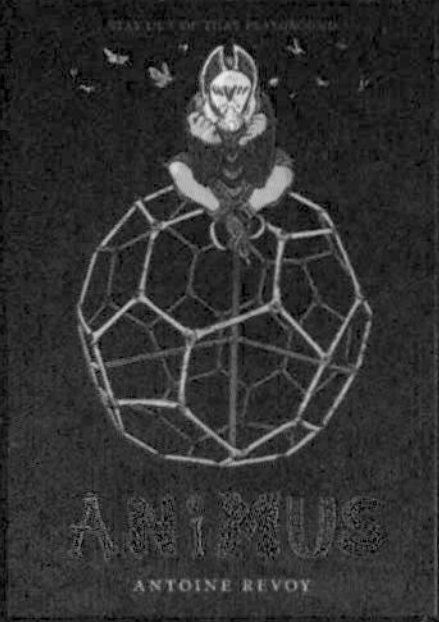
ANIMUS
ANTOINE REVOY

Animus
by Antoine Revoy

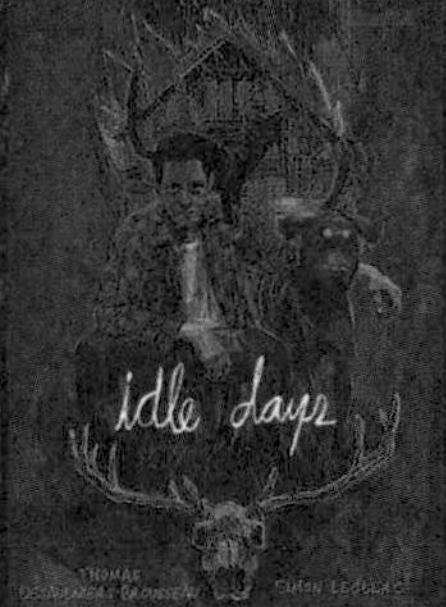
idle days

Idle Days
by Thomas Desaulniers-Brousseau
& Simon Leclerc

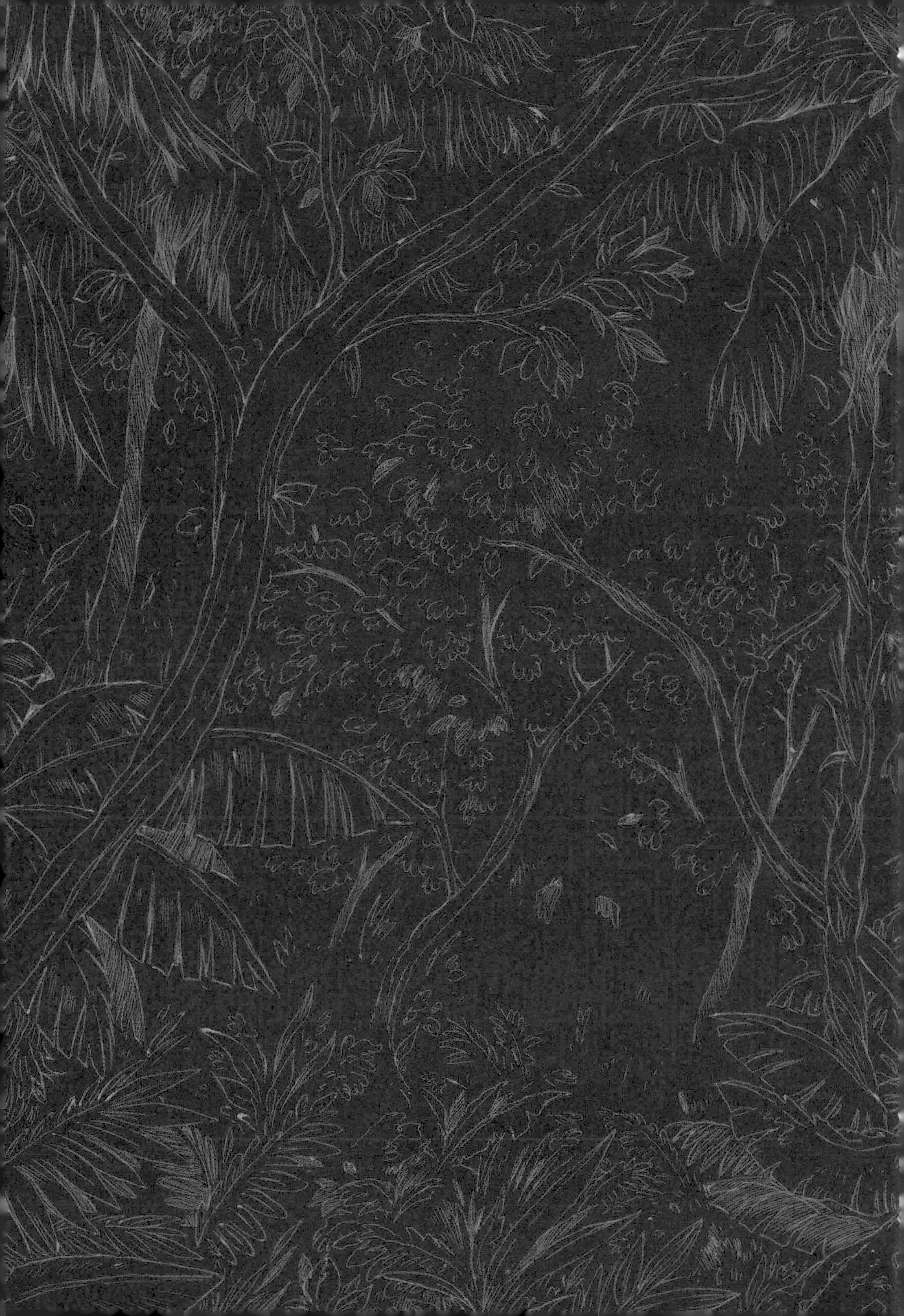